TELL ME WHAT YOU WANT

Being within the strong circle of his arms was no accident of sleep. Motionless, Joan savored the beat of Brandt's heart beneath her hand and the firm pressure of his thighs against her body. A sensual warmth began spreading from the hands on her back. She felt his face move through the golden silkiness of her hair and stop near her ear.

The catch in her breath told her she should break free, however innocent the embrace had been to begin with. But the exhilaration she felt in his arms was irresistible, an almost frightening excitement that lured her like a sweet taste of forbidden honey. She stayed right where she was.

from "A Lyon's Share"

Don't miss any of Janet Dailey's bestsellers

The New Americana Series
Sunrise Canyon
Refuge Cove

The Tylers of Texas
Texas Fierce
Texas Tall
Texas Tough
Texas True
Bannon Brothers: Triumph
Bannon Brothers: Honor
Bannon Brothers: Trust
Calder Storm
Green Calder Grass
Lone Calder Star
Calder Promise
Shifting Calder Wind
American Destiny
American Dreams
Masquerade
Tangled Vines
Heiress
Rivals

Two-in-One Volumes
Always With Love
Because of You
Bring the Ring
Can't Say Goodbye
Close to You
Crazy in Love
Dance With Me
Everything
Forever
Going My Way
Happily Ever After
It Takes Two
Lover Man
Man of Mine
Ranch Dressing
Something More
Stealing Kisses
Texas Kiss
That Loving Feeling
Try to Resist Me
Wearing White
When You Kiss Me
With This Kiss
Yes, I Do
You're Still the One

Published by Kensington Publishing Corporation

THAT LOVING FEELING

JANET DAILEY

ZEBRA BOOKS
KENSINGTON PUBLISHING CORP.
http://www.kensingtonbooks.com

ZEBRA BOOKS are published by

Kensington Publishing Corp.
119 West 40th Street
New York, NY 10018

All Kensington titles, imprints, and distributed lines are
available at special quantity discounts for bulk purchases
for sales promotion, premiums, fund-raising, educational,
or institutional use.

Special book excerpts or customized printings can also be
created to fit specific needs. For details, write or phone
the office of the Kensington Sales Manager: Attn.: Sales
Department. Kensington Publishing Corp., 119 West 40th
Street, New York, NY 10018. Phone: 1-800-221-2647.

First Printing: July 2010
ISBN-13: 978-1-4201-4447-5
ISBN-10: 1-4201-4447-2

10 9 8 7 6 5 4 3 2

Printed in the United States of America

Contents

THAT CAROLINA SUMMER   1

A LYON'S SHARE   171

That Carolina Summer

Chapter 1

The languid heat of the North Carolina sun lost some of its intensity when a soft breeze from the Atlantic blew in over the beach. Bending a knee, Annette Long smoothed lotion over her golden leg in long strokes. Her smoky gray gaze took in the large swimming pool area, and the guests enjoying the resort's luxurious setting.

A young couple splashed in the pool, shrieking with laughter as they tried dunking each other, but most others lazed in the lounge chairs provided by the hotel, doing nothing more strenuous than applying suntan lotion to their bodies, like Annette.

Finishing, she capped the bottle and turned to her younger sister. A faint, affectionate smile touched her mouth. As usual, Marsha had her nose in a book—and she'd chosen a conservative one-piece to sit by the pool and read. Not that Annette had expected her quiet, unassuming sister to flaunt her assets, even though she was eighteen and very pretty. Marsha just didn't do that. In fact, she resisted all of Annette's attempts to change her.

Sometimes it was difficult for Annette to believe

they were sisters, considering how different they were. Annette didn't share her younger sister's shyness. She was her complete opposite, boldly confident and assertive enough to go after what she wanted. They didn't look much alike either.

Annette's shoulder-length hair was the tawny shade of light sherry, styled in soft feathered curls. Marsha, a brunette, preferred a low-maintenance, somewhat boyish cut that didn't do much for her face. Her eyes were sky blue and innocent, but Annette's were gray, intelligent and knowing, with sparks of fire in their smoky depths.

Both sisters were slim and a little above average height, but Annette tended to show off what Marsha was inclined to hide. Annette's white swimsuit was a one-piece too, but it couldn't be described as conservative. Its sides were daringly cut out and it dipped low in the back.

They were as different as night and day. Their stepmother, Kathleen, had once described them as devil and angel, Annette remembered, although it hadn't been a derogatory comment about either of them. It was simply that Marsha was cautious, while Annette tended to make things happen rather than wait for them to occur. Occasionally that tendency got her into trouble, but she had always been clever enough to get herself out of it.

"Here." Annette offered the suntan lotion to her sister. "You'd better use this before you turn into a lobster."

"Thanks." Marsha set her book aside, laying it facedown, opened to the page she was reading, to keep her place. As she began rubbing the lotion on her arms, a look of dreamy contentment swept over her face. "Isn't it beautiful here, Annette? I didn't think

Dad was serious when he said we were all going to spend a month at Wrightsville Beach."

"Why not?" Annette leaned back in the lounge chair and closed her eyes to bask in the sun.

"Well, when he takes vacation time he usually likes to stay where we live, in fabulous suburban Delaware. I guess it's really not surprising when you think about how much traveling he does," Marsha said.

"True," Annette replied. "But he also knows Kathleen gets stuck at home when he's gone. It's only natural that she likes to get away for a while—especially now that Robby is older," she added, referring to their five-year-old brother.

"You're right about that. And like Dad said, with both of us in college, there aren't that many chances for us to vacation as a family."

"Well, big kiss to him for footing the bill. I intend to enjoy myself to the max," Annette declared.

At the sound of approaching footsteps, Annette looked up through her barely lifted lashes. A uniformed waiter assigned to the poolside guests stopped next to Marsha's chair, an empty tray balanced on his uplifted palm. Annette checked him out discreetly but thoroughly. In his early twenties, the waiter was blond, built, very good-looking—and fully aware of it.

"May I bring you ladies something to drink?" His flashing smile was intended to charm and Marsha blushed at his flirtatiousness.

Raising a hand to her forehead, Annette shielded her eyes from the glare of the sun. The movement immediately drew the waiter's attention to her as his admiring gaze skimmed the sleekness of her golden skin and the provocative style of her swimsuit. Marsha was invisible in a way, a fact that didn't escape Annette's notice—or surprise her. Guys like him usually ran to a type: fun-loving blondes, not quiet brunettes.

"I'll have an iced tea," Annette said with a faintly inviting smile. Maybe it wasn't fair to divert the sexy young waiter's attention from her sister, but it was partly protective. Marsha was so incredibly inexperienced when it came to men. She'd be way out of her league with this one.

"With lemon?" the waiter asked, giving her a smile that told Annette he found her very attractive.

"Please." Annette let her smile widen to show him that she got the message, even though he fundamentally left her cold. She glanced at Marsha, who wasn't doing a very good job of concealing her disappointment. "Do you want an iced tea too?"

"Yes . . . please." Marsha echoed the order in a small voice.

"Okay. Two iced teas coming up. I'll be right back," the waiter promised. "If there's anything else you need, the name is Craig."

"I think the tea is all for now. Thanks, Craig," Annette murmured dryly.

He winked and moved away to fill their order.

Annette rolled forward, draping an arm over an upraised knee to watch him go. She wasn't interested in him, but she knew Marsha was. For her sister's sake more than anything else, she wanted to be sure she had the young man's measure.

"Wasn't he gorgeous, Annette?" Marsha asked wistfully.

"Yes. And don't think lover boy doesn't know it," Annette answered. Craig took a little too much pride in his looks for her liking.

"How can you sound so blasé?" her sister marveled.

"I saw the way he looked at you. He did everything but drool."

There was no real envy in Marsha's tone. She'd become accustomed to men thinking her older sister was more attractive.

"As you get older, Marsha, you'll learn that guys like Craig are in love with themselves," Angela explained patiently. "They think they're irresistible."

As she watched, the waiter in question paused near another group of guests. One of the men among them caught her eye. Her pulse quickened with interest, her eyes lighting up. He was wearing black swimming trunks; the rest was all hard, sun-bronzed muscle. The man was tall, a couple of inches over six feet, wide shoulders tapering to nicely narrow hips.

As he turned slightly, Annette glimpsed his ruggedly masculine features—she liked that high-bridged nose and strongly carved jawline. The sun's rays glinted on his dark brown hair, revealing undertones of copper. Annette guessed he was somewhere in his early thirties. Her gaze strayed to his left hand, but there was no wedding ring. Which didn't mean anything, really.

"I really don't understand how you can be so analytical about men," Marsha sighed. "Haven't you ever seen anyone that turned you on?"

Two minutes earlier Annette would have answered no to that question. She'd always been too intelligent to let her imagination take over. Just about to turn twenty-one, she'd dated lots of guys, but never pretended, even to herself, that she was serious about any of the string of boyfriends. Annette had always been positive that she would instinctively know when she met *the* man. And the signals were going off like crazy this very second.

"Yes," she said. "I'm looking at him right now," she informed her sister with calm certainty.

"What?" Marsha blinked at her, not expecting that answer. "Who?"

"The man in the black trunks." A thread of excitement ran through her nerve ends, tying them together.

Marsha looked. "Who is he?"

"I don't know—yet." Annette qualified her reply, because she fully intended to discover everything she could about the stranger. That inquisitiveness was nothing new to her, but her boldness always made Marsha uncomfortable. She met her sister's uneasy gaze.

"You don't know anything about him." It was almost an accusation.

Annette gave Marsha a patient smile. "But you can bet I'm going to find out."

She continued her silent assessment of the man, noticing with pleasure how naturally sexy he was. In fact, he was so obviously male he seemed to have no need to prove it. He was saying something to a woman in the group. Annette couldn't hear the words, but the slight breeze carried the husky timbre of his voice to her ears. She liked the sound of it as it shivered through her, like velvet drawn across her bare skin.

A uniformed figure crossed in front of her vision, briefly distracting her gaze. Annette recognized the blond waiter returning with their drinks. He could be useful. She welcomed him with a wide smile.

"That didn't take long," she remarked.

"We take pride in keeping our guests happy." The routine reply was accompanied by a wink that left no doubt of his willingness to go beyond the call of duty.

He handed Marsha her glass and walked around the lounge chair to give Annette hers.

"Thank you." She set the glass down and reached for the check to sign it and charge it to the room. "By the way, who is that man over there?" Annette asked idly. "The one in the black trunks. He looks vaguely familiar, but I can't place where I've seen him," she fibbed.

"Oh, that's Joshua Lord," Craig replied.

Annette was careful to keep her gaze on the young waiter. The more attention she paid to him, the more information she'd get out of him. "Where have I heard that name before?" she wondered aloud, frowning.

"Probably lots of places. Josh owns this resort. The Lords are really rich. Descended from one of North Carolina's oldest families," he explained. He seemed eager to impress Annette by being on a first-name basis with one of them.

"Really," she murmured and sent a glance in Joshua Lord's direction. He was listening attentively to a bikini-clad redhead. "Is that his wife? She's gorgeous."

"No, that's not his wife," Craig informed her, not noticing Annette's fleeting smile of satisfaction. "He's not married. I get the impression that he's, uh, too busy to settle down." He nodded toward the man and woman still talking. "Josh is handson when it comes to running this place. He's always here."

"I bet all he has to do is crook his finger and they come running." Annette sipped at her glass of tea and smiled at the waiter, matching his knowing grin. "Do you mean he lives at the hotel?"

"Yes, he has a private suite."

"How convenient," she murmured, giving a throaty little laugh.

"It sure is," Craig agreed, but Annette was thinking how convenient it was for her. However, she didn't doubt Josh Lord made the most of having a hotel staff at his beck and call—it had to be like having an army of servants.

One of the guests at poolside called out, summoning Craig. His mouth crooked in a regretful smile. "Excuse me. I'll see you around."

"Bye." Annette watched him walk away, then let her gaze travel to Marsha. "Didn't I tell you I'd find out all about him?"

Marsha gave her a dubious look that revealed her inner misgivings. "Not quite. I mean, you got his name, where he lives, and you know he's single, but that's not everything. Besides," she added, "it sounds like Joshua Lord can have any woman he wants. What makes you think he'll be attracted to you?"

"Because I'm going to make sure he is," Annette said, laughing softly at her sister's somewhat shocked expression. "Don't worry, Marsha," she added. "It'll be easy."

"You've said that before." Marsha wasn't convinced.

"It's always worked out the way I wanted it to, hasn't it?"

"One of these times it won't," Marsha warned. "And you're going to find yourself in big trouble."

Annette just grinned at her and looked Josh's way again. Various plans were already beginning to take shape in her mind and would need to be thought through. She needed more information before she could settle on a course of action. In the meantime, she would have to be flexible.

As she watched, Joshua Lord detached himself

from the group and walked toward the pool. He had an easy, flowing stride—she had to admire the corded muscle rippling in his thighs and calves. There was a confidence in the way he moved, coupled with an aloof awareness of his surroundings. He really did look like he owned the place.

The couple that had been splashing around in the pool had climbed out to collapse in blissful exhaustion on a couple of deck chairs. There was no one else in the water when Josh Lord dived in. A second after he'd surfaced halfway across the pool, Annette was reaching for a scrunchie to pull her hair back.

"Where are you going?" Marsha asked, staring.

"For a dip," Annette replied with a mischievous gleam in her eyes. "You remember what Aunt Helen always said: Don't wait for your ship to come in—swim out to meet it."

"Oh, right. Aunt Helen was a lot of fun," Marsha said affectionately. "And do you remember her flower-petal bathing cap and ruched swimsuit with the pleated skirt?"

Annette smiled. "Yes, I do. Those were the days." She tucked the stray strands of her hair into the scrunchie. "Here I go. Want to come?"

"No, thanks." Marsha picked up the book she'd been reading. "Don't involve me in any of your schemes."

A faint smile played at the corners of Annette's mouth as she turned away and walked to the edge of the pool. Her sister's refusal was expected. Marsha wasn't athletic at all, preferring to be a spectator, not a participant. Nothing was guaranteed to drive Annette crazy quicker than sitting on the sidelines. She was a natural competitor—and the higher the stakes, the more she enjoyed the game. A hint of danger just added to the excitement.

Standing at the edge of the pool, Annette paused to study the lone swimmer now doing laps. She mentally timed the powerful stroke, but his pace was leisurely, which suited her purposes to a tee. Once he was clear of the immediate area, Annette arched and dived cleanly off the poolside, slicing into the water without a sound. She swam underneath for several yards and surfaced alongside him.

He looked her over with mild surprise. Up close, Annette could really see the male charm in his strong features—and better yet, the lazy sensuality of its chiseled lines. The attraction was potent. She guessed how wide-eyed and innocent she looked as she blinked the water from her lashes, well aware that her drenched ponytail was sending rivulets of water down into her cleavage. Casually, she flipped the ponytail back over her shoulder and raised her arms to tighten the slipping scrunchie. Then she smoothed away the water from her face.

Soaking wet, she looked good and she knew it. Her actions got his attention, although it was guarded.

"Hi." Annette spoke quickly before he could swim away. "Are you doing laps?"

"Yes." There was a faint narrowing of his eyes.

"Do you mind if I swim with you?" she asked, and offered the explanation, "It helps if I can pace myself against someone else."

"I don't mind." There was a glint of amusement in his dark eyes. He had to be used to women chasing him, maybe even sick of it. She would have to be a little more subtle.

"Great. Thanks." Annette struck out for the far end of the pool with a clean strong stroke.

All the hours she'd spent training on the college swim team were about to pay off. But not yet. Annette didn't attempt to outdistance him or even increase his previous pace. She wasn't foolish enough to believe she could outswim him even with her expertise in the water, but she could make him notice her for a while longer. First she wanted to settle into a rhythm.

For the entire length of the pool, Annette remained even with him, fully aware that he was holding back the same as she was—only he didn't know that. With each breath she glanced through the splashing water at the dark-haired swimmer opposite her and the slicing strokes of his muscular arms. Not a motion was wasted.

At the end of the first lap she did a racer's turn, not trying for speed. She was a half-length in front of him, the maneuver catching him off guard. This time Annette didn't try to take advantage of it as he quickly caught up with her. When their eyes met briefly on an accidentally synchronized breath, she saw a gleam of respect for her ability. Annette turned her face into the water and effectively hid her smile. He picked up the tempo slightly and she stayed with him.

She counted the laps, concentrating on her stroke. Past experience had taught her that she lost her kick after a mile. She waited until she had only two lengths of the pool left to go, then she made her move, putting everything she had into the turn and launching herself off the side of the pool. She was more than a length ahead of him when she surfaced and struck out for the other side. The race was on.

Before Annette made the final turn, he had caught up with her, just as she'd expected. But she had his full attention. Being challenged by a female usually did the trick—the male ego couldn't take it. She considered letting him win, but it wasn't necessary.

By the last lap he was easily outdistancing her. Annette used every bit of her reserve strength to keep up. The instant her hand touched the side of the pool she stopped, even though he continued. Her lungs were about ready to burst.

Buoyed by the water and a last surge of energy, she levered herself out of the pool with her arms, swinging her legs out of the water to recline at a right angle to the edge. Annette took in huge gulps of air, her breasts heaving with the effort to fill her lungs. Pulling off the scrunchie and letting her dripping hair hang free, she leaned backward on her elbows. Her head was thrown back, exposing the curve of her throat and catching the sparkle of sunlight on her wet lashes.

"Are you quitting?" It was a taunting challenge, and Annette half-turned, one bent arm supporting her weight. Josh Lord was treading water, eyeing her exhausted state with male complacency. His smile showed even white teeth, a sexy contrast to his bronzed skin.

For an instant she was irritated to see that he wasn't even breathing hard, but she forgot about that when his gaze traveled over her curves, lingering a scant second on the swell of her breasts.

"Yes," Annette admitted in a voice that was alluringly breathless. "A mile is my limit. Thanks for the workout."

"Any time, kid." He turned in the water and swam away leisurely, missing the outraged look in her eyes.

Kid? With another sudden surge of energy, she rolled to her feet and crossed to the lounge chair next to Marsha's. Her temper was simmering. Why would he take her for a kid? The more she thought about it, the angrier she got.

"What happened?" Marsha picked up on the stormy look in her sister's eyes, but not why it was there. "Did it backfire?"

"Not exactly." Annette stretched out in the lounge chair to let the sun dry her, closing her eyes. "I did what I set out to do."

Namely, to get Josh Lord to notice her. She had succeeded in that. But at the moment, this "kid" had to do some more thinking. It would seem awfully immature to brag in his hearing or directly to him about her turning twenty-one in just a few days, as if she expected him to take her out drinking.

Annette watched him out of the corner of her eye when he climbed out of the pool a few minutes later. His wet hair gleamed almost black, its burnished natural highlights temporarily hidden. The sheen of moisture on his flatly muscled body gave his tanned skin a polished look. His hard male physique was well worth a discreet but thorough stare. Turning her head, she did just that. She fought a quivering sensation that started deep inside her as she imagined what it would be like to be next to all that masculine gorgeousness.

He draped a towel around his neck but made no effort to dry himself. When he cast a glance in her direction, Annette felt a sense of satisfaction. Even if he considered her a kid, he was aware of her. For the time being she was willing to settle for that.

As Josh Lord left the poolside area to disappear down one of the walkways, Marsha set her book down. "Here comes Dad and Kathleen. Robby must have finally woken up from his afternoon nap."

Annette sat up as her father and stepmother

approached, a black-haired little boy tugging impatiently at Kathleen's hand to hurry her. She smiled, liking the picture the three of them made with her father's arm possessively around the shoulders of the attractive auburn-haired woman. It was always reassuring to see how much in love the two of them were.

Marsha waved to attract the couple's attention and Kathleen released her son's hand. Robby careened past the other chairs, a pint-size cyclone in baggy swimming trunks as he raced toward Marsha and Annette.

"Whoa!" Annette laughed and caught the boy around the waist to stop him. "You're not supposed to run around the pool. Sometimes it's slick—you could fall."

Her bathing suit was still wet and Robby noticed it immediately. "How come you didn't wait until I woke up to go swimming?" he said accusingly. "I'd wait for you."

"Get your water wings and I'll go swimming again—with you," Annette promised, turning him loose.

Robby barely gave Kathleen a chance to set the beach bag down before he was diving into it. "Not so fast," his mother admonished him for his carelessness with the other items in the oversize bag. "Fold the towels you dumped out."

"I'll do it, Kathleen," Marsha volunteered.

"No, Robby can do it." The rejection was softened by a smile. "You girls spoil him too much as it is."

"I thought that was what big sisters were supposed to do." Annette laughed. "Anyway, Marsha and I will watch him so you and Dad can spend some time together." She glanced at her father, so tall and handsome, and looked into a pair of gray eyes the same color as hers. "Besides, we don't want Robby giving Dad any more gray hairs." She had teased him about the white strand she'd found mixed in among the black the day before.

"Don't blame those on Robby," Jordan Long replied. "If anyone in this family is capable of giving me gray hairs, it's you, Annette."

"When have you ever had to worry about me?" she chided.

"Practically since the day you were born," he said dryly. "Speaking of that, have you decided what you want for your birthday?"

"Yes." An instant image of Joshua Lord came to her mind.

"What?" Kathleen prompted while she adjusted the water wings on Robby's arms.

"A Ferrari," Annette lied. She couldn't very well tell her father what she really wanted for her birthday.

"Try again," he suggested, and Annette laughed, knowing full well that her choice was going to be out of the question.

Chapter 2

Annette rolled over in the bed and dodged the glare of the early morning sun. She pulled the blankets over her head in an attempt to shut it out, but it was no use. Her sleep had been interrupted, and once awake, she was rarely able to go back to sleep.

With a groan she tossed back the covers and turned to look at the occupant of the room's other twin bed. Marsha was sound asleep. Annette wanted to throw a pillow at her out of sheer envy, but it wasn't her sister's fault that she was awake. She crawled out of bed and padded into the bathroom.

A few minutes later she emerged, her teeth brushed and the tiredness washed from her eyes. Before deciding what to wear, Annette walked to the window to see what kind of day it promised to be. Except for a few fleecy white clouds, the sky was bright and clear.

The second-floor window provided a view of the bay and the golf course that adjoined the resort complex. From where she was Annette could see the early morning joggers—and one in particular stood out, running alone. She'd recognize that length of muscled leg and that flowing stride anywhere. That gorgeous man had to be Josh Lord.

Her gaze skipped ahead of him to study his possible routes and instantly memorized them. Turning quickly from the window, she hurried to the dresser and pawed carelessly through the folded clothes in the top drawer until she found her turquoise blue jogging shorts and matching tank top. In record time Annette pulled off her T-shirt-styled nightgown and donned the jogging outfit, not bothering with a bra.

When she reached for a pair of heavy socks to wear with her running shoes, Annette caught a glimpse of her reflection in the dresser's mirror. She paused to look more closely. Her face was scrubbed clean of makeup and that, combined with the shorts and tank top, made her look awfully young.

"A kid, huh?" she murmured at her reflection and studied her shoulder-length blond hair. Reaching up, Annette loosely gathered her hair into two pigtails and made a face at herself. It was easy enough to see how he could have made a mistake like that, but there was no way she was going to go out looking like she just got out of braces.

She swept her hair back into a ponytail high off her neck. There. Now she looked like his competition. Returning to the bedroom area she shared with her sister, Annette tugged on her socks and shoes.

"What are you doing?" Marsha asked sleepily. "What time is it?"

"A little after six." With one shoe tied, Annette shifted position to tie the laces of the other.

Marsha frowned in her effort to focus her eyes on her sister. "You aren't going to go galloping around at this hour, are you?" She didn't believe in strenuous activity at any hour.

"Yep," Annette answered brightly, and shot her sister a wicked look. "You never know who I might run into."

"Let me guess," Marsha replied dryly and sank back into her pillows.

Annette started toward the door. "Wish me luck."

"With him you'll need it," Marsha called after her.

As Annette descended the exterior stairs to the ground floor, she silently conceded that in this instance her sister might be right. Luck would come in handy in catching Josh Lord. Without a second glance at a spectacular display of hot pink shrubs in full blossom, she trotted on. Playing a hunch, Annette headed toward the beach side of the resort, catching a salty whiff of ocean in the air.

Choosing the sidewalk instead of the sand, she rounded the curve and went past the cabanas. Her heart did a funny little leap when she recognized the man jogging toward her. The sleeves of a sweatshirt were tied low around his waist, baring a muscled wall of flat abs, his tanned chest glistening with healthy sweat. Annette saw the answering glint of recognition in his dark eyes when he spotted her. He didn't seem at all surprised to see her out jogging.

"Beautiful morning, isn't it?" she greeted him and shifted her course so she would pass him on the beach side of the walk. So far everything was going perfectly.

"Yes, it is," he agreed with a nod, not breaking stride.

Annette didn't slacken her pace either. But as she drew level with him to jog by, she deliberately stepped off the sidewalk onto the soft sand, throwing herself off balance on purpose. She faked a startled cry and tumbled to the ground, the sand cushioning her fall.

Very careful not to look around, she grabbed for her ankle and inwardly held her breath.

"Are you hurt?" His question came from a little distance away, but at least he had stopped. She managed to conceal the surge of triumph, though she did pick up on the skeptical note in his voice, as though he suspected the tumble had been for his benefit.

She cast him a quick glance and immediately lowered her head. Deep down, she wasn't all that proud of her silly ruse and she didn't feel ready to hold his steady gaze. "I'm okay," Annette insisted and flexed her ankle with fake caution. "I just turned it a little."

"Are you sure?" He waited as though sensing that something wasn't altogether right about this.

"Yes." Annette nodded but kept her face averted as she shifted her legs under her to rise, then paused to brush away the grains of sand clinging to her bare arms and legs. Even though she felt a little guilty, satisfaction filled her at the soft sound of his approaching footsteps in the sand.

"Let me give you a hand up." A large sun-browned hand reached out.

She looked at it, then hesitantly met his gaze before she put her hand in his. "This is embarrassing," she murmured as he helped her to her feet, conscious of his strength. He wasn't going to be easy to fool.

"What is?" he inquired.

"Falling down," she explained with a smile of chagrin. "Nobody can do it gracefully." The pretense of candor was meant to fool him and, for a wonder, it seemed to work. Annette knew she'd succeeded when she saw the amused indulgence in his expression. He released her hand but didn't let go of her, shifting his grip to support her elbow.

"Hey, it happens to all of us at one time or

another," he assured her, then suggested, "Why don't you test that ankle?"

She took a tentative step, deliberately favoring it. "It's a little tender, but I can walk it off." Annette wasn't going to pretend it was anything more than that. As she stood so close to him, she noted his body heat and healthy male smell. Both stimulated her senses, which were already overly alert to everything about him. Her side glance caught his watchful look, and she was dismayed to see a trace of suspicion in it.

"It could get worse. Sprains can be tricky."

She quickly protested, shaking her head. "But it's not sprained."

"I don't think you should run on it, though."

"Well, maybe not," she sighed. His hand fell away. "Thanks for stopping—" Annette paused and looked at him expectantly to see if he would supply his name.

"Josh."

"I'm Annette." She reached out to complete the mutual introduction with a handshake. When she didn't immediately withdraw her hand from the warm clasp of his fingers, Josh continued to hold it loosely. She wished there was something she could do to erase that glint of amusement from his eyes, but for the time being she was going to play it cool. "Thanks, Josh."

"My pleasure." His smile was brief.

She withdrew her hand and took a deep breath, which stretched the knit material of her tank top across the firm curves of her breasts. That got his attention. A flicker of annoyance appeared in his eyes. Annette wanted to laugh but she stifled the impulse. His gaze moved immediately back to her face, as though he guessed she had purposely been trying to get him to look down.

"Can I buy you some orange juice or a cup of coffee?" Annette offered. For a split second she thought he was going to refuse.

"Coffee sounds good. I haven't had my morning cup yet." Josh untied the sweatshirt around his waist and put it on. She was almost sorry when he did—it was a shame to cover up such a virile chest.

Her expression must have betrayed her thoughts, because he looked at her quizzically as he rolled it down with both hands. "Is something wrong?"

Annette started to deny that, then let a flirty smile curve her mouth. "I was just thinking that this is the first time I've seen you with a shirt on."

Just for an instant he looked irritated again, then he chuckled. "It is, isn't it? Okay, come on. Let's get that coffee. I'm done running."

"Oh, good. I wouldn't want you to stop because I was dumb enough to fall down." She followed him, trying to remember to throw in a tiny limp now and again. Not enough to make him worry but enough to make him believe her.

"So, are you staying here at the hotel?" he was asking.

"Yes, I am." She moved in the direction of the cabanas, where there was a walkway leading around the tall fence that screened the swimming pool from the beach. "Are you?" she asked innocently.

"Yeah." But Josh Lord didn't mention that he owned the place. "I believe they'll serve us outside on the patio if you'd like to sit there."

"Sure. That would be great."

"Where do you live when you're not on vacation?" Josh asked, and guided her around the pool to the umbrella-shaded tables outside the open-air coffee bar.

"Delaware, just outside Dover." She was pleased when he pulled out a wrought-iron chair for her to sit on.

"That's up the coast a ways," he remarked, waiting until she was seated before he sat down, his long legs nearly touching hers. "Is this your first trip to North Carolina?"

Annette nodded. "We flew in a few days ago. So far we haven't done much sightseeing, but we have a whole month for that." She was beginning to dislike his polite questions—they weren't going to get anywhere this way.

"We?" Josh asked blandly.

"My family—Dad, my stepmother Kathleen, my sister Marsha, and my little brother, Rob. And me." Annette knew that vacationing with her family made her seem young. But she couldn't lie about that. "Where are you from?"

"Here. I'm a native Tar Heel." Josh looked up as footsteps approached their table. She glanced up and recognized the blond-haired waiter coming toward them. Damn. It was Craig, the one who'd flirted with her at the pool yesterday afternoon. Double damn. He seemed surprised to see her with Josh Lord.

"Hello, Craig!" She greeted him with cheerful familiarity, hoping he would read between the lines and play along. "Did you draw the early shift?"

"Yes." He darted a curious but respectful look at Josh, whose gaze had narrowed slightly. "Did you want something?"

"I'll have a cup of black coffee," Annette said and looked all wide-eyed at Josh.

"The same," he echoed.

"Two black coffees coming right up." Craig backed away, seeming a little uneasy to be waiting on Josh.

When he'd gone behind the coffee bar, Annette was subjected to a few moments of silent scrutiny from Josh. "Do you know him?" he asked.

"Craig?" She shrugged lightly. "Not really. I met him yesterday at the pool."

The line of his mouth slanted in amusement. "You were busy yesterday, weren't you?"

She gave him a blank look. "What do you mean?" Then she pretended to get it. "Oh, because I met you there too. I guess my sister Marsha is the shy one in our family—I'm kinda not."

"It wouldn't hurt to be cautious," Josh stated. "I wouldn't get too friendly with the staff if I were you."

Annette wasn't sure if he was really warning her away from Craig. Obviously Josh didn't personally hire everyone on the staff—but he would undoubtedly have an employee who hit on the guests fired by somebody, probably the manager. This was getting interesting, but maybe she'd overdone it. Getting someone fired was not at all what she'd been aiming for.

"Why not?" She cocked her head to one side. It was hard for her to keep a straight face.

"Because they have work to do."

"Oh." Annette lowered her chin to keep from smiling. The handsome waiter hadn't seemed to care too much about that rule.

He came back with two mugs of coffee and made a big fuss about setting them down just so with napkins and spoons.

"Put it on my tab," Josh told him. The tone of his voice ensured that Craig would only nod in response.

"But this was supposed to be my treat," Annette

protested as Craig slipped away, unwilling to wait around while she argued with the owner. "I invited you."

"Um, I forgot," he said briskly. "Next time you can buy."

"Okay." She gave in readily to the suggestion even though she knew he didn't necessarily mean that there might be a next time. She took a sip of the steaming coffee. "And maybe next time I'll out-run you."

He seemed amused. "Don't make me feel old."

Annette favored him with her most charming smile. "Why do you say that? How old are you?"

"I'm thirty-three." When she laughed, he arched an eyebrow. "Did I say something funny?"

"Not really," Annette assured him. "It's just that you sounded a little like my dad for a second. And I know you're not his age. You aren't that much older than I am."

"And I'm not in college either." His tone was cool, but she knew perfectly well that he wasn't immune to her.

"So what do you do?" She changed the subject casually, taking another sip of coffee to let him answer.

"I'm in real estate." Which encompassed a lot of territory.

"Oh, that's interesting. My dad thinks that might be a good career for me. I don't know. I haven't decided yet."

"What does he do?"

It was hard for her to tell who was leading in this conversation. "He's a troubleshooter for an oil company. He gets sent to all the hot spots."

"So he must do a lot of traveling," Josh said.

"He does," Annette agreed. "That's why the whole

family vacations together when he comes back. We sometimes don't get to see him for months on end."

Craig headed their way with a pot of coffee. Josh looked up when he got to their table and covered his cup with his hand. "No more for me."

"Me neither." Annette sensed that Josh intended to bring their meeting to a close but she wanted to keep the upper hand. "I have to be getting back. My dad will start wondering where I am."

"I have a business meeting, sorry to say." Josh pushed his chair back from the table and got up.

"This early?" She realized that was none of her affair, and quickly thanked him for the coffee, adding, "And for rescuing me."

"Any time." He gave her a wink that made her squirm a little.

She laughed awkwardly. "Well, you have a great day," she said, standing up to leave.

"You too." His smile was pleasant but somewhat too businesslike for her taste. Maybe he really did have a meeting and was warming up for it.

Annette actually didn't feel like leaving and when Josh was gone, she sat back down to finish her coffee. She didn't notice that Craig was lingering on the sidelines until he came over to clear the table. He glanced in the direction that Josh had disappeared in, then looked curiously at Annette.

"You thought you recognized him yesterday," he remarked. "I guess it turned out that you'd met him before, right?"

"No." She shook her head in brief denial. "We just happened to run into each other while we were out jogging this morning and decided to have coffee together."

"That was fast," he commented.

Annette smiled but not in the friendliest way. "It was a coincidence."

Craig nodded, looking suddenly less sure of himself, as though he had misunderstood the situation. However, he was conceited enough to believe Annette was actually interested in him. His manner changed to winning charm and he lowered his voice. "We're not supposed to ask guests out, but a friend of mine is throwing a party tonight. Are you free?"

"I'm afraid not," she refused the offhand invitation.

"No problem. Maybe another time," he said with renewed hope.

"Maybe." But Annette doubted that time would ever come. She got up to really leave this time, tossing an airy "See you!" over her shoulder. But as she started through the breezeway between the hotel buildings, she met her father and Kathleen.

"Good morning," her father greeted her and let his gaze slide past her to the young waiter watching her walk away. "I see you've already made a conquest. Is he anyone I have to worry about? I don't need any more gray hairs, Annette. What's his name?"

"If you mean Craig, the answer is no, there's nothing to worry about. I'm not interested." She was relieved that her father hadn't arrived a few minutes earlier and seen her with Josh Lord. She had the uneasy feeling he wouldn't have approved and there was no reason her dad needed to know about him. She pretended to study his hair—he still had a great head of it. "Why? Did you find another gray hair this morning, Dad?"

"No. Let's keep it that way," he countered.

Annette laughed, then glanced at Kathleen, who'd been listening to them with amusement. "Where's Robby?"

"My wiggle worm? Marsha is getting him dressed and giving me a break," Kathleen replied, explaining her son's absence. "We were heading for the coffee bar. Do they serve breakfast there or do we have to stay inside?"

"I believe they do," Annette said. Craig had had menus tucked under his arm, so most likely she was right.

"Have you eaten?" Kathleen asked. "Want to join us?"

Annette was hungry and inclined to accept the invitation, but she knew her father and stepmother didn't have many chances to be alone. "I think I'll change first."

"We're going to Orton Plantation later on this morning, so wear your walking shoes," her father warned.

"I will," she promised with a smile and started off for the room she shared with her sister.

The door was standing open when she reached the room. Robby was sitting patiently on an unmade bed while Marsha wiggled one sneaker of his favorite grubby pair onto his foot.

"H'lo, Annette," he greeted her loudly when she entered the room.

"Good morning," she replied.

Marsha looked up at her as she reached for the other small sneaker. "Why are you smiling like that?"

"So far, I'm having a wonderful day," Annette said. "How about you?"

"Not too bad. I love the smell of children's sneakers in the morning," Marsha shot back. She set Robby on the floor when she was done.

"Ha-ha." Annette flopped on the bed.

"Tired? I don't want to know why," her sister said.

"Why is Annette tired?" Robby wanted to know. "Where did she go?"

"Ask her," Marsha said dryly. "On second thought—don't."

"Okay." Robby did a half backflip over one of the beds and came up with the remote control for the TV. Seeing his two sisters on the verge of a conversation he wasn't going to understand, he found a cartoon channel and fixed his attention on a cat and mouse wreaking havoc on each other.

"Mission accomplished? You ran into him?" Marsha asked in a low voice.

"I practically fell at his feet—literally." She got up and made an exaggerated show of limping across the room, favoring her ankle.

"Oh, no. You didn't fake a sprained ankle," Marsha said with indignation.

"No, just a little twist. But it got me a cup of coffee," Annette declared with twinkling triumph.

Marsha shook her head in disapproval. "You should think about what's going to happen when he finds out about your little tricks."

The mouse had flattened the cat when Robby looked up to ask, "When who finds out?" He craned his neck to look at his sisters. "You mean Daddy?"

"No, honey," Annette assured him. "Marsha and I are talking about someone else." Her little brother looked instantly bored and turned his attention back to the TV. She smirked at her sister. "I got him to talk to me. That's all I wanted."

"You got that cute waiter to talk to you too."

Annette gave a low laugh. "Hey, he served us coffee this morning. It was a little weird. I couldn't pretend not to know him."

"Annette—" Her sister let out an exasperated

sigh. "Sooner or later you have to stop this. I'm voting for sooner."

Annette only shrugged.

"All right. I get the message. I shouldn't get involved in this," Marsha stated crossly.

"Thanks." Annette sauntered to the closet to choose her clothes for the day.

"But keep me posted." It went against Marsha's nature to stay upset for long, but her concern for her sister was genuine. Her tone became placating. "Robby and I haven't had breakfast yet. Want us to wait for you while you change?"

The cartoon ended with a noisy musical jingle and the little boy switched off the TV, waving the remote like a fantasy weapon and making bang-bang sounds under his breath.

"Give me that before you break it," Marsha said. He handed it to her.

"I was only playing," Robby responded. "Marshie, do they have my favorite cereal here? That's what I want."

"It'll only take me a few minutes to change. Kathleen and Dad are at the coffee bar. I'll meet you two there, okay?"

"I don't want coffee," Robby said, fidgeting.

"Like I'd give you any," Marsha told him affectionately. "You're hyper without it. Come on, kid, let's go."

"See you," Annette called after them. "Don't forget to close the door on the way out." She slipped a pair of white pants off a hanger. She wanted to look good.

Just in case she ran into Josh Lord for a second time that morning.

Chapter 3

The lock defied Annette's attempts to open it with her keycard and the little red button flashed instead of the green. Hot, tired, and impatient, she swiped it again and tugged at the doorknob. Strands of sun-streaked hair escaped the scrunchie that held her ponytail, and the sweat she'd worked up exercising plastered them to her neck. Just to add to her irritation, her tank top was sticking to her back too.

When the lock resisted another attempt, Annette hit the room door with the flat of her hand in a fit of pique. She would have kicked it if her right foot didn't hurt so much from the blister on its heel. Her bad mood was caused by more than just heat and fatigue. Frustration compounded it.

As she yanked the keycard out of the slot, the door swung open. For a stunned instant Annette thought it had opened of its own accord, until she saw her bathrobed sister behind it, modestly using the door for a shield.

"Why didn't you just knock?" Marsha complained with a trace of lingering anxiety. "I thought someone was trying to break in."

"I didn't know you were here," Annette snapped and limped across the threshold, a raw pain burning where her running shoe had rubbed her right heel. She headed for the nearest thing with cushions. "The keycard didn't work."

"What happened? Did you sprain your ankle for real this time?" Marsha asked as she closed the door and Annette flopped in the chair by the window.

"No, I didn't." Annette sighed at the implied criticism, knowing she deserved it. But that didn't mean she wanted to hear it now. "I have a blister."

She untied her sneaker and eased it off her foot, feeling the first glimmer of relief. There was still a sock that had to be removed, which evoked a hissing breath of pain when she rolled it down over her ankle and off. As Annette twisted her foot across her knee to examine it, Marsha bent toward her and grimaced in sympathy.

"Ouch. Poor you."

"Count yourself lucky that you hate exercise," Annette grumbled as the inflamed area throbbed with exposure to air.

"Do you want me to get you a bandage for that?" Marsha offered.

"No. I have one somewhere—I'll find it in a minute. It's the gel kind, that supposedly works." She leaned back in her chair and let it support her head. "Three days of nonstop jogging every morning and this blister is all I have to show for it."

Marsha could fill in the blanks. "You didn't see him this morning either."

"Oh, I saw him all right," Annette admitted with frustration, "but from three blocks away. I couldn't catch up with him—not with this thing on my heel."

Marsha sat on the twin bed opposite the chair and

folded her hands in her lap. "Did it occur to you that it might be a sign? Maybe you should give up."

"No." Annette chewed thoughtfully on a fingernail, her mind working feverishly. "I'm just going to have to think of some other way to see him."

"You've jogged every morning and haunted the swimming pool every afternoon," her sister reminded her. "Maybe it just isn't meant to be."

"I can't accept that," Annette stated with a decisive shake of her head. "This is where you and I are really different, Marsha. You're content to sit and wait for Mr. Right to show up, and I'm not. Love just doesn't work that way, you know," she insisted. "You have to make your own opportunities."

On some subjects, Marsha was predictably stubborn. This was one. "But you can't make somebody love you, Annette. Either he does or he doesn't. What you're feeling is a crush. You hardly know this guy."

"Look." Annette leaned forward, feeling that she was explaining the facts of life to her younger sister. She had to sound wise to distract Marsha from the point she'd just scored. "Josh is interested, I know that—"

Marsha rolled her eyes.

"That's not a constructive response," Annette said, irritated. "Not that I care what you think. Anyway, he's got everything I want, so why wouldn't I follow up?" she finished.

Marsha didn't attempt to deny that. But she still got a dig in. "Follow up? You're chasing him!"

"Well, yes." Annette took a deep breath to contain her exasperation. She ventured an appeal to her sister's common sense. "It's the oldest game around. A man chases a woman until she catches him, you know that. But you and I are the only ones who know I'm chasing Josh Lord. You can bet I'm not going to let him find that out. He's going to think it's all his idea."

"It just doesn't look right," Marsha protested. "And I don't think it's fair either."

Annette sighed and shook her head. "All's fair in love and war, haven't you heard?"

"Yes, I have. I came across it in one of those books I'm always wasting my time on, according to you. It's a Shakespeare quote," Marsha retorted in a rare show of annoyance. "Sometimes, Annette, you act like you know everything worth knowing and I don't."

"But—"

"That old line doesn't justify what you're doing."

For a moment Annette just stared at her, a little dumbfounded. Finally she said, "You're my sister, Marsha, and I love you. There isn't anything I wouldn't do for you." She paused and gave a baffled shake of her head. "But sometimes it's hard for me to believe that anyone so incredibly naïve could be related to me. Marsha, you are really overprotective. Stop it."

Marsha eyed her warily. "What do you mean?"

"Because you're sitting here lecturing me about chasing men! Is that something you've seen me do before?"

"No," Marsha said, adding, "and maybe that's why I'm lecturing you. Although I wouldn't call it that."

"But doesn't it give you a clue that Josh is a special case?" Annette reasoned.

"I guess so." Marsha found herself unwillingly agreeing with her sister, and silently marveled at Annette's knack of getting people to see things her way. She was incredibly persuasive.

"Then, instead of being so negative, why don't you help?" Annette saw nothing wrong with asking for it and her tone slid toward patronizing. "I haven't had much luck at the swimming pool or the jogging path. I really would appreciate some new ideas."

After sulking for a few more seconds, Marsha thought for a minute, then offered, "What about where he works? Does he have an office somewhere?"

"He not only has an office, he has an entire office building," Annette informed her. "I went down to the hotel's business center and looked a few things up on one of their computers. I found an address for Lord Incorporated and yesterday morning I got a taxi out front and had the driver go by it."

"That's called stalking," Marsha said.

"No, it isn't. It's called research. And that's why I was late meeting you guys."

"And?" Marsha prompted.

"And the building is practically all by itself." Annette sighed. "There isn't a single shop or tourist trap within three blocks of it. I wouldn't have a believable excuse for being there. It isn't a place you can just happen to walk by."

"Hmm," was all Marsha said for a minute. Annette knew that a puzzle was all it took to get her sister interested. Marsha liked to think things through. "If we eliminate the office, what else is there? We know he jogs and swims. What about other hobbies or sports?"

Annette brightened and nibbled at her lip. "Good question. I think you're on the right track."

"Maybe he plays golf. There's a course right by the hotel."

"He probably does. The problem is, I don't," she said with a rueful smile. "And I'm not about to volunteer to caddy for him." She snapped her fingers. "I've got it! The tennis courts! I'd bet anything Josh plays!"

She bounded out of her chair, forgetting about her

aching heel, and ran over with one shoe off and one shoe on to hug her sister. "Thanks! You're a genius!"

"Maybe, but I don't see how—" Marsha broke off in confusion, frowning at Annette as she hobbled away from her. "You can't spend all your time hanging around the tennis courts in a teeny-tiny white dress waiting for him to show up."

Halfway to a much-needed shower, Annette stopped. "Did I bring a dress like that?" she fake-wondered.

"Annette!" Her sister threw a pillow at her.

"If not, I can buy one in the hotel shop. It's huge—they have a golf and a tennis section," she said with satisfaction. "And just so you know, anyone who wants to play has to reserve the court. All I have to do is get a peek at the sign-up sheet and I'll know the exact day and time Josh will be there."

It sounded simple but Marsha knew better. "And just how do you intend to get a look at the sign-up sheet? I doubt it's on a clipboard on the chain-link fence. You know how people like to sneak onto courts and pretend they belong there. Someone connected to the hotel has to maintain it, right?"

"You get dressed while I shower. Then you can come with me. I'll show you," Annette declared with a surge of confidence.

Marsha was half-convinced that her sister was a bulldozer covered in velvet. Somehow Annette managed to push aside obstacles as though they didn't exist. For the past ten minutes she had been talking to the tennis pro on duty about available court time for the next few days—talking and joking as if they were old friends, that is.

When the phone in the tennis section rang, Annette

casually turned the reservation book around so she could read it and smiled at the pro. "Don't mind me. Go ahead and answer that. I'll look over these free slots and decide which one we want to reserve."

He agreed without any hesitation and moved to the end of the counter to pick up the phone. Annette slid a glance of triumph at Marsha and began looking over the list. Josh Lord's name, written down in a big, bold hand that had to be his, practically leaped off the page across from the five o'clock slot the next afternoon.

When Marsha noticed that the court next to the one Josh had reserved wasn't booked, she murmured in a low undertone, "You lead a charmed life, Annette."

"I do, don't I?" She couldn't resist a smug little smile. The tennis pro hung up the phone and came back.

"How are we doing here? Did you find a time that works for you?" he asked affably.

"Yes, I did. Mark me down for tomorrow afternoon at four thirty." She gave him her name and room number. "And we'll need to rent two tennis rackets. And I'll take three cans of balls."

"Sure thing." He nodded. "Any preference in equipment?"

Annette shook her head with indifference. "No. Whatever you have on hand is fine."

"Okeydoke. One last thing—what's your grip size?" he asked.

Annette told him and added that Marsha's was the same, then thanked him happily. She pushed away from the counter to leave while Marsha stared at her in barely concealed astonishment.

"See you tomorrow," the pro called after them. Annette gave him a flirty wave and echoed his words.

They were outside on the sidewalk before Marsha recovered her voice. "When did I say anything about playing tennis?"

"I took it for granted that you would," Annette answered, a little startled that her sister seemed unwilling. "This was your idea. I can't play by myself, Marsha."

"I thought you were just going to find out when Josh was going to be there, then drop by," she replied.

"What would I do? Stand on the sidelines and watch him play?" Annette scoffed. "That's a little too obvious, sister dear. If I'm playing tennis I have a reason to be there—and he can't be sure I'm only there to see him."

"But I told you I didn't want to get involved in any of your schemes," Marsha reminded her.

"All you're going to do is play tennis! You brought your tennis sweater, after all. I saw it in your drawer."

"I was thinking of hitting off the backboard. That was about it."

Annette shook her head. "You could work on your ground strokes with me. That way everybody wins."

"Except Joshua Lord, of course. He can run but he cannot hide," she intoned. "I know the way you work," Marsha went on when Annette protested. "It all starts out so innocent. You lure people in and then you pounce. I have a feeling it's happening right now. But for some reason I'm numb."

"Oh, please. You're exaggerating, Marsha."

"No, I'm not," her sister said with the certainty of past experience. "Even if Joshua Lord notices you tomorrow, I don't see what good it's going to do. He's, what, ten years older than you?"

"Eleven years older."

Marsha sniffed. "That's worse. You're a guest at a hotel he owns and you're here with your father—what, do you think he wants to duel with Dad? Have you thought about Dad finding out, by the way?"

Annette tossed her head. "I'm almost twenty-one and old enough to make my own decisions."

"Yes, but your decisions stink sometimes," Marsha pointed out.

Annette thought it over, but only for a moment. "I'll work it out with Dad. After all, I'm not trying to get Josh Lord to marry me. I only want to go out with him."

"Dad still isn't going to be thrilled."

Annette scowled. "I'll cross that bridge when I come to it. But in the meantime, you have a sisterly obligation to help me out."

"No, I don't." Marsha looked at her sister's mulish expression—and understood the emotions behind it. "But I will."

Annette bit her lip, "Really?"

"Yeah."

"You'll play tennis with me tomorrow?"

Marsha smiled ruefully. "You know I will—although I should probably have my head examined for agreeing."

The hours Annette had spent at the swimming pool had turned her legs a healthy golden color and added a few platinum streaks to her blond hair. The result: her short white tennis outfit with black trim looked nothing short of fantastic. Annette had deliberately booked the adjacent court a half hour earlier than Josh's five o'clock slot, so she would be playing when he got there. Her side of the net faced the gate the arriving players went through.

As five o'clock got closer, she started getting nervous, wondering if he'd canceled or changed the hour. She didn't want to think so, after all the trouble she'd gone to. The handwriting in the book had seemed like his—she knew for a fact that it wasn't the pro who'd jotted down Josh Lord's name in those bold, clear strokes. He'd only scribbled hers. Somehow Josh signing up personally implied a higher level of commitment to her.

Fretting about it wasn't helping her game. She nearly missed an easy lob from Marsha and tried to bring her attention back to the uneven match. They were in the middle of a set when Annette saw Josh approaching the court, accompanied by a different tennis pro, not the guy from the shop. Her heart did a little tumble at the sight of him in white tennis shorts, and knit shirt stretched tautly across his chest. The sun glinted copper bright on his dark hair.

A faintly bemused smile played at the corners of his mouth when Josh recognized her. Annette smashed Marsha's next lob to the opposite corner, scoring an effortless point.

"That's game!" she declared, even though it wasn't, and trotted around the net to take a break and change sides.

"Are you sure?" Marsha frowned, standing stock-still at the baseline. "I thought it—"

"That's game," Annette repeated, and quelled her sister's protest with a glare. Marsha glanced around, noticing Josh's arrival for the first time.

"I guess you're right." She accepted Annette's bogus scoring and didn't dispute the claim.

Annette walked to the corner of the court near

the high chain-link fence and picked up the towel she'd left with her things. She pretended to wipe away nonexistent sweat from her face and neck as Josh, in the next court, unzipped the case protecting his racket. Tension licked along her nerve ends while she waited for him to glance her way. When he did turn his dark gaze toward her, the chiseled planes of his face seemed to fill her field of vision, excluding everything else.

"Hey, fancy meeting you here." She faked mild surprise at seeing him.

"I have the strange feeling that you're following me," Josh remarked, giving her an astute once-over. "Now why is that?"

"I was just going to accuse you of following me," Annette countered with a brittle laugh. "I was here first."

"Appearances can be deceiving." He didn't seem convinced.

Annette decided that the best way to allay his suspicions was to tease him. "Not in your case. You're so handsome," she cooed. It was over the top, but even outrageously obvious flirting made men happy. "Anyway, I'm old-fashioned."

"And what's that supposed to mean?"

"Just that I prefer a man to do the chasing." Annette's smoke-colored eyes looked at him with absolute innocence as she turned away. She'd gotten in the last word. Too bad if Josh Lord didn't like it.

She walked back to her court and called across the net to Marsha. "Are you ready?" At the affirmative nod from her sister, she batted a ball to her. "It's your serve."

Annette had a tough time concentrating on her game. She was much more interested in the match being played on the adjacent court. Marsha was an adequate player but she wasn't a challenging opponent. And Josh was a powerful distraction.

The match ended with Annette the easy winner. She would've liked to stay and watch Josh, but as she had pointed out to Marsha yesterday, it was simply too obvious. Plus, she was plagued by the knowledge that this hadn't been a very successful encounter. As she and Marsha gathered their things to leave, Annette tried to think of a way to salvage something from this lost opportunity.

She happened to look at Marsha's tennis sweater, a twin to her own, except that hers was trimmed in black and Marsha's had navy blue braid. She froze for an instant as an idea formed.

"Marsha, is your keycard in your sweater pocket?" Annette asked in an eager rush.

"Yes. Why?" Marsha gave her a funny look. "Did you forget yours?"

"No, I have it," Annette assured her. "But right as we leave the court, I want you to accidentally drop your sweater. Act like you have no idea that you did. Just keep walking."

Marsha frowned. "Exactly why am I doing this?"

"Because I want you to leave it behind—with the keycard in it—so Josh can find it when he leaves and return it," Annette explained.

"You can't be serious." Marsha stared at her, fully aware that Annette was completely serious. "I came along with you this afternoon just to play tennis. You didn't say anything about me losing my sweater on purpose."

"I just thought of it. And you aren't going to lose it, Marsha. You're just going to leave it behind accidentally. And if you're going to argue with me, would you please smile?" she urged. "I don't want Josh to know that we're up to something."

"No," Marsha agreed with a wide and faintly sarcastic smile. "We can't let Josh Lord know we're plotting against him. If you want to leave a sweater behind for him to find, drop your own—and leave me out of it."

"Marsha, I can't. It would be too obvious if I left mine," Annette reasoned with forced calm. "It has to be yours so he won't get suspicious."

"And what happens if he doesn't see it? Or someone else sees it and steals it?" Marsha retorted. "The keycard doesn't have our room number on it but why should we risk it?"

"Don't you get it? The front desk wouldn't tell just anyone who the keycard belongs to. But they would tell him."

Marsha grumbled, "The way I see it, I'm going to be out a sweater."

"I'll buy you another one," Annette offered. "A nicer one. Will you do it?"

"Give me one good reason why I should."

"Because you're my sister," Annette said. "And I've gotten you out of trouble lots of times."

"Almost as many times as you got me into it," Marsha reminded her with a sigh. She wasn't even sure why she was resisting the inevitable. Sooner or later, she always went along with her sister's crazy schemes—reluctantly.

"Please?" Annette remembered to say.

"Okay, I'll do it," she agreed and added the warning, "But if I don't get my sweater back, you're buying me a whole new outfit, not just that."

"Done deal." Annette beamed, her eyes sparkling like burnished silver. "Let's go."

As they walked to the gate in the fence, she glanced

at Josh. She was warmed by the discovery that he was watching her. It took all her self-control not to break into a smile. Instead, she lifted her hand in a vague wave.

Josh acknowledged the salute with a nod. When they started down the walk, Annette murmured instructions to her sister. "Let the sweater sort of slide out of your hand while you pretend you're talking to me."

"This is ridiculous," Marsha muttered. "What am I supposed to talk to you about?" She had never been any good at subterfuge or deception.

"It doesn't matter." Annette tried not to let her nervousness get the better of her. "Talk about anything. Talk about the tennis balls stuck in the chain-link fence. Count them if you want."

"One. Two, three—oh, the hell with it. I know I'm going to regret this," she said in a low voice as she let go of the sweater at last. It slid casually out of her hand and onto the walkway. "As a matter of fact, I know I am. But what I don't know is how you always manage to talk me into things. You'd think I would have better sense by now, right?"

The sweater was lying in the middle of a block of pavement. No one called their attention to it and Annette breathed easier.

The deed was done. It was time to soothe her sister's rattled nerves. "You don't have anything to worry about."

"What happens when he returns it? *If* he returns it?" Marsha questioned.

"I'll handle that," Annette promised. "You're going to be in the shower."

"For how long? Am I going to look like Prune Girl?"

"No," Annette said quickly. But she had no way of knowing exactly when Josh would return the sweater. And what if he sent the pro? She didn't want to think about that.

"Anyway, I'll thank him for you, so there won't be any reason for you to even speak to him." She was well aware that Josh would know it was a put-up job after one look at Marsha's guilty face. He was likely to guess as much anyway, but Annette intended to see that he had plenty of reason to doubt his conclusion.

She glanced over her shoulder. They were already out of sight of the tennis courts. "Hurry," she urged her sister, and quickened her pace to a running walk.

"Why?"

"Because *I* want to be out of the shower before Josh comes," Annette answered. "We only have one." She broke into a real run.

Her hands fumbled as she twisted her hair into a demure knot on the top of her head. Annette was sure she hadn't been this nervous on her first date in junior high. She had butterflies in her stomach and her knees were shaking. She secured her hair with a large clasp and stepped back to view her overall reflection in the mirror.

"How do I look?" she asked Marsha, nervously moistening her dry lips.

Her robe, a present from her stepmother, was made out of dotted swiss. Talk about innocent. And modest. It was buttoned up to the slender curve of her neck. With her blond hair swept up and off her face, and her clear gray eyes, the effect was pure and sweet.

"Like an angel," Marsha admitted in all truth.

Annette jumped when she heard the knock on the door. She breathed in deeply and looked at her sister for reassurance. Never mind asking for moral support, she thought. What she was doing wasn't exactly moral. On the other hand, it was a very small and eminently forgivable sin.

"Go get in the shower," she said quickly. "And don't come out until I call you."

"Don't worry. I won't." Marsha scurried off to the bathroom.

Annette's legs felt unsteady as she walked to the door. The security chain was on it and she left it in place, opening the door just a crack to peer outside.

It was Josh.

He was still in his tennis clothes, one brawny arm braced against the door frame. His dark eyes gleamed when he saw her, but the line of his mouth was straight.

"Hello." Annette tried to sound surprised to see him, but her voice wasn't behaving very well.

"Hello." He returned the greeting in a low, modulated voice. He didn't shift his casually relaxed stance, just waited for her to open the door.

"Oh—just a minute." She closed it to unhook the safety chain, then opened it.

Her heart was beating a rapid tattoo against her ribs as she moved into the opening, blocked from stepping too far outside by his masculine bulk. The dark mahogany of his hair was ruffled from playing outdoors—that and its thickness invited a smoothing hand. His gaze roamed over her, taking her in as though he liked what he saw and making it difficult for her to breathe normally.

"You need a sprig of lily-of-the-valley," Josh said dryly.

"Oh? Why?" Annette wondered if she sounded as foolish as she felt.

"You just do. To go with those big gray eyes and button nose and that sweet robe. You're as pretty as a picture."

Was he mocking her? Well, it wasn't as if she could fling open the door wearing nothing but sheer black lace and a come-hither smile.

"I just got out of the shower." Annette touched a hand to her hair, wishing for a brief instant that she looked a little sexier at the moment. The thought vanished when she caught the glimpse of something smoldering in his eyes, especially when he looked at her as though he was awfully interested in what was underneath all that modest dotted swiss.

"Fresh and clean, huh?" Josh seemed not to really care about anything she said.

She was very conscious of his natural scent drifting around her. Nice. If she had to name it and put it in a bottle, she'd call it Southern Sun. No, she thought, make that Southern Sun for Men—a warm, invitingly masculine scent, with a top note of handsome arrogance and a touch of smirk.

She told herself to stop thinking like an aftershave ad and also to stop staring at him. The last wasn't easy. The arm braced against the door frame was right in her line of vision. She could practically touch the fine, sun-bleached hair on his arm and wondered if they would be as silky to the touch as they looked. She shifted her gaze to his strong features, but that didn't ease the turmoil his nearness aroused in her.

"Did you want something?" Annette asked in a surprisingly steady voice. His glance fell to her lips and her heart stopped beating for a full second. Then his mouth tightened and the moment passed.

"You left this by the tennis courts." He lifted his other hand to show her the sweater and the room keycard between his fingers.

"I did?" She took it from him, her fingers tingling when they brushed against his.

"Just a little more subtle than a dropped handkerchief," Josh mocked the ploy to get him there, "and maybe more up-to-date."

Annette pretended to examine the sweater. "Except that I didn't drop it," she replied. "This belongs to my sister Marsha." She showed him the label inside the collar and the initial M stamped on the tag. "She must have left it."

When she lifted her gaze, she saw the flicker of uncertainty in his eyes. Her plan was working. Josh couldn't be sure the sweater had been left for him to find.

"It's lucky you returned it. Marsha is in the shower," Annette explained, her words confirmed by the sound of water running inside the hotel room, "or she'd thank you herself. She didn't even miss it."

"Then it isn't yours?" Josh still seemed skeptical.

"It looks a lot like mine," she said. "That's why I was confused when you first handed it to me. But mine has black trim to go with my tennis skirt. The trim on this is navy blue, so it's easy to get them mixed up."

"Yes, it is." Josh continued to watch her closely.

It took all of Annette's skill to keep from betraying herself. "We probably would've noticed Marsha's sweater was missing and gone back to look for it if I hadn't had my keycard with me."

He must have had the front desk clerk run it through the card reader to find out whose room it belonged to. Rank had its privileges.

"It helped that I found the other one in the

sweater pocket," Josh agreed with a continuing trace of suspicion.

"It sure did. Aren't pockets great? Women's clothes don't always have them. I guess the front desk helped you out with returning it, huh?"

"You could say that." Now he was looking at her with level amusement. "They know me around here."

"Oh—right. Of course. Hey, I don't know how to thank you. This is the second time you've rescued me. Well, my sister, really. I should offer you a reward . . . or something . . ." She trailed off, distracted by the interesting curve of his hard, masculine mouth.

"Or something," Josh murmured to indicate his choice of the latter.

A heady sexual tension enveloped Annette as his hand came up to lightly hold her chin, the touch of his fingers warm and firm. A tiny quiver ran through her at the contact. Josh leaned toward her, slowly bridging the space between them while his knowing gaze held hers. She was incapable of movement.

Her lashes drifted shut when his mouth settled onto her lips, his warm breath reaching them an instant before he claimed a kiss.

And what a kiss it was.

His mouth was tender and made no demands, yet the way he kissed was incredibly provocative. His easy-going skill revealed his superior experience, but he made no attempt to take her into his arms, not even when her lips softened under his light possession to invite him to do more.

Josh released her lips as slowly as he had taken them, and lifted his head to study her. The hand under her chin was caressing, his fingers gently stroking the feminine lines of her throat. She would have jumped into bed if he'd asked—thank goodness her sister was in the shower.

The corners of his mouth deepened with faint but sensual amusement. "That's what you wanted me to do, wasn't it?" Josh challenged.

It was, but for the life of her, Annette couldn't answer him. Her lips continued to tingle with the sensation left by his kiss. An elemental unspoken message passed between the two of them, but when his hand came away from her chin, the connection was broken. Josh straightened up, away from the door. And away from her, much to her chagrin.

His gaze flicked past her into the shadowed hotel room. "You should tell your sister to keep better track of her things."

"I will," Annette promised, but Josh had already turned to leave. "Thank you," she called after him.

As his long, unhurried strides carried him away, Annette remained outside the door a minute longer to watch him leave. Then she looked down at the sweater she'd forgotten she was holding, suddenly wanting to whirl it around her head. Elated, she ran back into the room, where she waltzed across the carpet and did just that, giving a jubilant laugh.

"It worked, Marsha!" she called. The sweater landed on the bed, propelled by centrifugal force.

"What?" came the reply, muffled by the noise of the shower.

"I said it worked!" Annette shouted.

"I can't hear you!" her sister yelled back.

"Turn off the water!"

It was several seconds later that Marsha ducked her head outside the bathroom door.

"Has he gone?"

"Yes, yes, yes," Annette said gleefully. "It worked!"

"Good. Another minute and I really would have turned into Prune Girl," Marsha declared.

Annette stared at her dripping-wet sister as Marsha wrapped a towel around herself. "Were you in the shower the whole time?"

There was a blank look at the question. "You told me to stay there until you called."

"You idiot." Annette laughed. "I meant that you should stay in the bathroom."

"That isn't what you said," Marsha retorted.

"Well, you weren't supposed to take me literally." It was very hard not to smile.

"Did he bring back my sweater?"

Annette picked it up and presented it to her with a little flourish. "Here it is." Then she couldn't contain her excitement any longer. "He kissed me, Marsha! He is just the most amazing kisser."

"And?" Marsha looked like she was waiting for Annette to say that Josh Lord had not only kissed her but asked her out on an equally amazing date.

But Annette didn't have bragging rights on that score, although personally she thought the dropped-sweater trick was worth more than a kiss. "That was all," she admitted. But the warm glow didn't lessen. "It's enough for now."

Chapter 4

The angling light from the morning sun glinted on the blue waters separating Wrightsville Beach from the mainland. Diving from overhead, a screeching gull swooped close to shore. Annette slowed her jogging down to a walk, stretching her legs now and then so the muscles wouldn't cramp. She headed off the path onto the sandy beach. The small marina belonging to the hotel complex was in sight just ahead.

It had been another fruitless morning with no sign of Josh. She would have quit jogging every day except that she didn't want Josh to think that she ran only in the hopes of seeing him. She wanted him to believe that it was part of her normal routine. Actually she was beginning to enjoy it and was physically invigorated by the exercise.

Thick strands of her blond hair had worked free of her ponytail. Annette slipped the scrunchie off and shook her head to let her hair tumble loose around her shoulders. Running her fingers through it, she lifted the silky mass to let the cool breeze reach the nape of her neck. Across the water, the mainland of

North Carolina stood out against the horizon and she paused to look at it.

Then she heard the sound of feet running through the sand toward her and half-turned to glance idly back. It was a second before it registered that the young guy with the burnished gold hair was Craig, the waiter. Without the uniform he looked like a surfer dude, in faded blue cutoffs and a fishnet T-shirt in a darker shade of blue.

"Hey there." His smile was wide, practically oozing charm. "I knew if I kept looking I'd find you out here somewhere, jogging away."

"You were right," Annette agreed with only a polite amount of welcome in her voice. He wasn't exactly the man she wanted to meet this morning, but when she resumed her walk, Craig fell in step beside her. "I take it you have the weekend off or at least today off," she remarked, with a pointed glance at his ragged cutoffs.

"The hotel rotates our schedules so everybody gets at least one full weekend off a summer. This weekend's mine," he explained. "Otherwise we just get an odd Saturday or Sunday each month."

"I see," she murmured, not really interested.

He draped an arm in a too-familiar way around her shoulders, paying no attention to her start of surprise. Annette wanted to shrug it away, but she doubted that Craig would get the message. She continued to walk, not entirely indifferent to his arm—in fact, she was annoyed by it.

"A buddy of mine is letting me use his Sunfish for the weekend," he said, his head turned toward her as they trudged through the sand. "It's going to be a perfect day for sailing. Want to come?"

Annette supposed that he expected her to fall all

over herself in eagerness to accept this last-minute invitation. "Sorry." The smile barely moved her lips as she refused. "My family's already made plans for the day."

"So?" He didn't seem to think that was an obstacle. "You're a big girl now. You don't have to go with them."

Annette stopped and turned to face him, forcing him to slide his arm off her shoulder.

"I don't have to go with them, but I want to," she stated.

"Aw, come on," Craig said coaxingly. "You know you'll have more fun with me." When she didn't seem impressed, he came up with his own reason for that. "I would've asked you yesterday but you weren't anywhere around."

"I doubt if it would have made any difference, Craig," Annette replied, trying not to be rude. "I happen to enjoy being with my folks."

"Yeah, but you can go with them whenever," he argued. "This is my only free time and I want you to spend it with me."

"Sorry. No."

He was too conceited to believe that she meant it, convinced that she only wanted to be persuaded. He tangled his hand in her hair. Annette didn't have a chance to do more than grab at his arm in protest before his mouth was crushed against hers. She wasn't in the least aroused by his hungry demand for a response and was glad when he abruptly broke it off before she had to kick him where it counted. He cast an anxious look toward the hotel's marina, then let her go.

His somewhat guilty behavior made her curious and Annette glanced in the same direction. A young girl, a member of the hotel staff, was sitting on the counter of a wood shelter on the dock where the hotel rented pedal boats and small sailboats to guests. She was looking in their direction.

"One of your girlfriends?" Annette teased him.

"Phyllis? No." He shook his head in an easy denial.

Annette made another guess. "I suppose the hotel has a policy against staff hooking up with the guests."

"Yeah," he admitted, but his smile indicated that he considered it a rule meant to be broken. "They aren't strict about it, though."

But he didn't repeat his invitation and Annette didn't bring it up. Her gaze went back to the marina, drawn to the two larger boats tied up at the front end. The nearest one was about a fifty-footer and the other was a little smaller.

"Does the hotel own those big boats tied up there?" she asked.

"Just the smaller one. The hotel charters it for fishing and harbor cruises," Craig informed her. "During the winter a lot of people come here for sport fishing. When someone hooks a marlin it's a sight to see."

"I bet it is," Annette agreed. "What about the other boat?"

"That's Joshua Lord's new toy." Craig shifted his stance, uncomfortable with that subject. Annette tried not to reveal her sudden increased interest in the boat. "Hey, I can't hang around here any longer or they'll put me to work," he joked. "Are you sure you won't change your mind and come with me today?"

"No thanks." She shook her head to reinforce the refusal.

"Suit yourself." He seemed to be making the point that she was depriving herself of his company and not the other way around. "We could have had a ball."

Her mouth twitched with amusement as Craig backed away to leave.

"See you around," he finally said. With a saluting wave, he headed off in the direction he'd come.

Snickering quietly at his incredible ego, Annette started off toward the marina. She walked onto the dock for a closer look at Josh Lord's impressive toy. As she passed the girl on duty, Annette smiled a silent greeting. Then her gaze moved to the boat, recognizing the sleek lines of a Hatteras.

She had just walked past the bowlines when the girl at the marina called to her. "Oh, miss! That end of the dock is private!"

Annette turned around to explain. "I was just looking—"

But she was interrupted by the familiar sound of Josh's deep voice. "It's all right, Phyllis," he told the girl. "She's a friend of mine."

Pivoting, Annette saw him standing on the afterdeck of the boat. A pair of faded denims hugged his thighs, riding low on his waist. The print shirt he was wearing was unbuttoned and hanging loose. There was a latent sexiness about him that was so magnetic she stepped toward him without thinking.

"Well, hello!" Annette paused by the gangplank. "I was just admiring your boat."

"Come aboard," Josh invited with a lazy look. "I'll give you a tour."

"I'd like that," she said, accepting the invitation and starting across, putting her hand in the one he offered to steady her.

His hand retained its hold on hers for a full second

after she was standing on the deck beside him. He looked down at her steadily, a half smile on his face.

"I imagine your waiter friend told you who I am," he said.

The remark made Annette glance back along the beach to where she'd met Craig. She suddenly wondered whether Craig had broken off the meeting because of the girl or because of Josh. It was obvious that Josh had seen them together, so it was possible that Craig had seen Josh and become worried about the security of his job.

"He did," she admitted, turning back to Josh and noticing his gaze drift to her mouth as if he were looking for a trace of Craig's stolen kiss. "But only in general terms. He wasn't all that specific." Annette hesitated, just a little unnerved by the almost physical quality of his glance. "Was there a reason you didn't tell me you owned this resort—among other things? Is it supposed to be a deep dark secret?"

"No." His smile widened. "I guess I expected our acquaintance not to last very long, so the information wasn't essential. But"—the challenging gleam in his eyes mocked her—"we seem to keep running into each other."

"We do, don't we?" Annette was aware that it would be a stretch to blame that on coincidence, so she didn't try. "Craig mentioned the boat was your pride and joy. She's a real beauty."

"Yes." It was a somewhat clipped agreement. Josh turned. "Let's go below and I'll show you the living quarters." He led the way down the steps. "Watch your head," Josh said, warning her of the low clearance. He had to duck but she didn't.

There was a subtle lushness about the quarters, hinted at by furniture covered in genuine leather and a solid mahogany bar and matching cabinets. Annette looked around at the rich appointments, her feet sinking into a thick blue carpet.

"The crew's quarters are in the forward section." Josh indicated the door leading that way with a brief wave of his hand. He moved aft. "Here's the galley." Its niches held gleaming new appliances that fit the limited space in ingenious ways.

Annette followed him down the companionway, past the head and the guest staterooms to the master stateroom. Her fingers brushed the brown velvet cover on the oversize bed. "Like it?" Josh asked.

"Yes. I'm very impressed." She felt a little self-conscious standing next to the bed with Josh watching her. She didn't mean it to look like an invitation.

"I planned on taking her out this morning, just for a short run," he said. "I'll probably be gone about an hour. Would you like to come along?"

"Oh yes." Annette accepted without any hesitation.

"Good." He smiled briefly. "You can cast off while I start the engines."

"Now I know why you asked me along." Annette grinned and followed him up the steps onto the afterdeck. "You needed a deckhand."

"That's right, so be quick about it." Josh laughed.

"Aye, aye, sir." She moved nimbly forward to release the bowline.

The engines sputtered and throbbed powerfully to life as Annette cast off the stern. Josh slid her a brief glance when she joined him by the wheel where he stood, his feet slightly apart.

"All clear," she said brightly.

Josh acknowledged that with a nod and began to expertly maneuver the large boat away from the dock. A full panel of state-of-the-art navigational equipment was in front of him as well as the engine throttles and gauges.

There were few other boats out in the bay—it was still early in the morning for the weekend sailors. Josh pointed the bow toward the distant mouth of the bay, keeping the boat at a reduced speed.

"The swells will be running a little rough this morning, especially when we reach the ocean. Are you a good sailor?" Josh asked.

"Yes," Annette assured him. "My sister is the only one in our family who gets seasick—and airsick." She hopped onto the little perch next to the controls. "What would you have done if I'd told you I was a total landlubber?"

"Taken you back to the dock," he said flatly. "I've got guests coming aboard this afternoon, so I don't want any aggravation."

"Guests, huh?" She felt a little twinge of jealousy. "Male or female?"

"Both." Josh arched his thick eyebrows in a knowing glance, as if he was reading her thoughts.

"A party. Sounds like it's going to be a blast," she lied.

"It's for grown-ups," he informed her, as if that was supposed to discourage her.

"I forgot to bring my driver's license, but I want you to know that I am officially, legally, about to turn twenty-one. So I am definitely a grown-up," she said tartly.

"Not quite." His deep chuckle warmed her in spite of her envy of the guests who would enjoy his company that afternoon.

"Is the party for business or pleasure?"

"No matter how they start out, they usually end

up a combination of both," Josh replied, and stepped away from the controls. "I'm going up on the flybridge. Want to come?"

Annette answered by following him aloft. A salty breeze whipped at her hair as she sat down on a cushioned front seat and curled her legs under her. Beyond the bridge ahead, she could see the first hint of breakers.

With the throb of the engines, the chatter on the marine radio and the rush of the surf, conversation was reduced to a minimum once they were underway. It was the shortest hour Annette could ever remember, the marina coming into view all too soon to suit her. As Josh came about to head in to the dock, she started to leave the bridge.

Josh called her back. "Stay where you are, Annette." He pointed. "Fred's ready with the line." He was referring to a man standing by on the dock with a thick, coiled rope in one hand.

She kept her seat while the boat was made fast, watching the swift coils of rope being looped over cleats and drawn tight. Once the engines were shut off, it seemed unnaturally quiet. Standing, she faced Josh, wishing there was a way to prolong the moment.

"I wish we were just going out instead of coming back," Annette admitted frankly. "Thanks for letting me come along."

"It was my pleasure." Josh smiled distantly, watching her with a hooded look, his hands resting casually on his hips.

Unable to find a reason to hang around, Annette attempted a bright smile. "Okay. I'm out of here. I hope your party's fun."

"I'm sure it will be," he replied. "You have fun on your date too, okay?"

"Date?" She looked at him in confusion.

His gaze narrowed. "Aren't you seeing Craig this afternoon?"

Annette hesitated and decided against denying it outright, catching a hint of jealousy in his eyes. "Isn't it against hotel policy for guests and staff to mingle?"

"Did Craig tell you that?" Josh asked mockingly.

"Yes," she admitted.

"Before or after he kissed you?" he challenged with a trace of harshness.

"As a matter of fact, it was after. You saw it, I guess." Her gray eyes eagerly watched every nuance of his expression.

"When a couple kisses on a public beach, someone is likely to see them," he pointed out.

"I think Craig saw you," Annette said. "Which explains why he left so soon after that. He probably thought he'd get in trouble."

"I have a hunch that you're trouble for just about every man you meet," Josh said.

A faint smile touched her mouth. "Including you, Josh?"

"Yes, including me," he admitted dryly, an amused light gleaming in his dark eyes.

Her next movement seemed idle but it brought her a little closer to him. She tipped her head back slightly to regard him with curious speculation. Her pulse raced a little under his steady gaze.

"You strike me as the kind of man who never does anything he doesn't want to do. The other afternoon, when you kissed me"—Annette paused for a second—"was it what you wanted to do?"

"You know damn well it was." There was a lazy curve to his mouth, as if he were silently laughing.

"I wasn't sure," she replied with a mild shrug, but a thread of excitement was running through her veins.

"Weren't you?" he asked huskily.

Then his hand was under her chin, as it had been that afternoon, but it didn't stay there long. It slid along her neck to tunnel under her hair while it urged her toward him. Annette needed little persuasion, flowing naturally into his arms.

His mouth burned on hers, erasing any remaining trace of Craig's kiss. His possession bore no resemblance to the chaste kiss of the other afternoon. Josh allowed for no innocence as he plundered the softness of her lips, taking them with a sexual appetite that left her in no doubt of his hunger.

The heat of his body enfolded her in languid warmth. His roaming hands pressed her curves to the hard contours of his length, awakening her to the delicious differences between a man and a woman and teaching her variations on that theme. Annette was reeling inwardly. His raw, utterly sensual embrace shook her to the core, changing every thought in her mind as to what it should be like to what it was really all about. It was all so shockingly new that she didn't know what she was thinking or feeling. Nothing was as she expected it to be.

When Josh dragged his mouth from her lips, he turned his head down to her neck and elicited fresh waves of pleasure on that sensitive skin. Dazed into submission, she moved to allow him access to the quivering pulse in her throat. Her fingers were curled in the material of his shirt, hanging on for dear life, her knees weak and trembling.

"I must be out of my mind," he muttered harshly against her skin. "You're, what, twenty, twenty-one? It doesn't seem right"—he kissed her neck again and again, and whispered against her ear—"but doesn't being wrong feel incredibly damn good?"

"Stop talking about how old I am," Annette whispered, afraid that he would stop whatever it was he was doing to her—and just as afraid that he would continue.

"I'm not wrong. And I'm not sorry." His hands gripped her shoulders and set her away from him. An odd mix of emotions blazed in his eyes. "I just don't think you know what you do to me. Didn't anyone teach you that it's dangerous to play with fire?"

"Yes." She managed a tiny nod.

"Then you ought to know you can't always put it out when you want to."

"I know," she said softly, not liking the way he thought of her as too young when she was old enough to do what she wanted. At the moment, she could think of no way to say that, without risking the infinite pleasure his caresses promised. A real woman didn't complain in a clinch and analyze every embrace.

"Do you?" he challenged. "To you, a kiss is one step beyond holding hands. But to me, it's a couple of steps away from bed. That's where this one will lead, you know." His gaze narrowed on the warmth that flooded her cheeks. "No, you don't know, do you?"

"Josh, I—" Annette wanted to change the subject, suddenly unable to handle the topic of sex.

"You thought it would be exciting and a little dangerous to flirt with an older man," he accused her roughly. "Did you have fun teasing me?"

"That isn't true!" she protested angrily, but Josh wasn't listening.

"It's not a game I like. Maybe you can get that waiter to play along." He turned her away and aimed her toward the dock, moving her forward with a tight grip on her elbow. "He's probably dumb enough."

His blazing anger only sparked hers. When he released her to adjust the gangplank so she could disembark, it burned her throat raw and stung her eyes with hot tears.

As Josh faced her again to escort her from the boat, Annette glared at him proudly. "I'm not a kid, no matter what you say."

His features were drawn in a hard mask as his gaze bored into her, then swept past her to shore. "No? I have a hunch that your daddy is looking this way," he muttered.

Annette jerked her head around to see what he was talking about, immediately spotting her father and Kathleen on the beach with Robby. What Josh said was true: her father's gaze was fixed on the scene and both of them.

"If he knew what you were up to," Josh said, "he'd give you hell. Which is precisely what you need!"

"And where you're headed!" Annette flashed, and turned to cross the gangplank to the dock, her body tensed and stiff with pride. But she didn't turn quickly enough to miss seeing the line of his jaw go white with anger.

There was some satisfaction in knowing that he was infuriated. But all his references to her supposed childishness continued to sting. She was going to exact revenge for every one. In her anger, Annette didn't remember that age wasn't the only issue. There was still the matter of her relative inexperience and how she'd tried to hide it from him.

As she walked off the dock onto the beach, Annette fought to subdue her aroused temper. At this point, she didn't want her father suspecting that anything unusual had happened aboard the boat. Like Josh, he wasn't an easy man to fool. She would need all her wits about her to keep his suspicions at bay.

Unable to postpone talking to him, Annette inhaled calm, steadying breaths and willed the constriction in her throat to ease. She blinked at the hot tears in her eyes and struggled to appear cool and collected as she approached the family group.

"Well, good morning." Kathleen greeted her as though nothing was amiss. "We missed you at breakfast."

"Would you help me build a sand castle, Annette?" Robby had dug a trench in the sand with his shovel, with the intention of building a moat. "Mom isn't very good at them."

"Thanks a lot, fella!" Kathleen laughed at the criticism.

"Sure. After a while, okay?" Annette promised her little brother, aware of the gray eyes, older and shrewd, that were watching her closely.

"Where have you been, Annette?" her father asked quietly—too quietly for her raw nerves.

"Out." But she knew he wouldn't settle for that ambiguous and slightly sassy answer. "For a boat ride," she added.

Robby looked up, disappointment crossing his face. "I want to go for a boat ride. Can I? Will you take me?"

"Later on we'll rent one of those pedal boats," Annette suggested in a futile attempt to distract the conversation. "Would you like that?"

"Boy! Yeah!" he agreed with wide-eyed enthusiasm.

But her father zeroed back in on the subject. "Who was that man on the boat with you? Do you know him?"

"Of course I know him." But Annette's laugh was brittle. "You don't think I'd go out on a boat with a stranger, do you? He's Joshua Lord and he actually owns this hotel—and that boat."

"Oh." Her father gave her a half smile as his gray eyes gleamed in curious speculation. "How did you gain entry to such exalted circles?"

"Oh, Dad, he's only a man, for heaven's sake. Not a god," Annette protested.

"He's a little old for you, don't you think?"

She didn't have to fake the mocking laugh that came from her this time. "He said almost the same thing, Dad, except that he turned it around and said I was too young for him. So I guess that you have nothing to worry about." She lifted her shoulders in an expressive shrug and smiled. Jordan Long offered no comment. Mentally crossing her fingers, Annette hoped the subject was closed. "Where's Marsha?"

"I think she's still in bed sleeping," Kathleen replied. "We knocked at the door when we left our rooms, but she didn't answer."

"She's probably still asleep," Annette agreed. "She was up until after three o'clock last night—reading a book." She backed away a step, preparing to make her departure. "I'll go wake her up. We'll join you after we've eaten breakfast."

"We'll be here on the beach," Kathleen promised.

As Annette walked away, Kathleen noticed how closely Jordan watched his oldest child. There was a quietness about him that she wasn't used to seeing. She glanced at Annette's disappearing figure, then back to her husband.

"Is something wrong, Jordan?" she asked.

He seemed to drag his gaze away from Annette before meeting her eyes. That mouth she loved so well was twisted in a wry, almost grim line.

"Yes."

"What is it?" Kathleen wanted more of an answer than that flat affirmative. "Annette?"

"I didn't like that look in her eyes," he replied. "She's up to something." His glance strayed to the boat tied up at the dock. "And I have a feeling that 'something' is Joshua Lord."

Kathleen remembered his comment that the man was too old for Annette and guessed the direction of Jordan's thoughts. "I wouldn't worry about Annette, honey. She's much too intelligent to be talked into anything." A quick smile crossed her mouth. "More than likely, Annette's talking him into something."

"One of these days she's going to meet her match, Kathleen," Jordan warned.

She sat back on her heels. "Really," she laughed. "I think you're actually hoping that she does. It bothers you when a woman outsmarts a man, doesn't it?"

"You come here and I'll show you what bothers me," he murmured in a suggestive mock threat.

Her breath caught in her throat as she started to sway toward him. Then Robby reminded her of his presence.

"Mommy, will you help me? I can't make the walls of my castle stand up," he complained in a disheartened voice.

"You're the one with the engineering degree, Jordan." Kathleen smiled. "Help your son."

He started to move to comply with her request, then paused to chuck her under the chin. "Wrong. He's *our* son—or have you forgotten that it takes two?"

"Maybe you'll have to refresh my memory," Kathleen suggested huskily. "Later."

"You can count on it." He ran his thumb across her lips and moved away to help Robby.

Later that afternoon, Annette took Robby out on one of the pedal boats as she'd promised. The bay was filled with families of afternoon sailors in crafts of every size and description. She kept their foot-powered boat close to shore, away from the congestion.

When she saw Josh's boat maneuvering away from the dock, she couldn't help looking. As it drifted slowly by the little cove where she was, Annette saw his guests. One in particular caught her eye. A raven-haired goddess in a scarlet swimsuit was draped all over Josh. Annette could well imagine the "business" that woman had in mind.

She was consumed with jealousy. If she'd been close enough, she would have plucked out every black hair on the woman's head, one by one. She hadn't guessed she could feel so much rage—or such pain—at seeing Josh with another woman.

"Annette, you'd better look where we're going," Robby said. "You nearly ran over a duck."

She looked to the front and saw the bird flying away. "Sorry," she murmured.

He looked at her. "Are you crying?"

"No, of course not!"

Her emphatic denial was at odds with reality. She blinked away the tears welling in her gray eyes.

Chapter 5

Annette rolled the toothpick-speared olive around her martini glass, staring absently at the hypnotic circles. Her dress of silver chiffon swooped low but somewhat modestly in the front, showing off the golden tan of her shoulders and arms. The salon's stylist had swept one side of her tawny hair away from her face for a touch of sophistication. An artful application of makeup had enhanced the smoke gray of her eyes and the fullness of her dark lashes.

But she was thinking about something other than her appearance, and was equally oblivious to the members of her family seated around the table in the hotel's dining room. There was talk and laughter, but Annette didn't hear any of it. They had gathered to celebrate her birthday, but she didn't feel much like celebrating anything.

"Don't you want that martini, Annette?" her father asked. His voice prodded her back to awareness of them. "Is it too dry?"

"No, it's fine," she assured him and let go of the toothpick to take a sip of the drink.

"Do you want to taste my Shirley Temple?" Robby offered. "It's good."

"No, thanks." She smiled wanly. "Too sweet for me."

"Does Annette have to wait until after dinner to open her gifts or can she have them now?" Marsha asked eagerly.

"That's up to Annette," Kathleen replied.

"It doesn't matter to me," Annette said with a polite shrug. "Whatever you want to do."

"I vote for right now," Marsha said, deciding for the rest of them. She picked up a large, beautifully gift-wrapped box by her chair.

Jordan Long studied his oldest daughter for a long moment. "I think everyone is more eager to give you presents than you are to get them." He glanced at his wife and said teasingly. "Are you sure it's her birthday?"

"I'm sorry, Dad." Annette realized she had to summon up some enthusiasm for the party, never mind the mood she was in.

"Open mine first," Marsha urged.

Her smile firmly in place, Annette took the box from her sister and pulled on a stray end of the bright ribbon bow to undo it. Marsha's eyes sparkled sapphire blue and her face was rosy with excitement. Annette couldn't help thinking how beautiful her younger sister was when she forgot to be self-conscious.

"Hmm. I suspect this is something to wear. Am I right?" Annette started the guessing game their family always played while opening presents. "I bet you bought me something blue, so you can borrow it."

Marsha laughed happily. "Open it and see."

When she lifted the lid and opened the rustling fold of tissue, Annette discovered she'd been close to right. A soft lilac-colored set consisting of a long-sleeved top and tank was revealed. "It's beautiful!" she said, assuring Marsha that she loved the gift, adding a laughing, "And it's not blue!"

"Now it's my turn," Robby insisted. "Open mine!"

Annette went through the full, wide-eyed pretense of wondering what was inside the paper-flat package, making Robby giggle with glee at her absurd guesses.

She opened the flaps by sliding a fingernail under the crisscrossed tape, and found his drawing of Wrightsville Beach, complete with the two of them in a pedal boat. Not that Annette recognized herself as either of the stick figures or recognized anything else in the picture, but Robby explained who was who and what was what, including an imaginary monster fish lurking below the boat that would have eaten them if he hadn't told it to swim away.

"You saved me and I didn't even know it!" she said to him, winking at Kathleen. "Thank you. That's a wonderful drawing. I'm going to hang it up on my bedroom wall as soon as we get home," she promised. "We'll make a frame for it and everything."

Robby beamed, positive he'd given her the best present of all. He had no way of knowing that her memories of the scene had a bittersweet edge.

"Here." Her father placed a small gift-wrapped box in front of her. "This is from me and Kathleen."

"I can't wait," Marsha murmured anxiously. "Go ahead. Hurry up."

"Do you know what it is?" Annette asked.

"Yes. Daddy showed it to me," her sister admitted.

Annette shook it gently, torturing her younger sister just for fun. "Hmm. It's small. It could be jewelry."

"Open it!" Marsha wailed, then shut up when a few people glanced their way.

Annette waited a few seconds longer, studying her

father, then Kathleen. Both looked at her. "It can't be a watch. You gave me one for graduation."

When she snapped open the jeweler's case, Annette didn't have to pretend to be delighted. Her response was genuine as she gazed, thrilled, at the diamond stud earrings inside. She looked at her father. "Are they real?" she whispered.

"Yes. Of course." He grinned at her as he spoke.

There was a small lump in her throat when she glanced at her stepmother. "It was your idea, wasn't it, Kathleen?" Annette asked with an affectionate smile, grateful for the comforting encirclement of family love. "I'm glad we picked you for a mother."

"Now wait a minute, Annette." Her father reached out to curl his fingers possessively around Kathleen's hand, resting on the table. "I know you like to take credit for finding Kathleen, but I ultimately did the picking."

"Dad, you're just like all men," Annette declared with a faint sparkle in her eyes. "You need a little help once in a while."

"Is that a fact?" He eyed her with amused tolerance.

"It is," she stated. "A woman has to put ideas in a man's head. There might be only four of us sitting at this table tonight if Marsha and I hadn't begged for a brother."

Her father chuckled and squeezed Kathleen's hand. "As I recall, I was thinking along those lines long before you two mentioned it."

Annette removed one earring from the velvet inner lining of the case and Marsha spoke up. "Ooh, let me help you put them on!"

With her sister's assistance, she didn't need a mirror, but she wished for one. "How do they look?"

she asked when both earrings were on her lobes. She had to rely on her family for a first impression.

"Fantastic!" Marsha assured her, and the others added similar praise.

Pushing out of her chair, Annette walked around the table to her parents. "Thank you, Daddy." She bent down and kissed his cheek, then turned and hugged Kathleen. "Thank you both."

When she straightened and turned to walk back to her chair, Annette found herself face-to-face with . . . Josh. For a heart-stopping second the smile on her lips froze as she stared into his enigmatic brown eyes. Tension vibrated in the air between them, making her heart beat faster. Seeing him so unexpectedly was a shock—and a thrill.

Her gaze wandered over his roughly hewn but handsome features and lingered for a second or two on the strong line of his mouth, remembering exactly how his kisses felt.

A little voice reminded her that her parents were watching and Annette forced herself to snap out of her daze. She became aware of his clothes—he was dressed in a dark evening suit and tie, his white shirt a sexy contrast to his sun-browned skin. The formal attire gave him a worldly air, a male urbanity that excited and challenged.

All the while Annette had been observing the changes in him, Josh had been noticing her sophisticated appearance. He took in the details—hairstyle, dress, makeup—until she blushed. Did he like what he saw? She had no way of really knowing. It was totally different from her usual athletic wear and minimal beauty routine.

Although it seemed they had looked at each other for long minutes, in fact only seconds had passed.

"Hello, Annette." Josh broke the silence.

She nodded demurely, summoning up poise she didn't feel. "Hello. Let me introduce my family."

His dark eyebrow arched in an affable way, but there was cool amusement glinting in his gaze. He took the wind out of her sails by introducing himself and smiling in a general way at everyone at the table. "I'm Joshua Lord."

She cleared her throat. "This is my dad, Jordan Long, and my stepmother Kathleen. You know my sister Marsha. And this is my little stepbrother Robby, Kathleen's son."

"Nice to meet you all," Josh said, shaking hands with Jordan who half-rose. "Please don't get up. I didn't mean to interrupt you."

Her father murmured a few words she didn't catch, but she noticed his air of reserve and the sharp inspection he made of Josh. He didn't seem favorably impressed.

Josh turned briefly to talk to two older men in business suits who'd reached his side, nodding to the hostess who hovered behind them to show them to their table. They went with her, after nodding politely to the Long family.

"My dinner guests. Sorry about that," Josh said.

Before that moment, she hadn't been aware anyone was with him. It staggered her to discover that she could be so unobservant, but Josh's presence had a way of blinding her to just about everything.

Her little stepbrother piped up, breaking the awkwardness of the moment.

"Are you here for Annette's birthday party?" Robby wanted to know. "Did you bring her a present?" He didn't wait for an answer. "Show him what I made you, Annette."

The line of Josh's mouth was half-curved in a smile when his dark gaze met hers. It slid to the table and the abandoned giftwrap at her place setting.

"You did mention you had a birthday coming up," Josh remembered. "I didn't realize it was today. Well, when you're really young, it's a cause for celebration. Happy birthday, Annette."

"Thank you." Inwardly she raged at his emphasis on *really*. He didn't have to keep making her feel like a kid. But she kept the thought to herself.

"Show him what I gave you," Robbie repeated, paying no attention to Kathleen's attempts to hush him.

"Robby drew me a picture." Annette reached across the table to pick up the drawing, motivated by her own self-interest to keep the subject of her birthday alive.

Josh obligingly admired it. "Hey, that's very good."

"She's going to hang it on her wall when we get home," Robby informed him with pride.

"Robby, can you tell Mr. Lord how old I am today?" Annette asked, shooting Josh a mocking look. It served him right for not inviting her to his boat party. She felt compelled to prove that she was, however, an actual grown-up even though she would have to admit that she didn't always act like one.

Her little brother readily supplied the information. "She's twenty-one years old."

Josh nodded.

"I can count that high," Robby declared, adding, "and higher than that."

Kathleen hastened to convince him that wouldn't be necessary while Josh studied the birthday girl.

"Amazing, isn't it?" Annette asked sweetly.

"He looks like a smart kid to me," Josh replied. "I bet he can count higher than a hundred."

"Now that would be my generation," her father said jokingly. "Or at least that's what it feels like sometimes. Ah, they grow up too fast, don't they, Kathleen?"

She murmured a laughing yes. He looked up at the man who'd stopped by their table, seeming to want Josh to move along and his next remark confirmed it. "It was a pleasure meeting you, Mr. Lord, but we shouldn't keep you from your guests."

It was easy to read between the lines of her father's polite words. Josh was being invited to leave. Annette wasn't going to object to that.

Josh's face crinkled in a smile. It was annoyingly clear to her that he thought it was funny her father (a) didn't approve of him and (b) was still vetting the men in her life.

"I was just about to head back. Hope you enjoy your dinner, people—my favorite chef is on duty tonight. And happy birthday again, Annette." Josh moved away to rejoin his party.

From her chair, Annette had a clear view of the table where Josh was seated at right angles to her. She could observe him all evening without half-trying.

"Is that man your boyfriend?" Robby asked.

"Oh, I wouldn't call him that," Annette replied, aware of her father's scrutiny. "He's just a friend-friend."

Robby thought that over and filed the information away.

"It's getting late." Kathleen deftly switched the subject, which she realized was a sensitive issue to her husband, to Robby's bedtime, which wasn't far away. "Maybe we should order."

"Yes, of course," he agreed, and signaled the waiter to bring menus to their table.

While those were passed out, the wine steward approached the table with a wine bucket and stand—and an iced magnum of champagne, placing it all by Annette's chair. Her father's gaze narrowed on the arrangement.

"We didn't order that," he informed the steward.

"No, sir," the man agreed and expertly popped the cork, which he set on the table. "Allow me to present this with the compliments of Mr. Lord." With a heavy cloth napkin wrapped around the bottle, he carefully poured just a little into a glass for Annette. *"Mademoiselle?"* It was a discreet request for her approval.

As she looked across the dining room to Josh, she lifted the glass to her mouth. Josh was watching her, their eyes meeting across the distance. Annette held the glass close to her lips, not sipping right away but inhaling its chilled bouquet as she enjoyed the tiny bubbles tickling her nose.

Josh raised his drink in a silent toast to her. When he took a sip, Annette quivered with the odd sensation that he was somehow drinking the essence of her. A little shaken, she lowered her eyes and sipped at the champagne, its intoxicating effervescence tingling in her throat.

"It's very good," she told the waiting steward.

After he filled her glass, the steward poured champagne for the others. Her father reached for the cork and put it in her evening clutch.

"Keep that for a souvenir," he said. "You only turn twenty-one once in your life."

Robby looked like he wanted it for reasons known only to a five-year-old boy, but Kathleen distracted him with the menu, helping him choose his evening meal.

"You seem pleased with yourself, Annette," her father commented.

"It's my birthday."

But he wasn't buying it. "That didn't seem to matter so much earlier."

"That was before I opened my presents," Annette countered.

"That was also before Joshua Lord stopped by the table," he murmured.

"Spoken like a dad," she said pertly. The waiter returned to take their orders and Annette was relieved to have the subject changed. Her father remained quiet throughout the meal, and he didn't mention Joshua Lord again. He was never out of Annette's mind, however, or her sight. And more than once Josh looked in her direction, which only added to the soft glow on her face.

When it was time to leave, the magnum of champagne was still more than half full. "Would *Mademoiselle* like to take it with her?" the wine steward inquired with exaggerated formality.

"Please," Annette answered with a nod.

"What are you going to do with that?" her father wanted to know.

"Take it back to my room and keep on celebrating my birthday," she answered him with breezy innocence. "The night is young. Who knows how late Marsha and I will stay up?"

He didn't look completely pleased or satisfied with that explanation, but he didn't pursue it. With the addition of the champagne bottle to her other presents, Annette accepted her sister's offer to help carry them. As the family left the table,

Annette smiled across the room to Josh. There was a responding quirk to his mouth and something else in his look that Annette was pretty sure she could interpret.

At the door of the room the sisters shared, they parted company with their parents and Robby, who continued to their suite around the corner. Inside the room, Marsha set her present to Annette on the dresser.

"Why don't you try it on and see how it fits?" Marsha suggested.

"I'll wait until tomorrow." Annette was preoccupied with other plans. She stopped in front of the mirror and checked her reflection, using her fingers to touch up her hairstyle.

Marsha paused to watch. "Are you really going to drink that champagne tonight?"

"Some of it." Annette opened her silver clutch and took out the tube of lipstick. Uncapping it, she twisted the stick up and began applying a fresh coat of luscious dusty rose.

Marsha frowned. "What are you doing?"

"Putting on lipstick. What does it look like I'm doing?" She blotted it with a tissue.

"Why?" Which was what Marsha had actually meant.

"Why do you think?" Annette countered. She found the cork in her clutch and shaved off some of its swollen side with manicure scissors, so she could get it back in again. Then she picked up the champagne bottle and a glass from the beverage service.

"Are you going out?" Marsha stared, knowing the answer was yes but asking the question anyway. "Where?"

"To meet Josh, of course." Annette started toward

the door, the chiffon skirt swirling around her shapely legs.

"But . . . how . . . ? When . . . ?" Marsha faltered, not sure even how to ask her questions.

"We didn't make arrangements to meet." Annette guessed the reason for her younger sister's confusion. "But he'll be waiting for me just the same." With a secretive smile on her face, she turned to wink at Marsha. "Don't wait up for me."

She was sweeping out the door before Marsha got a chance to ask how Annette knew Josh would be there. This time she was really worried about the kind of trouble her sister was getting involved in. She was playing in the big leagues now and who knew what could happen?

With Robby tucked in for the night, Kathleen moved quietly out of her son's darkened room and into the larger adjoining room where she and Jordan slept. He was standing at the window, looking out into the night. Something in his brooding stance made her go to him.

When she slid her arms around his middle from in back of him, she felt him stiffen in an instant of surprise at her touch, then relax. She laid her cheek against his back, enjoying the warmth of his body.

"A penny for your thoughts?" she murmured.

He stirred restlessly. She loosened her encircling arms as he turned away from the window to face her. His thoughtful gray gaze held a cynical gleam.

"I have a feeling Joshua Lord is worth a lot more than a penny," Jordan replied dryly. He curved an arm around her shoulders to hug her to his side.

Kathleen smoothed a hand across his shirtfront,

feeling the hard muscles of his chest beneath the material. It was a pleasant intimacy to touch him like this—to have the freedom of loving him.

"He's probably worth two pennies at least," Kathleen agreed in a playful tone. She too grew thoughtful as she remembered the meeting. "He's a very attractive man."

Jordan put a finger under her chin so he could look directly into her eyes. "You think so?"

"Yes," she admitted calmly. A teasing light danced in her hazel eyes. "Jealous?"

"Should I be?" he asked, not seriously.

"Not at all." Kathleen had no desire to let him wonder. Their time together was too precious to waste it playing games when they could be loving.

As if hearing her silent thoughts, Jordan kissed her warmly yet briefly, betraying the fact that his mind was still concentrating on something else. His caressing hand wound into her auburn hair and he pressed her head gently to his shoulder, rubbing his jaw against the silkiness he loved.

"Annette was certainly in a better mood after she saw him," he remarked.

"She seemed to be," Kathleen agreed.

"Has she said anything to you about this Lord guy?" He was trying to sound casual, but there was a stiffness to his question.

"No." Kathleen half-smiled but was careful not to let Jordan see it—or suspect it was there.

"What do you suppose is going on between them?"

"That's assuming that there is something going on between them," Kathleen said, reminding him that they didn't know that for sure. "Annette happened to mention the other day that Joshua Lord thought she was too young."

"So what?" Jordan didn't say it in a rude way, just bluntly. "He's about ten or eleven years older, right? That's the same difference as ours."

"Well, yes," she said. "Then what bothers you? I'm not sure I understand."

"Didn't you see the way he looked at her?" he demanded. "He wants her. I saw it in his eyes."

Her chin quivered with her effort to hold back laughter, but she couldn't. It spilled softly from her as he held her away from him. His challenging look indicated he was anything but amused by her reaction.

"Did I say something funny?" He seemed to be insisting on an explanation.

"I'm sorry, but you sounded so righteous." She tried more successfully to contain her amusement, but she still had to smile. "What do you think was in your eyes when you looked at me?"

"That's different," Jordan replied impatiently.

The dimples in her cheeks deepened with her effort to hide her silent laughter. "Naturally," she murmured. "Annette is your daughter—which makes all the difference in the world."

For an instant he looked angry, then amused chagrin stole over his expression. "I sounded very fatherly, didn't I?"

"Yes, you did." Kathleen smiled.

"I can't help worrying that he's too experienced for her," he explained.

"I wouldn't worry about it if I were you. It's probably just a vacation romance." Kathleen shrugged without concern. "We've been here—what?—two weeks?

And we'll be leaving in another couple of weeks. What can happen in a month's time?"

"If you're trying to reassure me, you blew it." Jordan winked at her. "Or have you forgotten that we fell in love in less than a month?"

"Remind me," she said invitingly. Jordan gathered her into his arms.

Chapter 6

The moonlight shimmered on the glassy surface of the Atlantic ocean while the night lights of Wrightsville Beach faded the stars in the sky. The air was fresh and soft, washed clean by sea breezes. The sensual warmth of the day clung to the night.

On the curving edge of the beach, Annette paused and balanced on one foot to slip off a high-heeled sandal, then shifted her position to remove the other. With the champagne bottle in one hand and her shoes and glass in the other, she wandered onto the beach. The fine grains of sand were cool beneath her toes when she stopped short of the tide line to gaze at the calm waters of the sea.

The unhurried sound of strolling footsteps broke the stillness of the night. Turning, Annette looked back at the hotel. A warm sensation of pleasure raced through her as she recognized the shadowed male figure as Josh. His stride didn't change as he angled across the sand to where she stood.

He stopped near her. Without the advantage of her high heels, Annette had to tip her head back to gaze into his eyes, troubled and excited by the look in them.

"I knew you'd be here." His voice was quiet and strong.

"I knew you'd come."

Instinct had brought them both where they could be alone together. Explanations weren't necessary.

"Would you like some champagne?" She indicated the bottle with a lifting gesture of her hand. "I only brought one glass so we'll have to share. Do you mind?"

"Not at all."

Josh took the bottle from her and worked the cork out with his thumbs, freeing it easily the second time around. Annette smiled approvingly and held out the glass for him to fill, her shoes dangling from a finger by their heel straps.

"Ladies first," Josh said, indicating he would wait to drink after her.

Annette transferred the glass to her other hand and carried it to her lips, sipping champagne while she continued to look at him. A heady excitement licked through her that had nothing to do with what she was drinking.

It had gone mostly flat and it wasn't very cold. But it served to bring them even closer together.

He watched her, his sensuous gaze taking note of her shining lips touching the rim of the glass with every sip, then moved down her throat to her breasts. Annette quivered inwardly, enjoying the illusion that Josh could see through the chiffon that covered them. The impression was lost when he lifted his gaze back to her face.

"Here." She offered him the glass when she was through, and it was her turn to watch him.

Her senses were alive to his presence, the way the moonlight looked on his face, the masculine fragrance of his cologne, the deliciously unnerving intensity of his gaze, and the even sound of his breathing.

"It's a beautiful night, isn't it?" she said as he re-filled the glass and handed it to her.

"Perfect," Josh agreed.

"Well . . ." She trailed off a little breathlessly. "Champagne, moonlight, and . . . a little romance. I can't think of a better way to get to know someone."

The question was a softly provocative challenge. In response, he took the bottle and glass and her shoes from her, and set everything on the sand. "There," he murmured. "Now all we have to hold is each other."

His hands spanned her slender waist to draw her to him. It seemed to Annette that she floated into his arms. It was all so effortless and it was happening just the way she'd planned it.

Josh's warm breath caressed her lips as his mouth hovered above them. Nothing was held back when he kissed her at last, not his experience and not his desire. Annette was enfolded in an embrace more potent than she had ever known. He fired her senses and melted her body to his solidly muscled flesh. His kiss was a revelation.

Her heart beat wildly as his roaming hands moved over her, arching her to fit her more intimately to his body. Without restraint, she ran her fingers into his hair, loving its texture, vital and thick.

Josh nibbled on an earlobe and moved on to the pulsing cord in her neck, making her shiver with pleasure. She stood on tiptoe, straining to receive every pleasure he could give. When he moved one hand over her ribs and stopped just below her breast, her breath caught.

Suddenly, Josh was the leader and she was the follower. Never in her life had she allowed that to

happen, but here and now, she was ready to surrender to the experience of allowing him to take
charge—and take her to a sensual high she craved.

Her body quaked and Josh felt the tremors, easing
her gently down until she was firmly on her feet, all
the while keeping her within the circle of his arms.
She couldn't look into his eyes, not when she felt so
vulnerable.

The rhythmic murmur of the ocean was the only
sound—neither of them said a word. Her hands were
spread across the front of his chest, the thud of his
heartbeat beneath her fingers reassuring to her. But
his breathing had a ragged edge. Nervously she mois-
tened her lips, tasting him and being unsettled all
over again.

"You don't practice what you preach, Josh," she
said softly.

"What do you mean?" His hands lightly stroked her
back, caressing and distracting.

"You didn't think Craig should kiss me in public
and here you are with me, doing just that."

But there wasn't a soul around, and that didn't
help Annette's nervousness.

"We are out in the open," Josh agreed. "Believe me,
I wish we were someplace private."

Her heart rocketed. What came next? Still, she
wanted to let him decide.

"My suite faces the water," he went on. "It's just a
short walk from here."

Her breath was uneven as she pushed the rest of
the way out of his arms, changing her mind in an instant. "I said I wanted a *little* romance, Josh. I don't
remember asking for a full seduction number by
moonlight."

A silence fell as Annette moved to pick up her

shoes. She shook out the sand inside them, feeling his gaze on her, watchful and quiet. She had never felt so unsure of herself. The beach could have been quicksand. She wished Josh would say something, because she couldn't think. Her pulse accelerated when he approached her.

"I think we've gone far enough for now," Josh said. "I wasn't wrong about your experience, was I? You've never slept with a man, have you?"

Annette felt uncomfortably warm and dodged both questions with a flippant reply. "I hear that men snore."

When he put a hand under her arm, she stiffened, but Josh's only intention was to guide her to the sidewalk. Once there he stopped, but continued to hold on to her arm.

"Put your shoes on," he instructed.

The moon highlighted his features, allowing Annette to see his expression. She knew her passionate response and subsequent skittishness might have irked him, but she couldn't see any sign of it. Under the circumstances Josh seemed remarkable tolerant of her hot-then-cold behavior.

The grip of his hand balanced her as she slipped on her shoes and hooked the straps behind her heels. She didn't feel quite so small with them on— literally and figuratively—since they seemed to return some of her poise.

"There are two ways people can learn how to swim," Josh said.

Annette gave him a puzzled look. The subject seemed totally out of place.

"One way is to throw them into deep water and hope their survival instinct will kick in. But that's a severe shock to the system and it rarely works."

He paused and it began to sink in that he was speaking metaphorically, comparing swimming to making love. He obviously meant well, even though she felt awkward and wondered where he was going with it.

"On the other hand, a person can learn to swim slowly," Josh continued. "It means starting out by practicing the basics and advancing by stages. Then it becomes second nature. And very enjoyable."

"Yes." Her smile was soft.

Because of his understanding, she fell a little bit more in love with him. In his own way he was telling her that he wanted her but he wasn't going to rush her. It indicated respect for her as a person and not just someone who triggered random male lust. If he respected her, Josh could love her and that was her ultimate goal.

"Let me pick up the champagne bottle and glass, then I'll walk you to your room," he said as he released her arm.

"Okay." Annette didn't object.

Her gaze followed his easy strides across the sand to the spot where he'd stashed the forgotten bottle and the glass. She felt almost starry-eyed. But then she'd known Josh was something special the minute she'd seen him. And time was proving her right.

When he returned, he put an arm around her shoulders and curved her to his side. Their legs brushed as they started walking slowly back. She really liked the feeling of his hard thigh rubbing against hers, their steps in synch despite the length of his legs. Simple things brought quiet joy, but the sensation was no less pleasing because of its simplicity.

Ahead of them was a mesh litter barrel, screened to blend in with the landscape. They stopped so Josh could deposit the champagne bottle and the glass inside it. They left the beach area and entered the hotel grounds, following the sidewalk. Moonlight silvered the pavement under their feet as they walked, talking idly.

"Your sister doesn't resemble you, does she?" Josh asked.

"No. We're a mixed-up combination of our parents." She smiled, trying to think of how to explain it in the fewest possible words. "Marsha has my mother's eyes and fair skin and my dad's dark hair. I have his eyes and my mother's hair. And Robby's a whole different story. We are unique, to say the least."

"I would agree," he murmured. "What happened to your mother?"

"She died when I was small. She had congenital heart trouble—nothing serious—but she caught the flu . . . and died," Annette said thoughtfully. "I don't really remember her. For a long time it was just Dad, Marsha, and me. Until we found Kathleen."

"You *found* Kathleen? I hope you're going to explain that."

"It's a long story," she assured him with a laughing smile. "To make it short, I guess you could say that Kathleen was hired to look after us—kind of like a nanny. After she and Dad got to know each—well, you can fill in the rest."

"You like her a lot, don't you?" he observed.

"Yes." It was almost an understatement. "She's mother, big sister, and best friend all rolled into one. I couldn't have picked a better wife for my dad if I'd tried."

The statement slipped out before Annette realized she'd said so much. She slid a brief look at Josh to see if he read anything unusual in her words. At this stage

it was better that he didn't know about the way she and
Marsha had helped their father's courtship along. But
Josh seemed to take her remark at face value.

When they reached the outside stairs to the second
floor, he let his arm slide to her waist, giving each of
them more freedom to go up at their own pace. They
passed the corner suite occupied by her parents. The
curtains were pulled and no light could be seen.

Before they reached the door to her room, Annette felt for her keycard, not finding it. "Shoot," she
said. "I forgot my keycard. I'll have to wake up
Marsha to let me in."

"Either she's still awake or she left a light on for
you," Josh said, drawing her attention to the glimmer
of light behind the window draperies.

"She's probably reading," Annette guessed.

With silent mutual agreement, they stopped in
front of her door and Annette turned. Josh's hand
slid with ease from the back of her waist to her
rounded hip. There was a velvet quality to his gaze,
warm and sensual. It had an immediate effect on her,
disturbing her in an inwardly thrilling way.

The hand on her hip moved her closer and his
other hand tunneled under her hair to cup the back
of her head. She raised her lips to his descending
mouth and slid her arms inside his jacket to circle the
middle of his body. His male length was as hard and
warm as his kiss—and there was an instant leap of
mutual desire between them, but Annette was prepared for it this time so its force didn't alarm her. Of
her own accord, she invited him to deepen the kiss.
His hand shifted again, to her lower back this time,
and he arched her firmly against him.

When he pulled his lips from hers, there was a

shaky edge to his rough breathing. His dark eyes blazed, even in the dim light.

"No more beginner's lessons for you," he murmured huskily. "You're ready for the advanced courses."

"Think so?"

Her provocative but oddly innocent words made him smile a little. Josh took his hand from her back and knocked on the room door behind her. Getting the message, she let go of him and stood apart.

"Who is it?" Marsha's voice was somewhat muffled by the closed door.

"It's me—Annette," she answered reluctantly. "I forgot my keycard."

"Just a minute." The reply was followed by the rattle of the safety chain and the turn of the dead bolt.

Before the door opened, Josh trailed a caressing hand across her cheek and let it pause to press his thumb to her lips and stroke them lightly. Then he was drawing it away.

"Good night, Annette," he murmured.

"Good night," she replied with equal softness.

He was walking away when the door swung in to admit Annette, but Marsha got a glimpse of his back before he disappeared. Her glance was sharp with curious interest when her older sister entered. She closed the door.

"You look positively mellow, Annette," she said with some surprise. Her eyes widened as Annette waltzed across the floor and stopped, hugging her arms tightly around her.

"I'm in love," she laughed. "If I had any doubts, they vanished tonight!"

"I take it the lucky man is Josh," Marsha guessed. "What happened?"

"Nothing. Everything." Annette didn't seem to be

aware of the extremes of her two answers. With a graceful turn she sank onto the bed and lay back on the pillows, fully dressed.

"Well, where did you go?" Marsha wondered if her sister was capable of an answer that made sense. "What did you do?"

There was no immediate reply, until Annette propped herself up on one elbow. Marsha took silent note of the mischief dancing in her sister's eyes.

"Josh invited me to his suite," Annette announced.

"Did you actually go?" Marsha was prepared to hear anything, even though sometimes she would swear her sister delighted in shocking her with outrageous statements.

"No, I didn't go." She lay back on the pillows again with that same dreamy smile. "Not this time anyway."

Marsha forced herself to ignore the qualification, certain she was being baited. "Does he love you?"

The question had a sobering effect on Annette. "I'm not sure." She sighed and looked at the ceiling. "It's hard to know. Sometimes I can't even think straight when he's near me," she admitted. "But if he doesn't love me now, he will—soon."

Marsha wasn't so sure, but she decided it was better to keep her doubts to herself. Annette had a way of making things work out the way she wanted them to, even when Marsha thought it was impossible. For her sister's sake, she hoped that would be the case this time, too.

When Annette began telling her about Josh, Marsha moved to her bed and sat cross-legged at the bottom of it. She listened while Annette confided her excitement and fears and happiness. She couldn't begin to count how many yawns she smothered before Annette's exuberance abated. It was well into

the wee hours of the morning before either of them
crawled under the covers to sleep.

It seemed to Annette that she'd barely put her
head on the pillow when the room phone began
ringing shrilly. She tried burying her head under the
pillow but couldn't shut out the incessant ring.
Marsha groaned in the next bed.

Dragging an arm from beneath the covers, Annette groped for the phone on the bed table. Her fingers plucked the receiver off the hook in midring
and brought it under the pillow to her ear.

"Hello," she mumbled grumpily.

"Up and at 'em, sleepyhead," Josh's voice chided her.

Her eyes opened as she fought off the drugging
tiredness. "Josh?"

"How many other men call you in the morning?"
he mocked.

She sat up, pushing the pillow to the floor. "This is
the first time you've called," Annette reminded.

"So it is," he admitted. "Are you jogging with me
this morning?"

"I—what time is it?" Between sleep and confusion,
nothing was clear.

"Six thirty."

Part of her wanted to collapse backward onto the
bed, but not the part in control. "I have to get dressed."

"Pity," he replied teasingly. "I'll give you fifteen
minutes, then I'm leaving without you."

"I'll be ready." She was already throwing back the
covers and swinging out of the bed. "Bye."

"Aren't you going to ask where to meet me?"

"Just tell me."

He chuckled. "I'll wait for you at the beach."

"In fifteen minutes."

"Okay. Now you can hang up," he mocked.

Smiling at the receiver, she did. As she started for the bathroom, Marsha raised her head, giving her a groggy look.

"Where are you going? Who was that?" she muttered thickly.

"That was Josh. He wants me to go jogging with him," Annette explained, hurrying to the bathroom.

Marsha frowned. "What time is it?"

Annette paused at the door long enough to answer. "Six thirty-five."

With a groan, Marsha flopped back into her pillow. "You must be crazy," she mumbled, but water was running in the sink so Annette didn't hear when her sister added, "or in love."

Marsha was sound asleep again when Annette left the room twelve minutes later to meet Josh.

The next few days they seemed intent on making up for lost time. They jogged together in the mornings before Josh went to his office, then met again in the evenings. Annette stubbornly ignored her father's disapproving looks and thinly veiled displeasure. Sometimes they went out and sometimes they stayed around the hotel—at the beach or on his boat.

This night, Josh had taken her into Wilmington on the mainland. As they strolled along, he held her hand loosely in his. It was a sleepy sort of evening, the long shadows of the setting sun spreading over the city.

"Getting hungry?" he asked.

Her answer was a nod. "You mentioned something about eating around here."

"The restaurant's actually just ahead." Josh motioned toward it. "Do you like Mexican food?"

"I like tacos." There was a teasing sparkle in Annette's glance.

"That's as bad as saying you like chop suey when someone asks if you enjoy Chinese food," he chided. But his look was warm with shared amusement.

"Gee whiz. Do you mean there's more to Mexican food than tacos, enchiladas, and refried beans?" She pretended to be surprised by the idea.

"Let's go in and find out."

"Let's," Annette agreed. "I'm starving."

Mariachi music was playing in the background as a hostess led them to a table. The air was filled with a spicy blend of delicious smells that whetted Annette's appetite. Sitting down in one of the brightly painted chairs, she opened the menu and skimmed the list, then paused and glanced up at Josh.

"I think you'd better make some suggestions," she murmured.

"Do you trust me to order for you?"

Annette hesitated, then agreed with a qualification. "All right, but you have to tell me what everything is."

The gleam in his dark eyes mocked her, but he made no direct comment. He ordered guacamole—that was familiar enough—and a platter of appetizers that were new to her so she could sample a variety. "Including a taco," he informed her.

"Thanks." She smiled, grateful for his thoughtfulness.

The order Josh gave the waiter included a carafe of freshly made sangria. The glasses that accompanied the chilled wine mixed with juice each contained a speared slice of orange and a stemmed maraschino cherry, which added to the fruity zest of the drink.

The emptiness of her stomach made Annette eye the fruit garnish hungrily. Finally, she decided not to resist and she slid the wine-soaked orange slice off its spear to nibble on its pulp.

As her teeth sank into it, her glance strayed to Josh. The gleam in his eyes made her smile. He was gazing at her juice-wet lips as if he longed to devour them, a look that unnerved her but in a sensual way. She set the orange rind aside, inwardly aroused.

"Do you have to look at me that way?" she murmured.

"What way?" Thick masculine lashes were partially lowered to screen the intensity of his gaze, but they didn't lessen his interest.

"As if you were eating me with your eyes," Annette replied, and twirled the cherry by its stem, drowning it in the wine.

"I'd like to take a bite out of you," Josh admitted with too much ease.

"Little nibbles are better," she said, amused by the blatantly sexual banter they'd slipped into. It was almost silly but nonetheless sensual.

"What are you going to do with that cherry?" His low question stopped her. She lifted it out.

"Do you want it?" Her tone wasn't as sophisticated as she would have liked it to be.

"What do you think?" He held her gaze and she felt a slow release of an unnamed tension under his steady look.

"You can have it." Holding the cherry by its stem, she handed it to him.

Instead of taking it, his fingers circled her wrist and guided her hand to his mouth so that she ended up feeding him the cherry. A thousand sensations ran through her body until she felt her toes curling with pleasure.

The waiter was approaching the table to serve their meal and Josh released his hold on her wrist. The conversation shifted to less suggestive topics, but the previous one wasn't forgotten. It lingered in her thoughts all through dinner and afterward.

Arriving at the hotel, Josh parked the car in his reserved space and switched off the engine. When he stepped out of the car, Annette waited in the passenger seat until he had walked around and opened her door like the gentleman he was. She craved his touch and with secret pleasure, she accepted his hand to help her out. Josh held on to it, keeping her at his side while he shut the door.

When he made no move to leave the darkened lot for the lighted walkways, her heart started skipping beats. He faced her, his hand settling on her hip while he brought her hand behind his back and released it. He bent his head and nuzzled her mouth, arousing a trembling hunger in her for more.

"Kissing in cars isn't that much fun." His low voice vibrated against her skin. "You can never get close enough."

Annette couldn't have agreed with him more. His powerful body pressed sensually against hers, keeping her between the unyielding but smooth metal bulk of the car and the living steel of his muscled form.

His mouth stopped teasing hers and parted her lips in driving possession. She could taste the last of the fruity wine they'd shared as Josh kissed her passionately, demanding more and more. She echoed his need, excited by the hard maleness of him against her soft curves.

There was a rougher quality now to the kisses he brushed over her neck and throat. His roaming hands seemed impatient, as though her clothes were a hindrance to the bliss they both desired. Annette was just as frustrated.

"This isn't enough for you either, is it?" Josh demanded.

"No." She was shaken by the force of her need and willing to admit it.

A faint shudder went through him as he lifted his head and framed her face in his hands. Passion smoldered in his eyes. Annette gazed at him with raw wonder.

"Let's go to my suite." The suggestion fell somewhere between a request and a command, insisting while giving her a choice.

"Yes." She was vaguely stunned that she could sound so calm when she had just made a momentous decision.

She hadn't been aware of his inner tension until she noticed the line of his jaw relax and felt the pressure of his hands ease. Josh let go of her long enough to curve an arm around her waist and direct her toward the hotel buildings. The contact provided much-needed support. Her mind was so filled with Josh, Annette wasn't conscious of thinking about anything else.

Another couple was strolling arm in arm along the beachfront sidewalk as they approached. At first Annette looked at them without really seeing them, until she snapped out of her half-dreaming state. A shiver of discomfort ran down her spine as she met her father's look.

"Well, hello. You're back earlier than we expected,

Annette." His smile of greeting didn't reach his eyes. "I take it the two of you decided to have an early night."

"Not exactly. It's such a lovely evening we thought we'd walk around a bit." She certainly couldn't tell him she'd been on her way to Josh's suite.

"Kathleen and I had the same thought," her father said. "We can all go together."

With a sinking feeling, Annette gave Josh a questioning side glance. The slight upward curve of his mouth held rueful humor and resignation.

"Sounds like a good idea," he told her father.

The four of them wandered through the hotel grounds together, talking quietly now and then. Annette couldn't ever remember a time when her father had appointed himself as her chaperon on any dates. It seemed a little uncanny that he did it that night.

Chapter 7

The sand was warm beneath her as Annette leaned back on her hands and watched her small brother send the red Frisbee sailing through the air. Robby laughed in delight when Josh went chasing across the beach after it. Annette was just as delighted, but for different reasons. Josh in motion was all sinewy, strong legs and muscled chest. The red disk landed in the sand. Josh scooped it up with one hand, spinning it around in a smooth movement and sailing it back in the direction of the boy's outstretched hands.

Robby tried to catch it and failed. When he tried to duplicate Josh's coordinated maneuver, he lost his balance and plopped on his bottom in the sand. Josh ran over, dropping down on one knee. "Are you okay?" He lifted Robby to his feet and helped him brush off some of the sand.

"Yeah," Robby mumbled, a little embarrassed by the fall, since he'd been trying to show off.

Josh rumpled the boy's dark hair. "Let's both take a rest."

"I'm not tired," Robby protested.

Josh grinned. "But I am. You can play in the sand awhile and I'll do the resting, how's that?"

"Okay."

While Robby went reluctantly to get his sand pail and shovel, Josh straightened and went over to where Annette was sitting. Blowing out a sigh and smiling at the same time, he sank onto the beach beside her and put his arms around his knees. His gaze went back to Robby, busy packing sand into his pail.

"I don't know where that kid gets his energy." Josh shook his head in weary amazement and slid an amused glance at Annette. "Does he ever run down?"

She smiled at the question. "Yup. At about eight thirty every night. I'm glad you didn't mind him spending the afternoon with us."

Her father had taken Kathleen and Marsha shopping. Annette knew from past experience that Robby hated shopping expeditions and did his best to lose himself in the racks of clothes and drive everyone crazy with worry.

"Of course. Did you think I would mind?"

"I didn't really know. It was a possibility."

She didn't mention her suspicion that this afternoon of babysitting had been her father's idea. After last night, she had the feeling he didn't want her to be alone with Josh, and everyone knew that an energetic, curious kid was a very effective deterrence to romance. It was entirely possible that she was just imagining her dad's involvement, though.

Annette turned to lie on her stomach. She uncapped the bottle of suntan lotion next to her beach towel and handed it to Josh. "Would you rub some on my back?"

"With pleasure."

Crossing her hands in front of her, she rested her

cheek on them. An involuntary shiver danced over her skin when Josh dribbled the cool lotion along her spine. His hands began spreading it around, gliding silkily over her back, almost caressing.

She closed her eyes as his strong fingers kneaded her shoulders, feeling her muscles relax under his gentle massage. "You can keep that up for at least another hour," she murmured.

"I can, huh?" His voice half-challenged her. "I might get carried away."

She lifted her head to check on Robby. Her little brother was flat on his belly, head down in a large hole he'd scooped out in the sand.

Good.

Josh's mock warning hadn't prepared her for the easy way his hands moved to the sides of her rib cage. His fingertips made discreetly tantalizing forays under the edge of her white swimsuit to investigate the swelling curve of her breasts.

"Mmm," she said dreamily.

"That's what I like to hear." The rubbing motion ended as he moved away. Annette murmured a protest, but he playfully slapped her behind. "No more," he declared as she rolled onto her side in startled surprise, covering that part of her bottom with her hand.

"That hurt," she complained, even though the stinging sensation had already subsided.

"Want me to kiss it and make it better?" he asked in a very low voice, and caught Annette without a comeback.

Robby picked that opportune moment to stop digging his giant hole to China and join them. "Are you rested now?" he asked Josh.

"Almost. Give me a few more minutes."

"Okay," Robby sighed, and trotted off.

Annette watched him go, then glanced sideways at Josh. "Robby likes you."

Josh looked at him briefly, then back at her. One of Josh's knees was bent, an arm resting on top of it. His other leg was stretched out on the sand, an arm braced behind him in support.

"Robby likes anyone who'll play Frisbee with him," Josh replied.

"No." Annette shook her head. "He likes you. Robby has an instinct for people. I've never known him to be wrong about anyone."

"Well, he's a great kid. Looks like he's growing like a weed, the way they're supposed to. Give 'em fresh air, plain food, and just enough attention, they turn out fine. That's my theory, anyway."

She eyed Josh, admiring not just the outer man but the inner one as well. "You'd be a good father."

"Is that right?" He turned to her, the arm leaving his knee to curve behind the middle of her back and pull her to him. He stopped when her swimsuit-covered breasts brushed against his chest. "What's on your mind? Would you be interested in having my baby?"

He asked the startling question against her lips and he wasn't joking. Annette couldn't think of a word to say but she answered him by surrendering to the imminent kiss.

Love seemed to create an explosion of light inside her, its bright warmth suffusing her body. She wasn't conscious of Josh lowering her shoulders to the sand while he leaned over her to keep the intimacy of the kiss going. She was blissed out when he dragged his mouth from hers. Dimly she heard the laughter and shouts of other beachgoers and looked around dazedly for Robby, who was once again preoccupied with a digging project a little distance away, his small back to them.

"Don't worry, I made sure he wasn't looking." Josh laughed in her ear. "He just got started on a canal to nowhere."

"So kiss me again," she murmured.

"Annette, don't tempt me. If your little brother turns around, we're toast."

"Butter me then. Where's the lotion?" She fumbled for the bottle but couldn't find it.

"You really are wicked, you know that? You just look innocent. But you're not."

"Neither are you."

The connection between them was all the stronger for it.

"Look, let's have dinner in my suite tonight," he said. "The beach isn't exactly private."

For once, Annette didn't object to her lack of options. She simply nodded a silent yes. His gaze darkened for a fraction of a second, then he let her go so she could sit up.

"I think I'd better go help Robby with that canal," Josh said dryly.

Annette watched him cross the short distance, glad that it wasn't only her who was aware how quickly things got intense between them.

But there were witnesses to the kiss other than the oblivious swimmers and sunbathers on the beach. Poised on the steps overlooking the stretch of sand, Jordan Long stood watching. The set of his mouth and jaw was as hard as iron. His gray eyes had darkened to charcoal black. Kathleen and Marsha were on either side of him. Marsha was eyeing him with apprehension while Kathleen's expression was more on the side of resigned tolerance.

He turned away. "Come on." He gestured for them to accompany him.

"I thought we were going to let Annette know that we were back," Kathleen said, reminding him of why they were there.

"Not right now we're not. I ought to punch him out." Jordan was rigid with paternal outrage. "Did you see the way he kissed her?" he demanded. "Right out there in public!"

"Jordan . . ." Kathleen paused as she searched for words that would calm him down. Marsha trailed behind them both, well out of range of her father's temper. "You've kissed me on a beach. Lots of times."

"Yes, I did. And you know damn well what I suggested afterward too!" he reminded her.

"Oh, don't be a hypocrite." Kathleen couldn't help smiling at her husband's indignation, although she tried not to let it show. "She is twenty-one."

"So?"

"You want your daughters to do as you say, not as you do. But she's going to make up her own mind about Josh Lord and you can't interfere."

He stopped to confront her, still simmering and looking definitely more annoyed by the glimmer of a smile in her expression. "Do you think I'm in the wrong?" he challenged her. "Lord's more than a decade older. He should know better if she doesn't."

"I understand why you're upset," she said soothingly, "but even so, Annette's not your little girl anymore. You have to trust her to do the right thing," she added, finishing with a few equivocal words. "Eventually she will."

"Trust Annette?" Jordan scoffed. "That girl gets herself into more trouble on purpose than most girls do accidentally. I wouldn't be surprised if she has some harebrained scheme in mind right now. That worries me almost more than Joshua Lord does!"

"You're just guessing that she might." But Kathleen didn't deny the possibility.

Jordan swung around to look at his other daughter. She had been trying to be unobtrusive, but he hadn't forgotten she was there.

"Do you know something about what's going on?" he demanded, aware that his younger daughter found it impossible to conceal anything for long, especially without Annette around to bolster her.

"Nothing like what you're thinking," she answered nervously.

His eyes narrowed. "And what am I thinking?"

"I don't know." She refused to speculate, but she did add an explanation of her answer. "I just meant that Annette and Josh haven't done anything." When her father continued to look at her, Marsha forced herself to be more specific. "He hasn't, um, made love to her or anything like that."

"I should hope not!" The words burst out before he seemed to realize he was playing the heavy for no very good reason. He lowered his voice. "Would you mind telling me what your incredibly impulsive sister is actually up to with Josh Lord? She barely knows the guy—she can't possibly be serious."

Without arguing, Kathleen laid a hand on his arm.

Marsha shifted uncomfortably and tried to avoid answering his pointed question before she settled for one she thought might mollify her father. "She says she loves him."

"God, no." He muttered the words and lifted his gaze heavenward.

"Jordan, don't you think you're overreacting?" Kathleen was beginning to get a little irritated with him. "Annette is entitled to fall in love if she wants to. There isn't some official age for it. And I don't think she made a bad choice when she picked Joshua Lord."

"So far he hasn't proved it to me," he retorted.

"He doesn't have to prove it to you!" Some of Kathleen's hidden fire flashed in her eyes.

"That's where you're wrong!" Jordan snapped. "And I intend to put the brakes on this little affair one way or another, and give her a chance to think about what she's doing. Josh Lord sure as hell won't!"

In the next second he was striding away, leaving Kathleen and Marsha standing on the sidewalk. Marsha looked worried when she met her stepmother's glance. Kathleen released her anger in a long sigh.

"He's really steamed, isn't he?" Marsha grimaced. "He shouldn't have taken it out on you, though."

"Oh, well." Kathleen managed a smile. "He's just venting. Sometimes it's best just to listen, but I had to say something. I just don't agree with him on this one. But we still love each other. And life goes on."

Reassured, Marsha gave her stepmother a faint smile in return. "I guess you're right. It's just that you and Dad are usually so happy together, it's a surprise to hear you argue."

"It happens," Kathleen said peaceably. "Let's go back to our rooms."

"Okay." Marsha fell into step beside her. "What do you suppose Dad's going to do?"

"I have no idea," Kathleen admitted. "After he's

calmed down, I'll talk to him again. I'm sure he'll listen to reason."

Marsha wasn't. Her father and Annette were a lot alike in that respect.

By late afternoon, Annette breezed into the hotel room. She had on a hooded but short caftan that added to her leggy look.

"Hi." She smiled the airy greeting at Marsha. "Kathleen said you got back over an hour ago. Why didn't you let me know?" She didn't wait for an answer, rushing another question after the first. "What did you all buy?"

"Just pants, nothing special. They're hanging up in the closet," she said, and watched Annette with a guarded look. "When did you talk to Kathleen?"

"Just a couple of minutes ago." Annette walked to the closet to see Marsha's purchase. "I took Robby to their suite to give him a bath and get him cleaned up before you guys got back. When I walked in with him, there was Dad. And Kathleen." She took out the hanger with the new pants. "Hey, these are nice. Blue, of course. Your wardrobe is getting in a rut, Marsha."

Marsha picked at a loose thread in the bedspread. "Did Dad say anything?"

"No." Annette glanced in her direction, suddenly noticing her sister's guarded attitude. "Why?"

"I was just wondering." Marsha shrugged a little too indifferently.

Annette knew there was something more to it than that. "What did you expect him to say to me?"

"Nothing," Marsha insisted.

"There must have been something or you wouldn't have asked," Annette persisted. "So what is it?"

"It's just that . . . we did go to the beach to let you know we were back early," she explained unwillingly.

Annette frowned. "But I didn't see you."

"No, but we saw you." Marsha paused and sighed. "Actually, we saw Josh kissing you."

"Oh." Annette lifted her head a little, like an animal scenting trouble.

"Dad was furious. That's why I thought he might have said something to you. Or even yelled."

"He didn't." And she wondered why not.

"I guess Kathleen talked to him. She said she was going to . . . after he cooled down." Marsha offered that as an explanation.

"Maybe," Annette conceded and pulled the caftan over her head. "I just don't understand why Dad doesn't like Josh. He barely knows him."

"I think Dad believes *you* barely know him," her sister pointed out.

"Well, he's wrong." She hung the caftan up in the closet and began sorting through her clothes. "You should have seen Josh today with Robby. He's a born daddy himself."

"Maybe that's what's got Dad so riled up," Marsha said almost in a whisper.

"What did you say?"

"Nothing." Marsha got up and went to the closet, flipping through the clothes on hangers just for something to do.

"What do you think I should wear tonight?" Annette asked happily.

"Are you going out?" The minute she asked it, the question seemed totally ridiculous.

"Yes, I'm having dinner with Josh." Annette was careful not to mention where. "He's seen me in just about everything."

"Why don't you wear my blue silk dress?" Marsha suggested.

Annette turned, her face lighting up, but she didn't accept immediately. "Are you sure you don't mind? It's your favorite."

"No, go ahead. You'll look terrific in it."

"Thanks."

Reaching in the closet, she took out the shimmering blue dress and carried it to the dresser mirror. She held it by the waistline against her bathing suit to see how it would look on her. Marsha was right. It was terrific—the fabric, the color, the style.

"Oh, Marsha, it's gorgeous," Annette breathed. "Thanks for letting me wear it. I promise to lend you anything you want out of my closet, any time." Her expression became affectionate and thoughtful. "You know, we're not much alike, but you always come through when I need you."

"What are sisters for?" Marsha smiled.

Chapter 8

Annette waited until her family had gone to dinner before she left the room to walk to Josh's suite. Her stride was light and free. She could have been walking on air for all the notice she paid to the ground beneath her feet. It was a perfect July night—a soft breeze blowing in from the sea, night birds singing in the trees, and a gorgeous sunset filling the sky with reds and oranges. She laughed aloud when she realized she was humming to herself.

Arriving at the door to his suite, she knocked twice and waited, but not for long. She heard his footsteps and the turn of the lock before the door was pulled open. Her bright gaze swept over him.

His white linen shirt was unbuttoned at the top, contrasting nicely with his bronze tan and the fine dark hair on his chest. The sleeves were rolled up to reveal his forearms, and dark jeans, a bit loose, covered his long legs.

The lazy half smile on his mouth disarmed her. "Right on time." Josh reached out to take her hand and invite her in.

His suite was like a luxury apartment, complete

with a living room, a dining area overlooking the bay, an immaculate kitchen, and—naturally—a bedroom. Annette could see it through an opened door.

The thick draperies were pulled open to let the vibrant colors of the sunset illuminate the suite. The white damask cloth on the table gleamed with the scarlet rays of the setting sun. The table was set for two, polished silver shining and crystal goblets glittering. In the middle, a matched set of silver holders supported a pair of slim blue candles.

"I thought we'd eat later, after the sun goes down," Josh said, following the direction of her gaze.

"I agree. It would be a shame not to use the candles." And sunlight, even in strikingly passionate hues, didn't seem nearly as romantic as candlelight, but Annette didn't feel she needed to say that.

"In the meantime we can have some champagne." Josh led her by the hand into the living room. "This time it will be properly chilled."

She caught the oblique reference to the tepid champagne they had nonetheless enjoyed during their encounter on the beach, and smiled at him.

Releasing her hand, he lifted the bottle out of the bucket of ice on the coffee table. A pair of wineglasses sat on a tray. Annette picked them up while Josh attempted to work the cork out of the heavy bottle. It defied him at first, then the pressure inside shot the cork into the air, ricocheting it off the ceiling. Froth bubbled from the neck. Annette quickly held out a glass to catch the overflow.

"Aren't you lucky I was prepared?" she laughed. By some miracle not a drop was spilled.

"I knew you would be," Josh replied and set the bottle deep in the nest of ice. "How about a toast?" Facing her, he touched the rim of his glass to hers, the fine crystal chiming at the contact. "To the rest of the evening," he said softly.

"To the rest of the evening," Annette echoed and carried the glass to her lips, sipping while she held his gaze over the clear rim. The bubbles tickled her throat. She had to cover her mouth to contain a choking cough, trying to laugh at her predicament. "I knew those bubbles would get me someday," she said hoarsely, when she was able to talk again. "But I always thought I would embarrass myself by sneezing."

"I can't imagine anything embarrassing you," Josh replied.

"It takes a lot," she admitted in a more natural voice.

"Come on." He slipped an arm around her waist. "Let's sit on the couch."

Skirting the coffee table in front of it, Josh guided her and got her settled on the firm cushions. When they were both seated, his arm was around her shoulders. His body heat warmed her right through her dress, sensitizing her nerve ends to the solid feel of his flesh.

It seemed impossible to be any more aware of him, but she was. Yet there wasn't any nervousness, even though this was the first time she'd ever been alone with a man in his apartment. She'd been to parties in college, of course, held in rat's-nests that didn't deserve to be called apartments, rented by scruffy guys who set out cheap canned beer and no-brand chips and called it a party. And there had always been a horde of other friends there.

This was different. Gloriously different.

"What are you thinking about?" Josh asked, his gaze on her.

"How comfortable I am," she said. She took another sip of champagne and didn't choke on the bubbles this time.

"You managed that without a cough or a sneeze," he said approvingly. "Ready for a refill?"

"No," Annette said, setting down her empty glass. "I can't drink much on an empty stomach—it always makes me giddy. You don't want to have dinner with a tipsy blonde, do you?"

He didn't seem too upset by the idea, but he shook his head and said, "Of course not," before finishing his glass.

She studied the muscles moving in his throat as he swallowed the cold champagne—he had muscles everywhere. Which was nice. Her fingers curled with the desire to touch him.

"If you'd like some more, don't let me stop you," she offered.

"Why? Do you want me to get tipsy?"

"That's an interesting thought," she murmured provocatively.

He gave a low chuckle. "And I always thought a man was supposed to get a woman drunk."

"I like to do things differently," Annette said with a semishrug. The weight of his arm around her shoulders limited the movement and kept her close to him.

"Do you?" He set his glass down on the end table next to hers. "In that case, you can kiss me."

She started to laugh, then realized Josh was serious. On second thought, she rather liked the idea of being the one to initiate an embrace. The hand that had been so eager to touch him curved around his strong neck, applying slight pressure to bend his head to hers.

Her lips found the warmth of his, and it no longer mattered who was doing what. Josh turned to her, reaching for her. His linen shirt was deliciously light—her caressing hands took in every subtle contour of his powerful shoulders and back.

She was drunk, but that was from being so close to him, free to do what she wanted. Wild vibrations swept her as Josh nuzzled her neck and rediscovered the pulse point at the base of her throat. The wayward roaming of his hands created sensual havoc, exciting and arousing her to fever pitch.

His hand slid along her thigh, trying to mold her to him. "This is almost as bad as fooling around in a car." Josh sighed in frustration, and lifted her onto his lap.

The kissing and caressing continued with greater freedom. Her hands made a tactile exploration of his hewn features, memorizing the cut of his jaw and the solid cheekbones and discovering the softness of his thick lashes. Lengthening shadows outside darkened the room as a rich purple twilight became night. Josh stirred, his hand smoothing the hair near her face. "Are you hungry?" The question held concern, but it was said reluctantly.

"No." And she wondered if he had wanted her to say yes.

"Good." Josh answered her silent question with fire in his dark eyes. "I wasn't looking forward to making love on a full stomach."

The breath disappeared from her lungs. His arms tightened to keep her cradled against him as he got to his feet, holding her securely and effortlessly. Her hands linked around his neck as if she'd done it a thousand times. It was his place, he knew it well, and he carried her to the bedroom without the benefit of a light.

Inside the room, he set her on her feet. His hands settled onto the soft curves of her shoulders, stroking them lightly. Her heart was thudding against her ribs as Josh bent his head and kissed her with warm, slow desire. Annette swayed toward him, but his hands kept her away. Lifting his head, he looked at her deeply.

Then he turned her in a half circle. His hands moved and Annette closed her eyes as they glided down her back, unzipping her dress. She shrugged sensually and it slid off her shoulders, falling to the floor. The near-total darkness of the room intensified the erotic intimacy of Josh undressing her.

He brought her to the bed and stripped back the covers, lying her down on the silky tautness of the sheets. Kissing her, he sat on the edge of the bed, leaning to her. His hands moved restlessly over her softly full curves, stimulating her skin until she wanted to writhe with pleasure. But she held still.

When he straightened to sit erect, Annette reached out, trailing a hand over his hair-roughened chest. Josh finished unbuttoning his shirt and removed it, tossing it aside. His skin felt hot to the touch, on fire, as she was. The touch of her hand brought him back to her.

His mouth rocked over hers, then wandered to the pulsing vein in her neck. Her hands moved caressingly over his shoulders and neck, fingers running in and out of his thick hair. A quivering rush of emotion swelled within her when his hand cupped the roundness of one breast. As his mouth made a foray over its peak, Annette bit her lip to silence the wanton murmurs of delight, not very successfully. His hard male lips came back to her throat as if to investigate the faint sounds.

"You are so incredibly beautiful, Annette," he murmured huskily.

His words broke the lock she'd placed on her own voice. "I love you, Josh," she whispered with overwhelming certainty.

He was motionless for an instant, his mouth against her skin, no longer kissing every inch of her. Slowly he levered himself up. Even in the darkness she was conscious of his gaze searching her face. At first she thought he didn't believe her.

Her lips parted to say it again.

But Josh spoke first. "I should have known," he muttered wearily. He sat up quite straight, raking a hand through his hair.

Annette was bewildered. "What do you mean?"

He hadn't turned away from her or stopped looking at her. "Why did you pick this minute to say that?"

"Because it's what I feel." She frowned in confusion. "I thought I should tell you."

"But why now?"

"What difference does it make?" She didn't understand what possible significance that had. But a coolness began to steal over her bare skin without the arousing warmth of his hands to keep it at bay. "You aren't making any sense." She didn't like being on the defensive. And should she have to defend her love for him?

"It's hard to explain, Annette. If you would just answer the question—"

"Are you cross-examining me? Why am I being subjected to this?" she challenged him.

"If I didn't make myself clear, I apologize. I'm just wondering why you had to declare your love for me at that precise moment," Josh replied grimly and reached over to switch on the lamp by the bed.

Annette was bathed in light, startled and self-conscious about being naked when she hadn't been before. She yanked up the covers.

"I had no ulterior motive," she protested. "I just wanted to tell you."

Looking at him in the light, she could see the effects of their lovemaking. His thick hair was wildly tousled and passion softened his dark eyes to velvet brown. There was a sensual fullness to his masculine lips—the many kisses they'd shared had done that.

She felt bereft. He was no longer holding her or touching her or making any attempt to eliminate the distance between them now.

"I may be overthinking this," he began.

"Just tell me," she said warily.

"All right. We are—were—about to have sex for the first time. You're a virgin. If you tell me that you love me before I claim the honor of being your first lover . . ."

She barely noticed when he trailed off. So it wasn't going to happen. That one word "were" was a cold little clue. Annette clutched the covers tightly.

He blew out a regretful sigh. "I know I'm not making sense, not even to myself. But you telling me that you love me makes everything very complicated. I'm talking about emotions, Annette. You're just so damn young and naïve."

"So?" Her voice was icy.

"I'm afraid that you'll think I ought to marry you or something, in return for—"

"I wasn't going to ask that. I said what was in my heart. Sorry if I scared you." She wanted to turn her face into the pillow and howl. But she kept her eyes on the face of the man who'd just betrayed her—and his own weakness.

She really didn't have the experience to understand why he'd pulled back at the last second and hurt her by doing so. Annette studied him, searching his impassive face for some sign of emotion for her.

"You do want to seduce me," she murmured with a sinking heart. "But not marry me. Ever. So why on earth did you ask me if I wanted to have your baby?"

Josh didn't answer right away.

"You did ask. Unless one of us is crazy. I don't think it's me." A hard lump closed her throat.

"Oh God." He sighed and let his shoulders slump. "I did say that, didn't I?" He wouldn't even look at her. "I don't know why. Maybe I just went a little crazy for a few seconds. You seem to have that affect on me."

"Interesting how it's all my fault," she said bitterly. "Considering how experienced you are and how many other women have probably rolled around in this bed with you." At this point, she felt like she could sense them in the bed, and she shuddered. "Dozens? Hundreds? Not too many virgins, though. Maybe not any."

Her shrewd guess hit home. Josh groaned and buried his face in his hands for a few seconds. Then he came up for air. "No. For all the reasons we are discussing at the moment."

"I'm not sure I would call this a discussion," she said in a shaky voice. "It's more like a bad dream."

"Then is it so wrong to try and wake you up?" He turned to her at last. "Please listen, Annette—"

"I don't think I want to. It was really stupid of me to think I was something special to a man like you."

"Believe it or not, I am trying to protect you! Don't give your heart away—that's a hard thing to hear, but

I know what I'm talking about." His voice was ragged. "And as for the rest—"

"My precious virginity, you mean. Well, I still have that," she said acidly. "So I guess I'll save it for some other lucky guy. I wonder who he'll be. Definitely not you," she added with savage calm. "All you wanted was an affair, with clear boundaries. Sex, yes. Love, no. Commitment, forget it."

"Y-yes." His strong voice hitched for a fraction of a second.

"Why didn't you tell me that before you got me up here?" she asked. "Or was there a handout on the dresser that I missed?"

Utterly furious, Annette rolled to her feet, picked up a pillow and whapped him hard across the face with it, happy to see him spit out a feather when she threw the pillow on the floor. She would have been happier to break his nose.

"Until th-this afternoon," he gasped out, standing to tower above her, "I thought you understood a lot of things that I didn't bother to spell out."

"Well, I didn't!" she flashed. "Where are my clothes? I want my clothes!"

The room around her seemed to shift as Josh walked to the dress she'd stepped out of, picking it up along with her underwear. He took his time to collect it all, then handed everything to her. Annette felt hot under his steady regard.

"Turn around so I can get dressed," she ordered.

"You're naked," he said. "What am I going to see that I haven't seen?"

"I don't want your eyes on me one second longer."

He dropped them and did what she said, staring at the floor under his feet, his hands thrust deep in his pockets.

He seemed deeply ashamed. And he should be, she thought, jerking on her panties and missing a hook on her bra clasp. The dress went on next, twisted. She didn't give a hoot.

But she was unbearably aware of the strong, tapered back turned to her, and the handsome head he was hanging. Even though he wasn't watching her, his presence and compelling sexuality struck her more intensely than ever.

Then something he'd said came back to her: *Until this afternoon.*

"Wait a minute. You said something like, oh, you thought I understood you were only interested in an affair . . . until this afternoon. What happened? I wasn't with you then."

"After I left you today, I had a visitor," he replied.

"Don't be so coy," Annette said with disgust.

Impatience rippled through his tense muscles. "This is ridiculous," he muttered. "I'm not going to talk to the wall. Whether you like it or not, I'm turning around." Josh faced her, his eyes straying over her tangled clothes. "You can't go out like that."

"Don't tell me what I can and can't do either. Don't even make suggestions. Who came to see you?" Annette repeated the question, a gnawing suspicion already forming. She wanted to be wrong.

"Your father," Josh answered.

She felt as if a thousand-ton weight had just landed on her. "He came to see you?" She almost didn't want to know why.

"He wanted to find out what my intentions were as far as you were concerned. He said something about him being old-fashioned. Maybe protective would be a better word."

"I don't doubt that," Annette retorted.

Josh looked at her levelly. "I understood what he was getting at. It was kind of weird when he started talking about marriage, and you, and how you weren't as sophisticated as you pretended to be. But I listened. I had to."

"And?"

"I got stuck on that word—marriage. All of a sudden, I connected it with you. Before he started explaining, I wouldn't have. You seemed like a free spirit—a beautiful young woman who did things her own way." He gave her the ghost of a smile. "I guess I got spooked. You do deserve to have what you want out of life. I don't think I'm the right guy for—you know. If that's what you want, you deserve to have it."

Her father had really done a job on Josh. Big-time.

"That doesn't explain you inviting me up here. Why didn't you tell me about my father's visit when I got here?"

A wry look came over his face. "Like I said, I'm not the right guy. I wanted you. So—" One bare shoulder lifted in an expressive shrug. "I told myself your father didn't know what he was talking about. I think fathers would sometimes prefer their daughters to become nuns. And I told myself that he hyped this marriage thing because he couldn't accept the idea of you having an affair." Josh paused to study her. "It really didn't occur to me that you didn't know the score."

"Until I said that I loved you." Annette remembered the moment—and the change in him—with aching clarity. She almost wished she could take back those words, but that was impossible. At the moment she was hurting inside, and the backlash from the pain was anger.

"Bad timing," he said. "You wanted me to say I loved you then, didn't you?"

"Only if you meant it," she retorted, and adjusted her dress.

"Hey, a lot of men would say it without meaning it, just to have you. I remember doing that once or twice when I was young and stupid. I still regret it. Ultimately, it creates too much hassle," Josh told her with steady calm. "The minute you said that, you stopped me cold. All I could think was that your father was right and I was wrong."

Her fingers tugged at the balky zipper behind her back, trying to force it to close. Frustration brought a latent violence to her actions. She was dying to finish dressing and get the hell out of there, trembling with pain and growing anger.

"Let me do that before you break the zipper," he volunteered roughly, walking toward her.

At the touch of his hands, Annette jerked away from him. "I can do it!" Her gray eyes blazed with deep hurt. "I don't need your help!"

The grip of his hands was firm as he overpowered her objections and turned her back to him. "Just shut up and let me do it, Annette. It'll be a lot faster."

That was a persuasive argument. She stood rigidly, fighting the sensation of his fingertips on her lower spine. Within seconds, she heard the quiet sound of the closing zipper traveling up her back.

"Do you want me to fasten the little hook at the top?" Josh asked.

"No." She stepped away from him. The dress would look fine whether that was done or not. His hands at her sensitive nape . . . no, no, no. She couldn't take it.

Annette looked around for her shoes. She was

distraught enough to storm out barefoot and not know it.

"Be honest, Annette," Josh challenged her. "You were willing to go to bed with me because you thought I'd be so crazy about you and so honored"—the inflection in his voice put a question mark at the end of that word—"and I would have been honored to be the first, if you really want to know. But you might have pinned a whole lot of romantic hopes on that, marriage included. Look, your father knows you better than I do. Which one of us was wrong?"

"I'll have to get back to you on that," she hissed. She felt like a fool—a naïve and easily deluded fool.

She finally spotted her shoes and scooped them off the carpeted floor.

Agitation seemed to steal her natural grace. When she tried to put her shoes on, she had to hop in a ridiculously ungainly way to keep her balance. It was a small humiliation in an evening filled with big ones.

"I'm sorry it turned out this way, Annette," Josh offered a grim apology.

"Look," she snapped. "You've made it clear you aren't interested in me. Let's leave it at that."

"I guess I didn't make myself all that clear. I am interested in you. I'd like you to stay here tonight. I'd love to make love to you," he stated.

"I can't believe you used the word 'love' twice in one sentence," Annette said bitterly.

He ignored the jab. "But what I'm not interested in is waking up tomorrow morning to a knock on the door and—"

"Please!" At this point, she wanted to scream. Loudly. But meeting the hotel detective who was sure to show up if she did was not high on her list of fun things to do. She settled for vehemence. "My father isn't going to be standing there with a shotgun and a preacher!"

"But he is going to say that I took advantage of you and worse. I can do without that scene."

"So can I!" she insisted, her pride storming to the front.

"Good. Then we can both be spared that." A toughness tightened his jaw and his eyes grew dark. "One more thing—the next time a man asks you to go to bed with him, make sure you do it because it's what you want. And don't think because he takes your virginity that he wants to marry you."

"Good advice!" Annette was nearly spitting from the raw hurt raking her insides. "And you can bet you won't be that man!"

A grim kind of anger flashed across his face. "Am I supposed to be upset by that remark?" Josh demanded. "Are you trying to get me to want you more? You must be hoping to get something from me—let me guess. A declaration of something? Like love?"

Was she? Annette honestly didn't know what she was trying to accomplish anymore. Except . . . it was possible she wanted him to feel some sense of loss, because she felt destroyed. It wasn't fair that she was the only one in the throes of pain.

"No!" She fiercely denied his claim. "I don't want anything from you! Not your kisses! Not your love! Nothing!" But even as she said it, she knew she was lying. And she hurt all the more.

He'd calmed down—which infuriated her—to a state of quiet exasperation. "Like I just said, I'm sorry it turned out this way. Maybe we'll meet again sometime."

"Yes." Her throat nearly closed in agony. "Maybe we will—after I've had a couple of affairs. But you're way ahead of me in that department."

His mouth thinned. "Annette—I'm letting you go—"

"You're not letting me go!" She choked with rage at the thought that he was *allowing* her to leave. "I'm walking out!"

It was the best exit line she'd had. Annette used it, whirling away to march from the bedroom. The blood was roaring in her ears. It was so loud that she couldn't hear if Josh was coming after her. She tried to pretend she didn't want him to. Still stronger pain hit her when she reached the front door of his suite and realized Josh had not followed her.

Out she went, seething with fury.

Irrationally, she remembered that her father had triggered this devastating scene with his visit to Josh. It was Jordan Long's fault that everything she'd hoped for had come to an abrupt end before she had a chance to make Josh love her. It could have worked.

The two men she cared the most about had hurt her—for typically idiotic male reasons. And Annette wanted to get back at them. She was determined to, blindly insistent about going into action without taking time to consider the situation from all sides.

Reaching the door to her father's suite, Annette pounded on it with her fist. All her pent-up pain trembled violently through her and the hammering helped. She kept it up even after she heard her father's muffled voice.

"Just a minute," he called in vague irritation.

Her fist hit the door one last time before it was swung open. Her eyes burning, she looked at her father's frowning expression as he paused in the middle of tying a knot in his robe's belt. Gray eyes, gray as hers, took in her paleness and the way she was shaking.

"Annette!" His obvious concern quickly became

anger. "What happened? What did he try to do?" He reached out to pull her inside. "So help me, I'll—"

With a violent shrug of her arms, Annette flung aside his hands. "How dare you!" she stormed. "Who gave you the right to talk to Josh about me?"

He stiffened at her attack, lifting his head. "I'm your father. That gives me every right."

"No, it doesn't! You had no business interfering in my personal life!" Annette raged at him. "It has nothing to do with you! Don't you ever do it again!"

"You are my daughter," he began as Kathleen hurried anxiously to his side.

"And don't think I'm not sorry about that! I wish I'd never been born, if you really want to know!" She tried to ease her hurt by saying every mean thing she could think of. Hot tears were finally spilling from her eyes and running down her cheeks.

"Keep your voices down, both of you," Kathleen ordered. "You're going to wake up Robby."

"I don't care!" Annette didn't lower the volume at all. "It's time he found out what kind of father he has!"

"Young lady, you just crossed a line," her father warned.

The hotel wall that separated the suite from the sisters' room wasn't thick enough to block the noisy argument. Marsha was propped in a sitting position on her bed, nestled into the pillows, listening and flinching now and then, the paperback novel in her hands forgotten.

She didn't understand why it was always a gigantic shouting match every time her sister and her father fought. Her shoulders hunched at all that anger vibrating right through the wall. Robby started crying to add to the furor.

Some loud remark from Annette was punctuated by the slamming of a door. A sudden silence followed. The argument was over, to Marsha's great relief. Angry footsteps came to the door; the keycard slid into the lock. Marsha started to get out of bed to open the door for her sister, but it was already swinging in.

Annette swept across the threshold on a wave of temper and banged the door shut. She didn't even look at Marsha as she crossed the room and began undressing with jerky movements.

This brooding silence always followed blistering arguments. Marsha had learned it was better to leave her sister alone if she didn't want to get broadsided by her temper. Quietly she walked to the door and locked it for the night.

Under the covers again, Marsha picked up her book and pretended to read it while she listened to Annette getting ready for bed. When Annette crawled under the covers, Marsha glanced hesitantly in her direction.

"Want me to turn off the light?"

"I don't care," Annette answered coldly.

Sighing, Marsha set her book aside and switched off the bedside lamp. For a long time she lay there trying to piece together the fragments of the argument she'd overheard. It had been something about her father talking to Josh.

There were times when she envied her sister's bold confidence and thirst for adventure. But she was very glad she wasn't Annette right now. Rolling onto her side, Marsha closed her eyes.

Chapter 9

While Marsha took her time to get dressed the next morning, Annette lay in bed with her hands, under her head, staring at the ceiling. There was no expression on her face, but Marsha wasn't fooled. There was raw pain in her sister's eyes, and a glittering anger. Those busy wheels in Annette's mind were turning, and Marsha was leery of all that implied.

She couldn't take the silence anymore. "Aren't you going jogging this morning?" she asked.

"No." The single word was hard and decisive.

Marsha hesitated, biting at her inner lip. "Do you want to talk about it?" She eyed her sister, feeling sure that Annette shouldn't keep it all bottled up inside like that.

"No, I don't want to talk about it." Not once did her gaze stray from the textured pattern of the ceiling.

There was a knock at the door and Marsha went to answer it. Kathleen was standing outside when she opened the door. She smiled and glanced past Marsha, spying Annette in the bed.

"We're on our way to breakfast," Kathleen said. "If you're ready, we might as well walk together."

"I haven't brushed my hair yet," Marsha answered. "I'll be a few more minutes." She glanced over her shoulder at Annette, who hadn't moved.

"Aren't you coming, Annette?" Kathleen asked.

"No." The monosyllabic answer was flat, allowing no opening for a discussion.

"Honey, I know how you feel—" Kathleen began, the warmth of understanding mixing with a firmness in her voice.

"No, you don't." Annette cut across her words with a hard incisive stroke.

There was a trace of impatience in her stepmother's eyes as she glanced at Marsha. "She'll be all right," Marsha murmured the assurance. "She just needs a little time."

"Maybe we all do," Kathleen said in an equally subdued tone.

"Go ahead to breakfast," Marsha urged. "I'll join you as soon as I'm ready."

Kathleen nodded a silent agreement and turned away. Quietly Marsha closed the door and turned to go back toward the beds.

"You really should eat some breakfast, Annette," she advised.

"Marsha, please," her sister flashed in exasperation. "I don't need any lectures from you about diet or exercise. Just go."

"Suit yourself. But I thought you might feel better if you had something to eat," Marsha retorted with a trace of anger at the undeserved snap.

"I'll eat later." Annette was less abrupt this time, retreating into her thoughts and shutting her sister out.

There was some consolation in the thought that sooner or later Annette would talk to her, but it wasn't much comfort as Marsha entered the bathroom to brush her hair.

Dark sunglasses shielded her eyes from the glare of the afternoon sun as Annette lazed in a lounge chair by the pool. Her indolent pose was completely faked. She continued to seethe inside, and toy with schemes for revenge.

Out of the corner of her eye she saw someone coming toward her chair. She turned to see Craig. Dressed in his waiter's uniform, he had a look of reserve on his handsome face. He favored her with a polite nod at first, nothing more. She wasn't really surprised by his lack of friendliness, considering the way she'd ignored him lately because of Josh. But that aloofness could be overcome.

He stopped beside her chair. "Jack said you asked to see me." Jack was the other waiter who had been on duty at poolside.

Swinging her feet to the paved sundeck, Annette sat sideways in her chair and perched her glasses atop her sun-streaked hair. As she stood up, she gave him her most alluring smile.

"Yes, I did," she admitted, then looked around at the other guests by the pool before returning her gaze to him. "Is there someplace private where you and I can talk?"

Interest flickered in his eyes, and then he narrowed them just a little. "I guess you must want to find out more about Josh Lord."

Okay, he wasn't totally stupid. That *was* the reason she was paying attention to Craig.

"Josh is a bore," she declared, wrinkling her nose. "No, I don't want to talk about him."

His expression began to soften, and that golden-boy charm of his kicked in. Craig actually seemed to puff up a little at the idea that Annette might prefer him to Josh Lord and all his money.

For her part, she was a little disgusted by how easy it was to manipulate a man if you pushed the ego buttons just right.

"There's a place behind the game room. It's kind of secluded and out of the way. We could talk there," Craig suggested.

The game room was where the video games were with a couple of vintage pinball machines for the diehards. It sounded ideal—close by and practically no chance of being observed. She wanted to get this conversation over with.

"Let me get my things. I'll follow you. Discreetly." The lilt in her voice seemed to promise him something he undoubtedly wanted.

"Okay." Craig was grinning now. "I'll meet you there."

There was something almost leering in the way his gaze traveled over her white swimsuit. But nothing could penetrate the shell she'd retreated into to protect her shattered heart.

As he ambled off in the direction of the game room, Annette bent to pick up her beach robe and bag. She took her time folding them to lie smoothly over her arm, then set off after him.

When she walked around the corner of the game room, Craig was standing next to the building waiting for her.

"What happened between you and Josh Lord?" he asked curiously. "You two seemed to be a pretty hot item for a little while."

"There were a few things we didn't agree on, so I

bailed." Annette shrugged and sauntered closer. "I didn't need the aggravation and he didn't have anything that you don't have." She stopped and ran a finger along the underside of his uniform's lapel. "Besides, I think you and I could have more fun. That is"—she paused as though she might be too presumptuous—"if you'd still like to go out with me."

"Sure," he answered quickly, then tried to conceal his eagerness. "It might be kinda fun."

"Are you busy tonight?" Annette continued to let her finger move under his lapel, slowly going up and down.

"I was thinking about going over to a buddy's place for a kegger. We play beer pong and get totally wasted, usually. It's going to be a blast. You're welcome to come along." Craig made it sound like he was doing her a huge favor by inviting her to a raucous party in somebody's grubby basement. Ugh.

"Actually," she sighed, and her finger stopped its movement. "I thought we could go somewhere a little more private than that. Someplace where we could be alone, just the two of us. I think you know what I mean."

"Like . . . uh . . . where?" His hand moved to the bare curve of her waist and stopped on the cut-out side.

"Maybe some other friend's place? A friend who's not there?"

"Oh. The guy I room with has, uh, company tonight. I've been sexiled, so that won't work," Craig said. "And my other friend who might let me use his bedroom is the guy who's throwing the kegger."

"There must be someplace we can go," she said, wide-eyed and looking a little sad.

He thought, but not for long. "One of my buddies

is a night clerk on motel row. Rooms by the hour or for the night." He studied her closely as he said it.

Double-ugh, either way. But in the mood she was in, Annette supposed it didn't matter.

"Are they all booked this time of year? Would you know?"

"I'll call him. It's policy to hold one room back for regular customers—businessmen who come there a lot," Craig explained. "He owes me a favor," he bragged. "What time do you want to meet and where?"

"Is nine o'clock too late?" She allowed his hand to draw her close to him but arched her back, fidgety as a cat, to keep some space between them.

"That's fine. How about if I pick you up by the parking lot exit?"

"I'll be there at nine o'clock on the dot," Annette promised, and kissed him lightly on the mouth, then slipped out of his hold, leaving him wanting more and expecting it. She waved to him and walked around the corner of the game room.

Bending down, Marsha gave Robby a hug and a good-night kiss. "See you in the morning," she said. "Sweet dreams." Then she straightened to leave. "Good night, Dad, Kathleen."

They echoed her parting phrases as she left them to walk to her own room. Unlocking the door, she went in. A tray of dirty dishes sat on the round table by the window. Marsha guessed that her sister had ordered dinner from room service, since she had refused to have the evening meal with the family.

"Annette?" she called.

"I'm in the bathroom," her sister answered.

The door was standing open so Marsha walked over. Annette was leaning close to the lighted mirror and applying a thick coat of mascara to her lashes. Marsha stared at the pink halter-style sundress and white sandals her sister was wearing.

"Are you going out?" Marsha asked in disbelief.

"Yes. I have a date." Annette stepped back to inspect the result of her primping in the mirror.

"But—I thought you and Josh—" Marsha began in bewilderment.

"I'm not going out with Josh," her sister stated in the flat voice that had become her preferred method of communication for the last twenty-four hours. "That's over. We didn't have as much in common as I thought and neither of us is any good at compromise."

"Then who—"

Annette didn't let her finish. "I'm going out with Craig."

"Craig," Marsha repeated, because it didn't seem possible. "The waiter?"

"Yes." Annette brushed past her into the main part of the room. Dazed by the unexpected announcement, Marsha followed.

"But I thought you didn't like him." As a matter of fact, her sister had made it plain that she didn't. But she'd never known Annette to do anything without a reason—she was a natural-born schemer that way. Something was up. A thought occurred to Marsha. "Are you trying to make Josh jealous?"

"Nope." Annette laughed at the suggestion, but there wasn't any humor in it. It sounded brittle and phony to Marsha.

"Then why are you going out with Craig?"

Annette made a project out of making sure her

room keycard was in her purse. "I never realized what a problem being a virgin was," she said airily. "I figured out a solution."

Marsha's mouth dropped open in shock. "You can't be serious," she protested with a squeak of horror. "You don't expect me to believe that you cold-bloodedly intend to—"

"Take it from me," Annette interrupted, "the cold-blooded way will cause a lot less heartache than the hot-blooded one. At least you won't want—or expect—the man to marry you afterward."

Marsha didn't like that kind of logic, but she was beginning to understand what had probably happened between Annette and Josh. "But don't you want to—"

"Save your breath if you're going to say 'save myself for the man I marry,'" Annette replied mockingly. "Nobody's cared about stuff like that for a million years. No, my problem is that the man I want to marry me doesn't want to marry me."

"But . . . does Craig know what you have in mind?" Marsha was in a state of semishock. She couldn't believe her sister was saying these things—or really intended to do them.

"He'd be awfully dense if he doesn't," Annette retorted, suddenly sounding impatient. "What else would he think I wanted when I agreed to go to a motel with him?"

"A motel? You mean the no-tell kind of motel?" Marsha really was shocked now. This couldn't be her sister talking. "Annette, what are you thinking? Don't do that."

"The place doesn't make any difference, Marsha." Impatience and irritation seemed to lace every word.

"You've been reading too many romances. Grow up. Love isn't real."

Being criticized by Annette was nothing new to her, but this time there was more sting to the barbs. "You're telling me to grow up? When you're the one who's going to some sleazy motel—"

"It's an okay place," Annette said stubbornly. "It's on motel row and I wouldn't call it a no-tell. Granted, it's not a palace. But Craig has a friend who's a night clerk and he'll probably get the room for nothing or next to nothing."

"You can't go through with this," Marsha said flatly, suddenly very calm and determined.

"I can and I will," Annette stated and started for the door.

Marsha rushed to block her way. "I mean it, Annette. You aren't thinking straight," she said fervently. "Look, I know you're upset because of Josh and I get that you want to hurt him, but you're going to end up hurting yourself more. Think about it. I happen to be right."

For a fleeting second a crack appeared in her sister's defensive shell. Marsha got a glimpse of the stark pain underneath the cynicism, but Annette was nothing if not stubborn. She realized that her sister was determined to go through with this. Marsha could talk until she was blue in the face and not steer her away from the self-destructive course she was on.

"Would you mind getting out of my way?" Annette asked frostily. "Can't keep Craig waiting."

There wasn't any way Marsha could stop her, short of physical force, and even that might not work. Reluctantly she stepped to the side, letting Annette pass. She felt helpless as she watched her sister walk to the door and pause.

"Don't wait up for me," Annette declared with deliberate flippancy. Marsha wanted to scream at her not to go. But she didn't.

"You're crazy," she said quietly instead.

The instant the door closed behind Annette, Marsha almost lost it. She ran a hand through her hair, searching for some way she could stop her sister when reason had failed. She couldn't just let the stupidest scheme her sister had ever cooked up happen. No way.

Her mind recalled a remark Annette had made not all that long ago: *You're always there when I need you most.*

Whether Annette knew it or not, she needed Marsha now. But what could she do? How could she help? She wished she had Annette's cleverness at coming up with ideas—no, actually, she didn't. Common sense was what was best.

But time was slipping away.

It was out of the question to go to their father. After that spectacular quarrel, there was too much chance that involving him would lead to another with more severe consequences. Annette was already furious that he'd interfered in her budding relationship with Josh. And in her present mood, she just might decide to break away from the family altogether.

Marsha couldn't go to Kathleen, the second obvious choice for help. She was positive her stepmother would insist that her husband be told what was going on. Which brought her back to the starting point.

She chewed at a fingernail, desperate to find an intelligent way to resolve this awful mess. There simply wasn't anyone else who could help. Annette wouldn't listen to her or their father. And there just wasn't anybody else—

Josh!

His name flashed in her head with the suddenness of a switched-on light. All of this had started with him. He was ultimately the cause of Annette's nutty behavior. He was probably the only person that Annette would listen to, but would he help? Her already tense nerves tied themselves in tighter knots because she knew she would never find out unless she asked him.

A phone call would give her a degree of anonymity. Marsha didn't like the idea of confronting him in person with the news of Annette's latest escapade. It was possible that she wouldn't be able to convince him over the phone that the situation was desperate. It was sure to be an uncomfortable experience, but she knew she had to see him.

And besides, the front desk didn't put just anybody through to his private line. Her desperate message, if she left one, would languish in voice mail for days.

Yet she struggled with the decision a few minutes more before she gathered up the courage to seek him out. With her keycard tucked safely in her purse, Marsha switched off the lights and left the room.

She could just imagine what they would think at the hotel desk when she asked where Joshua Lord's suite was. Polite but poisonous. Marsha taxed her brain to remember what Annette had said about it—not much—but she was pretty sure she could at least get herself to the right floor. And it had to be the highest floor—he owned the whole hotel. Once she'd gotten that far, she'd befriended an entrepreneurial member of the housekeeping staff to the tune of twenty bucks and been directed to the right door.

A storm of doubts swirled in her stomach as she

approached it. There were lights on inside, so at least he was home. She crossed her fingers that no one was with him and knocked at the door.

Within seconds her summons was answered and the door opened to frame a shirt-sleeved Josh Lord. A slight frown narrowed his dark eyes when he saw her. His features were drawn and tense, minus any polite welcome. There wasn't even a flicker of recognition in his look.

"Yes?" It was a peremptory demand for her to state her business.

"I'm Marsha Long." She clutched her purse with nervous fingers. "Um, I'm not sure if you remember me, but I'm Annette's sister."

"I remember you," he stated, but his aloof expression didn't change. He made no attempt to put her at ease.

This was going to be harder than she thought. For a panicky instant, Marsha didn't know where to begin. He didn't look like he'd be willing to help her at all.

"I need to . . . to talk to you about my sister," she managed finally.

If anything, his hard expression got harder. "I have nothing to say on that subject," he replied in a cold voice. "You wasted your time coming to see me."

When he started to close the door, Marsha sprang forward in desperation. "No! Please!" she protested, and pushed a hand against the door to keep it from shutting. "I need your help!"

The request made him pause. "My help?" Josh repeated, and his flare of interest gave her a little bit of hope.

"Yes," she said, bringing her hand down. "Look, Annette just left to go out with Craig, one of the waiters here at the hotel," she began.

His interest immediately waned. "She can go out with anyone she wants to. That has nothing to do with me."

"Yes, it does," Marsha insisted anxiously. "She's only going out with him to spite you and Dad."

"That's her business." Again the door started to close.

"No, you don't understand!" she burst out in a rush. "She's going to a motel with him!"

Josh visibly stiffened. The sharpness of his gaze seemed to pierce her. "What did you say?"

"She's going to a motel with him." She repeated the sentence in a less melodramatic tone. "I tried to talk her out of it, but she wouldn't listen to me. She's got this wild idea in her head . . . that's it's better to . . . do it . . . with someone she doesn't care about." Marsha blushed furiously as she stammered over the words.

"She decided that, huh?" He snapped out the words with steely emphasis. "And was it part of her plan to send you over here to tell me all about it?"

"No!" She breathed out the denial in a burst of alarm, realizing Josh had a knack for seeing through Annette's plotting and maneuvering.

What if she couldn't convince him that this time the situation was genuine and not manufactured by her sister? It couldn't become a case of the boy crying wolf too many times!

"I swear Annette doesn't know I'm here," she vowed, and automatically raised her hand as if taking a pledge. "Honestly, she doesn't."

"You sound very convincing." But skepticism continued to narrow his gaze. "But you are Annette's sister, aren't you?" It was practically an accusation.

"I admit that sometimes . . . Annette . . . arranges for

things to happen." She struggled with the confession of her sister's guilt—and her own. "And . . . sometimes she talks me into helping her out."

"Like with the sweater," Josh guessed.

"Yes," Marsha admitted. Agitation surfaced as she tried to convince him that this time it was different. "I'm trying to help her now, but not because she wants me to. It's because she's my sister and I don't want her to make a terrible mistake." All the apprehension that was twisting her into knots threaded itself into her voice. "She doesn't even like Craig— and she's planning to go to bed with him!"

The corners of his mouth tightened in a kind of angry impatience. "You believe that she means to go through with this?" he demanded.

Marsha sighed brokenly and shook her head in vague confusion. "I don't see how she can. But with Annette—I sometimes think I wouldn't put anything past her." She looked at him, her rounded blue eyes filled with anxiety. "After last night, when she broke up with you and had that awful quarrel with Dad, she's been . . . different. I don't know how to explain it," she finished lamely. "I think you're the only one who can stop her. Will you help?"

Josh didn't answer directly. "Do you know what motel they were going to?" His insistence on more information was as good as a yes.

"No." Marsha shook her head as a quiver of relief went through her. "All she mentioned was that Craig had a friend who was a night clerk somewhere on motel row."

"That's a start," he muttered, and turned away from the door, leaving it open.

Marsha hovered on the threshold, unsure if she was supposed to enter or if Josh was coming back.

She watched him stride across the living room and stop to pick up the phone. Half-turning, he looked to see where she was and motioned her into the suite.

Stepping inside, she closed the door. During the ensuing one-sided conversation, Marsha was able to gather that Josh was talking to one of Craig's co-workers, a buddy who knew the waiter pretty well, to find out which motel on the strip employed the clerk. Obviously he obtained the information, because the minute he hung up he was moving toward the door.

"Are you coming?" He shot the question at Marsha and she nodded, too intimidated by his bad mood to speak. With a barely suppressed violence, Josh yanked the door open. "So help me," he muttered under his breath, "if this is another of her tricks, I'll wring her damned neck!"

Annette hugged the wall while Craig unlocked the door to the motel room with the battered brass key and pushed it open. Her skin immediately felt chilled and she blamed the cold feeling on the motel's air-conditioning and the skimpy sundress she was wearing. A little clumsily, Craig put a hand at her waist to guide her into the room.

"Hey, this isn't bad." He made the pleased declaration as he looked around. "It's even got a king-size bed."

She couldn't help noticing the way the huge bed dominated the room. It seemed appropriate that it was covered with a scarlet spread with a couple of small cigarette burns in it. The other sticks of furniture in the room were barely noticeable next to it.

The paper bag under Craig's arm rattled noisily as

he let go of her to set it down on a long dresser that
had seen better days. He hadn't mentioned what was
in the bag, but she'd already guessed it contained a
bottle of liquor.

Switching on the TV set, he glanced at her. "We'll
be able to watch it in bed."

Whoopee. His remark drew her attention to the
fact that the screen faced the bed. Not a plus. Craig
began surfing stations to see what was on. It seemed
ridiculous to her to pretend that they'd come here to
watch TV.

But she went along with him. "Yes, we can."

Satisfied with whatever was playing on one channel, he moved away from the TV and took the bottle
out of the bag. "Is whiskey okay?"

"Sure." Annette wandered farther into the room
and looked around, but the bed was all she really saw.

"I'll get some ice." Craig picked up the cheap plastic bucket the motel provided to the rooms and
paused. "There's a vending machine outside. What
kind of mix do you want with your whiskey?"

"Whatever you're having will be fine." She didn't care.

Before leaving the room, he stopped to kiss her.
"Don't disappear while I'm gone," he said with a wink.

When the door closed behind him, Annette
rubbed her hand across her mouth to wipe away the
damp trace left by his lips. She walked to the bed and
set her purse on the nightstand. Half-turning, she sat
down and pressed her hands on the mattress as if she
were testing it in a store.

She felt only numbness, blanking out what was
around her, not wanting to feel or think anything.

A few minutes later the key turned in the lock, signaling Craig's return. She studied him as he walked

in, abstractly noting his standout good looks, totally unaffected by them.

"One stiff drink coming right up," he said cheerfully.

Suddenly she didn't know why they were going through all these motions. TV and drinks—ugh. That wasn't why they were there. Basically, she wanted to get the whole business over with as fast as possible.

"Why don't you fix it later, Craig?" Annette stood up and reached behind her neck to unfasten the halter straps of her sundress. In the back of her mind was the nagging thought that she'd probably welcome the drink later.

She wasn't aware of his startled glance as he set the ice bucket and can of soda beside the whiskey bottle. And she didn't notice the way his avid gaze licked over her when the straps fell loose. She was too busy unzipping the back of her dress.

Almost in a trance, Craig moved toward her, unbuttoning his shirt as he walked and tugging it off. Stepping out of her pink dress, she draped it over a chairback. Under the dress she had on a strapless bra and a lacy half-slip. Her fingers were on the elastic band of her slip when the touch of Craig's hand on her shoulder made her pause.

She turned her head to look at him, her gray eyes blank, completely lacking the passion that burned in his. Annette offered no resistance when he took her in his arms and began smothering her lips with kisses. His hands were all over her, crudely touching and feeling.

A jarring feeling of revulsion welled inside her as Annette submitted to his lust-crazed maneuvers. She'd thought she could pretend he was Josh, but she realized a little too late that she couldn't. He wasn't Josh, not by a long shot. Annette turned her head away from his greedy mouth, her hands pushing at him.

Craig misinterpreted all of it, taking her actions as a signal for him to do more. He unfastened his pants and started to unzip them, his gaze riveted on the agitated rise and fall of her breasts within the supporting cups of the strapless bra.

"You are so incredibly beautiful, Annette," he declared hoarsely.

Oh God. Was that ever the wrong thing for him to say. Those were the very words that Josh had used. No matter what she'd thought before, Annette knew she couldn't possibly go through with this ugly charade. She had been a fool to lead him on, and she had only herself to blame for that.

"No." She took a step backward, utterly repulsed.

Craig stopped what he was doing and reached out to grab her hand. "Hey, where are you going?" he laughed, and pulled her back. Immediately Annette started to struggle and Craig fought to hold on to her, suddenly confused. "What's the matter with you?"

"Let me go!" she demanded angrily.

"What are you talking about?" He roughly attempted to overpower her unexpected resistance. "This was your idea, remember?"

Chapter 10

Someone rattled the motel room door, freezing both of them. As Annette turned her head to look at it, the door burst open with explosive force. The color drained from her face as Josh charged in. His hard features were livid with anger when he saw her in Craig's arms. But she wasn't imprisoned in them for long, because Craig was shocked into letting her go. Josh advanced on them with purposeful strides.

"How did you know I was here?" Her voice was a thin thread.

An instant later she had her answer when Marsha ventured hesitantly into the room. Her cheeks flamed with the realization that her sister had ratted her out to Josh and told him where he could find her. Humiliation prickled her as Annette considered what Josh must be thinking about her now.

"What's he doing here?" Craig demanded an answer from Annette.

But she wasn't given a chance to explain that she hadn't expected Josh to barge in. Her wrist was seized to pull her out of Craig's reach. Without wanting to, Annette looked directly into Josh's angry eyes.

"I'm taking you back to the hotel." It was clear that he wasn't interested in any arguments.

"Now wait just a damn minute!" Craig bristled in protest at the way Josh was assuming he had the right to control whether Annette stayed or left. "She came here with me and she'll leave with me."

"Like hell she will." Josh let go of her wrist and turned on him with a snarl.

"I know what you're probably thinking," Craig retorted. "But she came here of her own free will. I didn't twist her arm."

"Maybe that's true, but she isn't staying." Josh gave his competition a once-over and his lip curled with disgust. "Better zip up your pants before they fall down."

Craig turned beet red and quickly fastened them as Marsha hurried to Annette's side. "Are you all right?" she whispered.

"How could you tell him?" Annette practically choked on the words. Her sister had betrayed her. Well, maybe she had it coming—she felt a tiny flash of surprise at finding out that Marsha had a spine.

Her sister's soulful blue eyes filled with tears. "I'm sorry, but I didn't know what else to do," Marsha whispered.

"Marsha, get her purse," Josh ordered, and grabbed the sundress off the chair to shove it into Annette's hand. "Put this on."

He stood between her and Craig, a living wall intent on keeping them apart—as if it were necessary. Annette kept her head down to avoid eye contact with her angry rescuer as she slipped the dress on and tied the straps behind her back. She didn't get any further than reaching for the bodice zipper before his hands turned her around and pushed her fingers out of the way.

"So far your father doesn't know about this dumb stunt," he said in a low voice, pulling the zipper roughly closed.

She spun around in shock, her gaze rushing to his. "You aren't going to tell him?" Annette breathed in panic.

"Why not?" he replied grimly.

"You just can't!"

It was bad enough that she'd been so stupid—maybe obsessed was a better word—to think she could go through with this. Her sense of shame doubled with Josh's appearance on the scene. If her father knew what was going on, she would just about die of mortification. How could Josh threaten her this way? His challenging stance hinted that he would.

"I thought you came charging in to rescue me from a fate worse than death," Annette hissed sarcastically. Out of the corner of her eye, she saw Craig edge away into the bathroom and heard the puny click of a dimestore lock. Josh could kick that in too if he wanted to. No doubt that was next on his macho list. "You are despicable, Joshua Lord!"

"Yeah? You wouldn't win any prizes, either, but you're damn well going to get what you deserve," he warned.

Annette favored him with a scalding glare. "If you tell all, so will I. Craig isn't going to be the only guy getting caught with his pants down. Just you wait until the reporters and bloggers find out all about the handsome scion of the oh-so-illustrious Lord family. They'll have a field day."

That actually seemed to hit home. He clamped his mouth shut but she could see a muscle twitching in his jaw. Marsha just stared at both of them, frozen. But Annette couldn't resist a final jab.

"I bet your doctor dad won't love seeing his perfect son on the cover of a supermarket tabloid."

Josh found his voice. "He doesn't read that crap."

Annette snorted. "Don't count on it." She turned to her sister, summoning up whatever pride she had left to walk out of there with her head held high. "Come on, Marsha. We're catching a cab and going back to the hotel."

The instant her attention was diverted, Josh moved in. He grabbed an arm before she could scramble out of his reach, and grabbed Marsha's arm too. Both sisters squeaked in unison, but only Annette clawed—ineffectually—at him.

"You and your sister are going back to the hotel with me," Josh growled somewhere near the vicinity of her ear.

The pressure he was applying arched her backward, giving her little room to kick at him. Besides, Marsha might get in the way. It was impossible to struggle, and that seemed to be his intention. Frustration drove her nearly to tears. She scrubbed them away furiously with her free hand.

"Here." The dull rustle of some kind of paper followed the sound of Josh's voice. At first Annette thought he was speaking to her. But he'd let go of Marsha and was taking something out of his pocket and putting it on the dresser. He raised his voice to call to Craig. "Tell your creepy friend at the desk to replace the lock I kicked in. This oughta cover it."

There was no reply from the bathroom, but she realized the sound she'd heard was money.

She was propelled out the door. Marsha, that traitor, got to walk. Once they were in the outer hallway of the motel, Josh didn't let go, just moved his iron grip to her wrist. Annette was grateful there was no one there but the three of them. She and Josh certainly made a sweet couple. She could almost hear the imaginary whispers: *Trucker and hooker? Heartbroken husband and cheating wife?*

"You let me go, Joshua Lord." Her voice was low and trembling, near the breaking point, but he didn't deign to reply.

Behind them, Marsha was half-running to keep up. It was clear that she had defected to the enemy—and it occurred to Annette that her sister undoubtedly had a cell phone in her purse and would definitely call their dad if things got out of hand. First, Marsha had betrayed what Annette had told her in confidence by going to Josh. Now she was allowing Josh to manhandle her out of this situation without offering a single word of support for Annette's stand against him.

Annette was devastated. And, in truth, as angry with herself as she was at everybody else.

His car was parked in the lot. She recognized it as they approached. She thought about breaking free—it would have to happen at the moment Josh released her to get in the car. There was no way she was going to let him march her into her father's presence like some delinquent. But Josh knew the way her mind worked.

He motioned for Marsha to climb into the backseat. Without letting go of her wrist, he pushed Annette into the front passenger seat and pressed a button on his key to child-lock all the doors. She yanked at the handle anyway, furious.

"Sorry," he called to her as he walked around to the driver's side.

With her escape thwarted, Annette glared at him through the stinging tears in her eyes. The profile next to her was uncompromisingly male, showing no softness or yielding in its rugged angles. She had never suspected he could be so ruthless and uncaring.

"I don't know what I ever saw in you," she declared in a low voice made husky by the awful tightness in her throat.

Tearing his gaze from the street and its traffic, Josh shot her a look. "I don't see any halo above your head."

"You aren't really going to drag me in front of my father. You're just trying to scare me." Annette desperately wanted that to be the case.

"You need more than a good scare." The words were threaded with a trace of humor.

That had to be wishful thinking. She swung her gaze to the front, staring blindly out the windshield. "I hate you." There was an unmistakable tremor in her voice.

"Go right ahead and hate me," Josh said with cold unconcern. "It isn't going to make any difference."

"I must have been crazy to think I loved you," Annette declared tautly.

"Why don't you just shut up?" Josh asked in a friendly voice, shooting her a silencing look.

The silence in the car became thick and oppressive. Sitting in the backseat, Marsha looked like she was waiting for something to explode. The atmosphere was volatile. Her glance kept darting from Annette to Josh, but they exchanged not another word or look.

When they arrived at the hotel, Josh parked the car and got out to walk around, making a show of gentlemanly conduct in the way he helped Annette to get out. She had gone numb. Let him do what he wanted. Her fury and rebelliousness seemed to have vanished, now that her planned rendezvous had come to this odd conclusion. In its place . . . there were no emotions at all.

Annette rose gracefully, her face composed. He could have been escorting her to a dance. She even let him take her arm. Again Marsha tagged behind them. She had no idea if Josh intended to carry out his threat to deliver Annette to their father. The doubt was erased when he led the way to the suite occupied by Jordan and Kathleen Long.

At the door, Josh let go of her arm and put his hand at her waist to make sure she stayed by his side and didn't bolt. Annette stood rigidly, but her flesh burned at the contact. It was too familiar, too possessive. It reminded her of things she'd do well not to recall ever again. A renewed sensation of feelings coming back to life made her tremble deep inside.

"Why are you doing this?" The question betrayed emotion, but she stayed where she was.

Josh merely looked at her at first, his dark eyes unreadable. "Do you really want to know?"

"Yes."

He sighed before he replied, "So the Lord Corporation doesn't get slapped with a multimillion-dollar lawsuit, among other reasons—which I'm not going to go into now." He rapped on the door with firm authority.

Just slapping him, period, sounded awfully tempting at this unbelievably awkward moment. But at the sound of someone stirring inside, Annette made no move to avoid this confrontation with her father. Josh tightened his arm around her waist anyway. Her body was brought alongside the length of his side and she had to fight the involuntary reaction of her senses.

"Who is it?" her father asked before he opened the door.

"Josh Lord." He raised his voice slightly. "I have your daughter with me." He failed to mention Marsha, hovering in the background.

The door swung inward and Annette's gaze ricocheted away from any contact with her father's. She had glimpsed his frown of disapproval at the sight of the two of them together. She didn't want to contemplate his reaction when he learned why they were there.

"What is this?" he demanded. "What's going on here?"

"May we come in?" Josh asked tersely, ignoring the questions. "Your daughter has something she'd like to tell you."

Her father seemed, not surprisingly, confused but also concerned. He moved out of the way silently to admit all three of them. But Josh had to push her inside. After a couple of seconds of resisting, Annette thought of more than one alternative that would serve Josh right, without deciding on any—things were happening a little too fast for that. Nonetheless, she walked all the way into the room of her own accord. Both her father and Kathleen were in their robes.

"So what did you want to tell me?" her father prompted.

"Nothing." She sat down in a chair and crossed her arms, sending Josh a belligerent look. "There's something he wants me to tell you."

He gave her a cross look. "Annette, I hope this isn't some kind of parlor game. Just talk to me."

She searched her mind for the right words, but

couldn't think of a thing to say that wouldn't make her sound ridiculously childish. Josh took the initiative.

"Annette went out tonight," he began.

"You did?" Her father's face registered his surprise.

She stubbornly refused to answer. Josh walked over to her chair and bent down, resting a hand on either armrest and forcing her to meet his look. "Which explanation do you want him to hear?"

"It's none of his business—or yours!" Her only protection seemed to be anger, but that was bound to backfire.

"All right. If that's the way you want it." Josh straightened and turned to face her father. "Annette visited a motel tonight with one of the waiters from this hotel."

"Really." To his credit, her dad found the self-control not to play the outraged father. But it took visible effort for him to answer calmly. "Well, she's twenty-one. She can go to motels if she wants to, although I don't have to like it. But I don't get what you have to do with this," he added with an authority that overshadowed Josh's. "So what's your story? Start with how you knew. Then tell me why you're here with Annette. And her."

Jordan glanced at his younger daughter and raised an inquiring brow. Marsha pressed her lips together and said nothing.

"Marsha came and told me where Annette had gone and I was concerned for her," Josh replied evenly.

"You knew about this?" Jordan Long asked, more puzzled than ever.

"Yes, I knew," Marsha admitted.

Jordan held up both hands. "Whoa. Let's get one

thing straight. Was Annette hurt in any way or was she in actual danger at any point? My guess is that she wasn't, but I want to be clear on that point."

"No. Never," Annette muttered, twisting her hands in her lap.

"Glad to hear it," her father said, exchanging a look with Kathleen. "Okay, continue."

"I—I went out with Craig," Annette began hesitantly. "He's a waiter here."

"That's not a crime," her father said. "Let me guess—you were in the mood for some fun. And he looked cute in his white suit."

Annette knew perfectly well that her father didn't ever want to know the details. And there was no reason she had to share them. She pushed herself out of the chair, the turmoil inside her becoming more than she could contain. "I don't see what all the fuss is about," she bluffed. "Nothing happened!"

"Settle down. I believe you. But I can't say I'm thrilled that you went to a motel room with someone you obviously don't know very well," her father replied.

"I'm sorry if you're upset, Daddy, but where I was and who I was with really isn't your business." Annette glared at her sister and Josh. "Or theirs."

Kathleen stepped forward, her hazel eyes soft with concern. "Annette, what's going on? The three of you wouldn't be here in this room if what happened really was nothing important."

The gentleness of her stepmother's voice almost proved to be her undoing. Kathleen's words were the first real promise of sympathy she'd received and Annette suddenly wanted to cry. The tactics she'd considered while they were on their way to the suite door weren't going to impress anyone in this room. She couldn't make him look bad for rescuing her—

which he had done—when the situation with Craig threatened to spin out of control. It would be nothing more than another way to get revenge for Josh's rejection of her.

"Why did you go to a place like that? Why him?" her stepmother continued.

Annette lowered her head in remorse, her voice becoming husky when she answered, "I thought it was what I wanted to do."

"And it turned out that it wasn't," Kathleen guessed.

Annette started to admit that much until she caught Josh watching her with his expressionless dark eyes. She glanced away. "Josh came before anything happened," she said tightly and refused to explain more.

The stubborn streak in Annette wouldn't allow her to confess that she had changed her mind before he arrived. He might interpret that to mean that she actually cared about him or something. And she didn't.

"I still don't understand," her father muttered, but he was interrupted by a knock at the door. Swearing under his breath, he strode across the room to answer it.

A respite was the last thing Annette wanted. Her legs were shaking and she felt sick. And foolish. Returning to the chair, she sank into it as her father opened the door.

"Mr. Long?"

Annette lifted her head, thinking at first that it was impossible—that couldn't be Craig. But she knew his voice. Holy cow. What next?

"Yes?" her father asked irritably.

"I'm Craig Fulton," he began, then went on, "I was with your daughter tonight. I knocked on her door to make sure she got back all right, but nobody answered. I wondered if—"

"*You're* the guy she was with?"

"Yes, sir," Craig's voice admitted. "Is she here?"

"She is." There was anger in the terse answer.

"May I come in, sir?" he requested. "I'd like to explain what happened."

"By all means." The agreement was almost a challenge as her father swung the door wide open.

Annette paled. She had no idea what Craig wanted to explain. But whatever he said wouldn't do anything for her reputation. She realized that he most likely wanted to clear himself, probably so he wouldn't lose his job at the hotel. Her glance went to Josh. Sure enough, he was watching her, instead of the two men at the door. She looked away just as quickly, fully aware of his low opinion of her.

"Are you all right, Annette?" Craig asked, as though he were concerned about her welfare.

When she looked at him, she saw the nervousness in his face that she hadn't heard in his voice. He did have courage, even if he lacked class. But Annette wasn't sure whether he was being brave or stupid coming here like this.

"I'm fine." Her answer was a little clipped. "What are you doing here?" He had to see that she was in trouble.

"I wanted to be sure you got back okay," he said, repeating the explanation he'd given her father at the door. His glance slid to Josh, alert as always. He didn't seem to have missed a thing.

"You were going to explain about tonight. Let's hear it," her father said in a challenging tone.

"Yes, sir." Craig angled himself to face both Annette and her father. His attitude was very respectful, his posture erect. "I know how it must seem—I mean, about Annette and me being alone in a motel room. But we just wanted privacy to, uh, talk over some things."

She dared to look at Josh and realized she could practically hear the words he was holding back: *Talking? Was that why Annette was in her slip and your shirt was off? You two were just getting comfortable, huh?*

Annette didn't have to look at her father to sense his total disapproval.

"We both realized that it was wrong to—to—" Craig stammered and trailed off, unable to come up with a phrase that wouldn't get him thrown down the stairs by her irate dad.

"To fool around," her father said bluntly.

Craig turned scarlet. "Yes, sir. More or less. I mean, I'm an employee and she's a guest and—"

"I get the point," her father interrupted him. "And that is a serious issue, which I will turn over to Joshua Lord, who is more or less your employer, although I suppose he doesn't hire or fire staff."

Josh nodded but didn't add anything.

"So correct me if I get any of this wrong," her father said, rubbing his chin and looking back and forth among the three of them, ignoring Kathleen and Marsha for the moment. "You and you"—he pointed to Josh and Annette—"had a lover's quarrel. So you"—he pointed at Craig—"made a move. Or, knowing Annette, she moved first."

"Dad!"

"Then you"—the pointing finger moved back to Josh—"checkmated him at the motel. Right so far?"

Josh inclined his head in a nod of agreement. Craig seemed to be about to speak again, but he looked a little more desperate than before. As for

Annette, she was wavering between anger at her father and Josh, and guilt for getting Craig into this fix. She had been sneaky and it wasn't right that he should pay the whole price. Somehow she would have to fix things with Josh or someone under him in the hotel hierarchy.

"I want you to understand, Mr. Long," Craig blurted out, "that I'm not interested in just a casual relationship with your daughter. I care about Annette very much."

Impatience and irritation rippled through her. The only person Craig cared about that much was himself and Annette knew it. It wasn't her name he was interested in clearing but his own.

"Will you stop being so noble, Craig?" she flared. "In another minute you're going to be volunteering to marry me or something crazy like that."

Craig opened his mouth to respond, looking scared half to death by this point, but Josh cut in, "And that can't happen, because Annette is going to marry me."

The calm statement jarred Annette to her feet—and made her father sit down with a sigh. "Things are getting interesting. But that could work," he murmured to Kathleen, who went over to him to put an arm around his shoulders.

"What?" Annette was furious. After what Josh had put her through tonight, it was outrageous that he would say that in front of her father, even as a joke. "I wouldn't marry you if you were the last man on earth!"

"Whew," he said cheerfully.

At least she knew he was joking. She still felt irrationally hurt.

Josh turned to Craig. "Listen, Fulton, it was big of

you to show up and make that little speech. I think you might be wasted as a waiter. Check in with Human Resources in the morning and see if we have any gigolo openings."

"But—"

Josh jerked his thumb toward the door. "Out. You're not fired, but you are going to be written up. You know what the rules are."

"Oh—okay—" Craig beat a hasty retreat, not bothering to say good-bye to the Longs.

"So you want to marry Annette," her father said musingly. "Josh, I really should give you my blessing but—what if she comes back? You'd better be damn good to her."

"I will," Josh said.

"Is this a conspiracy?" Annette asked in a low, disbelieving voice.

Her father grinned wickedly. "Of course not."

"Stop it," Kathleen said reprovingly to her husband. "They hardly know each other and it's Annette's decision, not yours or his."

"I suspect they know more about each other than we think." Jordan gave her a wry but very affectionate wink. Then he looked around the room and let his gaze rest on his younger daughter. "It's time you called it a night, isn't it, Marsha?"

"Oh—I guess so." She wiggled the fingers of one hand to wave good-bye and decamped hastily, not daring to look in her sister's direction.

Rising, her father brought his wife to her feet at the same time and turned her in the direction of the adjoining bedroom. "We really aren't getting any younger, Kathleen. I don't think I can ever remember being as crazy as those two, can you?"

He named no names, but it was clear he was talking about Josh and Annette.

"Where are you going?" Annette demanded. "You can't leave me here with him."

The gray of her father's eyes gleamed. "I think my future son-in-law can handle the situation without my help."

"What?" She practically shrieked the question this time. "I'm not going to marry him!"

"Yes, you are," Josh stated, attracting her gaze back to him. "Eventually. Not now. Calm down, will you?"

His certainty infuriated her. It wasn't right that he should be so sure of her, so positive she would agree. He had dragged her here as if she had no say at all, then somehow gotten her father on his side. They were in cahoots. They had to be.

"I won't calm down!" Silver fires blazed in her eyes.

There was only one chair in the alcove to the side of the darkened room where their son Robby was sleeping. Jordan guided Kathleen to it. "We're going to be in here for a while, so we might as well make ourselves comfortable." He spoke softly, so he wouldn't disturb the sleeping boy. Taking the chair for himself, he drew Kathleen onto his lap.

"You certainly reversed your opinion of Josh in a hurry," she murmured, and curved a hand around his neck, absently stroking the dark locks of his hair.

"Until tonight he hadn't proved to me that he was the right man for her. But he has guts. After all, he stood up to—"

Kathleen snorted. "That waiter? Excuse me, but I don't think Craig is much of a rival."

Jordan nuzzled the side of her neck, making her

giggle. "Let me finish. What I was going to say is that he stood up to Annette. He refuses to let her bait him and he doesn't seem to mind when she goes off on one of her wild tangents. I get the feeling he adores her, no ifs, ands, or buts about it, just the way she is. That's a start."

Kathleen laughed very softly into his hair. "You could be right. But it's only a start."

"It's a good one—as good as anyone gets. It's plain to me that she's head over heels in love with him. I know my girl."

"Well, impulsive as she is, it's not a good idea to rush her into things. After all these years, she's my girl too."

Jordan gave her a chaste but soulful kiss. "And I am incredibly grateful to you for staying the course. With me. And with her."

Kathleen smiled when he let her go a little bit. "Just give them time."

He nodded against her neck, murmuring, "They can take all the time they need. It's nice and dark in here."

His hand moved along her arm and caressed her rounded shoulder in a leisurely way. "The next problem could be adjusting to the idea of becoming a grandfather," he whispered.

"She's much too young yet," she whispered back with mock severity. "But years from now, when that day comes, you'll make a very sexy grandfather."

"That's because I'd be very happily married to a sexy grandmother," Jordan assured her and let his lips find hers in the dark to show just how powerful the attraction was.

* * *

Annette strained in Josh's hold, her hands flattened against his chest. "You're crazy if you think I'm going to marry you." She repeated the denial the instant her father and stepmother left the room. "Just because I thought I loved you—"

"You do love me," Josh interrupted with unwavering sureness.

"I don't!" she snapped.

His mouth crooked. "Do you want me to prove it?" he taunted.

"No, I—" She broke off her denial, saving her energy to resist as his hold on her shifted.

The iron band of his arm circled the back of her waist to bring her against his body while he combed his fingers into her tawny hair to hold her head still. Annette tried to elude his descending mouth and failed.

Her lips stayed stiff under the persuasive pressure of his mouth as he coaxed her to respond. It was agony to resist the sensual warmth of his kisses. The thrill was melting her and firing her nerves. And she suddenly wondered why on earth she was fighting such pleasure. Wantonly, Annette began kissing him back.

Josh insisted on total surrender, not content until she was clinging to him and caressing him with tender fierceness. Only then did he draw back while she shuddered with the intensity of her longing. His encircling arms continued to support. "You said you hated me," he murmured.

"I do sometimes," she answered honestly. "But I also love you—or maybe I just think I do. I'm all mixed up."

He shook his head. "You're young. Which was no excuse for me to act like a total jerk when you said what was in your heart. I deserved everything you threw at me, including that pillow."

"Oh, Josh—"

"Do you think we can start over?"

A barely audible cry of anguish came from her throat. There were tears in her eyes when she lifted her head to gaze at his ruggedly handsome face. His intent gaze seemed to drink her in. "When we were alone you told me you don't want to be married and then you say the opposite in front of my family. Which Josh am I talking to right now?"

He hesitated, but his gaze held steady. "The one who figured out what he really wanted: You."

"Not just an affair?"

"No. And let's forget about Craig, random redheads, and all the other distractions. I'm only talking about you. And I love you. I want you, on your terms, whatever they are." There was a definite twinkle in the depths of his eyes. "You're good at making yourself clear, Annette. So what do you say?"

She couldn't quite believe he meant it, not after the things he'd said the other night. "Did my father put you up to this?"

He laughed and shook his head. "Nope. I had no idea how he was going to react."

"So why did you drag me to his suite?"

"He was bound to notice sooner or later that you and your sister were both gone. I know you're twenty-one but she isn't. And he's a protective guy, from what I can tell."

"Overprotective."

"Yeah, well—I remember the look he gave me when I barged into your birthday party. Like he was going to remove some vital organs if I didn't move on."

"And tonight? He seemed to think you were harmless."

Josh blew out his breath. "He was glad I brought you back, put it that way. It's a guy thing, kind of hard to explain. But I think he gave me a lot of credit."

"More than that. He practically offered you my hand in marriage."

Josh chuckled. "Not quite. Your father isn't stupid and he got what was going on. Maybe before you did."

"Oh, excuse me for not understanding instantly. It's a girl thing. We prefer actual explanations, not secret handshakes."

"Annette, he wants you to be happy—and safe. And you're the oldest and you're supposed to set a good example—" He paused for breath. "But I wouldn't mind one or two daughters just like you."

"Would that ever serve you right, Joshua Lord," she said vehemently. "Don't forget, sisters are sneaky. You won't ever win. But why are we even talking about—having children?"

He smiled broadly, dazzling her even more. Inwardly she was still astonished by the wondrous discovery that he really did love her when she'd thought it was all so hopeless.

"Because I think you do get what I'm talking about: love. The real deal. Are you ready?"

"Do you really want to marry me?" she asked. Doubt and hope were mixed in equal measure in the rushed question. "I mean, you know, after a few years, we could start thinking about it, and get in some travel along the way, and maybe live together, and I could start my career, and we could practice on the kid thing by getting a puppy—"

"Let's keep it simple. The answer is yes."

"Josh." His name was an aching little cry of sheer pleasure.

Further discussion of the subject ended. Annette gave herself up to the delights of his embrace and love circled them in a golden halo.

A Lyon's Share

Chapter 1

"Joan, it really is okay to have fun once in a while. Trust me on that."

Joan Somers only shrugged in reply and took a final bite of her sandwich.

Her friend Kay sighed impatiently. "You're not listening to me. Name one thing you planned to do tonight that can't be put off until tomorrow."

Joan Somers refused to meet her roommate's accusing gaze as she gathered the crumpled wrapping from her sandwich and the empty milk carton on the lunchroom tray.

"That's not the point. You know how I feel about blind dates," Joan said.

"Oh, get over yourself. Ed can't be classified as a blind date. He's John's brother," Kay argued.

John Turner was Kay's fiancé, a likable guy, but in Joan's opinion—which she kept to herself—dull and unexciting. His one endearing quality was his loving devotion to Kay, something that he managed to show in a hundred different romantic ways. Still, it was unlikely that Joan would find his brother's company any more thrilling than his. It was a safe guess that neither Turner was her type, although at twenty-five, she was beginning to wonder if she had a type.

"Why don't you ask Susan instead?" Joan suggested as they slid their empty trays into a receptacle for that purpose. "She's great at small talk." The company receptionist was famous for it, in fact. It was hard to get past her desk without chatting with her.

Kay snorted. "Have you ever known Susan to have a free hour on weekends? She always has men panting after her. Friday night? Forget it."

"That's true," Joan agreed. A twinge of self-pity reminded her that she was the only one in the company who seemed to spend most of her weekends alone.

"You have to go out tonight," Kay pleaded. "John just found out this morning that Ed was flying in to meet me. I can't rustle up a date for him on such short notice except for you."

"Gee, thanks," Joan said. "It's nice to know I'm considered that reliable."

"You are, though. What's wrong with that?"

Joan shook her head. "Never mind. Anyway, Ed's coming in to meet *you*. So why don't the three of you just go somewhere for dinner?"

"Ed is John's brother, not his uncle." Kay delivered that nonexplanation and got up, tagging after Joan as they both left the lunchroom.

Joan glanced at her watch. "Let's discuss it after work tonight," she said. "I have to get back to my office."

"I can't wait until five o'clock." Her roommate ignored the hallway that branched to their right, which led to the computer department where Kay worked, and followed Joan into the upper management sector of Lyon Construction. "John is picking me up after work and we're going straight to O'Hare to meet Ed at baggage claim. I have to know now."

Joan was backed into a corner and she knew it. Even before she agreed, she knew she was going to say yes. There was no real reason not to. Joan prided herself on being practical and logical, which made superstitious avoidance of blind dates seem kind of silly.

Simply because she'd met Rick Manville on a blind date four years ago and thought she was his one-and-only, until by accident she'd come across his long list of one-and-onlies . . . well, she was never going to be that naïve again. And she'd been more humiliated than hurt. Thinking back, she could almost laugh about it. Almost.

"Joan, you really have to come tonight," Kay insisted again. "John and I are counting on you."

The wide-eyed, soulful look that Kay put on when she really wanted something reminded Joan of a cocker spaniel begging for attention. Kay could be extremely emotional at times, even though she was a computer nerd and total tech whiz.

She regarded her friend and roommate for a moment as they both stopped at the outer office door. In many ways, Joan and Kay were complete opposites: Kay, with her dark pixie curls, was petite and bubbly, with an outgoing personality, but Joan was statuesque and full-figured, her long hair coiled in a practical bun at the back of her neck. When she took the pins out to brush it before bed, its glorious natural color had the deep gold of amber, but she almost never wore it down. Her eyes were a warm brown, though without the lively sparkle of Kay's.

As far as their personalities, Joan considered herself just as friendly as her roommate, although generally speaking she was a lot quieter. It just wasn't as easy for her to connect socially with men she didn't know, something that was never a problem for Kay. Even when it came to work, Kay flung herself into projects with abandon while Joan would efficiently organize each step.

But at the moment their differences didn't matter. Kay needed help and Joan knew she ought to jump at the chance to have a night out. She'd spent too many weekends alone lately. Still, she hesitated to say yes. Joan pushed open the door to her office and walked in with Kay on her heels.

"You can't say no," Kay repeated. "We want to—"

The rest of the sentence was lost as she caught sight of the man standing beside the open drawer of the filing cabinet. Kay's face brightened into a smile.

"Hello, Mr. Lyon."

But her cheery greeting didn't change his expression. He nodded to Kay before his deep blue gaze moved to Joan. Tall and ruggedly handsome, Brandt Lyon radiated an aura of boundless energy and competence that was simultaneously unnerving and reassuring.

"Joan, will you please tell me where the Statler file is in all this mess?"

Clearly, his fingers had been raking the thick brown mane of his hair in frustration, because it was standing on end. At the moment his hands were braced on his hips in an attitude of challenge.

His question and criticism got Joan's chin up a fraction of an inch. Annoyed, she walked over to the metal cabinet where he was standing.

"If you'd stay out of the files, they wouldn't be in such a mess," she replied crisply, and began reinserting several folders that had been yanked out halfway. "And the Statler file wouldn't be in this drawer since this is strictly for suppliers." She flicked her fingernail against a tab in front. "It's labeled right. S for Suppliers, not S for Statler."

With the drawer in reasonable order again, she closed it and pulled open the one beneath it, aware of the tall, broad-shouldered man at her side.

"So what do you file Statler under if it's not S?" he asked. "Am I supposed to pick any other letter of the alphabet randomly and hope for the best?" He sounded exasperated. "I don't have all day."

Joan remained unruffled. "Just so you know, you look under a heading first, then under the alphabetized subheadings. Or you can simply ask me." She began to flick through the tabbed files while he watched.

"You weren't here," he growled.

She gave him a calm look, unwilling to admit that she couldn't locate the folder. Where was it?

"Looks like you can't find it either," Brandt said a little smugly.

"Yes, I can." Joan straightened and went to her desk. Her tortoiseshell-frame glasses were lying beside the phone. She often laughed that she could see a country mile, but not an inch in front of her nose. It didn't seem funny now, though. "I just can't read the tabs without my glasses." She slipped them on and kept looking.

In a few seconds, she handed him the Statler folder. He flipped it open and perused the contents page clipped to the inside front, missing her prim smile of triumph.

"Some day," Brandt said absently as he headed for his office, "you're going to have to draw me a map so I can find things in that metal monster of yours."

Her lips were pressed tightly together as the connecting door closed behind him. Then, with only

Kay to hear her, Joan put her hands on the waist-band of her tailored tweed skirt and addressed her next words to her now-invisible boss. "And on that day, Brandt Lyon, I will quit and you will have to look under S for Slave to find a new me."

Kay burst out laughing, but soon stopped at Joan's warning glare. "Whoops, sorry, am I too loud? I don't want to get you in trouble. You amaze me sometimes, Joanie."

"Why?" Joan walked around her desk and put her bag into the bottom drawer. "I'm not always a good girl."

"You should do that more often—talk back to him, I mean."

"Not if I want to keep this job. I happen to like it."

"Do you? Imagine telling your boss to stay out of his own files—I wouldn't have the nerve." She chuckled. "Of course we don't have a clanky old cabinet like that in the computer department."

"Consider yourself lucky."

"Does he still insist on keeping hard copies of everything?"

"How did you know?"

Kay waved a hand at the neatly stacked files every-where. "I can see the evidence. It's actual and vir-tual—I maintain his computer on the company network. Did you know we call him Backup Man?"

"Not to his face."

Kay grinned. "Well, no. Anyway, you should ask him for a couple of new cabinets. Unless you two aren't getting along well at the moment."

"We are," Joan replied, adding, "well enough."

"Are you?" Kay launched into an explanation of that simple question. "I mean, you're obviously not pals. Everything is strictly business. A robot could do your job and he wouldn't notice. And you're just as bad. He's very good-looking. Sexy, even. And you've never said a word on the subject." Kay gave her a sly look. "C'mon, aren't you a little bit interested? Or curious about his love life?"

"I'm his assistant. I'm not supposed to be interested."

"That's not an answer," Kay pointed out.

"You noticed," Joan said serenely.

"Well, if I were you, I would make a move." Kay sighed.

"Really?" Joan slipped her glasses off. "And what would John think if he knew you had eyes for the company CEO?"

"He would be jealous, wouldn't he?" Kay giggled. "But he knows I'm a big flirt."

"I sometimes think that's an understatement," Joan said ruefully.

"Hey, speaking of John, what about tonight?"

Joan frowned slightly. "All right, all right, I'll go. But don't ask me to entertain Ed the entire weekend. It's going to be only for tonight."

"Thanks!" Kay got all charged up again. "We're going straight to the apartment from the airport. I'm guessing we'll be there by seven thirty, depending on traffic, so if you could be ready when we get there—"

"I will."

The intercom buzzer sounded. "Yes?" Joan answered.

"Please come in to my office." Brandt's disembodied voice echoed a little.

Kay was halfway to the door to leave when she turned around to add a parting remark. "And wear something sexy, too!"

For a split second, Joan could only stare at the button she'd just pushed, holding her breath and hoping that her roommate's words hadn't been picked up by the intercom speaker.

"I'll be right there, Mr. Lyon," she murmured.

Breaking off the connection, she slipped her glasses back on and gathered her pencil and paper. At the door to his office, she paused to straighten her skirt, then went in.

Brandt's expensive leather chair swung around as she entered. His computer screen was filled by an open spreadsheet he'd been working on. She knew she would have to file it as a hard copy when he was done. Brandt really was a big believer in backing up documents and files on his external hard drive, discs, and good old paper as well. Remembering to do it sometimes made her job a little more complicated, but it was certainly true that they had never lost a single document to system glitches.

His gaze swept over her.

Joan could guess what he was thinking. Her signature tortoiseshell glasses and neat chignon were the opposite of sexy. He probably figured he'd misheard Kay's silly comment.

The gleam of speculation disappeared, and his look held nothing personal at all. As Kay had taken such pains to point out, they were strictly employer and employee. With an efficiency that matched Joan's, he went through his schedule for the afternoon, handed her a disc of the document files from his computer for her to print out and send around interoffice and elsewhere. He added a jotted list of phone calls he wanted her to make on his behalf.

The businesslike mood was quickly reestablished. He said nothing to confirm or deny that he'd overheard Kay. That swift appraisal of her when she'd walked in the door might not have happened at all.

Yet at five o'clock, Joan stepped into the doorway of his office one last time to make sure there was nothing else he needed before she left for the weekend. His casual remark stripped the doubt that remained.

"So, are you going out tonight, Joan?" Brandt asked after assuring her that he was set up and she could go.

"I sure am. It's Friday," she replied, trying to make it sound as if her date, if she could call it that, wasn't a once-in-a-blue-moon occasion.

"Enjoy yourself."

There was no mockery in his statement, not even teasing, but she didn't like the indifferent tone he used. "I generally do, Brandt. Good night."

The wind had a bite of the cold north in it as Joan waited on the corner for her bus. But the late November snowfall had mostly melted earlier in the week, leaving the ground frozen and barren on the first day of December. Dusk was encroaching on the gray sky. The heavy overcast didn't permit the golden pink colors of sunset to peep through the clouds.

Her weekends generally were quiet respites from work, punctuated by girls' nights out now and then or an admittedly rare date. Standing at the bus stop looking at the rush of Chicago traffic, Joan felt gloomy and lost. She knew why—that last comment from Brandt Lyon.

Enjoy yourself.

It didn't come naturally and she hardly ever found the time—but that could just be habit. When she'd graduated from college with a BA in business administration, she'd had to find work right away to start

paying off her student loans. She'd ended up in a tiny
cubicle at a large insurance firm processing documents, working twelve-hour days for nine months.
Fun? No. Never. Not at all.

Then she'd spotted an online ad for a private assistant to a CEO. On that day three years ago, she'd contacted the Lyon Construction Human Resources
department, sent in a resume, and aced the first interview.

Two days later, she was asked to come back to meet
with Brandt Lyon. He'd been rummaging through
the very same file cabinet looking for a folder when
she'd gone in. He hadn't wasted time with introduc-
tions or small talk as he told her what he was looking
for and asked her to find it. It had taken her only a
few minutes to puzzle out the admittedly haphazard
system and produce the required folder.

By then Brandt had been talking to someone in another city, holding the call long enough to thank her
and ask her to wait for him outside. She'd done so, a
little nervously, surprised to find that her prospective
employer was relatively young, since he'd been in his
early thirties. There was such a positive air about him,
a sense that he always got things done one way or another. Joan smiled when she remembered that look
of exasperation on his rugged face when he hadn't
been able to find the folder he wanted from the filing
cabinet.

At about that moment, he'd come into the office.
She'd been uncomfortably conscious of the appraisal
in his dark blue eyes and wondered if he was the type
who chased women he worked with. She had even
thought that it might be a thrill to be caught. And
then he'd said something that surprised her even
more than his youth.

"I wanted someone older with experience."

Joan remembered the way her heart had quickened at the sound of his quietly spoken but firm words. His voice was one that people listened to and automatically sat straighter without realizing it.

"Oh. I'm really qualified for the position, Mr. Lyon," Joan had replied, hoping she sounded professional and not scared half out of her interview shoes.

"We'll see how you do." He'd nodded and turned away.

"Do you mean I have the job?" She had been so positive he was going to turn her down that she hadn't been sure she'd heard him correctly.

"You did apply for it, didn't you?" Brandt had answered with marked patience. Joan nodded and right after that, he'd added, "Then you've got it, starting right now."

In the beginning, she'd assumed he'd made a snap decision because he needed an assistant right away. The woman she was replacing had been badly injured in an auto accident. Gradually, Joan learned through the office grapevine that he'd had a background investigation done on her before calling her in, so as not to waste his time. Still, she secretly believed that her ability to instantly fathom the filing system had been the clincher.

Kay had been hired only the day before and as the two latest additions to the Lyon staff, they gravitated toward each other despite their very different positions and personalities. Within a few months they were sharing an apartment.

Joan readily admitted—to herself—that in the first few months of her new job she had developed a crush on her boss. Brandt Lyon was a dynamic guy who didn't seem to be fazed by anything. Every obstacle or crisis was met head-on and resolved intelligently, or removed from his path. His last name conjured up the image of a jungle cat and he really was a lot like a lion. His strength and power were held in check, displayed only when there was need for both, and not in anger. His ruggedness, the features that weren't handsome but compelling, made the comparison more apt.

Yes, she had cherished secret hopes in the beginning that he might be attracted to her, but it had always been business. Joan herself had set the foundation for their relationship. She had been overly conscious of her inexperience, for one, and had done her utmost to look capable. When she'd started, her wardrobe consisted of sweaters and skirts, which she upgraded to tailored suits, right for the job but not very womanly.

Her amber golden hair was no longer caught by a scarf at the back of her neck, but coiled into a tightly pinned bun that hid its shimmering color. Glasses were a necessity and she picked frames that conveyed the same capable image. Her awareness that she was attracted to Brandt made Joan all the more conscious of the way she addressed him—she was afraid he would guess.

But Brandt Lyon's total lack of interest in her life outside the office and her duties there didn't encourage romantic fantasies. Joan was grateful that the practical side of her nature had kept her from confiding her secret feelings in anyone. Not even her roommate guessed how close her teasing remarks had come to the truth.

Admiration and respect were the only emotions that Joan let herself feel for him. But she still knew that she remained a little sensitive to his indifference.

Stubbornly, she wanted him to see her as a woman and not as his assistant.

The bus stopped at her corner and Joan pushed her way through the passengers to the folding door in the rear. The wind chased her to the apartment building, its cold breath trying to penetrate the scarf around her neck. Inside the building she bypassed the elevators for the stairs leading to the second floor and the apartment she shared with Kay.

Kay liked to describe the décor as Early Leftovers since the two-bedroom apartment had been furnished with discards from their respective sets of parents. It was a hodgepodge of styles ranging from a heavy Mediterranean-type couch to a colonial-reproduction rocker with uncomfortable spindles. A white stove and a copper-colored refrigerator fought it out in the kitchen.

At least they each had their own bedroom. That was a huge plus. Joan removed her heavy winter coat and pushed it into the crowded closet on its hanger, then slipped off the jacket of her suit and tossed it on the rose-bedecked chenille bedspread.

She traipsed halfheartedly back to the kitchen area, trying to summon enthusiasm for the upcoming evening and her date with John's brother. She started to fix a pot of decaf coffee and changed her mind when she was measuring out the dry grounds, quickly adding a few spoons of caffeinated to the filter basket. Dozing off was not an option, no matter how tired she was.

Even though she knew she was long since over her crush on Brandt Lyon, Joan knew she would compare Ed Turner with him. In three years she hadn't met any men who could outrank Brandt. He was in a class of his own.

Not that she'd dated often enough to compare him with many men. Joan had never been much of a social butterfly, even in high school, when everyone dated everyone else. She'd been too tall for nearly all the boys her own age. Once she was out of school and through college, she discovered it wasn't as easy as she had thought it would be to meet single men. She didn't like going clubbing with other girls just to try her luck—the noise and the drinking and the press of gyrating bodies made it impossible to talk, which was the reason she spent most of her evenings alone in the apartment.

At the office, ninety percent of the guys were married and the other ten percent Joan didn't care about. Besides, her position as Brandt's assistant was something of a handicap. She was occasionally pursued, but most avoided her because of her closeness to the head of the company.

Joan glanced longingly at the half-finished book lying on the table beside the sofa, knowing that she didn't dare pick it up. She loved to read and might become so engrossed in it she would lose track of time and not be ready when Kay and the Turner brothers got back from the airport. She had looked forward to finishing the rest of that book tonight. Joan sighed, then laughed. The sound echoed in the room.

Isn't that just great, she told herself. *I'd rather read a book than have a life.*

Resolutely she walked into the bathroom and turned on the bathtub faucets, pouring an extravagant dollop of bubble bath into the stream and watching it foam up. Searching through her closet, she found a coffee-colored silk pantsuit and laid it out on the bed, removing the gold metal belt from the hanger's hook first. Wear something sexy, Kay had decreed. Joan was going to do her best to comply.

The coffeemaker had finished brewing a few minutes after she was through with her bath. Sitting on the blue velvet sofa with her coffee cup on the scarred table, Joan began removing the pins from the coiled knot of her hair. It shimmered like molten gold once it was freed, the overhead light picking out the sunny highlights. She brushed it until it crackled and snapped.

Her father had once said the length of her hair was the only unpractical thing about Joan. With her hair down over her shoulders, she always felt so feminine. A shorter hairstyle would have been a lot less work, but she'd never have the nerve to whack it off. Only when it was long did the unusual but natural shade of her hair look its best.

When Kay, John, and his brother finally arrived, Joan was glad she'd taken extra time with her appearance. Even John, accustomed to seeing her in jeans and sweaters, looked twice. The coffee brown pantsuit accented the gold of her hair and the velvet shade of brown in her eyes. The clinging silk did wonderful things for her curves and her slender legs.

"Kay, you never told me your roommate was a blonde." Ed Turner was holding Joan's hand, his hazel eyes checking her out with obvious appreciation.

In looks, he resembled John, though he was a couple of inches taller—they had the same light brown hair and similar features. Yet John's face always gave the impression of kindness and Ed's expression was more raffish. Joan wasn't sure she liked that gleam in his eyes either. Then she told herself not to be so prim and proper.

It was nonetheless true that her bad experience

with Rick Manville had made her cautious around the wolf-type. Their easy admiration and constant compliments were employed all too often to get past a woman's emotional defenses.

Not this time. Not her. Joan managed a smile, but she pulled her hand free of Ed's hold.

"Did you have a good flight?" she asked him. Travel seemed like a neutral topic—well, maybe not around the holidays. She took the white fun-fur coat that Kay handed her and waited for him to answer.

"It was on time, which in this day and age makes it an excellent flight," he joked, quickly taking the initiative to help her with the coat. Once she was snuggled into it, Ed patted her on the shoulders and winked. "I had John make reservations for the best eatery around. We might have more to celebrate than their engagement."

"We'd better get going," John said, but it was more of a suggestion than a statement. "Pierre's doesn't hold reservations for latecomers."

John drove, since he was the one who was most familiar with the area and Kay sat in the front seat next to him, which left Joan alone in back with Ed. She didn't have to make small talk, since he was very willing to carry the conversation. He wasn't boring, she'd have to grant him that. She remembered the uneasy silences that had descended during most of her nights out with one guy or another. Ed had a knack for putting her at ease, but she suspected that, like Rick, he'd practiced it on quite a few willing women.

At the dinner table, Ed was even able to draw out his brother John, who was generally not all that talkative. He had both Kay and Joan laughing over stories of their boyhood. From the restaurant, the two couples migrated to the lounge area where the mood was more intimate and the conversation was less boisterous.

It was nearly midnight when John suggested that they leave. Joan was smiling contentedly, unable to remember when she had enjoyed an evening out so much. She still didn't altogether trust her flirtatious escort, but her ego had basked in all that glorious attention.

Only when they'd risen from their table did Joan notice the couple on the small dance floor. The fragile blonde in a cloud of pink caught her eye—she was the epitome of everything dainty and feminine that Joan wanted to be. Then she noticed the man holding her in his arms. It was Brandt Lyon, the masculine line of his mouth curved into a smile.

Her stomach turned over with sickening suddenness. Of course, she'd always known there were other women in his life. For a man like Brandt Lyon, that was a given. On odd occasions, she'd even taken phone messages that confirmed it, but she'd never seen him with a date.

At that moment the woman snuggled her head against his chest. Joan watched his gaze lazily sweep the room while he made some whispered comment to his partner. Then, for a fraction of a second, he looked Joan's way. She waited in breathless anticipation for his nod of recognition before his attention reverted to the woman he held.

She bit her lip. He hadn't recognized her. Out of the office, she was essentially invisible to him, she supposed. And in it, all the wishing in the world wouldn't make him see her as anything other than his efficient assistant.

Then Ed's arm moved around her shoulders, urging her toward the door. His touch snapped her back to reality. Her crush on Brandt Lyon had fizzled out a long time ago. She had to stop hoping. The truth was that even if he did suddenly see her as a woman, she could never compete with the likes of the blonde in his arms.

It was a waste of time to want someone who was out of her reach. Joan pushed aside her romantic yearnings and summoned up her stronger, practical side. Ed Turner was nice, much more than she'd expected. It was time she stopped comparing every man she met with Brandt Lyon.

Infatuations were strictly for teenagers. Now that she was, gulp, twenty-five, she was older and supposed to be wiser.

Chapter 2

Kay teased Joan unmercifully about her vow not to entertain Ed the entire weekend. In fact, Joan ended up going to the airport to see him off that Sunday. She decided that she had needed to see Brandt Lyon with another woman to completely end her infatuation. And Ed had been all too willing to fill the gap—not in any serious way, however.

Joan still believed he thought of himself as a play-boy, not that she'd minded. Although she had to admit she was rather surprised by the flowers he sent after the day he left and all the calls from Cleveland on Wednesday. He'd even made plans to fly back to Chicago the weekend before Christmas. It was obvi-ous she'd impressed him and that filled her with con-fidence.

Outside her office window, flakes of snow were swirling in a light wind. The weekend promised to be white and Joan began to daydream about her plans for the following day. She and Kay were going shop-ping for the rest of their Christmas gifts. She won-dered if she should buy something for Ed, nothing expensive or personal, but a little something.

The intercom buzzed commandingly. "Joan," Brandt Lyon's voice sounded crisp over the speaker, "bring in the printed estimate Jenson left with you on the Danville hospital. And I need the estimates from ten years ago, too, believe it or not. The client is complaining about rising costs, but he's wrong."

"Be right there." Joan flicked off the intercom switch as she rose from her desk. She was nearly at the filing cabinets when the buzz of the intercom called her back. "Get Lyle Baines in here. The figures on this hospital bid he just e-mailed me don't look right. I want to go over them with him before we submit anything."

The idle mood of the first hour of the morning disappeared as Joan went running back and forth between the printer, her computer, and the files to find what Brandt needed. He'd zeroed in on an error in the computations for the hospital construction bid and now everything had to be double-checked.

At noon Kay stuck her head inside the door asking Joan if she was going to lunch. Joan glanced at the closed door and grimaced.

"I doubt if they know what time it is. Can you bring me back a sandwich, Kay?"

"I bet they haven't looked outside either." Kay smiled. "Have you? Looks bad to me—we could be in for a major storm. Check the forecast. And tell him. Maybe he'll let us go home early." With a cheery wave, Kay closed the door.

Joan looked out the window. The gentle fall of drifting white flakes had turned into a wind-driven curtain of snow. That was nothing out of the ordinary during a Chicago winter, but she followed Kay's advice and clicked on to a weather Web site to double-check. Uh-oh. The storm had doubled in size in just a couple of hours, howling down from the north. Very heavy snow was forecast and blizzard warnings were in effect.

Her next click, on her neighborhood Web site, got her live video of side streets already closed by drifts; and a click over to the city government site confirmed that officials were recommending early closing for schools and businesses.

Rapping once on the inner door, Joan went into the private office. Brandt Lyon was bent over his desk, his jacket and overcoat thrown across a side chair, his tie loosened. The top buttons of his white shirt were open and his sleeves rolled up. The fingers of one hand continued to race over his keyboard as he plugged in figures to a spreadsheet on his computer screen.

"What is it?" The leonine head didn't look up from the monitor.

"There's a blizzard on the way. They're recommending that all nonessential businesses close. Schools, too."

The burly figure of Lyle Baines was sitting at the small drafting table that faced away from the window. He turned around and stared at what was happening outside the window. "Oh, hell. Will you look at that? Brandt, people are going to have to get home and pick up their kids and whatnot."

"Then we'll close," Brandt said absently. Joan gave both men a brief update. Finally looking up, Brandt rubbed the back of his neck and listened thoughtfully. The blue of his eyes was intensified by the faint, weary circles below them. Joan was drawn, as always, by the strength and perseverance etched in his irregular features.

"Send a broadcast e-mail, would you, Joan? Everybody

go home, be safe, stay warm . . . the usual." He turned his attention to the older man. "We should be finished in another hour or so, Lyle, unless you want to go right now. Up to you."

"I don't have to rush home," Lyle said. "My wife's in Peoria with our daughter." Then he smiled proudly. "Our first grandchild just arrived—a boy. I was going to drive there after work tonight, but so much for that."

Brandt smiled in sympathy, then raised a questioning brow at Joan.

She understood. "Right away." She wouldn't mind an early closing and she turned to send that e-mail.

"Oh, Joan—" Brandt called her back. He gave her a rueful smile. "Can I ask you to stay a little longer? I need you to go over this bid when I'm done and that's going to require extracting more folders from the metal monster."

Joan glanced out the window, silently wondering how long the buses would be running in a storm this size. They usually got through, sometimes by following a plow—people had to get home somehow and it took a lot of snow to shut down the transit system in a city like Chicago, even on the outskirts where they were.

"Sure," she said.

"You commute by bus, don't you?" Brandt asked, perceptively guessing exactly what she'd been thinking about.

"Yes."

"Don't worry about getting home. I'll give you a ride when we're through. My SUV has four-wheel drive and antilock brakes, if you're worried."

She smiled. "Okay, that's a deal." Knowing there was nothing behind his offer than thoughtful consideration, Joan murmured her thanks and left the room, glad that she was over her ridiculous infatuation. Once upon a time, she would have been giddy with hope at the thought of Brandt Lyon taking her home.

The building emptied quickly as the news spread. At one thirty, Brandt sent Lyle home too. It was close to three by the time Joan finished entering the corrections to the construction bid. She clicked on the icon for the printer, but had to take a few minutes to fix a paper jam before she had all the pages of the complex bid in hand. Then she shut down her computer and straightened her desk, while he looked it over and finally signed it and slipped the whole thing into a manila delivery envelope.

Done with it, Brandt went to the window in his office and stared out. Or tried to. The outside world was essentially invisible, obscured by blowing snow.

He looked over his shoulder at her and went for his coat. "Let's get out of here. Sorry I kept you this long."

She scrambled into her warm things, tying her scarf around her neck as they hurried out to the front door. He locked the door to the company offices while she waited, noticing that the receptionist and the security guard were both gone. The blast of wind as they stepped outside nearly knocked Joan off her feet. His arm circled her waist in support and they walked somewhat unsteadily toward the adjacent parking lot. The driving snow made it almost impossible to see and Joan had a feeling Brandt was guiding her to his car on instinct alone.

"Too dangerous," he gasped and stopped, shielding her from the wind. In just a second, he had turned her around and was leading her back to the building. Her teeth were already chattering in the breath-stealing, frigid wind and she heaved a huge sigh of relief when he half-pushed her back through the main door, one step behind her. It took all his strength to shove it shut again and another minute to find the master key for the heavy bolt in his pocket.

"Whew. That was a close one. Looks like we'll have to wait it out here in the building. I don't want to take the risk of being stranded in the car."

"Me neither." She moved away from him, brushing snow off her coat and shaking out her scarf.

"At least we have food, heat, and light," he was saying. Joan had thawed out enough to think a little. Her last look at the weather forecast had confirmed the worst: the blizzard would continue through the night and into Saturday, which meant she and Brandt might be together for the next twenty-four hours or more.

She tried to make light of things. "You mean food from the vending machines? I guess we won't get scurvy if we eat chips and cookies for a day or so."

He chuckled. "I hope not. But there might be some fruit in the conference room. And somebody probably has a can of corned beef hash in their desk."

"I have my cell phone. And I want a picture of you eating a stolen can of hash." She laughed.

"Send it to everyone. Hell, print it out and post it on the company bulletin board." He slapped her on the back in a friendly way. "Give them something to talk about. Let's get back in and make a few calls, speaking of that cell phone."

"The office phones ought to work."

He shrugged. "If the lines don't go down, they will. You've never been through a real Chicago-style blizzard, have you?"

She thought for a minute. "I guess not." Her small town had been socked in for days some winters, but a big city was different. This was exciting—and she had to admit that she was looking forward to his exclusive company for what promised to be a big chunk of the weekend.

Joan walked a few steps behind him through the strangely empty spaces of Lyon Construction, forcing herself to remember that admiration and respect were the only feelings she wanted to have for him. He was her employer. She would be wise to leave it at that.

They came back to the offices they'd just left and hung up their coats, brushing the last melting crystals of snow from the backs. She stepped rather quickly away from him. "I'm going to call my roommate so she doesn't worry."

He nodded. It occurred to her that he didn't seem to have anyone to call, or at least he wasn't saying if he did.

She picked up the receiver of the phone on her desk to see if it was still working and was pleased to find out that it was. She called the apartment and Kay answered on the second ring.

"Joan, where are you?" her roommate demanded frantically.

"I'm at the office," she answered. They hadn't wanted to pay an extra charge for caller ID on their landline, which was why Kay had asked.

"Whew. I imagined you stuck somewhere in a snowbank, like half the population of Chicago." Kay sighed in relief. "But don't tell me you're working. Can Brandt bring you home?"

"He tried to," Joan explained, ending with, "we had to go back inside."

"Do you mean"—Kay was probably bouncing on the couch with glee—"that you two are stranded there alone?"

"Please." Joan pressed a weary hand to her forehead. "Don't get carried away. It's no big deal. And we're safe." She was having trouble enough with her own imagination without subjecting herself to Kay's flights of fancy.

"Ooh, it is just the two of you!" Laughter bubbled in the voice on the other end. "It's like a reality show! Love in a blizzard! Thrown together by the elements!"

"Shut up," Joan said with an exasperated sigh. "Brandt Lyon is my boss."

"That's what I'm talking about," Kay crowed.

Joan lowered her voice to respond but made her next point very clear. "Hey, for all the attention he pays to me, I doubt he's aware I'm female. I'm his efficient and practical assistant, remember? Being stuck in the office means I'll end up with more work to do, that's all."

Kay still couldn't contain herself. "I don't think so," she replied happily. "Keep me posted."

"If the phones stay on."

"You have a cell."

She could hear her roommate switch on the TV and the distant sound of a weather report.

"Hey, Joan, this is a gigantic storm. The weatherman is smaller than the satellite picture of it. Really, call me if you can."

"I will, Kay. But I'm sure we'll be fine here. I'll be home as soon as the roads are clear."

They exchanged good-byes and Joan hung up first, wondering what Brandt was up to. She might as well get some work done, actually. It beat being bored and there was absolutely nothing to see outside the windows but snow, snow, snow, blowing every which way.

She riffled through the paperwork she'd stacked, concentrating on it and not noticing Brandt until he was standing by her desk. Her downcast eyes caught sight of his pants and she blushed, deeply embarrassed—she wasn't one to start there when it came to looking at people, for heaven's sake.

"Did you check in with your parents too?"

Nice of him to ask, but she wasn't sure how she felt about him listening in. "No, but I will. How about you?"

"I sent an e-mail to my mother telling her we're hunkered down here and doing fine. She'll alert the extended family, I can count on that." He smiled. "Don't work too hard, okay?"

She nodded. "Just catching up. There's really nothing else to do."

He went back into his office and she vaguely listened to the sounds of papers being moved around and the occasional creak of his swivel chair. She was preoccupied with trying to remember her side of the conversation with Kay, thinking that she'd spoken very softly when she'd said she doubted if he knew she was female.

But . . . he still could have heard her.

Joan told herself firmly that there was nothing she could do about it now if he had and focused intently on her paperwork again. She took a break to e-mail her parents just as he had done, enjoying a little flurry of family messages back and forth, mostly about the blizzard. Everyone reassured everyone else that they were safe and warm and had stocked up on food and milk and beer. Although her parents were a little concerned about her being stuck in an office building before she told them she was with her very capable boss and not going to starve or freeze. She signed off and got back to what she'd been doing.

"Joan?"

She jumped and knocked a pencil off her desk. For a second time she hadn't heard him come to her desk and, looking down for the pencil, she understood why: he'd slipped off his shoes and was padding around in socks on the carpet.

"Quit sneaking up on me," she said with a smile. But there was a funny feeling in her stomach.

"Sorry. I didn't mean to startle you. Want to make a raid on the lunchroom or are you still busy?" His smile was affable, even warm. Even Brandt Lyon didn't work all the time, she thought.

"Sure. I'm pretty much done."

"Hang on—I'll put my shoes back on."

She stood up while he did and stretched a little, easing out the tension in her back.

"Ready?" He waited for her to go out the door in front of him and they walked down the hall together.

It was a bittersweet feeling to discover that being with him under these circumstances felt almost like a date—the mood was relaxed, despite the raging storm outside. They were safe in here, trapped through no fault of their own by spectacularly bad weather, but making the best of it. Kay'd had a point—Joan did like being alone with him, although the echoing emptiness of the suite of offices was anything but romantic.

"Yes. I'm hungry too." She kept her tone just a bit cool and controlled, on her professional best behavior as usual.

Brandt didn't say much until they entered the

lunchroom and looked around. The tables were clean—most of the employees hadn't bothered to eat before they left for the day.

"I don't see that fruit I thought was here," he mused.

Joan walked over the row of waist-high cabinets and started opening doors, peering inside. She laughed and pulled out a bowl. "Here it is. Very high quality, too. Pure plastic."

He looked sadly at the decorative apples and bananas in the bowl she set on one of the tables. "Too bad. Let's check the fridge."

The shelves were almost bare, unfortunately. Besides a small container of half-and-half, there were two wrapped sandwiches that someone had left untouched, from a couple of days ago, if she remembered right. "There's our dinner," she sighed as he came to peer over her shoulder. "But we won't have to drink our coffee black. That's good."

"I like black coffee," he protested. She made a face. "And look at this. I found single-serve potato chips and cookies in a box the vending machine guy left in the closet. We can save our quarters."

"For what?" she chuckled.

He tumbled his loot on the table while she set the food out and he found a knife in a drawer, halving the sandwiches. "We should keep some for tomorrow. Who knows, right?"

Joan nodded. "Good point. Half is plenty for me, anyway." She made a pot of coffee and brought over two cups.

"You're indispensable, do you know that?" he said. His praise made her smile.

"Efficient, too. And practical."

She stopped smiling and turned red. "Okay. You heard me talking to Kay."

He was munching on a potato chip and nodded before he finished it and replied, "It's your own fault, you know."

It was really unnecessary to ask what he meant, but she did anyway. "What is?" she asked, widening her eyes with fake innocence.

"The fact that I take you for granted," Brandt replied calmly, leaning back in his chair with an ease she couldn't begin to feel. "I do know you're female, by the way. But you really don't flaunt it."

She played with a potato chip, the rosy glow in her cheeks adding a vibrancy to her face. "Look, I didn't mean for you to hear any of that."

"I know." He grinned and munched another chip.

"Anyway, I'm not supposed to flaunt anything. This is a business, not a—a dance club or something. And as far as taking me for granted, I don't expect any special recognition for doing my job. I mean, it's what I'm paid for." She shifted uncomfortably in her chair.

"You're probably due for a raise. By the way, how old are you?"

"Twenty-five."

"How long have you been working for me now?"

"Three years."

"Really?" A brow raised in surprise. "I have to say I appreciate your putting up with me for that long. Maybe you are blending into the background too well, though."

"A good assistant is supposed to," Joan replied, nibbling on her sandwich.

"It's never good to notice someone's efforts

after they've left," he said smoothly. "Which makes it difficult for me to take advantage of you now."

"Uh—what?" She stared at him.

"Sorry. Poor word choice." He grinned. "We don't have anything to do but work to pass the time, so I was thinking we could catch up on some of the less important correspondence. That was all I meant."

"Oh. Sure." She relaxed visibly—but at the same time, experienced a funny little pang of disappointment. "I'm done. Even half of this was a little too much food for me." She wrapped the wax paper carefully around the remaining part of her sandwich and got up to put it back in the refrigerator, then came back to clear the table, with help from him.

Back to the office they went. She was glad to tackle the routine letters to keep her thoughts from wandering in dangerous directions. She'd set up shop in his office, jotting down what he said to formulate into letters when she went back to her computer. His long legs were stretched out on the ottoman that matched his leather throne and he referred occasionally to the file in his lap as he dictated to her.

Joan stifled a yawn, wondering where they would sleep tonight. She had no idea of the time. Brandt was resorting to stock phrases to get through the last of the letters.

". . . Re: your previous bid . . . pending shipment of materials . . . five dragons and a cherry pie . . ."

Joan blinked. "What did you just say?"

Brandt laughed loudly. "Just checking to see if you're awake."

"Sorry. I wasn't paying attention."

"You must be exhausted." He closed the folder and tossed it on his desk. "Why didn't you stop me earlier?"

"Just doing my job." She flexed her tense fingers and loosened her death grip on the pencil.

"From the sound of the wind, we'll have all day tomorrow to finish whatever needs to be done. I think that it's time we called it a night."

The moment of truth had arrived. The suite of offices boasted only one couch and it was right here in Brandt's office, in back of her. She knew instinctively that his gentlemanly nature would mean he'd insist that she take it. She hadn't decided whether she should refuse and go looking for the yoga mat under Kay's desk and bed down on that. Either way Joan knew she wasn't going to get much sleep.

"Are you ready for the argument?" Brandt asked.

He'd read her mind. "What argument?" she asked anyway.

"Over which of us is going to sleep on the only couch in the building," he answered with a completely straight face. "I know we could each sleep in a chair and solve the problem, but my mother would never forgive me if I didn't insist that you take the couch."

"I couldn't—" Joan began, her hands raised to protest his statement.

"Yes, you can. And you will." His quiet authority silenced the rest of her words. "That's an order."

Joan removed the tortoiseshell glasses that made it difficult to see his face clearly at a distance. She searched his eyes for a telltale sign of amusement at her unfortunate tendency to blush, because his intent regard only made heat rise in her cheeks.

"If you insist, Mr. Lyon." Maybe it was best to joke her way out of this one—and just accept that the situation was awkward.

"I do insist, Ms. Somers."

Strong hands closed over the arms of his chair as Brandt levered himself out of it, flexing his shoulders as though he too felt the strain of an extra-long session of office busywork. Through her lashes, Joan discreetly studied his build. His height, easily two inches over six feet, made the breadth of his chest seem not so intimidatingly . . . male. The stamp of pride and authority in the chiseled, angular planes of his face were striking from any point of view, reminding her of an eagle.

As though he sensed her scrutiny, he turned his head to her, one eyebrow rising a fraction of an inch. Her pulse fluttered erratically. To cover her confusion, she began fussing in a random way with the notepad and miscellaneous papers she still held.

"What are you doing?" he asked.

She swallowed back her nervousness and said coolly, "Just going over my notes while they're still fresh in my mind."

"Enough. Let it go until morning." He gave a dismissive wave. "If you have trouble with the fine points, you can ask me then. Besides"—one corner of his mouth quirked upward—"you can't read any of that without those glasses that are in your lap."

Joan quickly flipped the notepad cover over the pages. The sudden movement sent her spare pencil flying across the room to land at his feet. Feeling like a complete klutz, she walked over to retrieve it from his outstretched hand when he picked it up, seeing the laughter in his eyes. As she bolted for the connecting door, the phone rang.

"I'll get that," he said. His low voice was laced with indulgent amusement.

The door between their two offices didn't swing to and latch after she'd darted through it. The absence of any other sound in the building allowed his voice to carry clearly to where she was.

After an initial, rather impersonal greeting, the tone of his voice changed subtly, becoming almost caressing. "You weren't seriously expecting me to show up, Angela, were you? Anyway, I was just about to call, and yes, I'd rather be snowbound at your place for the weekend."

The image of the petite blonde immediately danced into Joan's mind. Her throat constricted painfully as she thought how well Angela's name fit her. So delicate, so pure—so not like Joan. She scowled at the seductive pitch of the soft male laughter that followed the pause after Brandt's last comment. Joan got up and made sure the door between them was closed all the way before she succumbed to the pangs of envy.

She got busy with tidying up, carrying her wastebasket out to the larger can in the hallway and dumping in the crumpled paper. Retrieving a binder clip that had been accidentally tossed away took another few seconds. Then she went back.

Good. The button light on her multiline phone went out, signaling the end of Brandt's conversation. Within a minute, the connecting door was open and Brandt Lyon walked in.

"My office is yours, Joan," he said with a sweep of his hand. "But you might want to use your coat as a pillow. The couch doesn't have any."

With a self-conscious nod of agreement, Joan walked around her desk to the coatrack, removed the fun-fur coat and folded it in front of her like a shield. Even as she did it, she knew the reflexive gesture was silly, since Brandt had made it plain she had no reason to protect herself from him.

When she reached the open door, she glanced awkwardly over her shoulder. He winked at her as he shook out his overcoat for a blanket and claimed the visitor's armchair, settling his long form in it right away.

"Good night." Something about the way he said it quelled any argument from her about their separate but unequal sleeping arrangements.

"Good night," she replied in a voice that lacked conviction.

With the door closed behind her, she walked hesitantly to the long leather couch. For the first time, she noticed the heavy sheepskin jacket that had been thrown in the corner of it, something he wore on weekend getaways that had ended up here.

She'd use her own. The rugged-looking jacket probably smelled too much like him for her peace of mind. Drawing a deep breath, she arranged her coat in a plump, furry square at one end and slipped off her shoes. She put her suit jacket over the back of a chair before removing the pins that held her long hair in place. Letting it down always relaxed her, even though she couldn't brush it out the way she usually did, and she gave a tired yawn.

Hoping that was a sign that sleep was not far off, Joan flicked the wall switch that turned off the overhead light, throwing the room into complete darkness. She felt her way back to the couch and lay down.

The man in the outer office was all there was between her and the desolate emptiness of the rest of the building. Thinking of that made her feel odd inside. The howling wind sounded much louder than before, venting its fury on the double-paned windows until she swore she could hear the faint screeching of icy sleet against the glass. The chair in her office creaked loudly and Joan guessed that Brandt was trying to find a comfortable position in it.

It was more than an hour before her alertness receded and sleep claimed her. Even then it wasn't restful as a nightmarish dream began to unfold in her mind.

In it, she was clinging to Ed Turner, pleading with him not to send her back—where wasn't clear. Incongruously, a lion roared someplace in the background. But Ed kept insisting that the lion was entitled to his share of her time and he pushed her in the direction of the unseen beast.

When she tried to escape, a large paw descended from the darkness and dragged her back, without injuring her. The gargantuan proportions of the roaring lion made Joan quake with fear. As long as she stayed between the lion's paws, he ignored her, but whenever she attempted to sneak away, a mighty paw pulled her back. And the dream lion had cobalt blue eyes that saw her no matter where she hid.

Fear that she would never escape the lion grabbed at her with icy fingers. Joan shuddered violently in its grip. *Wake up. It's only a dream,* she kept telling herself, but the terrible coldness wouldn't go away. Finally her lashes fluttered open and she tried to focus in the darkness, needing to see some familiar, reassuring object that would end the reign of freezing terror.

The luminescent dial of her watch gleamed on her wrist, but the numbness in her arms and legs seemed to be spreading. She shivered again and hugged her arms around her middle. As she drew in a deep breath, the coldness of the air struck her. Tentatively she touched the couch where the warmth of her body heat hadn't reached. The leather was icy cold.

She realized that there really was no light at all—
not the tiny dot-sized one on the monitor or the ON
button of the computer. There was no faint glow
from the function screen of the phone either.

Unfolding her coat and wrapping it around her
shoulders, she rose stiffly and stumbled toward the
door and the light switch beside it. Nothing happened when she flicked it. The blizzard still raging
outside had knocked out the electricity.

Quickly she opened the door between the two offices. "Brandt?" she whispered softly, trying to see if
he was still in the chair. "Brandt?" she called again in
a slightly louder voice.

She reached out into the darkness as she felt her
way to the desk and then the chair. It was empty, with
only a little warmth remaining in the cushions.

Where was he? She nearly ran into the open door
leading into the hallway. Her hand maintained constant contact with the wall as she tiptoed into the dark
void, praying she wouldn't get lost. "Brandt!"

Only the echo of her own voice and the whistling
north wind answered her. She ventured farther into
the darkness, trying to fight off the terrifying sensation that she was now completely alone in the building. "Brandt!" A frightened note crept into her cry.
She wondered frantically where he'd gone and called
again, almost shrieking this time. "Brandt! Brandt,
where are you?"

A beam of light pinned her against the wall, blinding her as effectively as the darkness had done.

"Calm down and don't panic, Joan. I'm right
here," his even voice replied.

Joan exhaled a shaky breath. "I wasn't panicking—
but you weren't in the chair," she said defensively. "I
called and called, but you didn't answer."

"I wasn't far away," he said. He directed the flashlight beam away from her face. "Better put your shoes on. You can't run around in thirty-degree temperatures with bare feet."

Instantly Joan became conscious of the cold tile floor. She hadn't put on tights today, just panty hose. Her freezing toes curled under and she shivered.

"I couldn't find them in the dark," she lied. "Where were you anyway?"

"In the basement, flipping every damn circuit breaker in the box," he replied. "It took me awhile. The elevators aren't working. I wanted to make sure that the power failure was an outside thing." His hand took hold of her elbow as he turned her back toward their dual offices. "The phones are out and the storm must have knocked down a power line. It might not be just this building, though. Could be that a much bigger area is affected—I didn't see lights anywhere when I looked out. It happens," he said grimly.

Joan drew her coat tightly around her neck as she tried to ignore the warmth of his touch. "Why isn't the furnace working? I mean, it's powered by natural gas." She remembered him saying that once to a visiting building inspector who'd stopped by to talk to him for some other reason. Joan had never actually been in the basement.

"Yes, but the thermostat controls and the blower to the heating system are electrical," Brandt answered. "I'm afraid it's only going to get colder. Wait here a minute," he ordered.

In the next instant the comforting beam of light was gone as a door closed. Joan was left shivering in the dark hall, her legs turning into numb sticks as the coldness of the floor seeped into her feet. She heard a rushing sound—had part of the roof caved in? What next? Then the light shone on her again.

"What w-were you d-doing?" Her teeth had started to chatter.

"Turning on the taps in the restrooms. With the water running, maybe the pipes in the building won't freeze." He took hold of her elbow again as they walked the last few feet to her office.

The carpeted floor felt blissfully warm compared to the smooth tiles in the hallway and the pressure of his hand didn't ease until they were well into the adjoining rooms. Joan walked unaided to the couch, aided by the flashlight beam, which stopped on the sheepskin jacket in the corner, then moved back.

"Glad I left that here."

She nodded. "Okay, I'm sitting down. Shouldn't you shut that off to save batteries?" she asked worriedly.

"Not just yet. I have several packs of D batteries in my desk, as it happens. You know me—Backup Man."

Joan nodded, managing a faint smile at the nickname bestowed on him by the computer department. So he did know it.

"What time is it?" she asked, then realized she could have looked at her battery-operated watch. Oh, well. He probably had one too. She sat down on the cold leather upholstery and curled her legs beneath her in an effort to warm her feet.

"Almost one thirty."

"Is that all?" She shivered and snuggled deeper into her furry coat. "It's going to be below zero in here by morning with no heat. What are we going to do?"

A heavy silence followed her question. Then Brandt walked slowly to the couch, stopping in front of it to look at her upturned face. The flashlight in his hand offered faint ambient light and she was grateful for it.

"We can keep warm," he said quietly. "Together. It's the only logical thing to do."

Her heart pounded painfully hard as she stared at the unreadable expression in his eyes. She tried desperately to push her fears aside and react calmly to his suggestion. Spending a night snuggled up actually was a practical solution—but it was likely to cause all sorts of other problems. At the moment, she wasn't looking up at a respected, take-charge boss. She was looking at a virile, well-built man who was planning to hold her in his arms so they could share body heat for as long as possible.

When she finally managed to reply, her voice was weak. "We can use both our coats as blankets."

"Yes, and the sheepskin jacket over there in the corner. Everything will help." Brandt smiled. Cold as she was, she felt warm enough to be melted by that smile for a second or two.

Self-consciously, she stretched out on the couch, pressing herself into the back cushions as Brandt set down the flashlight. Then he was spreading his overcoat over her legs, topping it with the sheepskin jacket. Joan held rigidly still as he lay down on the outer edge of the couch, turning on his side to face her. Her coat only partially covered him, but that thought vanished. The male body pressed against her radiated heat.

His arm slid around her waist to draw her closer, making her more fully aware of every muscular inch. The warmth of his breath was a soft caress against her cheek. Joan knew he could feel the rapid beating of her heart just as she felt the steady rhythm of his.

"Your feet are cold. You should have worn your shoes," he murmured softly.

Unwillingly, Joan drew her toes away from the material of his pants, his intimate comment disturbing her more than the touch of his hands.

"Leave your feet there." She felt the movement of his mouth as he spoke. "They'll be warm soon."

Since it was impossible to find a place for her feet where they wouldn't brush against him, Joan let them slide back to their former position as she wondered how she would ever relax enough to fall asleep.

Chapter 3

During the night, their positions shifted. Joan awoke to find her head resting on the shoulder opposite her, her face pressing into the fake fur collar of her coat. Her arms were curled around Brandt in a careless embrace while his hands were locked behind her back to hold her there. Gradually she became aware that he'd buried his face in her tousled hair.

She tried to squirm into a less intimate position, only to have the holding power of his arms increase. Her skirt had inched up around her thighs, making her doubly aware of the muscles in his legs. Brandt stirred beside her and she held her breath.

"Brrr," he murmured. "I feel like the first caveman— his name was Joe Cave, did you know that?"

She wondered if he was still dreaming. "No," she said softly.

Brandt cleared his throat, his voice husky with sleep as he continued, "On cold mornings, Joe Cave used to gripe like crazy about getting up and leaving his nice warm cavewoman in their fur-lined bed. He knew what he was griping about."

Joan smiled against his chest. "Joe, huh? What was her name?"

"Josephine. She tended to swipe all the fur covers."

"Did I do that?" Joan giggled.

"Yes," he said, resting his stubbly chin on her smooth hair.

She was so touched by his groggy attempts to amuse her, especially considering the circumstances. But she refused to read anything into it. Just staying here was dangerous to her sanity.

"Sorry, Joe," she said, "but both of us had better get up." A huge shiver ran over her when he shifted position slightly. "Brrr is right. W-w-we can't stay here all day."

"Why not?" He smiled against her hair, she could feel it. Then the chest beneath her head lifted as he took a deep breath and loosened his hold on her. "Don't answer that. You're right. We can't stay here all day."

Joan twisted backward, balancing herself on one arm to allow him room to get up. Frigid air stole the warmth that had been generated between them. As Brandt slid from beneath their improvised covers onto the floor, Joan resisted the impulse to snuggle into the coziness of her coat.

"Don't get up." His hand pushed her back on the couch when she started to rise. "Stay there and keep warm as long as you can."

She frowned. "What are you going to do?"

The freezing air in the room was biting her face and nose, but Brandt seemed impervious to it as he stood above her in his rumpled business clothes, an aura of vitality about him that impressed her.

"I'm pretty sure there's a catalytic heater in the

shed by the equipment yard," he replied in his take-charge voice.

Joan glanced toward the window, noticing the thick white frost covering the panes, and hearing the wind growling fiercely on the other side. That wind would be blowing the fallen snow, reducing the visibility to near zero.

"Do you have to go out?" she asked anxiously.

He held up his arms and pumped his biceps in a mock-manly gesture of strength. "Yes. I am Joe Cave. I will protect you." When she began to laugh, he added, "I'll follow the fence to the shed. I won't get lost."

No, Joan thought. He wouldn't get lost. Even in a battle with the elements, Brandt Lyon was likely to come out the victor. He was joking around to distract her, that was all. But she had been brought up in a rural area in this, the northern part of the state, and knew how dangerous it could be to venture out in a storm of this magnitude. Even if she could reach help on her cell phone, help couldn't necessarily reach them—people had been lost within a few feet of safety, unable to see. The velvet depths of her eyes shimmered with fear.

The smile went away from Brandt's face and his jaw set in a hard line. "Don't let your imagination run away with you," he said firmly. "And I will need that heavy jacket, so you'll have to curl up in that fur thing and my overcoat until I get back."

As he reached for his sheepskin jacket, Joan tried to draw her legs beneath her coat, but it was too short. Before she could shift into a sitting position and tuck her legs under her, Brandt removed the jacket, revealing the bareness of her legs where her skirt had ridden up. She pulled it down and crossed her ankles. She was modest and there was nothing she could do about it. Obligingly, he added his overcoat to the mix.

"Don't be embarrassed," Brandt said. "You have great legs."

"Thanks. You—um, you'd better take my scarf," she stammered, sneaking a hand from under her coat, wishing he didn't have the ability to disconcert her so easily.

The gray wool scarf was sticking out of the pocket of her coat. Brandt removed it, then reached over and crooked a finger under her chin to raise it.

"Stop worrying," he commanded. "I'll be back before you have a chance to miss me."

Joan doubted that. The instant the office door closed, a frightening sense of desertion spread over her. It was this aloneness that made her huddle deeper into her coat, not the biting nip of the air stinging her nose. The minutes passed with interminable slowness as she listened intently for some slight noise that would signify his return. The impulse was there to wait for him by the rear door, but her practical nature wouldn't let her give in to it. Without the benefit of his body heat, she was already beginning to feel the cold. With less covering her legs, she would be chilled to the bone if she strayed from the couch.

She thought about calling her family on her cell phone—maybe they could reach emergency personnel in the Chicago area who could get to her and Brandt. Joan decided against it. The police, fire, and medical crews had their hands full in weather this bad, what with stranded drivers and people injured in the storm and a million inevitable mishaps of every type. The two of them were not in imminent danger.

No, she'd save the precious charged battery of her cell in case a call like that really needed to be made. Her uninformed family would worry themselves sick if she contacted them. Kay would just have to deal with her not calling.

Twenty minutes went by before she heard his footsteps in the outer hall. She said a silent prayer of gratitude and then a human snowman walked into the office. Snow caked his trouser legs and only patches of brown could be seen on the sheepskin of his jacket. His thick hair was capped with white snow and fat flakes clung to his brows and lashes. His hoary breath filled the cold room with billowing clouds.

Brandt's blue eyes seemed brighter, but that could be the look of triumph in them. He set a small heater on the floor.

"You found it," Joan murmured, afraid of tearing up if she voiced her relief at his safe return.

"Yup. Here's hoping it works." His broad shoulders blocked her view of the heater as he knelt beside it. Within a few minutes, Joan felt the first emanations of blessed warmth . . . then heat. The snow on his clothes began to melt, puddles forming on the carpet.

"You're going to catch pneumonia in those wet things," she said anxiously.

"That's an old wives' tale." Brandt shrugged out of his jacket like a giant grizzly bear coming out of hibernation. "Pneumonia is caused by bacteria or viruses, not wet clothes. Anyway, they'll dry." He walked to the couch, picked up her shoes from the floor beside it, and put them by the heater. "We'll get these warm before you have to put them on."

His thoughtfulness sent a warm glow of pleasure through her. That combination of real strength and tender consideration was rare. Maybe, Joan decided, when men were as self-assured as Brandt Lyon, they could manage being kind without doing damage to their egos.

"What's it like out there? Anyone around?"

"Not a soul, as far as I can tell. But that doesn't mean anything, because I couldn't see anything, or hear any snowplows. Basically, we might as well be in Antarctica. We're on our own, Joan."

"I figured," she said in a small voice.

"But we should be okay if we take some precautions. We could get a call out on my cell or yours, but what's the point? There's a lot of people who are much worse off than we are, count on that."

"I figured that too."

She watched him use her scarf to rub most of the snow from his hair and carelessly brush the flakes that hadn't melted off his pants. Before she could conceal her silent study of him, his gaze glittered over her.

"This heater can't keep both rooms warm. We'll have to decide which office we're going to use," he said.

"The one we're going to work in. We ought to keep busy," she pointed out. "With the power off, about all I can do is clear out the inactive files." The prospect of sitting idly for an entire day with a high-energy guy like Brandt doing everything for her was too daunting to contemplate.

"Okay. We'll move the heater into your office." He reached down for her shoes and handed them to her. "I'll open a window. Just an inch or so."

"Why?"

His reply was curt. "Because the heater burns the oxygen in the air. We'll need some ventilation if we don't want to suffocate." He watched her slip on her warmed shoes. "How does that feel?"

"Wonderful. But I'm worried about the heater."

"Don't be."

An hour later the temperature in Joan's office had risen to the point where she no longer needed to wear her furry coat to be comfortable. Brandt had disappeared again on an undisclosed errand after setting up a foldaway table in her office. Pausing for a moment by the heater to warm her fingers, Joan wondered how she would have fared if she had been stranded by herself, dependent on her own resourcefulness.

The door to the hall opened and closed quickly, a cold draft accompanying Brandt. She looked curiously at the tray in his hands.

"No electricity, no coffee. But look what I found in the freezer section of the lunchroom fridge—we forgot to look there yesterday. Sweet rolls and juice, courtesy of the breakfast brigade."

"I wish you hadn't mentioned coffee." Joan made a face, walking to her desk to rummage through the center drawer for her comb. "I just don't feel like myself until I've had my first cup."

"Yourself being the cool, efficient paragon who rules the office?"

He sounded like he'd had five cups of coffee. The comb in her hand stopped in midstroke through the slightly tangled locks of her long hair.

"I don't rule the office," Joan asserted, feeling completely incapable of ruling anything, ever. "Not without caffeine in my system, I mean."

"Maybe we can brew coffee with cold water—I've done that, camping. Takes a while but it's not bad. That can be my next project," he said with satisfaction.

"You're good at finding things to do." She went

back to combing her hair, finding it soothing. It seemed to just about hypnotize Brandt.

"I like what you're doing right now," he said softly. "You have beautiful hair."

"Thanks. It needs washing."

"No, it doesn't." She began to coil it, but he protested. "Leave it down, Joan. Please." His voice was suddenly husky and he crossed the distance between them when she wasn't looking. "It'll keep your ears warm." His fingers gently pulled sleek strands of her hair free from her unresisting hold. His comforting nearness made it hard for Joan to object. "What a color—like amber. Your hair's too pretty to be hidden in that bun. It's like spun gold when it's down."

"The color's natural," she said as if he'd asked if it came from a bottle.

He laughed softly. "I guessed that."

Joan fought against her reawakened senses. How she craved his touch . . . but she ought to know better. She willed her rational mind to kick in, but her senses overruled it.

"Please wear it down." He wasn't giving up.

"It's not practical. It keeps getting in the way of everything I do."

"Really?" He let go of her hair and turned her around to look at him. "But you never wear it down, so how do you know that?"

"Oh, all right. If you insist." She shook the rest of her hair free in frustration and dumped the pins on top of the desk.

The instant she capitulated, she knew she'd made an irretrievable mistake. The glossy hair flowing free over her shoulders made her feel feminine and vulnerable, a state of mind she needed to guard against or she would fall completely under the power of his animal magnetism. The invisible, necessary barrier between employer and employee had been breached last night when she'd slept in his arms. She desperately needed to repair her defenses.

Summoning up what was left of her self-control, she ignored him the rest of the morning, completing the filing from the wire basket on her desk. On the surface, Joan was successful, but an inner radar kept her aware of every movement Brandt made as he pored over the blueprint Lyle had left spread out on the drafting table. It was interesting to work without computers, thanks to the power outage—she felt like she was doing the thinking for a change.

"I'm hungry." His low voice shattered the silence, causing Joan to spin around to look at him. "What are we having for lunch?"

It was an ordinary question, but the sound of his voice got to her. The cold discomfort of the long hours made her want something she couldn't have more than ever.

In the mood she was in, the blue depths of his eyes seemed to pull her into a whirlpool of emotional chaos. The unavoidable intimacy between them made it nearly impossible for her to react naturally. Something warned her that she was much too susceptible to his attraction, but she couldn't think of what she might do to prevent it.

"I don't know," she answered quickly, even though she did know: the other halves of those sandwiches, just as cold and another day older. She got busy with the everlasting files again to keep herself from succumbing to a different hunger—a hunger for his touch.

"I'm going to the lunchroom to reconnoiter. Hold the fort."

Later, as she nibbled the unappetizing sandwich, Joan realized that it was this constant sharing that was undermining her resolve. A businesslike distance was impossible to maintain when they were sitting out a blizzard that showed no signs of blowing itself out. She was conscious of his stirring interest in her or maybe it was curiosity. Brandt seemed to be regarding her in a new light, discovering that she was human behind her façade of efficiency—and acting a whole lot more human himself.

But was she making too much of his attention or reading romance into it? There wasn't anything wrong with friendship, if that was what was developing between them. So what if Brandt Lyon had finally realized she was a woman? That didn't mean he was suddenly going to be on his knees with adoration, considering her average looks—not when he had someone like Angela in his life.

"A penny for your thoughts." Brandt's voice snapped the thread of her musings.

"They aren't worth it," Joan protested self-consciously.

"Anything that can keep a woman quiet for fifteen minutes must be worth at least a penny."

She favored him with a disapproving stare. "Watch it. Unless you want to spend the night in a snowbank."

"Come on, Joan. What's on your mind? Tell me."

"If you must know . . ." She glanced up from her sandwich into the vivid blue of his eyes, now lazily veiled by thick lashes. "I was wondering how much longer the storm would last."

"Getting tired of my company?"

"Not as tired as you must be of mine," Joan retorted, not able to match the lightness in his voice.

"On the contrary." He seemed very pleased that

she was talking to him. "As a matter of fact, I'd like to get to know you better."

"Really." It was safe to assume that meant being asked questions. And he didn't disappoint her—but what he wanted to know totally surprised her.

"I was wondering how a woman like you has avoided the altar."

Her mouth opened and she stared at him, unable to think of what to say for a moment. She strove again for a light one. "Oh, it's more a case of the altar avoiding me."

"Aha. Then you aren't all about work, all the time. Thought so." He gave her a wry but charming smile. "Some day your prince will come and I'll have to find myself another assistant, because he won't want to share you. But promise me you'll stick around a little longer. I'm just getting used to you."

It was an arrogant thing to say, even though he was kidding. "I haven't quit yet," she said stiffly.

"Please don't."

Joan only shrugged. They were venturing into sensitive territory. He didn't seem to realize how sensitive.

"Anyway, you must have someone special in your life," he continued.

She blinked back the sudden sting of tears, pride surfacing with a rush. She couldn't tell him of her empty weekends, of the countless nights she had spent by herself. Those half-forgotten words she'd spoken last week when she'd hinted that her weekends were always occupied had returned to haunt her. White lies, any lies, always seemed to backfire.

"I don't know if—" Joan hesitated, then plunged forward, hoping she wasn't digging herself into a hole and silently apologizing to Ed Turner for using his name—"I'd call Ed a prince, but I am fond of him." That statement at least was the truth.

"Have you known him long?" The tilt of Brandt's leonine head indicated a casual interest.

"No, he's the brother of my roommate's fiancé." Yikes. She sounded like a foreign-language instruction manual. Joan frowned and picked at the uneaten portion of her sandwich.

"And your roommate is Moreland from the computer department, isn't she? Sorry—I know who she is, but her first name escapes me."

"Yes, that's right, Kay Moreland," Joan answered with some surprise. She'd never suspected that he was even aware that she had a roommate.

"Are you bringing Ed to the Christmas party?"

That question caught her off guard too. "Well, he lives in Cleveland."

"But he flies back and forth to see you," Brandt commented.

"And his brother." Joan got up, wanting to end the conversation any way she could.

The swivel chair behind her desk squeaked loudly in protest at her sudden movement.

"That chair needs to be oiled," he said, walking over to rock it back and forth.

For some reason the comment sounded like a reminder of something she should have done. But she drew the line at office furniture repair, whether he knew it or not.

"I may look like an Amazon, but it's too heavy for me to turn upside down to get to the part that squeaks like that," she said sharply.

There was a piercing quality to the look he gave her that communicated his controlled annoyance. She stared defiantly back. Joan had always been conscious of her size ever since her teenage days when she had towered over the boys in her class.

His eyes narrowed as they studied her. "I was talking about the chair, not you. Sorry if I hit a nerve. I didn't mean to."

"Well, I am too tall. Maybe too everything. It isn't something that can be ignored," Joan responded stiffly.

"Oh." Brandt nodded thoughtfully. "Now, why is it that short women dream of being leggy and statuesque and tall women want to be dainty and petite?"

That was more of a statement than a question. But she answered him, with a shrug. "I suppose it's human nature to want what you can't have. But I have accepted the way I am."

"Then don't ever apologize again for being a tall, beautiful blonde." The crisply spoken advice and the tacked-on compliment seemed to accuse her of false modesty and Joan reacted with indignation.

"Oh, please. That's over the top, Brandt." She held her head high and glared at him. "How can you say things like that when you've barely noticed me for the last three years? You just haven't. Why should anyone else?"

Brandt's knee was hooked over the corner of her desk as he half sat and half stood against it, his strong hands folded on his thigh.

"I noticed the NO TRESPASSING signs, put it that way. Don't get me wrong—you're amazingly efficient and always businesslike, which is why I hired you in the first place. So I didn't go past them. I don't believe in mixing business with pleasure, ever. My personal life and my work are entirely separate." He paused and looked at her carefully. "Maybe you're the same way."

She understood. His precise, clearly voiced statement was the guiding rule in any well-run business office. But it sent prickles up her spine to know—from what he'd just said and a lot of the little things he'd done in their time alone—that Brandt Lyon did consider her attractive and had most definitely noticed her.

At the same time, he made it clear that her looks made no difference. He would never want her to be anything more to him than a loyal, capable assistant. She knew perfectly well why that was best. If a romantic relationship had developed between them, her position at the company would have become untenable. For both of them.

"I agree with you completely." Her reply gave away nothing of her inner emotion.

"Do you?" The words were muttered and Brandt gave a heavy sigh of . . . it could be exasperation. She couldn't read his averted eyes.

As usual, he turned his attention to what needed doing, squatting down to take hold of the swivel chair's stem support and standing up to flip it as if it weighed nothing. He set it against the desk, upside down, and gave the wheeled base a spin.

"Do you have any all-purpose oil?" he asked.

The detached voice forced Joan to conclude that she'd only imagined the previous question. Being in Brandt's exclusive company for this long really was beginning to rattle her.

"There's a little bottle in the middle desk drawer," she answered. She'd bought an all-purpose, compact tool kit when she'd started the job. Prepared for everything, that was her. Except Brandt Lyon.

While he worked at oiling the squeaky moving parts of the swivel chair, Joan began again to sort out drawers in the filing cabinet, wondering when and if they were ever going to replace or dump the damn thing. It had been in the office since forever, but it did what it was supposed to do.

Sort of like me, she thought crossly. Only she was nowhere that old.

Joan told herself not to be silly and focused on her task: she removed inactive files and placed them in stacks on the table he'd brought in earlier. Only one part of her mind was devoted to the task. The rest was trying to sort out what she was beginning to think of as her Brandt file. She took mental inventory of his comments about her, pro and con.

He'd kept her safe through the biggest blizzard to hit Chicago in years, held her all night long to make sure she was warm and made her laugh in the morning instead of being grumpy, asked her to wear her hair down just so he could admire it, didn't think she was too tall, and told her she was beautiful. And he'd gone out of his way to praise her work and her methodical approach to it.

Her preoccupation made her somewhat less than methodical at the moment. She barely noticed that the top drawer didn't close tightly when she pushed it forward to go through the second drawer. Her mouth twitched in amusement as she found a misfiled folder right away. It was one she had given Brandt the other day and he had, typically, replaced it in the wrong drawer. Removing it, she reached down to the third drawer of the four-drawer cabinet.

The instant her fingers released the catch on the drawer handle and began to pull it open, the unlatched top drawer began sliding forward. The metal frame groaned in protest as the extraordinary weight of the three drawers combined at once. That was the only warning Joan got before it tilted forward. Her hands reached out to try to check its fall, succeeding for a second to keep it at an angle.

Then much stronger arms lent their power to hers, righting the toppling cabinet and shoving the drawers quickly back into place. The aftershock of realizing how very close she'd come to having the massive cabinet fall on top of her sent shudders of fright through her whole body. Her knees were wobbling and weak. Then those same strong hands that had saved her were gripping her shoulders.

"Are you all right, Joan?" There was a frown of sincere concern in the face looking into hers.

Her trembling hand brushed tiny beads of sweat from her forehead. "Yes," she answered shakily. "I think so." His shirt buttons blurred in front of her as she unconsciously swayed closer to him. "It . . . it all happened so quickly."

"Why did you try to stop it?" Brandt's voice was husky. "You should have jumped aside and let the damn thing fall."

"I didn't think," Joan answered with a choked sob.

His soft chuckle resembled a rueful sigh as he folded her comfortingly against his chest. "What the hell am I saying?" he murmured. "It's not like it was your fault. I should have had that thing retrofitted with autolocks a long time ago. Or junked it."

She only nodded, still not thinking clearly.

"You're much too trusting," he was saying. "I had a feeling that monster would turn on you one of these days."

Joan smiled weakly into his shirt, her fingers curling around the lapels of his jacket. His lighthearted remark about the filing cabinet eased her inner quaking. But as the shivers subsided, a tingling awareness of his embrace replaced them.

Being within the strong circle of his arms was no accident of sleep. Motionless, she savored the beat of his heart beneath her hand and the firm pressure of his thighs against her body. A sensual warmth began spreading from the hands on her back. She felt his face move through the golden silkiness of her hair and stop near her ear.

The catch in her breath told her she should break free, however innocent the embrace had been to begin with. But the exhilaration she felt in his arms was irresistible, an almost frightening excitement that lured her like a sweet taste of forbidden honey. She stayed right where she was.

"Are you sure you weren't hurt?"

His calm voice almost made Joan wish she could claim some minor injury, but she shook her head. Sensible to a fault, as usual. Her fingers spread against his chest one last time as she pushed herself away, or at least as far away as the hands on her back would allow.

"I'm all right. Really." She gave him a nervous smile of assurance.

His roughly stamped features were indistinct. But the nearness of his mouth made her pulse race. She wondered desperately what it would be like if Brandt kissed her. There was no question in her mind that he would be very, very good at making love, good beyond her wildest dreams. Her lashes fluttered down so that her expressive brown eyes wouldn't reveal her wayward thoughts.

His hand left her shoulder blades to brush back the long hair that had fallen over her cheek. "I like the fragrance you're wearing," Brandt mused. "It suits you."

"I . . . I'm not wearing any perfume," Joan answered

in an embarrassed whisper, again at a loss as to how to cope with his casually intimate remarks.

"You're not?" His face moved ever so slightly closer to the side of her neck where she was acutely conscious of his soft inhalation along her skin. "You smell so good." He shrugged and released her.

"Oh—maybe it's my hair." She turned away to conceal the confusion she felt. "I shampooed it the other night. I used a new brand—I liked the fragrance."

If Ed or any other man had made a comment like his, Joan would have laughed it off. But coming from him, it got to her.

Brandt's lithe strides had carried him back to her desk and the overturned chair. "By the way," he said, all business again, "from now on you'd better open only one drawer of that metal monster at a time."

A rush of angry heat filled her cheeks. "It's not like I made it happen on purpose, Brandt!"

He turned slowly around, studying her with disconcerting thoroughness. "I never said you did."

The way he said the words, in a tone of slight reproof, irked her. "What I meant was—" She broke off. What had she meant?

"I can figure it out by myself, thanks." Brandt smiled. "I know when a woman is tricking me into holding her in my arms."

"I didn't!"

His expression was calm. "My mistake, then. Sorry."

There was little she could say in return without putting her foot in her mouth again. Joan turned away to get back to work, feeling awfully frustrated.

Chapter 4

In a forgotten corner of a conference room shelf, Brandt had found a box of candles. Four tiny flames were bravely fending off the encroaching darkness in Joan's office. Their wavering light wasn't enough to work by, but it illuminated the stale fare of sandwiches and chips.

Brandt was behind her desk, leaning back in the now unsqueaky swivel chair, while Joan studied the candle flames. She needed something to do, and the flames were soothing as a subject of meditation.

"Tell me about your family, Joan. Do they live in Chicago?" His gaze roamed over her face, not missing the way she avoided meeting his eyes.

He was making small talk, filling in her uneasy silence. Conversation seemed like a good idea, if only to keep certain thoughts in check. Answering his questions might take her mind off the softening effect of the candlelight on his rugged features. It seemed to heighten his attractiveness and make her more aware of his sensual virility, unfortunately.

"No, my parents live in a little town about ninety miles from here," she answered in response to his question. "I have an older brother in the army. He's stationed in Germany right now. My younger brother's in his last year of high school and my baby sister is in her first, so they're both living at home."

"What does your father do?"

"He and my mother run a small general store. It's a family business. Jean and Bob, my sister and brother, help out after school and on weekends." The smile she gave him was hesitant. Her folks were anything but glamorous.

"It sounds like a very warm, settled environment." Brandt leaned forward to ease his back, his gaze flicking smoothly over her face. "You don't seem like the type to crave the excitement of the big city."

"But I do like it," she said defensively. "The Chicago Art Institute is great and I love the pier with the Ferris wheel in the summer and all that vintage architecture in any weather. And there's always window-shopping on the Gold Coast. Plus grill joints like Ed Debevic's—"

He grinned and quoted their famous slogan, "Get in here!"

"That's the place."

"I have to admit they have the best chow for us carnivores." He gave a growl that wasn't scary at all and she had to smile. "Do you ever get bored working this far outside the city?"

Not with you around, she wanted to say. But she didn't. "Never."

"Good. Land was much cheaper out in the boonies, so that's why we put the company building here. So what else brought you to Chicago?"

"College. And jobs. When I graduated, there weren't any job openings in my hometown, and I stayed on here."

"Good decision. But life can be lonely without family and friends," he commented.

Joan knew just how right he was, but she waved it away. "Oh," she said, "I've made lots of friends and I visit my family once a month."

Brandt leaned back in his chair again. "I guess I'm too used to having my parents nearby. You've met my mother, haven't you?"

"Yes," she admitted, remembering the day the tall, angular woman had entered her office, a feminine version of her son. She had been very warm and friendly to Joan, not treating her with a superior attitude at all.

"My father is a doctor," Brandt continued in the same thoughtful way. "Semiretired, working mostly as a medical consultant now, but he'll never quit completely. He enjoys his work too much."

"I thought Lyon Construction was started by your father."

"No, my uncle. He passed away a few years ago. I worked for him in the summers when I was a kid, went to college, majored in engineering and did day labor on construction sites to learn the business from the ground up, so to speak," he added with a wink. "I joined the company when I graduated."

"Do you have any brothers or sisters?" Her curiosity about his personal life was sparked by all this information.

"A sister. Venetia followed in Dad's footsteps and became a doctor. She's practicing in Arizona."

"Not married?"

"No, she's like me. She enjoys a certain amount of solitude." There was a dark glow emanating from the depths of his eyes as he shot her a questioning look.

"Aren't you going to comment on the loneliness of a bachelor's life?"

"I can't throw stones when I live in a glass house," Joan murmured.

"Don't you want to marry, settle down, and raise a family?"

"Sure. Some day." She shifted uncomfortably in her chair. "But that decision involves finding the right man."

"Haven't you met him yet? What about this Ed guy you mentioned before?"

She gave a slight negative shake of her head and Brandt responded with a rueful smile. "Uh-oh. I guess I put my foot in my mouth. Sorry about that. I should have known."

"Known what?"

"You don't have the look of a woman in love. You know, that soft radiance. It usually accompanies the other symptoms."

"You make it sound like a disease." She tried to laugh off his astute observations.

"In some ways it is. The loss of appetite, the restlessness, the funny aches, the pangs of uncertainty . . ." He trailed off. Was he joking around again?

"You sound as though you know." The fragile image of the blonde named Angela immediately came to Joan's mind and she experienced one of those funny aches that Brandt had just mentioned.

"I'm acquainted with it." He smiled dryly and got to his feet, walking over to the outside window and staring through the frosted panes. "It sounds as though the wind is letting up. Maybe the blizzard is history. It would be nice if it would blow on out of here tonight."

Joan gazed at the broad shoulders tapering to lean

hips. What would it be like when the storm was over? she wondered. Would she be the same tweedy, tailored Ms. Somers, the busiest bee at Lyon Construction? Or had they progressed to a point where it would be impossible to return to that level of businesslike distance?

She was sure they had. In fact, she was afraid her own emotions had gone beyond the point where she could control them. Her reserve had been penetrated. That seemingly strong barrier between her and Brandt was gone.

"At least we'll be warm tonight," she said with false brightness, glancing at the heater sitting in the middle of the room.

"Not from the heater, we won't." Brandt had spoken so quietly she wasn't sure she'd understood what he said.

"What?"

He twisted sideways, the flickering candle flames not revealing all of his face. He studied her wary expression.

"We won't be able to have the heater on all night, Joan."

"Why not? You opened the window a bit for ventilation."

"It's not that," he said. "We just don't have much fuel left. Not enough for tonight and into tomorrow," he clarified, "and there's no telling when the power will go on again."

Sensibly, logically, Joan wanted to admit that Brandt was being practical, but she didn't even have to close her eyes to visualize the sweet sensation of lying by his side. That shared heat was overwhelming.

"I didn't know that." She frowned with worry.

"That's because I didn't tell you." The bland expression on his face made his inner thoughts unreadable. "I really didn't want you to stress out over it."

"I wouldn't have," Joan murmured, her quick glance skittering off his face.

Brandt continued to study her thoughtfully, his gaze riveted on the softness of her lips in the candle-light. His hands were thrust into the pockets of his pants, pushing open the suit jacket and emphasizing the muscular flatness of his abs. He drew in a deep breath and turned away.

"I'll get our coats and warm them in front of the heater before we call it a night," he announced as he opened the inner office door.

The sudden draft of cold air sent little shudders racing over Joan's skin. There was no objection she could make, not when she'd willingly agreed to the same arrangement the night before.

It seemed as if a week had passed since yesterday. A little more than twenty-four hours ago she had been in complete charge of her unadventurous life. Now she felt insecure and lost, trapped in random events that had her slowly twisting in the wind.

Her heart was pounding against her ribs when Brandt came back in with their coats in his arms. She wished desperately that his calmness was catching— she could use some of it right now. But then, she thought, he wasn't affected by her the way she was by him. No man had ever made her senses come alive the way Brandt did.

Joan felt the need to speak, but the impulse died in her throat as Brandt glanced at her and smiled, a lazy smile that dissolved her apprehensions. She chided herself for worrying. It was all one-sided.

Rising to her feet, she helped him drape the coats over the side chairs so the inner linings would be exposed to the heat. When that was done, she clasped her hands together, holding them above the heater as though they were cold.

"I almost wish we'd decided to use your office today so at least the room would be warm." Her mouth curved weakly into a smile as he moved away, behind her now.

"Yeah. If the couch weren't so damn cumbersome, I'd drag it in here." Brandt's gaze was centered on the middle point between her shoulder blades. She could sense it as if she had eyes in the back of her head. "In a few minutes," he continued in that same quiet, unassuming voice, "I'll take the heater into my office and get the worst of the chill out of the room."

If there had been a clock in the room, Joan didn't think its ticking could have drowned out the sound of her heartbeat. Last night there hadn't been any real opportunity to dwell on the thought of sleeping with Brandt. There had been no premeditation involved. Now, knowing that within a few minutes she would be walking into the office, slipping off her shoes and lying down on the couch to wait for Brandt to stretch out beside her, she was sure she would betray her intense, constantly changing feelings about him.

She started visibly when Brandt stepped forward to remove the coats from the chairs. He didn't say anything as he wrapped them together to retain the heat they'd absorbed. Calming down some, she watched him pick up the heater and carry it to his office.

When he hadn't returned in a few minutes, Joan knew she couldn't wait any longer. Her nerves were already raw. Extinguishing all but one candle, she draped the toasty-warm coats over her arm and picked up the candle.

"Leave the door open," Brandt said, not even glancing up when she entered the room.

He was bending over the heater and she could only guess that he was turning it off. She set the candle on the table beside the sofa, not letting herself be distracted by the magnetic attraction of his presence. The air in the room could still be described as brisk, but it was much warmer than it had been.

"I'll go and shut the window in your office while you get ready." His voice came from the direction of the open door.

"Okay," Joan said, thinking she ought to make some reply.

Taking up her position along the back of the sofa, she arranged the coats over her legs and was trying to keep an ample amount of the topmost coat available for Brandt when he quietly entered the office. There was an electric quality to the air, akin to the charged moments before a thunderstorm.

The candle was blown out, casting the room in darkness. For a moment Joan was completely blinded by the lack of light. Then there was a sensation of supple, controlled movement as Brandt's weight was lowered onto the cushions. Instinctively she held her breath, bracing herself for the contact with his hard form. There was no hesitation in the way he settled himself beside her, adjusting the curves of her body to fit his. Her breathing, when it returned, was ragged. Being so near and forcing herself not to reveal the effect he had on her was bliss—and torture.

"Comfortable?" he asked in a husky voice that moved the air near her face like a caress.

"Yes," Joan breathed, barely able to.

"It's warmer than last night." His easy, deep tone was undoubtedly meant to relax her.

"Yes," she answered again, but it was the heat in her cheeks and neck that was causing her the most discomfort. A fire seemed to have been kindled within the most sensually responsive part of her body.

"Good night, Joan," Brandt said.

The simple words had a familiar, even friendly ring, as if she and Brandt had been married for ten years or so . . . but hearing him say them into her ear was a novel and utterly delicious experience. "Good night, Brandt."

Closing her eyes, she listened to and felt the steady rise and fall of his chest. He smelled wonderful, a mixture of good aftershave—it had lingered for more than a day, because he still hadn't shaved—and pure him. She prayed for sleep to deaden her overstimulated senses. Her muscles ached from trying to hold herself away from him, or at least not to relax against him.

His right arm was resting over her waist. Unbidden, dangerous thoughts came to her—what would it be like to feel him caress her through her clothes . . . and then her bare skin? A quicksilver thrill of delight danced over her whole body.

"Are you cold?" Brandt asked softly.

Automatically her head moved in the direction of his voice, stopping when her cheek brushed against his mouth and chin. Or maybe that happened the other way around. "A little," she lied, unable to explain her sensual shiver any other way.

He edged the rest of his body closer, scorching her skin right through her clothes. There didn't seem to be any part of him that wasn't touching her and exciting her. Her heart stopped, then started again with a swift rush.

"Is that better?" The movement of his mouth against her cheek, so very close to the corner of her mouth, just about paralyzed her.

A barely audible "yes" came from her dry throat.

"What's the matter?" His soft, guarded tone only added to her confusion.

Opening her eyes, Joan tried to focus them on the face next to hers. "Nothing," she said in a faltering voice.

In an effort to distance herself from the disturbing closeness of his mouth, she drew her head back into the corner of the sofa, keeping her face toward him. His right hand left her waist to brush a few tangled locks of hair from her cheek.

"You're trembling," he said gently.

"Please. It's nothing," she whispered. Frustrated tears welled in her eyes.

"I don't believe you," he said flatly.

"Let's just go to sleep, Brandt," she insisted with a throbbing quiver in her voice.

"Not until you tell me what's wrong."

The seductive strength of his low voice almost closed her throat. How could she possibly tell him that she wanted him to make love to her, wanted to feel the caress of his hands and the warmth of his lips?

"Brandt . . ." The aching sigh in the way she said his name revealed more than she realized.

The sudden tenseness of his muscles was immediately evident to her. In the dark, she could only sense the slow movement of the head beside her as it came closer. Her lips trembled at the light touch of his mouth against them, feather light, not a kiss but a hesitant caress.

When his mouth moved an inch away, it was the moment to rebuff his advance. But she couldn't. She had fought so long against the attraction that she simply didn't have the willpower to deny it any longer.

His hand curved around the side of her neck, his fingers sliding into her tumbled hair as he raised her head the fraction of an inch that was needed to meet his descending mouth. She felt a bursting wave of heat at the immediate possession of his kiss, a dazzling unleashing of explosions.

As his body weight shifted above her, Joan slipped her arms around his waist, spreading her fingers over the taut muscles of his back. His mastery and sensuous passion gave him unlimited power and she moaned softly in surrender as the command of his mouth parted her lips. She was a captive in ecstasy, and Brandt rewarded her by taking her to dizzying heights.

But it wasn't only from her lips that a response was demanded. Gentle, exploratory caresses deliberately kindled more flames in the rest of her body, slowly building her desire to a crescendo of need that would match the urgency of his hunger. Yet his very gentleness, his sureness, vanquished any lingering fear.

When his fingers undid the last button of her blouse and pushed the material aside, Joan could only sigh with gratification at the touch of his cupped hand on the rounded curve of her breast. The heady gloriousness, the deep sense of rightness at what was happening, dissolved all modesty. The whole universe could have collapsed at that moment and she would not have cared as long as she was in Brandt's strong arms.

As his mouth brushed over the hollow of her throat, beginning a slow, meandering trail to the shadowy cleft between her breasts, a bursting light filled the room. For a moment, lost in a sensual wonderland, Joan thought she had only imagined it. Then the cessation of Brandt's loving touch prompted her to open her eyes.

The fluorescent overhead lights had come on.

His head remained buried in her neck for an instant longer. Then he cursed briefly beneath his breath and pushed himself upright and away from her. She stared at him in tortured stillness, watching him as he sat on the edge of the sofa, his breathing uneven, raking his hands through his hair before using them to rub over his face.

"That's as effective as the cold light of day."

The bitterly spoken words drew a silent gasp of dismay from Joan. So Brandt felt nothing but regret. His desire for her had lasted only moments, and intense shame washed over her. How foolish of her to think his passion had been sparked by more than just lust.

Hot tears of humiliation scalded her cheeks as she fumbled beneath her coat for the buttons of her blouse, her skin still tingling from the slow, intimate strokes of his hands over her nakedness.

"Joan, I'm sorry." His voice was lower than she had ever heard it. "You must think I'm—"

"Please don't apologize!" She lashed out sharply. That he should do so was unbearable. "Spare me that!"

Covered enough for modesty's sake, she pushed herself up on the sofa, driven by an overwhelming need to run, hide, get away somehow, before tears sizzled over the heat in her cheeks. But Brandt pinned her against the cushions in one swift move, his fingers digging roughly into the flesh of her arm.

"You aren't going anywhere." Blue fire blazed in his eyes as they moved over her face, stopping at her lips, still warm and swollen from his kisses. "Not until we talk this over."

The hard set of his features indicated the tight hold he had on his temper and emotions. The sight of his face could still raise hell with her senses, but she kept her expression cold and proud.

"There isn't anything to talk about," she said, refusing to flinch under his powerful grip.

"You know damn well there is!" He spoke softly, almost under his breath.

"Please—" She broke off. Was it necessary for her to be so polite? She reached up to push his hand away from her arm. "What happened wasn't important."

"What nearly happened, you mean," Brandt reminded her cuttingly.

In spite of her attempts at self-control, color stained her cheeks, a silent admission that what he said was correct. She didn't want to look at him.

"But it didn't, did it?" she said. "So we have nothing to be ashamed of. You're a man, I'm a woman, we got close and things got physical. So what? It's really no big deal."

"Do you actually believe that?" His eyes narrowed as he withdrew his arm.

"Of course I do." It was partly true, Joan believed, as far as he was concerned, but not at all for her.

"I swear, I never met anyone as coldly analytical as you are." Brandt shook his head grimly, looking at her angrily for a flash of a second until he rolled to his feet. "You can turn your emotions on and off at will, can't you?"

Sheer nerve was the only thing keeping Joan from turning into a blubbering mass of tears. "And you can't?" she challenged him. Somewhere in the basement, the distant furnace had kicked on, sending warm air surging through the room.

"What are you talking about?"

"Oh, just what we've been talking about off and on for the whole time we've been stuck here."

"And that is—?"

Leave it to him to double-check. "You hired me because I was efficient, practical, and not prone to panic without a damn good reason. Are you about to fire me for the same reasons?"

She almost wished he would. In fact, she prayed that he would, so she wouldn't have to face him day after day, thinking about the time when he'd almost made love to her.

"No." He managed to get a sarcastic inflection into the one word. Brandt still wouldn't look at her. "I'm not going to fire you."

The moment passed and his long strides ate up the distance to the connecting door. Joan knew he was ending the conversation to go back to his former sleeping place in the chair in her office. The need for revenge put a sharp edge on her voice.

"Would you turn off the light when you leave? I want to get some sleep." It was a request that bordered on a command.

Brandt stopped by the door before reaching out to viciously flick off the light switch as he went into her office, slamming the door behind him.

Darkness enveloped the room. Joan wanted to curl up and forget everything that had happened. But she couldn't. She huddled deeper into her coat, letting tears of misery flow. The silent release didn't ease her emotional state. Nothing could.

Neither of them was really to blame for what had happened. She and Brandt had played equal roles in this adventure, if you could call it that, but for different reasons. Yet Brandt's cardinal rule had been broken. The line between his business and personal life had been crossed, something that could never be forgotten.

Joan couldn't possibly forget. She loved him. It was foolish, impractical, and futile to do so, but she loved him.

Chapter 5

The clouds outside were gray, not the slate gray that held snow but the oyster gray of high overcast. The wind had subsided to tame puffs that sent the top snowflakes dancing and swirling over drifts piled many feet high by the harsh north wind.

The shimmering gold of Joan's long hair was subdued to a dull shade by its return to the severe bun at the nape of her neck. Her glasses were set primly on the bridge of her nose, more to conceal the telltale redness of tears and the blue shadows of sleeplessness than to improve her vision.

Washing up with soap and water had restored much of her courage, but not enough of it to meet Brandt's eyes squarely when she walked into her office from the outer corridor. Fortunately, she didn't have to. His gaze flicked briefly and remotely over her.

"The snowplows are clearing the streets," Brandt told her, shoving his arms into the sleeves of his sheepskin jacket and shrugging it on. "I'm going to shovel the SUV out. Might take me a while."

An acknowledgment seemed to be expected, so

Joan said a crisp, "All right." As she went to her desk, he walked away.

Everything had changed. Only hours ago, Brandt had thoughtfully provided food and warmth, talked to her, teased her, pleased her—and the last straw, persuaded her, very seductively, to leave her hair tumbling down over her shoulders.

His sweet coaxing and attentiveness were gone and the loss of both made Joan want to cry. But tears wouldn't ease the desolation. She'd proved that to herself last night. The fault was hers. She should not have let all that gorgeous, rampant masculinity swamp her common sense.

She'd been well aware of her feelings for him and should have been on her guard, but his warm, friendly attitude had melted her defenses.

Brandt had said he wasn't going to fire her. But wouldn't it be best if she handed in her resignation before he changed his mind? Or could that be construed as an admission on her part that what had happened meant far more to her than she'd wanted him to believe? The answer seemed to lie in whether she had the strength to deal with him in the structured daily routine of the office without letting him discover the depth of her emotion. Maybe after a few months, she could resign and find a better job somewhere else. It would be dangerous to stay working for him forever, given how she felt.

"Damn!" she whispered, clenching her hands into tight fists on the desktop. The problem was going to be surviving the upcoming weeks while still salvaging a few scraps of her pride.

Then she got hold of herself. These constant recriminations over things that could happen to anyone had to stop. To keep reliving those painful moments after the electricity had been restored was serving no purpose. She had no idea how long Brandt would be gone, but she had to occupy her mind with something besides obsessing over him. She poked a random key on the computer keyboard and the monitor flickered to glowing life.

Getting started again on polishing the letters Brandt had left for her as scrawls on a notepad, ready to be turned into documents, was her task of choice. The sight of his handwriting gave her a pang, but she squelched it firmly. She was barely through the third letter when he walked into the office.

"Are you ready?" His quiet, calm voice stopped her fingers for a split second before they continued to race over the keyboard.

"I'll be finished in a minute," she replied, keeping her eyes on the notepad.

When all the letters were printed out, Brandt was beside the desk, handing her the fun-fur coat that had been in his office. Her already wounded nerves smarted at his eagerness to be rid of her, but a swift glance at his rugged face revealed none of the impatience she had expected to see. He stood silently by as she put the coat on, his hands thrust deep in the pockets of his sheepskin jacket, the lighter overcoat folded in his arms, a withdrawn expression in his eyes.

He ushered her to his car, which was parked in front of the building, its motor still running. The cold, invigorating air made the warm interior seem stifling as Joan settled into the passenger seat.

"Where do you live?" Brandt put the car in gear and turned into the street. It had been plowed in haste and there was only enough room for one vehicle to get through. But the city was still snowed in and they saw no one else out until they were well away from the Lyon building.

Joan gave him the directions and leaned back in the seat. Her side vision gave her a glimpse of his hawklike profile, but she kept her gaze mostly to the front. In other circumstances, she might have enjoyed the white purity of the landscape that had transformed Chicago's streets into a wintry wonderland. The snow that hadn't drifted was firmly packed in thin layers on patches of asphalt, making driving somewhat treacherous in spite of the snowplows' diligent efforts to scrape the streets. The strong hands on the steering wheel were competent and he was obviously experienced at driving in bad conditions. The two miles to Joan's apartment took longer than usual to cover, but nothing went wrong.

The pavement leading to the front entrance of the old brick building hadn't been cleared off. Pristine white drifts showed that no one had ventured out yet on this gray morning after the huge storm. Pushing open the car door, Joan silently wished that some premonition had made her wear snowboots last Friday. Wading through those drifts with unprotected legs and office shoes wasn't going to be fun.

Before the soles of her leather pumps even touched the snow, Brandt was out of the car and around on her side. She glanced at him in surprise, fully expecting him simply to drop her off and let her make her own way into the building. A gasp of astonishment came from her as he reached down and easily swung her from the car seat into his arms.

He only smiled at her quick, "Put me down!"

His long strides were already covering the short distance from the snow-covered curb to the apartment building's entrance. "There's no reason you should freeze your feet."

"I'm too heavy," Joan protested, but they had already reached the door and Brandt was setting her down. In another swift move, he swung the wooden door open. "You're tall, but you're not heavy," he said without any emotion as he turned his blank gaze on her.

Her pulse refused to settle back to its normal pace. Just when Joan had thought she'd regained control of her senses, he had to go and cradle her against that rock-hard chest and carry her. She almost wanted to smack him. He stood solemnly in front of her, blue eyes unreadable, the staircase to her second-floor apartment behind him. She looked at it to conceal her confusion.

"You don't need to come into the office until noon tomorrow," he told her. An apartment door slammed on the floor above.

Joan stiffened, tossing her head back. "I don't expect any special favors just because I got stranded at work for most of the weekend," she asserted coldly. "I'll be in the office at eight tomorrow as usual."

He seemed remarkably unimpressed by her dedication and it ticked her off. "Suit yourself. See you at the water cooler."

A few seconds after the outside door closed behind him, Joan realized that she hadn't said thanks for the ride or the knight-in-shining-armor bit at the end. In spite of everything, Brandt was entitled to basic courtesy. But it was too late now. He was already behind the wheel and driving away.

"Wow! Were there icicles in your voice or what?" Kay's exuberant question sounded from the stairs. "And after the way he carried you to the door too!"

Joan glared at her friend, who was wearing a robe and giant fuzzy slipper-socks to brave the elements. "His idea, not mine."

"Yeah, I figured," Kay enthused, "I was watching from the window. He was so masterful about it. Lucky you."

"He only did it because I didn't have boots on and the sidewalk wasn't shoveled," Joan said.

Her explanation didn't erase the impish smile from Kay's face as Joan hurried past her up the steps. There was about to be a deluge of questions. She needed to move to collect her wits after the soul-shattering intimacy of being in Brandt's arms not all that long ago.

"Is the coffee on, Kay?" she asked as she pushed the door open and entered their apartment. "I haven't had a cup since the electricity went off Friday night. I have a raging headache."

"Caffeine withdrawal. It's the worst. Hey, wait a minute—what did you just say?"

"The electricity went off."

"Holy cow! I didn't know that. I heard parts of the city lost power, but it didn't occur to me you didn't have it at the office. Didn't Backup Man have a generator?"

"He had a flashlight."

Kay grinned. "My, my. The nights must have been awfully long. But I didn't worry when you didn't call." In the act of pouring Joan a much-needed cup of coffee, she kept yapping away, her sparkling brown eyes widening. "Hey, how did you keep warm? Did you set fire to heaps of old files?"

"Good idea," Joan said wearily. "But no. We didn't think of that."

"The furnace doesn't work without electricity to operate the thermostat. Did you and Brandt Lyon get all hugged up? Oh my God, I bet you did." Kay rushed to the couch with the coffee cup. "Is that why you were so cold to him? Did he try anything? Was it fabulous, being marooned in a storm?"

"I think you have to be on a desert island to be marooned and desert islands are warm," Joan said crisply. "We were freezing, even though we had our winter coats on."

Her excitable roommate didn't need to know that they'd used the coats together.

"But Brandt found a space heater and fuel in the equipment shed," she went on. "If there was a generator—well, they're huge things. He couldn't exactly drag it up the stairs himself."

"Even so." Kay made a wry face. "What a boy scout. Always prepared, huh?"

Joan's fingers tightened on the comfortingly warm mug she was holding. She took a sip and put it down. "You could say that."

Her roommate was nothing if not persistent. "So he didn't try anything—oh, that's a shame. But maybe next time. Chicago in the winter is one storm after another."

"Don't remind me." She got up, stretching a little. "I feel so grubby after wearing those clothes for nearly three days. I'm going to take a long, hot bath, if you don't mind."

"Go right ahead." Kay cleared away the cup and coaster as Joan wandered away to the bathroom.

Monday morning marked the return of the strictly business atmosphere between Joan and Brandt. His gaze didn't convey irritation or contempt, and he seemed totally in control of his temper otherwise. He treated her in the same friendly but indifferent way he always had, which made it easier for Joan to fall into the same pattern for the most part.

The main topic of conversation throughout the company was the weekend storm, with everyone trading stories on where and how they'd been trapped by the blizzard and how difficult it had been to get home. Joan was grateful for the privacy of her own office, away from the rest of the employees. It saved her from relating her own tale without lying. Mercifully, Kay had agreed not to talk about what little Joan had told her, knowing full well how easily office rumors could get started and how they never seemed to stop.

It was almost noon when Brandt came out of his office to request some older files from the metal monster. Joan had just handed them to him when Lyle Baines walked into her office, a cheery smile creasing his face.

"Sorry to be so late reporting in, Brandt, but the snowplows didn't make it to my street until after ten this morning," he explained. "That really was a first-class blizzard. One for the record books, I bet. Hope you two made it home all right."

After Brandt had nodded an unspoken greeting, he opened the top folder to study its contents. "Actually, Joan and I got stuck here until Sunday morning."

"Really?" Lyle Baines swallowed his astonishment as he turned to stare at Joan.

What? she wanted to say. Had Brandt's name suddenly appeared on her forehead? She only nodded.

She was dismayed, though, that Brandt would carelessly share what she had taken such pains to keep secret. Lyle Baines was too nice to gossip, but Joan had a feeling that someone else might have overheard. The news would quickly spread through the grapevine.

Brandt paused in the doorway. "Come into my office, Lyle. I had a chance to study the 3-D specifications for the Parkwood Mall this weekend, and I want to go over them with you before you start putting the prices together."

Joan retreated to her desk, avoiding Lyle's quizzical gaze as he slowly obeyed the authoritative voice of his boss. Only when the connecting door closed behind both of them did she let her shoulders slump.

It wasn't until the following day that Joan felt the results of Brandt's offhand remarks. When she entered the lunchroom with Kay, there was instant silence as all eyes were turned to her. Then there were whispers and even a little muffled laughter. Joan maintained an outward air of composure, knowing that to react would add fuel to the fire.

Of course, when Kay got wind of the rumors, she was loudest in her friend's defense. Joan knew that Brandt never heard what was said about them. No one would dare to carry tales to the lion, including herself. She wanted to avoid further humiliation more than anything.

During the week, the gossip died down, for want of anything new to add to it. Joan was glad she'd kept a cool silence through it all. Her tactic—ignoring the snide comments—worked well.

A few of her bolder coworkers did question her directly, though. How did she and Brandt spend the time? Did they play, cough-cough, board games the whole time? What did they do when the lights went off? Joan simply said they'd gotten a lot of work done, which was true. And she pretended indifference to all

the rest of it. Her usual professional demeanor gave
her answers credibility.

By Friday afternoon, Joan was congratulating herself for getting through the week. Not that it had
been easy, because it hadn't. Some moments had
been pure torment.

There had been times when Brandt's hand had accidentally brushed hers as they exchanged folders or
other documents and she felt a rush of warmth at his
touch. Or moments when he would be signing letters
she'd typed and printed out, and she would steal a
few seconds to enjoy the sight of his thick, wavy
brown hair, and his strong, self-assured face. Above
all, she let her gaze linger on the hard masculine
mouth that had so devastatingly awakened her latent
desire and love.

At around four o'clock on Friday afternoon, Joan
began the filing and finishing-up of the work on her
desk in preparation for the weekend. Clearing the
OUT tray was a major task in and of itself. She only
smiled absently when the payroll clerk stopped by her
office with her weekly paycheck. It was an old-
fashioned ritual that Lyon Construction still offered for
employees who didn't trust automatic direct deposit.

Preoccupied by everything she hadn't done yet,
Joan removed her checkbook from her bag and slid
the check, still in its envelope, into it. On an impulse,
she flicked open the unglued flap and peeked at the
amount. It was almost half again as much as usual.
She froze.

For a moment she could only blink at it in bewilderment. Then a slow anger began to seethe. She
had no doubt that Brandt had authorized a boost to
the usual sum to appease his conscience. Buying her
off would take care of his guilt.

Joan rose and stalked to the connecting door. Her sharp rap was answered right away by Brandt. "Come on in." He looked up at her and then back at the papers in front of him. "What's up?"

She was too angry to speak and his uninterested tone didn't help. The squareness of her shoulders and the tilt of her chin were dictated by pride as she walked to his desk and let the check flutter out of her fingers and down in front of him on the desktop. He glanced at it and pushed it toward her absently, all without looking up again.

"That's your check," he said as though she was showing it to him for verification.

"I know—it's made out to me," Joan responded tautly. "But the amount is incorrect. I want you to call Accounting and have another check issued for my usual salary. And I'm not going to make the call for you."

The barely disguised anger in her voice got his full attention. He gave her a searching look that noted the glittering fire in her eyes.

"That is the correct amount." His eyes narrowed as the line of her mouth tightened. "Even though it was unscheduled, you did work overtime last weekend."

"I have no intention of accepting any money for last weekend, no matter what reason you dream up, Brandt!" She crossed her arms over her chest, ready to do battle.

He leaned back in his chair. "I didn't dream up a reason, as you put it," he responded evenly. To her fury, he seemed to be admiring her warrior woman stance. "The fact is, you put in a lot of extra hours for the company on Friday night and Saturday. The additional money is fair compensation. I don't see how you can argue with that."

If it hadn't been for her pride and her sense of the rightness of things—the gossip had only just subsided, after all—Joan might have accepted his explanation. As it was, she couldn't and wouldn't.

"I don't believe you. And I won't accept money just because you regret—"

"That's enough out of you." His comeback stopped her outburst cold. Only the slight tensing of his muscles in his jaw hinted that his anger had been aroused. "If you don't like my explanation, okay, but the check is yours and the amount is correct. What you do with it is your business."

"I'll show you what I'll do with it!" Joan declared stormily.

With one swoop, she retrieved the check from his desk and tore it into small pieces. Hot tears scalded her eyes as she turned and dashed to the door.

She was almost out when she was caught by the arm and spun around to stand face-to-face with Brandt.

"You know, Joan," Brandt said with infuriating calm, "I'm tempted to make you tape that check back together. But I can't do that, can I?" He let her arm go, but she didn't run away.

"No, you can't!" Her breath caught and she said nothing more, her senses instinctively awakened by his nearness. She was almost intimidated by his height and solid presence, but not the angry exasperation in his carved features.

"Well?" he asked. "Now what?"

Pride lifted her chin. "I'm not sorry, Brandt."

"I'm not waiting for an apology from you, believe me." He managed a wry smile. "Obviously you think I'm trying to buy you off or something like that."

She felt quick color rise in her cheeks as she fumed in silence.

"But that's not true," he continued. "And I'm not going to apologize either. As far as what happened between us on Saturday night, we—I wanted you, Joan. And I acted accordingly. You were willing, to say the least."

Joan glared at him with renewed fury. "Brandt, what were you thinking? Someone in Accounting is going to spread the news of my, shall we say, unexpected raise. And once the rumor gets going, someone else is going to add a juicy reason why."

"That money was for overtime, unexpected or not. Look at the check stub. And in case *you* were wondering, I don't pay for sexual pleasure."

Her lips pressed together to hold back a cry of shame. The high color in her cheeks drained away, leaving her unnaturally pale.

"That was out of line," he sighed. "I apologize for that, Joan."

"Please." Her hand rose in a weak wave that was meant to ward off any more cutting remarks. "Just call Accounting and have a check reissued."

Brandt gave a curt nod and went back to his desk. "I'll do it if you listen in." He motioned for Joan to sit down and sat down himself.

She sank into a chair, surprised by his sudden capitulation. Brandt Lyon wasn't a man to give in once he'd taken a stand. Conscious of her quick heartbeats, she watched him punch the buttons to reach someone in Accounting.

His gaze flicked over her as if to make sure she was still there before he spoke into the phone. "Connelly? Brandt here," he said in his authoritative voice. "Joan ripped up her check—yeah, by mistake. Would you cut another for her and bring it in for my signature?"

There was a pause during which Brandt looked at

Joan, who squirmed a little under his pinning gaze. "Yes. In exactly the same amount as before," he added firmly. "And would you circle the overtime code? Uh-huh, for when she does her taxes. Thanks."

Resentment flared immediately as Joan realized he'd tricked her into believing he'd agreed to her request, and forestalled further argument by getting Connelly to come over, while he was at it. She bounded to her feet and raced out, ignoring his order to come back.

She didn't waste any time straightening her desk as she grabbed her purse and dashed to the coatrack. With her coat thrown over her shoulders, she reached for the doorknob to the outer hall when Brandt appeared in the inner office doorway.

"Joan, get back in here!"

She flashed him a fiery glare. "I'm leaving early. Don't forget to ask Connelly to dock my next week's paycheck." With her sarcastic rejoinder ringing in the air, she went out, slamming the door behind her and not caring who heard it.

She was pretty sure Brandt wasn't about to chase her through the hallowed halls of Lyon Construction, but she still hurried to the main front door. She cast an apprehensive glance behind her as she walked quickly out of the building. Except for Susan, who was jabbing at buttons on the phone console with her usual bored expression and chatting with someone on her headset, there wasn't anyone around.

It was freezing out when she arrived at the bus stop. She'd only waited a minute when a bus lumbered up to the curb in a steam cloud of hot exhaust, and she quickly got on board.

Kay arrived at their apartment more than an hour and a half later, stopping on her way home to pick up an outfit she had on layaway. The detour undoubtedly kept her from wondering why her roommate was already there, for which Joan was grateful. The spat over the check—and the so-called overtime added to it—evidently hadn't made the late afternoon news around the office.

"Thank God it's Friday!" Kay sang out as she flung herself and a bulging shopping bag onto the couch. "But I have a million things to do. John is going to be here in an hour to take me to the movies and I have to be up bright and early in the morning so we can pick up Ed at the airport. Are you going with us?"

"I thought I would." All the same, Joan couldn't summon up much enthusiasm about Ed's arrival—something she had looked forward to until last weekend. She turned away before Kay could read her thoughts and started to set the dinette table for their evening meal. "The goulash is heating up in that pan on the stove. We can eat whenever you want."

"Goulash!" Kay moaned. "I wish we could afford steaks. No, scratch that. I wish *John* could afford to take me out to a fancy steak restaurant, but he doesn't have an expense account. Not yet," she amended. She sighed and pushed herself into an upright position. "Lead me to the goulash. I'll eat and then I'll shower."

For all her complaining, Kay devoured the goulash and green salad Joan had prepared. Never one to slack off on the housework, Kay cleared the dishes and stacked the pots and salad bowl, leaving the actual washing to Joan when she insisted she didn't mind.

Joan made short work of the minimal kitchen cleanup, then decided to tidy the front room. Kay was out of the shower and dressing by the time Joan was done plumping up pillows and collecting magazines in a basket. At the quick rap on the apartment door, Kay bounded from the bedroom.

"Yikes! John's here and my hair isn't even combed!" she yelped to Joan, beating her to the door all the same.

"He won't mind waiting a few extra minutes." Joan smiled over her shoulder before she spotted a dish she'd missed in the kitchen and headed in there.

She heard Kay open the door, but she didn't turn around until she heard her roommate's breathless, "Oh, hello." The door was ajar, but at an angle that blocked her view of whomever was there. Obviously not John.

"Is Joan here?"

Joan's stomach churned at the sound of Brandt's voice. A crazy surge of heat rushed through her body. She turned on the cold tap at the sink and let the water run over her fingers, then patted a few drops on her cheeks. Forget that, she thought, scrubbing them off. She didn't want him to think she'd been crying.

"Yes, of course," Kay answered, her voice still charged with surprise. Hinges squeaked as she flung the door all the way open to let him in. "Hey, Joan, look who's here!"

She had to turn around. Her mouth quirked nervously in something that she hoped resembled a smile. She would have to put a good face on this or Kay would get way too curious.

Brandt seemed too large for the small apartment standing just inside the doorway. Maybe it was that overcoat he had on, she thought, telling herself right away that wasn't the reason. It was who he was—and what he meant to her.

"Oh, hello," Joan said casually. Her voice failed her

for a few seconds as he continued across the room to the kitchen. "Ah—what are you doing here?"

"As if you didn't know," Brandt murmured for her ears alone.

Joan flushed uncomfortably and darted a quick look at Kay. The petite brunette had been watching them in fascinated silence, but she retreated hastily to the bedroom at Joan's glance. The sound of the door closing only increased the sensation of unwanted intimacy, and Joan wished she could call Kay back. She turned to the sink, washing the lone dish meticulously just to have something to do with her hands.

Brandt moved quietly closer, resting an elbow on the counter as he leaned back, effectively taking over the tiny kitchen. His gaze stayed on her profile until she turned her head, unwillingly, to look at him. Joan started as his hand raised, and she frowned when it moved into the inner pocket of his suit jacket under the overcoat.

"I have a new check for you." The amused inflection of his voice mocked her as he set an envelope on the counter.

Joan swallowed. "Is it made out correctly?"

"Yes it is," Brandt responded with infuriating calm.

"Somehow I don't believe you," Joan said in an undertone.

In that lazy but totally focused way he had, Brandt studied her thoroughly. "After three years of working for me, Joan, you should know that I generally get my way."

"Not this time." She raised her head proudly, a move that accented the graceful curve of her throat.

The lines around his mouth deepened with thinning patience. "Why can't you accept the check instead of making an issue out of it?"

There was another knock on the door and Joan quickly turned away from Brandt, self-consciously wiping her hands on her jeans. Who knew where the dish towel had gotten itself to? She didn't care that Kay was already emerging from the bedroom to answer the door. She needed a few moments' respite from Brandt's unnerving presence.

Her eyes pleaded with Kay not to rush off with John once he was inside and fast hellos were exchanged all around. But for once, John put himself in charge and insisted that they leave immediately so they wouldn't miss the beginning of the movie.

To her chagrin, Brandt seemed to pick up on Joan's agitation when Kay and John left and they were really alone.

While Joan had been focused on John and Kay, Brandt had seized the chance to take off his overcoat, since no one had asked him to. The physical impact of his darkly elegant attire stole her breath. Black tie. Hmm. Who was that for? He was dressed for an occasion, not the office. She wasn't entirely sure this suave, handsome stranger was the man she worked with daily.

"Aren't you going out this evening?" he asked idly.

His question struck a nerve. "You can answer that yourself." Joan looked down pointedly at her brother's cast-off sweatshirt, then tugged the bottom over the waistband of her snug but ripped jeans. She felt gauche and shabby next to him. "I'm not exactly dressed for a date."

"Some people would call that a fashion statement," Brandt said diplomatically. "And you always look good to me."

"I bet," she retorted. "I'm sure your dates don't dress like this."

Brandt was no longer leaning against the counter, but standing a few feet away. Joan brushed past him to squeeze out the sponge and finish up.

"So, who's the lucky girl tonight? Let me guess— the china doll I saw you with a few weeks ago?" There was a decided edge to her voice.

"Hmm. Let me think." A sardonic gleam darkened his eyes. "You must mean Angela. She does kind of look like a china doll. Unfortunately, I didn't see you."

"Is it unfortunate?" she flashed. "You don't believe in mixing business with pleasure, right?"

His face was suddenly grim and she knew she'd crossed an invisible line again. Her hand brushed a strand of burnished gold hair back to where the rest was secured by a clasp.

"Oops. Maybe you don't like to be reminded of that," she said sweetly. "Don't let me keep you. Your date is waiting."

Her sarcasm seemed lost on him, because he only smiled. "Nice try, Joan. But not enough to distract me. I did come here for a reason." Brandt studied her stubborn expression. "What are you going to do with the check?"

"I suppose I'll have to accept it," Joan said grudgingly.

He crossed the few paces that separated them. She wanted to turn away, but like a butterfly in a net, she couldn't fly away from his compelling gaze.

"Do I have your word on that?" Brandt demanded quietly.

For a mutinous moment, Joan didn't give it. But she guessed he wouldn't leave until he got her to promise.

"Yes. I won't tear it up again." Joan got the words out.

"Or stick it somewhere and forget it?" His mouth quirked at one corner. He seemed to be expecting her to go back on her promise.

"I have bills to pay and I need every dime I earn. Believe me, I'll cash it." She glared at him resentfully.

Brandt smiled. "That wasn't so hard."

"I had to agree, didn't I?" she answered, fighting that sudden leap of her pulse at the magic smile. "How else would I get you to leave?"

"Are you so eager to see me go?" he mocked.

"You want to," she said firmly.

His gaze swept the room, then moved over her pale face. "You never know. What if I stay?"

"I can't believe you'd choose me over precious little Angela."

His hand caught her wrist as Joan started to walk away. When she tried to pull free, his hold tightened and Brandt smoothly twisted her around and pulled her close. The move was easy for him, but then he was incredibly strong. That impression was replaced by a sensual, pleasurable inertia that kept her where she was.

"I have to get used to the fact that you're sensitive and insecure, don't I?" he murmured. "That capable act fools me sometimes."

How badly she wanted his arms around her, protecting and comforting and stimulating all at once. She hardly dared to breathe, afraid she would reveal her craving to be cared for. Aching with need, she kept her eyes lowered, not fighting.

With an impatient movement, Brandt released her and walked swiftly to the chair where his overcoat was. Inwardly Joan reeled from the sudden shock of standing alone.

"I have to pick up Angela. I'll be late if I don't leave now," he said sharply.

"Of course. It wouldn't do to keep her waiting." Her voice was low and controlled to hide the quiver of pain.

"That's right," Brandt said. "Unlike you, she wants my company."

He went quickly to the door that led into the outer hall. As his hand closed over the doorknob, he hesitated and turned back. It was very hard for Joan to meet his indifferent last look at her.

"Will you be all right alone here in the apartment?" The question was asked with grudging concern.

Joan was chilled by his oh-so-manly arrogance. "I'm going to be so busy tonight I doubt I'll even notice I'm alone," she said crisply. "Ed is flying in tomorrow morning and I have a ton of things to do before he arrives."

Brandt's gaze raked her face. "Lock and bolt the door when I leave," he ordered.

Joan did.

Chapter 6

The filing drawer of the metal cabinet was slammed shut as Joan walked into her office. She looked just in time to see Brandt glance at his watch.

"I'm five minutes early," she informed him coldly, going to the coatrack to hang up her coat.

When she turned around, he had propped his rangy frame against the cabinet. The hard line of his mouth was faintly curved in a smile.

"You're always punctual, Joan." His arms were folded over his chest. "But I did think you might cheat a bit this morning. Must have been a full weekend for you."

In truth, it had been a bore from beginning to end. Too many forced smiles and laughs. Too much pretending that she was actually enjoying Ed's company or his kisses.

"I don't let my personal life affect my work," Joan responded curtly. Going to her desk, she took her reading glasses from her bag and slipped them onto her nose. "Now, what was it you wanted from the filing cabinet?"

"You're all business today, Joan." The dry comment

mocked her attempt to distract him. "So how was your weekend? Everything you hoped for?"

"Please. You're not really interested in the details of what I do with Ed. And I don't want to hear about you and Angela."

There was altogether too much truth in her reply. Her entire weekend had been haunted by the thought of Brandt making love to the blonde.

His carved features hardened. "I want the completion schedule on the Blackwood project. Bring it in to my office." Then he straightened away from the cabinet and walked with long strides to the open door of his office. "Let me know when the cold war is over," he tossed back.

Joan was stung. "I don't know what you're talking about," she retorted.

Brandt stopped in the doorway, his eyes narrowing as he met her haughty look. "I'm not accustomed to getting hit with severe frostbite just because I asked a casual question," he snapped.

"We never confided in each other before and I see no reason to start now." Her voice matched his clipped tone.

"Touchy, aren't you?" His own annoyance had increased. "All I had in mind was an ordinary conversation. I would ask you how your weekend went and you would say just fine or great or something like that. And then, because I'm the boss, I would say something stuffy like, well, the fun is over, it's back to work for another week."

Joan flushed scarlet, firmly put in her place by his self-deprecating assessment. "Then I misunderstood. I'm sorry."

"Making mountains out of molehills is hardest for the mole," he said dryly. "And it's all uphill."

She nodded, still embarrassed. "True enough." Her mouth moved into a tentative smile. "Let's just drop it."

"Fine with me." A dancing gleam appeared in his eyes. "But I really do need that completion schedule. And we do have to get back to work."

Their truce was surprisingly solid. The constant tension no longer crackled in the air. True, it was bittersweet for Joan, but at least she didn't feel that she had to guard her every word on the chance that Brandt might misconstrue her meaning.

Besides, in the week of Christmas, it seemed so wrong to squabble. The holiday was supposed to be about peace on earth—and love, in a general sense. Where he was concerned, that emotion was quite specific. Her heart overflowed with love for Brandt, but in another month she would hand in her notice and no longer be a part of his life. And she would rather he thought of her as a casual friend than the instigator of a cold war. He would be less likely to question her motives.

Her fingers paused over the keyboard and she wished she hadn't reminded herself of her imminent departure. A minute before she'd felt full of Christmas spirit, looking forward to the joyous warmth of the holiday. She was determined not to let herself sink into a nameless depression, not even for an hour. Tonight she was taking a bus home to be with her family on Christmas Day. She didn't want that precious time to be overshadowed by pointless yearning for a man she couldn't have.

The door to her office opened and Kay floated into

the room, looking like one of Santa's helpers with her pixie curls and bright red dress and beaming smile.

"Aren't you ready? Almost everyone is in the lunchroom now, except you and Brandt Lyon," she scolded lightly.

Joan smiled back. Kay loved a party, and the annual Christmas fete at the office was the perfect outlet for her outgoing, bubbly personality.

"As soon as I finish this letter, I'll be done for the day," she replied.

"Who cares?" Kay sighed. "It doesn't matter if it gets done today or not. Tomorrow is Christmas and it isn't going to get delivered to wherever it's going. Besides, you could e-mail it."

"Nope. Has to be a hard copy for legal reasons. It'll only take me a few more minutes to finish it and then I won't have it waiting for me when I come back," Joan argued logically.

"Well, I'm not going to wait for you." Kay wrinkled her nose and glided toward the door. "The party starts at one thirty and it's now one thirty-five."

"I'll be there as soon as I can," Joan promised.

When the letter was done, she printed it out and set it with the others awaiting Brandt's signature and cleared her desk. Kay's bright spirits were a little contagious. She smiled to herself as she picked up the letters and went to the connecting door. She rapped lightly and entered at Brandt's muffled okay.

He was leaning back in the large leather chair, a suggestion of amusement in his eyes that Joan found disconcerting. He waved her over to his desk.

"These are ready to be signed," she said, placing the letters on his desk. "I'll see that they get out today."

"You're all done after this, aren't you?" He picked up a fountain pen and began to sign.

"Yes," Joan said quietly, liking the way the old-fashioned pen made precise, flowing strokes over the paper.

"You're late for the party," Brandt commented, not glancing up.

"So are you." A few days ago, before their truce, she wouldn't have been able to respond so lightly and naturally.

"Yes, but the boss is supposed to arrive late and leave early, so the employees can have a good time." He signed the last letter, but instead of handing them back to her, he began folding and inserting them into their attached envelopes, removing the protective strip from the self-sticking flap of each one with a flourish and sealing them. Then he looked up at her and smiled.

That smile sent shock waves through her system and she had to take a deep breath to compose herself. "I guess it's only natural that we're self-conscious when you're around."

Deliberately she added herself in as one among many other employees, although she didn't exactly fit. Her closeness to "the boss" meant her position in the company was unique.

"Are you self-conscious around me?" The letters were ready to go, but he kept them in his hand.

"Well, not so much. I mean, other people here know you, but from a distance," Joan qualified.

His gaze moved freely over her face and slightly guarded expression. "So to you, I'm not some omnipotent god with the sword of dismissal in my hand," he teased.

She decided to dodge that. "You're my employer," she said simply.

Her hand reached out for the letters. There was something omnipotent in his hold over her heart and senses, but he was a man, not a god. Almost reluctantly he gave her the envelopes.

The paper was warm to the touch where he'd held them, something that unnerved her a little. She had to get out of his office. "Okay," she said briskly. "That's taken care of. I think I'll head to the party now."

"Not yet." He rose from his chair and walked around the desk to where she stood. His compelling gaze held hers as Joan looked at him in confusion. "There's something I want to give you first."

"Oh?" Her voice was weak and barely audible as she watched him reach into his pocket and withdraw a flat, narrow case that looked expensive. Very expensive.

Behind the amused gleam in his eyes was something else that made her pulse race. Her hands fumbled as she took the box from him, and she stared dazedly at the name of a famous jewelry store scrolled across the fine-grained red leather of the lid.

"Open it," Brandt said.

He waited, watching. Joan fiddled with the clasp for a few seconds, then snapped the lid open. A white gold circle of linked ovals twinkled on a bed of dark velvet. Dangling from the bracelet was a whimsical and quite wonderful charm, also of white gold, in the shape of a filing cabinet. The drawer handles were studded with two tiny diamonds each in lieu of screws.

"Custom-made. I hope you like it," Brandt said. He looked at the twinkling bracelet and then at her.

Joan pressed her lips together, foolish tears of happiness filling her eyes. His gift touched her heart more than she wanted to admit. Since the very first day she'd entered his office, the filing cabinet had sometimes been the subject of disagreements when Brandt would misfile a document in her absence or create an uproar when he was unable to fathom the system, and sometimes it was useful. Either way, it was what brought them together.

"It's perfect," she assured him in a choked voice, trying to blink back the tears as she smiled at him. "Thank you."

A single tear slipped from her lashes. Brandt reached out and gently wiped the wet drop away with his thumb, letting his hand remain on the soft curve of her neck.

"You aren't going to misunderstand my motives for giving it to you, are you?" he mocked lightly. "You're still receiving your regular Christmas bonus just like every other employee of Lyon Construction. But this gift is from Brandt Lyon to Joan Somers only. In the spirit of Christmas, that's all."

For a frightened moment, Joan thought he was warning her and then she realized he was referring to the scene she'd made when he had paid her for the weekend they were stranded at the office.

"I understand," she murmured, still with a catch in her voice. Her finger touched the smooth links of the bracelet. "From one friend to another."

The lines around his mouth deepened into a wide smile, but some unspoken emotion kept the smile from reaching his eyes. "Let me help you put it on." He reached into the case for the bracelet.

Joan was beyond any protest as she offered her wrist to him. Deftly Brandt circled the bracelet around it and fastened the clasp. All she could think at that moment was that the pretty links chained her in a way that he perhaps never intended, chained her heart and soul. Soon he would own all of her and she would never be free.

Staring down at the strong hand holding hers, she wondered if it would be so very bad to really belong to Brandt, then flushed at her complete lack of pride. The silence that had fallen became too much for her, and Brandt's probing gaze didn't help.

"I . . . I suppose we'd better go to the party," she said softly, then realized she'd coupled herself and Brandt, unthinkingly.

"It's Christmas, a time for rejoicing," he said cryptically. At her puzzled frown, his mouth crooked a bit in a smile that wasn't a smile. "As in making merry and having fun. And maybe it's even time to let your hair down, Joan—literally. It's bad enough to have the boss around to spoil the fun, but you don't have to look like a schoolmarm."

Her hand flew to the smoothly coiled bun at the back of her neck.

"Yes, that," he said. His gaze raked the full length of her as her hand dropped to her side. With a smooth swiftness that didn't allow time for a protest, he turned her around and slipped the jacket of her green-and-gold tweed suit from her shoulders.

"What are you doing?" she asked breathlessly as the pressure of his hand brought her around to face him.

For a brief moment, he ignored her question, looking at her more thoughtfully now that she was minus the jacket. "You're going to a party," he said, and unfastened the top two buttons of her pale green silk blouse. His bold action made her gasp faintly, but he didn't take it any further. Still, she hardly knew what to think—and she wasn't going to be impossibly prissy and button herself right back up.

"That's better," he was saying cheerfully. "Now, do you want to let your hair down? I'd be happy to help."

She didn't doubt for an instant that he would and stepped quickly back out of his reach while her fingers fumbled for the pins in her hair. She couldn't understand why she was giving in so easily to his demands. Maybe it was because her intuition told her there was nothing more behind his request than the reason he'd stated—that, and the fact that she was reluctant to argue with him.

"Excellent." He gave an impersonal nod of approval as the last hairpin was removed and the molten gold flowed down her back.

Joan didn't see even a glint of admiration in his eyes. But then, what did she expect? For him to break into flowery compliments about her hair?

Strangely disappointed, she turned away. "I have a brush in my desk," she murmured, walking there to retrieve it from the center drawer. Brandt joined her, meandering over to the window where he stayed, gazing silently outside until he heard the desk drawer close.

"Are you ready?" he asked over his shoulder, hands clasped behind his back.

"Yes," she said, then, quickly, "no." Reaching into the side drawer of the desk, she self-consciously took out the flat, gift-wrapped box.

"A present for me?" Brandt guessed, looking tickled by the idea. "From you?"

"From all of the employees." A pale pink flush appeared in each cheek. "I—I didn't personally buy you a gift."

"I didn't expect that you would." The corners of his mouth twitched briefly upward. "If you had, I really would've wanted to know why." His gaze flicked to the wrapped box in her hand. "Did you pick it out?"

The red foil paper seemed to burn Joan's hand as she visualized the very expensive pen and pencil set inside. Considering the elegant bracelet and custom-made charm that now adorned her wrist, she wished she'd chosen something less impersonal.

"Yes," she admitted softly.

"Then I'm sure it's an appropriate gift for a group of employees to give to their boss." There was laughter in his low-pitched voice. "Come on." He came around to the front of her desk. "It's time I put in an appearance."

As she and Brandt entered the lunchroom, decorated in red and green for the occasion, Joan was awkwardly aware of heads turning to stare. It wasn't that she and Brandt had arrived together and late; it was her hair. Down, it tended to get noticed.

Several of the women besides Kay had seen Joan after work looking like this. Among themselves they'd wondered about her reasons for dressing so primly. The rest, including all the male employees, had never seen her in anything other than her self-imposed uniform and regulation hairstyle.

After the initial stillness, there was a general gravitation toward them. Brandt's hand occasionally rested on her back in an impersonal way, causing speculating looks from more than a few people. Her vague feelings of embarrassment grew and she confined herself to murmuring "Merry Christmas" now and then, and smiling nods of greeting.

She had completely forgotten the flat box in her hand until one of the women nudged her, saying, "What about the gift for Mr. Lyon?"

Instead of delivering the little speech she was

supposed to make, Joan held out the box to Brandt and said only, "This is from all of us at Lyon Construction. Merry Christmas."

Brandt winked broadly at the employees gathered around. "I wondered how long you were all going to make me wait for my gift."

His hands were completely occupied with the bright foil wrapping and Joan took the chance to slip to the far side of the room. Brandt seemed unaware of her departure and she wondered if he'd really meant to keep her at his side or whether she'd misinterpreted it.

The pleasure he expressed to the group when he opened the present sounded genuine, but hearing the tiny jingle of the bracelet around her wrist, she didn't experience any sensation of gladness. There was regret and a hint of inner sadness in her eyes as she gazed at the back of his head, then his profile when he turned slightly.

Then Brandt glanced over his shoulder. "You picked this out, didn't you, Joan?" he said as though he didn't already know. The people in front of her stepped to the side as he turned to face her. "You have excellent taste."

"I hope you like it." That would have to do—she couldn't think of any other reply.

"You'll have to remind me not to lend these to anyone, ever." He smiled, not seeming aware of how uncomfortable she was with everyone looking at her.

"Of course."

A sudden light gleamed in his eyes as he glanced above her head. "Now that's an invitation," he said dryly. "I wouldn't be human if I turned it down."

His statement bewildered Joan until she looked up and saw the ball of mistletoe hanging from the ceiling light fixture. Her cheeks were stained crimson when she brought her chin sharply level. In that fleeting second, Brandt had moved to her side. The room was agog with amused interest.

Helplessly Joan gazed into his bluntly carved face. "No, Brandt," she whispered.

"Where's your Christmas spirit, Joan?"

Her lashes fluttered down in dismay as his fingers closed over her chin. Her pulse thudded loudly in her ears. Then the warmth of his mouth was firmly covering hers for a not-exactly-chaste kiss that went on several seconds longer than propriety dictated. The onlookers cheered and whooped.

When the kiss was over, Joan reeled slightly toward him, but his hands lightly braced her shoulders, steadying her. Her eyes opened in embarrassed resentment as she met his watchful gaze.

Brandt chuckled softly. "Go ahead and slap me. That was worth it."

She would have liked to, if only to save her own pride.

"It was only an innocent Christmas kiss," he said to a guy from Accounting. The guy looked at him like the statement didn't add up.

She would have to agree. To her, the kiss was far from innocent, but Joan couldn't say that. There was very little she could say, so she opted for the usual.

"Merry Christmas." She inclined her head graciously and moved her mouth into a false smile.

Then Brandt turned to another male employee from a different department, subtly distracting attention from Joan. Kay appeared at her side, took one look at Joan's strained expression and began to chatter, maintaining the monologue until Joan was able to respond. Slowly Brandt worked his way around to most of the others, ending up on the opposite side of the room. The distance wasn't enough to ease her intense awareness of his presence.

Until Brandt left the party a half hour later, she felt as if she couldn't take an unrestricted breath. She would have liked to leave right after he did, but doing that would mean talk. Suspicion that something was going on between her and Brandt had surfaced again.

At his departure, some of the single men at the company began drifting to her side. Joan couldn't tell whether they were attracted by the way she looked or curious to find out if she really was the boss's office toy. None of them had ever appealed to her, and the faintly leering looks they were giving her now didn't help.

Tom Evers was the most persistent one. He gave her the impression that she should be overjoyed to have his undivided attention and he was still hanging around her an hour later. She flashed a silent look at Kay, signaling her for help, and her roommate responded right away, distracting him long enough for her to make an escape.

Her bus was leaving in an hour and a half for her hometown. She would just have time to pick up her overnight bag and another one filled with gifts at her apartment and catch a taxi to the bus depot. The last thing she wanted was for Tom Evers to offer her a ride. She might have to be blatantly rude to get him to accept a refusal, and this was not the time to make an enemy of one of her fellow employees.

The suit jacket Brandt had taken from her was where he'd left it, slung over the back of a straight chair in her office. She quickly slipped it on and retrieved her purse from the desk drawer, taking a precious few extra seconds to get the correct change for the city bus. As she started around the desk, Tom Evers appeared in the doorway. His stocky but muscular body blocked her way.

"So this is where you ran off to," he said, smiling at her suggestively. "You could have told me you wanted to go somewhere alone. I know a more comfortable place than this."

Joan hesitated for a fraction of a second, too aware of the length of empty hall that separated her office from the company lunchroom. Then she walked unhurriedly to the coatrack.

"I wasn't looking for a place to be alone. I'm leaving," she told him sharply. "I'm spending Christmas with my parents and I have a bus to catch."

He sidled closer. "I'll give you a ride home."

"No thanks," Joan replied.

"You sure?" he asked mockingly.

Her eyes blazed for a second, and she tried to step around him. Tom Evers had no intention of letting her get by.

"Don't I get a Christmas kiss, Joan?"

Ugh. A kick was what he deserved. "Get out of my way."

His hands shot out to grip her shoulders. He was only a couple of inches taller than her, but much stronger. She struggled hard to get free, sickened by the smell of hard liquor on his breath. They didn't serve that at company parties—he must have smuggled in his own.

"Let me go!"

The angry cry had barely left her lips when the connecting door burst open. Before she could gasp her relief at the sight of Brandt, he was pulling her out of the other man's hold, practically bouncing him off the wall in the process. The wind hadn't been completely knocked out of Tom, though, and his malevolent gaze darted from Brandt to Joan.

"She's your girl, huh?" He straightened up with some difficulty.

"Get out!" Brandt ordered in an ominously low voice. "And consider yourself terminated as of now. I'll deal with the details after the holidays."

"Yeah? You can shove it," was Evers' parting shot. "She's not worth the hassle." He walked stiffly out the door.

Quaking shivers chased over Joan's skin and she wrapped her arms around herself to control them. The memory of Tom's hot breath made her stomach churn. The places where he'd touched her felt contaminated.

Gentle fingers touched the flaming heat in her cheeks and she automatically pulled away from them. Then she realized Brandt was standing in front of her. His broad chest seemed so safe that she swayed against it without thinking.

"Are you all right, Joan?" His arms lightly encircled her. "Do you want me to call the cops?"

"I'm all right. No, don't call them—what if he files a formal complaint? You roughed him up but good." She felt better in his comforting embrace.

He smoothed her hair. "I shouldn't have kissed you in public."

It was getting too comfortable in his arms. Her hands pushed weakly against his chest and Brandt let her go. She gave him a grateful look.

"Thanks. I really am all right."

His gaze was guarded and so was his smile. "At least I was in my office. Good thing I overheard."

"I'm glad." Joan picked up the coat and purse she'd dropped.

"Do you have a bus to catch or was that an excuse to get rid of Evers?" Brandt asked.

"No, I really am going home for Christmas. My parents are expecting me." She glanced at her watch. "I have plenty of time to pick up my stuff at the apartment and make the bus."

"It might be hard to get a taxi." He looked at her inquiringly. "I was just leaving myself. How about a ride to your place and then to the depot?"

"I—" Joan was about to refuse, then found herself saying, "Yes."

The traffic both ways was heavy, what with everyone rushing all over the city in the annual Christmas chaos of last-minute shopping and company parties and family get-togethers. The ride turned out to be a lifesaver, as Joan had only ten minutes to spare when they arrived at the depot. Brandt went with her to the gate, insisting on carrying her overnight bag and the one with the presents, handing both over when she got in line with the other passengers to board.

"Merry Christmas, Joan," he said, offering his hand in good-bye as the boarding call for her bus blared over the loudspeaker.

"Merry Christmas, Brandt."

She wished she could have another hour to spend with him before leaving town, some extra time to help her relax after what had happened with Tom, but she knew she couldn't. Reluctantly she released his hand, tears filling her eyes as the line moved forward.

She thought about Brandt all the way to her hometown, staring out the bus window at the bleak fields of winter without really seeing them.

Chapter 7

The Christmas spent with her family had been pure contentment. The family tradition of putting the star on the top of the tree on Christmas Eve had been saved until Joan arrived. Her mother had set out a feast of wonderful things to eat and drink: homemade eggnog, fudge, popcorn balls, and Christmas cookies for everyone to gorge themselves on. It had been a blissfully happy reunion with all of them staying up until well after midnight, laughing and talking and reminiscing.

In theory, Santa Claus still visited the Somers house. Even though the younger generation of Somerses were all grown up, there was still a silly toy in every stocking on Christmas morning. Joan's father insisted that there was a little bit of child in everyone and kept up the fiction of Santa's mysterious night visit. The rest of the family knew for a fact that he was only after Santa's plate of extra cookies.

The best present of all had been when her older brother Keith called from Germany on Christmas morning. Of course, there it had been Christmas afternoon. Only once did Joan allow herself to wonder where Brandt was spending the holiday—probably, like her, with family.

With Christmas falling on a weekday, it was right back to work. Brandt's manner was business as usual, except for an offhand, "Did you enjoy your Christmas?"

He actually seemed bent on making up for the lost time. But a lot of people had taken a few days off in the interim, and that meant she'd have to scramble to get routine things done.

By late Friday afternoon, she felt as if she'd worked an entire week in two days. Yet she wasn't looking forward to the weekend. There would be too much idle time to think and she would rather work herself to exhaustion than suffer the pangs of unrequited love.

Her loss of concentration was brief, but it had only taken a minute for Joan to screw up a phrase in the boilerplate contract she was updating on the computer. With a tired sigh, she pulled up the original from her document files and compared the two side by side on her screen, correcting the mistake.

When she'd saved both, the phone rang. "Brandt Lyon, please," a sweetly feminine voice requested.

Joan cradled the receiver under her chin, glancing at too many unopened e-mails. "I'm sorry, but Mr. Lyon is in conference. May I have him return your call?"

"Are you his assistant?"

"Yes I am," Joan confirmed.

"Perhaps you could help me," the voice cooed. "This is Angela Farr."

Joan stopped staring into the screen.

"Brandt has tickets for a concert tomorrow night. Would you know which performance they're for? My parents are anxious to have Brandt join us for dinner and I don't know whether it would be best to make a reservation for dinner before or after the concert."

The question and its many implications knocked the contract right out of Joan's mind, but she couldn't summon up a reply. She felt a cold chill come over her as she thought how well the delicately melodious voice matched the fragile blonde.

"I'm sorry," Joan said. She hoped and prayed her voice didn't sound the least little bit envious or resentful. "Mr. Lyon handles all his personal appointments himself. I don't have that information."

There was a regretful sigh. "Would you tell Brandt that I called and ask him to get in touch when he's free?"

"Of course."

"He has both my numbers. Thanks so much."

"Not at all." It took a lot of willpower not to slam the receiver down.

Joan didn't need anyone to explain that things were getting serious between Brandt and Angela if they were already at the meet-the-parents stage. Driven by frustration, she pulled up the contract on her screen again just to have something to do and found six more mistakes in her redraft. Joan swore under her breath and started over. She had it nearly completed when Brandt returned from the conference room with the project superintendents.

"Do you have the Hadley contract ready?" were his first words to her.

"Almost," Joan replied, her tone angry and tight.

Brandt frowned. "I thought you'd have that finished by now."

"I was nearly done, but I found some errors. And I was interrupted by phone calls."

The messages were lying on her desk. Brandt

picked them up, sifting through them. Joan saw him
hesitate when he got to the note about contacting a
certain fluffy female.

He caught her watchful look. "Angela Farr called?"

"Yes, she did. Twenty minutes ago," Joan responded, trying to keep a professional crispness in
her tone and not betray her stinging jealousy. "She
wanted to know which of tomorrow's performances
you had tickets for."

Blue and probing, his gaze swept her controlled expression, then went back to the messages in his hand
as he turned to leave. "Bring that Hadley contract in
as soon as you're done."

With only a third of a page to finish, Joan had the
contract printed, separated into copies, and stapled
within a few minutes. She walked to the connecting
door and her hand turned the knob an instant
before she started to knock. Brandt's voice floated
out to her.

"Angela," he was saying forcefully. "I'm sorry, but
I have to fly to Peoria tomorrow. Jake Lassiter, the en-
gineer out of Springfield, Missouri, is meeting me
there to go over the owner's changes on an interior
layout. What? Listen, if I could send someone else in
my place, I would."

A pause followed as Angela made an unheard response to his statement. Discretion ordered Joan to
close the door and wait until Brandt was off the
phone, but she disobeyed it.

"Yes. That too. If I thought I could make it back in
time, I wouldn't be canceling our plans, would I?" he
asked with a thin edge of exasperation. "Your father's
a businessman, I'm sure he'll understand." Another
pause. "Angela, I'm not going to argue with you. I

have a thousand things to do. It's called making a living. We'll discuss it tonight. And I am sorry."

Joan heard Brandt hang up and she rapped lightly on the door. When she entered his office, he was holding the receiver again and punching in another number. At least she hoped it was another number. Just how much of a claim did Angela Farr have on him? He barely glanced at the contract she slid onto his desk, nodding a brisk approval and waving her away.

"Craig Stevens, please. This is Brandt Lyon returning his call."

Joan closed the connecting door behind her, deriving no pleasure from the discovery that Brandt wasn't meeting Angela's parents tomorrow night. He was still seeing her this evening.

If her weekend were a paint color, she would have to call it Melancholy Blue. Not even a bright, sunshiny Monday could chase away her depressed mood. And Brandt spent all of Monday and Tuesday with Dwayne Reed from his estimating staff, going over the prices and cost estimates that had to be revised because of the changes to the Peoria job. Joan couldn't decide if she was happy or sad to see so little of him. With her heart twisting itself into knots, it hurt as much not to see him as it did to see him.

Joan was lolling in a bubble bath when Kay called out that she and John were leaving. Joan wished them both a good time, then felt the silence seep into the apartment as the water grew lukewarm, then close to cold. Sighing heavily, she thought that spending New Year's Eve alone was going to be a habit.

Kay had suggested arranging a date for her with one of the men John worked with, but Joan had quickly vetoed that. For once, Kay hadn't pushed her to accept. Since the office party, Joan knew Kay had guessed some of what was happening. But she wasn't about to cry on anyone's shoulder. Lots of women had fallen in love with the wrong guys before and gotten over it. She would too. In time.

The silence was getting to her. Joan drained the chilly, bubbly bathwater and turned on the hot tap full blast, splashing around and making a racket, then giving a little yelp when it got too hot. She ran some cold water for a final overall slosh-and-rinse that cheered her up somewhat. After clambering out and toweling briskly dry, she unpinned her hair and slipped into the warm velour robe that her parents had given her for Christmas. In the combined kitchen, living, and dining room, she switched on the small TV set that was on loan from her brother while he was in Germany. Not finding the remote, she didn't bother to change the channel from the football game in progress. Random noise. What she wanted.

As she fixed a huge bowl of buttered popcorn, Joan wondered idly whether Brandt and Angela were celebrating the New Year in private or at a party. The refrigerator door banged as she tried to shut out both thoughts from her mind. With a glass of Coke in one hand and the bowl of popcorn balanced in the other, she walked back to the couch.

Propping a book in her lap, she had barely settled back against the cushions when she heard a single set of footsteps coming up the stairs. She smiled in sympathy for whomever it was that had to spend New Year's Eve alone too. Then she thought wistfully that it might be someone's date. It was almost nine o'clock, but some parties didn't start until late. It took her a full second to realize that the subsequent knock she heard was on her apartment door.

Frowning with bewilderment, she set down her book and padded in her bare feet to the door. She left the chain latch hooked and opened the door the few inches it allowed to view her unexpected visitor.

"Brandt?" She blinked quickly to be sure she wasn't imagining him.

"May I come in?"

He didn't disappear and the voice matched. Joan slid the chain latch off and opened the door, still expecting him to vanish somehow. He was wearing jeans and a sweater—she had seen him in evening wear and business suits but never this casual. No sheepskin jacket—a parka was hooked on his finger by the hood and slung over his shoulder. The sweater was probably cashmere—it looked that soft. It matched his blue eyes. He had on dark jeans and boots that would get him through snow if there was any—both emphasized the muscular length of his legs.

"I saw the light in your apartment from the street and wondered if you were home." He came inside and closed the door in back of him.

"Oh." Not much of an answer, but he still hadn't said why he was here. His unexpected visit didn't feel like stalking or anything—it was just a visit, she was sure of it.

He wandered past her with a smile and stood in front of the TV. "Is it a good game?"

"I don't know. I just turned it on a couple of minutes ago."

"Looks like it's really about to get going." He was holding his parka now, like he didn't know where to put it.

"Let me take that," she offered. "We can watch the

game together if you like." The words were barely out of her mouth when he was sitting down.

She was happy enough to see him, but still confused. Had he and Angela gotten into a fight about something? She couldn't think of any other reason for him to come here. But it wasn't exactly flattering to be his default date. Even so, here he was.

"How about a Coke and some popcorn?" she offered.

Brandt seemed to come back from some distant place. "Sure." His gaze slid to her in acknowledgment for a brief instant.

"Soda is all we have. No champagne or anything. Sorry about that." She wondered why she was apologizing.

"Sounds great." His absentminded answer was just loud enough to be heard over the hyper sports announcer, who talked much too fast.

She went to the refrigerator and fussed for a little while with the ice and the soda, pouring from a large plastic bottle and letting the foam settle before she brought him the glass. Brandt was already helping himself to the popcorn. His quiet thanks left her with nothing to do but seat herself again. He seemed disinclined to make small talk. She couldn't guess whether he was that into the game or thinking about something that had happened before he showed up here. She was more inclined to think that something had happened. She tried to pretend to be interested in football, but she really wasn't. Brandt's presence was a potent distraction.

"Did you enjoy the visit with your family on Christmas?" he asked suddenly.

"Yes, very much," she answered, fiddling with the pages of the book beside her. "My brother called from Germany on Christmas morning. I think that was the best present he could have given my mother."

"Was this the first Christmas your family hasn't all been together?"

"Yes." She glanced at him in surprise. "How did you guess?"

"Just something in your voice. Bet you were happy when he called too. You must be close to your brother." There was a suggestion of a smile in his otherwise expressionless face.

"I am," she admitted. "We always were, except for a few years when he couldn't stand girls, especially sisters. That didn't last." She hesitated, unwilling to let the conversation die. "I suppose you spent Christmas with your folks."

"Yes, I did. My sister Venetia wasn't able to make it home. She called, but that was before I arrived for the traditional family feast."

"My mother made fudge and cookies and all that." Joan leaned her head against the back of the couch and grinned. "I probably gained five pounds in one day."

He nodded, then looked around before he changed the subject slightly. "Wasn't Ed able to fly in for New Year's Eve?"

"No." Joan hadn't asked Ed to come and he hadn't suggested it. In fact, he hadn't said a word about when he would be back.

"Hmm. So you'd rather stay at home on New Year's Eve than celebrate with someone else?"

"I wouldn't put it quite like that. But I didn't have other offers," she answered truthfully. "What about you? I thought you and Angela would have had plans for this evening."

Brandt reached for a handful of popcorn and munched

it. She waited for his eventual reply, wondering if she should have asked, but somehow she just had to know why he had stopped by.

He tossed the last fluffy kernel in his hand into his mouth and ate it, then sat back. "Would you mind if we didn't discuss Angela tonight?" he asked.

So they'd had an argument. That fit. Joan drew a deep breath and answered, "I didn't particularly want to discuss her. I guess I was just curious why you were here instead of at some fabulous party."

"I prefer your company." His dark blue gaze pinned hers. The lines around his mouth deepened into smiling grooves at the disbelieving look in her brown eyes. "Don't look so surprised, Joan."

"I can't help it. I am."

He chuckled softly. "If I didn't come to see you, why else would I be here?"

There wasn't any other reason that Joan could think of, especially since it was obvious that he wasn't here to discuss business. So she made no response.

No matter what he said, she couldn't shake off the feeling that an argument with Angela was the real reason for Brandt coming to her apartment. And she didn't think she liked being used as a means of solace or revenge or whatever he was after.

The ensuing silence, broken by an occasional comment from him on the game, couldn't be described as companionable. One couch cushion separated them, but for Joan's nerves, that wasn't nearly enough. When the delayed newscast came on, she sat through the world and local news, but got up as the sports came on with highlights of the game they'd just watched.

That brought an immediate, questioning look from Brandt. "Just thought I'd wash the popcorn popper and butter pan," she explained hastily. Glancing at his empty glass, she added, "Would you like some more Coke?"

"Please." He handed her the glass.

While the water was running into the sink, she refilled the glass and carried it back to him, then returned to shut off the faucet, wishing she had a sinkful of dishes to wash instead of just a few. All too soon there was only the popcorn popper left. As Joan reached for it, Brandt handed it to her. He had crossed the room with catlike quietness. Surprised, she nearly dropped it.

"I thought you were on the couch," she laughed shakily.

"Would you like some help?"

"No," Joan said. "This is the last thing."

Brandt stayed near the sink, watching her scrub the popcorn popper. Not the most fabulous New Year's Eve for either of them, she thought wryly. But it was better than being lonely. Maybe.

"Have you lived here long?" he asked.

"Nearly three years. Kay and I moved in together just after I came to work for you. We both had smaller places that were still too expensive and were too far from work. When we saw this one on Craigslist, we jumped on it," she answered with forced calm.

"When is—Kay getting married?"

"She wants to be a June bride." Joan smiled. Kay did do a few things by the book, and her wedding was going to be traditional in every way.

"What are you going to do?"

"I'll have to find another roommate," she replied as she rinsed the suds from the sink. "But it's going to be hard to find someone as easygoing and fun as Kay."

"Not even your boyfriend?" His mouth twitched with amusement at her look of indignant surprise. "Oh, sorry. So you're not planning to take that relationship to the next level, I guess."

Joan swallowed hard. "That's none of your business, but the answer is no. Ed is more than a friend, but—"

"He just isn't Mr. Right," Brandt stated with obvious satisfaction.

There was a trace of temper in her eyes as she turned to face him. "Would you mind if we didn't discuss Ed?" She deliberately echoed the words of his request concerning Angela, and the bright gleam in his eyes told her he'd noticed that.

With the dishes done and the sink cleaned, Joan would have returned to the couch, but his hand lightly touched the long sleeve of her robe, halting her as effectively as a high-voltage wire.

"I like your robe. Did you get that for Christmas?" His approving look burned the length of her body, a potent reminder that she was wearing practically nothing underneath the soft velour.

"My parents gave it to me," she admitted with an odd, breathless note in her voice.

His hand fell away, but her breathing didn't return to normal. She forced herself to go over to the TV and change the channel—God only knew where the remote was—from the New Year's celebrations starting all over the country to some old Humphrey Bogart movie. As she straightened up, Brandt was standing in her path to the couch, a serious, watchful look in his eyes.

"Do you want me to leave, Joan?"

Oh, God. She never wanted him to leave. It was a totally unfair question.

Striving to sound offhand, she replied, "You're welcome to stay as long as you like."

"You'd better rephrase that," Brandt said dryly.

Her pulse raced and a wave of heat swept over her face. She swiftly looked away from the troubling intensity of his gaze.

"You don't have to stay, if that's what you're thinking," she said stiffly. "I was just trying to be polite."

"Oh, you're very polite. But not enthusiastic," he chided in a grim voice.

"Well, what do you want me to say?" The question was rhetorical—it wasn't as if she wanted to please him.

"That depends," he began. "If you're being polite to me because I'm the CEO of Lyon Construction, then my answer would be to leave now. On the other hand, if you're talking to me as a man, I'll stay as long as you want."

"Don't talk in riddles," she snapped. She went around him, afraid the confusion in her heart would make her read more into his words than he meant. Swiftly as a big cat, he captured her and brought her close.

"Sorry," he murmured. "Let me make myself perfectly clear."

His hand slid beneath her long hair, tilting her head back to give her a scorching kiss. Joan could sense the hunger in his exploring mouth and responded in kind, unable to resist his lips or his caressing hands for deliriously long moments. Gently he released her and drew her down to the couch, where he cradled her across his lap.

Mesmerized by the unfathomable light in his eyes, Joan stared at him, waiting tensely for another kiss and not disappointed when he possessively covered her lips. Her pride was gone. Physical desire hadn't destroyed her defenses, but the intensity of her hidden love for him did.

She lay in his arms, pliant and responsive to his expertly sensual lovemaking. The desire for total surrender was inescapable, and she wanted nothing more than to be completely his.

Somehow, she managed to remember that he had rejected her once—and that memory became stronger.

On fire with arousal, Brandt didn't seem to guess that her response had changed from willing submission to a subtle struggle to be free of his embrace. She moved out of his arms, though, standing a little shakily beside the couch, her brown eyes misting with love as she turned away.

"I need a drink," she said, more to herself than him. She never made it to the cabinet. The hands sliding around her waist brought her to an abrupt stop. She inhaled sharply as Brandt buried his head in the side of her neck. Her fingers closed over his wrists, but she didn't attempt to remove his hands from her waist.

"I don't think you do," Brandt muttered huskily as his lips teased her throbbing pulse. "I know I don't. All I want is to make love to you. Is that wrong?"

"Oh, Brandt," she whispered. She couldn't summon up a definite yes or no, besieged by her own uncertainty.

The pressure of his hands turned her around, molding her against the length of his body, letting her know how much he needed and wanted her. Her hands slipped around his neck, a wild singing in her heart blocking out all sound. She was overwhelmed by emotions, eager to surrender. He kissed her again and again.

A key turned in the lock and the apartment door

was opened. A tiny, startled "Oh!" seemed amplified a thousand times louder when Joan finally registered it, a second after Brandt stiffened against her.

Her hands dragged themselves from around his neck and she felt the ragged beating of his heart as her fingers trailed over his chest. She still hadn't guessed the cause of the sound and her gaze moved over his face. But he was looking at the door, suddenly wary. Joan turned in confusion.

A red-faced Kay and John had returned and looked back, standing just inside the door. Like a child caught playing with matches, Joan put her hands instinctively behind her back as if to hide the evidence, and moved out of the interrupted embrace.

"I'm so sorry, Joan," Kay muttered fervently. "I didn't guess that—that anyone else would be here."

Especially not Brandt Lyon, Joan added silently, her cheeks flushing scarlet. She drew a shaky breath.

"It's all right," she said aloud.

"Speak for yourself." Brandt muttered almost inaudibly with a piercing look at Joan. Then he turned to Kay. "Hello and good-bye is all there is to say, I guess."

He grabbed his parka from the couch but didn't put it on, not quite ready to run the gauntlet of Kay and John. There wasn't much those two could do but walk all the way in, a silent apology still in Kay's eyes.

"Can I talk to you for a minute, Joan?" Brandt asked brusquely.

Joan stood still for only a second. "Of course," she breathed, moving self-consciously to his side.

Brandt didn't stop in the open doorway but continued into the hall, reaching behind her to close the door. Not wanting to meet his eyes, she stared at the carpet beneath her feet. The silence between them was almost ominous. She could feel Brandt's brooding gaze studying her.

"Will you come with me?" His blunt question stopped her heart for an instant.

She should have said an outright no. Instead she asked, "Where?"

He didn't answer right away, waiting until Joan glanced up. "To my place." His calmness was unnerving.

"No." She didn't trust herself to add one more word.

His sigh reopened the wound in her heart. "Why?" he demanded quietly.

She turned completely away from his searching gaze. "It's just that—Brandt, don't even ask. You shouldn't have come here tonight."

She couldn't answer his question. But now that she wasn't blissfully wrapped in his arms, now that she could think, she knew she didn't want to be the woman who soothed his hurt feelings when Angela had had enough of him for one night. It was the only logical reason for him to stop by on New Year's Eve. He had no other motive that she could imagine.

"Then why didn't you kick me out?"

"How could I?" Joan gave a bitter sigh.

"By answering honestly when I asked whether I should stay or go," Brandt snapped impatiently.

Tears stung her eyes as Joan forced out an obvious answer. "And how does an employee tell her boss to leave?"

"Is that what was on your mind?" The lack of anger in his voice made his words all the more cutting.

"Well, yes." There was some truth to her statement.

But it wasn't the whole truth. She stuck to it anyway. "I don't want to lose my job."

He shrugged into his parka. "You won't. But you did seem to be enjoying yourself during that red-hot kiss. Good a way as any to keep a job, wouldn't you say?" He flipped up the hood, but it fell back, leaving his hair spiky. It went with his exasperated look.

"You have absolutely no right to say things like that," Joan whispered. "I'm pretty damn sure you got dumped tonight, or something like it. You came over to get next to me so you could get back at Angela, whether she knew it or not. Did you enjoy your revenge?"

"Not really," Brandt shot back. "It seems safe to assume I was a stand-in for Ed."

Joan said nothing. Her heart was shattering into a thousand pieces. She could have endured his indifference, but after tonight everything had changed between her and Brandt. He believed she'd deceived him.

His hand gripped her shoulder and he turned her around, clasping her chin to position her for a totally unexpected farewell kiss. Hotter than the first. Then he released her, his diamond blue eyes hard and cold.

"Happy New Year, Joan," he said cynically. Then he strode down the hall to the stairs.

Chapter 8

When Joan returned to work after the New Year holiday, the atmosphere around the office had changed radically. On the surface, Brandt was as professional and businesslike as always, but his eyes held an odd expression whenever he glanced at her, which wasn't often. She told herself to forget about it and not be so thin-skinned.

But by the end of the first day, Joan knew the situation was intolerable. There was no reason to postpone her resignation. Brandt would undoubtedly be glad to see her leave.

Kay was more than sympathetic when Joan relayed her decision. They had talked and talked over the holiday. Kay had bitterly opposed Joan's returning to work on the second day of the new year. She insisted that there was no need for her to give notice, not after the way Brandt had acted. With a resume like Joan's, Kay said, she'd be able to get a job anywhere, and if that didn't happen right away, Kay's salary would cover their expenses if they budgeted.

But Joan was adamant about giving two weeks' notice unless she could find a qualified replacement in the meantime. Eventually Kay stopped arguing about it, although she still believed that Joan was wrong.

Her intention was to type her letter of resignation as soon as she arrived at the office the next morning, but the instant she came in there seemed to be a hundred and one things Brandt wanted done yesterday. Joan didn't have a free moment until her lunch break. Once the letter was typed and printed out, she kept waiting for a chance to give it to him, but he had his weekly meeting with the project superintendents and it dragged on forever. At closing time he was still in the conference room. Friday was just as bad.

For the entire weekend, the resignation letter stayed tucked away in a folder. On Monday morning she went in to the office determined that the first thing she was going to do was give the damn thing to Brandt. Taking the mail, the day's appointment book, and the all-important letter, she knocked on the connecting door and entered when she heard his low-voiced okay.

Brandt was on the phone and motioned for her to sit down. She took a seat in front of his desk and shifted the letter to the top, wanting to get it over with first. Her mind was going over all her well-rehearsed explanations, so she paid no attention to his business conversation. When he hung up, Joan took a deep breath in preparation for her speech, but she didn't have a chance to open her mouth.

"Is there anything critically important in the mail? As in things that need my immediate attention?" Brandt said, already rising from his desk.

She took her letter from the top of the pile she was holding and hesitated. "No, but—" she began.

"Cancel my appointments for today," he interrupted, going to get his coat. "If you need me, I'll be at the Chalmers Street site."

"What?" Joan said blankly. She couldn't very well stick the letter under his nose to force him to read it.

"That was Lang on the phone," he replied, knowing that Joan knew Bob Lang was the project superintendent on that building site. "One of the service elevators malfunctioned. It fell three stories to the basement and two of our guys were trapped inside."

"Oh my God. Are they seriously hurt?" She rose to follow Brandt out, all thought of the letter in her hand gone.

"One is unconscious and the other probably has a broken leg. The paramedics stabilized both men at the scene—most likely they'll be on the way to the hospital by the time I get there." He was struggling into his coat as he opened the hallway door.

"Do you want me to call their families?"

"Bob did. And I'll speak to everyone personally." He was half-running and it wasn't easy to keep up with him. "So you have to cover for me here."

"Yes, of course—"

"I'll be out of the office all day. We can't raise the elevator without the safety inspectors on the scene and the other elevators will have to pass inspection. Bob's contacting them now."

"I understand—"

Only when Brandt had dashed out the door and Joan was back at her desk preparing to make the necessary calls to cancel his appointments did she remember that she still hadn't delivered her resignation. Fate seemed to be conspiring against her and she didn't want any more time to reconsider her decision. No way was she going to tear up her letter the way she'd torn up that check he'd replaced and prolong her misery.

Later, Bob called in to confirm that one of the construction workers had suffered a concussion and the other man had broken his leg. Brandt had made a whirlwind visit to the office and headed back to the site. And the letter was still locked in her desk drawer.

Brandt wasn't in the office the following morning when Joan got in. The constant waiting made her nerves even more tense. Still, it didn't count as suffering, considering what had happened to the guys on the site. Not as carefully as before, she slid the letter into the morning's mail and added the appointment book in preparation for Brandt's arrival. She was on the phone when he walked in. Her heart constricted at the lines of tiredness etched in his strong face. He paused beside her desk, waiting until she hung up.

"Bob Lang will be here in about ten minutes," he told her. "I want Lyle Baines in my office when Bob and I go over the safety reports. Make sure he's available."

"Mr. Connelly is supposed to go over the accounts with you this morning," Joan reminded him quickly.

"I already put him off until this afternoon." An impatient frown added to his preoccupied look. "You get Baines."

Joan picked up the receiver and punched in the extension while Brandt waited. From the corner of her eye, she saw him pick up the mail and appointment book with her letter of resignation sandwiched between the two. She said quickly, "He's not picking up. I'll go over those with you in a minute."

"That won't be necessary," he responded and walked to his office door.

At that moment, Lyle Baines answered and Joan

was unable to stop Brandt. She'd always intended to hand him her resignation personally, not have him discover it with the morning mail. The instant she'd passed his message on to Lyle, she rose hastily from her chair, trying to think of a pretext to intercept the letter before Brandt found it. She couldn't—and fate was against her once more as the ringing phone distracted her. Joan picked up and began to jot down an irritatingly long message. The intercom buzzed loudly at the same second that Bob Lang walked in the door, followed by Lyle Baines.

Unwillingly, Joan flicked on the intercom switch. "Bob and Lyle are here to see you."

"Ask them to come back in half an hour. I want to talk to you."

The authoritative tone in his voice came clearly over the speaker. Both men had heard, so there was no need for Joan to repeat Brandt's clipped words. She accepted their silent nods of agreement with an uncomfortable smile, tension knotting her stomach as they left.

The connecting door had barely closed behind her when Brandt spoke. "I have an explanation coming, Joan." The letter of resignation was pushed to the front of his desk, toward her.

"I'm sorry." She stood up straight, pretending a confidence she didn't feel. "I meant to give it to you personally, not like that—just mixed in with the mail, I mean."

"Yeah? It's dated last Thursday. Why am I getting it now?"

Her chin tilted slightly. "I would've given it to you on Thursday, but you were in the conference room all afternoon and I didn't want to leave it for you to find when I was gone," she explained crisply. "And ever since, you've been very busy or out of the office."

His finger tapped a corner of the letter impatiently. "You didn't explain your reasons for leaving."

She looked at it instead of him. Warmth began spreading over her face and she wished she'd put on her glasses before coming in. They were a shield of sorts, after all.

"I thought that would be obvious," she murmured.

"Not to me," Brandt returned smoothly.

"You can't expect me to work for you after— after—" Her initial outburst died away into an embarrassed whisper. Her hands clenched nervously and she turned at a right angle away from the desk.

"After what?" he prompted.

"After the other night," Joan finished tautly.

"Which night are you referring to?"

"You know very well I mean New Year's Eve," she burst out angrily. Why was he pretending to be stupid?

"As I recall," Brandt leaned back in his chair, at ease and in charge, "that night you were concerned about losing your job. And now you want to give it up. I don't get it."

"It's a free country. I can change my mind."

"Do you have another job lined up?"

"I wasn't going to look for one until I gave notice here," she told him sharply.

"I suppose you'll want to use my name as a reference." A thick brow arched in question.

"I believe my work has been satisfactory." There was a flash of pride in the way she tossed her head.

"Above and beyond the call of duty," Brandt said with a dry smile.

"Would you stop implying things?" Joan asked bitterly.

"Okay. Let's spell it out. You let me kiss you and didn't protest for a second, and it happened more than once. I took advantage of your invitation, put it that way. But I didn't take advantage of you."

"Don't split hairs, Brandt. You sound like a politician who got caught in the act."

He grinned this time. "We didn't get caught. But I think we both enjoyed what happened."

"Maybe."

"More than maybe. I'm pretty sure I can tell when a woman is being kissed or doing the kissing." He leaned forward to pick up the letter. "Please don't make any more rash moves, okay? I'd hate to lose a great assistant because you wanted to have some fun."

Was that all it had been to him? Joan bit the inside of her lip so he wouldn't see her do it. "Too bad. Two weeks is plenty of time to find a replacement."

"Is it?" One corner of his mouth quirked. "But what if I can't?" With slow deliberation, he tore the letter into quarters and tossed it in the wastebasket.

"Don't do that." She glared at him. "I can print out another one with a new date. And another one. Eventually you'll get the point."

"I'm well aware of how stubborn you can be," Brandt said, "but I really am asking you to reconsider your decision. If you still feel the same way next week, let's discuss it again."

"I'm not going to change my mind!"

"Joan—you're making my life complicated. I wonder if I'll ever understand you." Then he sighed and bent over the spreadsheets on his desk. "Now get Lang and Baines in here, please."

Joan never did tell Kay that Brandt hadn't exactly accepted her resignation. She had every intention of resubmitting her letter on Monday morning, so she told her roommate that her two weeks' notice would begin then. Kay thought it was unfair and said so in no uncertain terms.

On Friday night, Kay started trolling employment Web sites, insisting that Joan update her resume and post it on some. Given the dismal state of the economy, she ought to begin applying right away, Kay said, adding that Joan might as well begin on Saturday morning.

There wasn't any plausible reason not to apply for likely openings, but Joan didn't look forward to it, though she told herself over and over a change would do her good. She needed to make the transition from this job to the next as soon as possible.

Yet she felt a sense of relief when Ed Turner arrived unexpectedly from Cleveland on Saturday morning. All Kay's big plans were set aside for a weekend of fun that included Joan and Ed with her and John. Most of Saturday afternoon was spent in a friendly argument between the four of them about where they would go for dinner and whether to take in a movie or a live band afterward at a local club.

Finally it ended in a compromise: Ed and John agreed to cook an Italian dinner for all of them at the apartment.

The incongruity of seeing the staid, quiet John in a frilly apron and his older, somewhat wilder brother Ed in a long bib apron from Joan's mother got both Joan and Kay laughing in near hysteria. The evening promised to be generally unromantic, but that was infinitely preferable as far as Joan was concerned.

Kay was rescuing the cooked spaghetti that Ed was just about to pour into the sink after nearly boiling the strands dry when there was a knock at the door.

"Oh no," John moaned. "It must be the apartment

manager. He probably smelled the spaghetti water boiling over and called the fire department!"

"Either that or he's coming to the rescue with a fire extinguisher," Kay giggled, waving at the vague scent of scorched cooking in the air.

"Or worse," Joan said in a pseudo-whisper as she hurried to the door. "It might be that old lady down the hall. She's probably outraged that we're entertaining men in our apartment and called the cops."

There was a loud burst of laughter from the other three at that statement. Joan was doing her best to conceal a smile as she opened the door. It vanished as she stared at Brandt.

"Hello, Joan," he said quietly, looking at her and then past her, hearing the others chatting.

"Ah, Brandt—"

"Who is it, babe?" Ed's voice came ringing clearly between them.

The look in Brandt's eyes immediately hardened into something cold and withdrawn. Joan ignored Ed's question, knowing the door blocked Brandt from view.

"Did . . . you want something?" she asked in a lowered voice.

A slight frown drew his brows together. "I wanted to take you to dinner tonight." His piercing gaze shifted from her face to the room behind her. "I should have called."

Joan stiffened. "Why would you want to take me out? Doesn't Angela have first claim on you?"

His mouth tightened. "There were some things I thought you and I should get straightened out. Obviously I was wrong."

"What things?" she asked, desperately needing to know.

Brandt didn't answer right away. He studied her face, lingering for heart-stopping seconds on her parted lips. Her shoulders quivered lightly at the almost physical touch. He averted his gaze, staring down the empty corridor outside the apartment.

"I wasn't going to invite you to my place, if that's what you're thinking," he replied grimly.

"That's not fair," Joan breathed. "I didn't think that at all."

"Didn't you?" he said harshly. "Weren't you already questioning my motives, the way you already have?"

"Brandt—" His name was spoken in a beseeching plea for understanding.

She wanted to explain that she couldn't trust him because she cared so deeply and knew he didn't reciprocate the emotion. For her, just having dinner with him would be too much to bear. But she wasn't going to say that. At that instant an arm draped possessively around her shoulders.

"I'm sorry about the noise," Ed was saying to Brandt. "I'm sure Joan explained that we'll keep it down." He saw Brandt's gaze shift with hard amusement to the frilly apron Ed was wearing. "My brother and I playing chef tonight. We had a kitchen disaster that got us all laughing."

"Ed." Joan touched his hand, realizing that Brandt's air of authority had caused Ed to mistake him for the manager. "This is my boss, Brandt Lyon."

"Oh geez, I'm sorry." Ed smiled broadly at his own mistake. He took his arm from around Joan's shoulder and extended a hand to Brandt in greeting. "I suppose it was a guilty conscience that made me think you were the manager. I'm Ed Turner. Joan's told me a lot about you, Mr. Lyon."

Joan was aware of Brandt's intent inspection of the

man beside her. At the last statement, his cobalt blue gaze moved to her.

"Has she?" he murmured, shaking Ed's hand courteously. "Nothing complimentary, I imagine."

There was a quick flow of color into her face, but Ed laughed easily. "Hardly. Joan's really loyal. She talks about you with respect. Admiration, even." He glanced from Brandt to Joan. "So, what's up? An emergency at the office?"

"I had a couple of quick questions to ask Joan before Monday. Relatively minor, but I didn't want to wait," Brandt replied. "She's set me straight. Sorry for barging in like this."

"No problem," Ed declared, waving the apology away. "Hey, if you're not doing anything, come on in and have a glass of wine with us. We're going to have to start over on the dinner preparations, though. Okay with you, Joan?"

There was little else she could do but nod agreement. Brandt hesitated for a moment, then shrugged. "All right. Thanks."

When the apartment door closed behind the three of them, Kay called out from the kitchen side of the room. "Did you make nice to Mr. Grady?" Then she glanced over her shoulder, startled to see Brandt. Her open mouth shut like a trap at Ed's next remark.

"Joan and I invited Brandt to have a glass of wine with us," he announced.

Bright brown eyes darted a fiery look at Joan. Kay seemed to be asking a silent question: *Have you lost your mind?*

But then Kay had never been one to hide what she was feeling and there was open disapproval in her expression when she greeted Brandt. Even John's hello seemed reserved. Only Ed was clueless, not picking up on the sudden tension in the room.

As Joan passed around glasses of wine that John poured, she was all too conscious of the cool blue eyes that followed her every move.

Their apartment was noticeably short of extra chairs. Brandt was seated in the rocker and Kay was perched on the footstool in front of the couch where John sat down. Ed was sitting on the opposite end of the couch. The only vacant place for Joan was the cushion beside Ed. She wasn't going to banish herself to one of the chrome dinette chairs. That would be a tacit admission that Brandt's presence unnerved her, so she chose the couch.

Ed's arm was resting along the back of it. There was a hint of amusement in Brandt's look, but the slight curl of his lip added an edge of contempt to it. Joan realized that the arm so near her shoulder had to indicate a familiar intimacy to Brandt. Whatever. She sensed that her boss was getting a certain satisfaction from her discomfort. He'd known her long enough to read her emotions fairly well. She had to wonder whether he would deliberately sip his glass of wine just to stress her out more, but he finished before the rest of them.

The smile that he managed for everyone else's benefit looked friendly enough, but Joan knew what his real smile looked like—genuine and warm—and this wasn't it.

He thanked them all for their hospitality as he got up. She half-expected him to ask her to see him out on the pretext of asking one last business question or two, but he didn't. He was at the door in a hurry, saying only, "Good night, all. Joan, I'll see you on Monday morning."

* * *

The very day that Brandt had torn up her first letter of resignation, Joan changed the date on the document file and printed out another. On Monday morning she was glad she hadn't waited because she found herself strangely reluctant to submit it to him. If she'd had to do it all over again, even though it took only seconds, she probably would've procrastinated a lot longer than that.

Her resolve hadn't wavered and she was still sure she was doing the right thing. But Brandt's unexpected visit to her apartment had raised her hopes—for what, she didn't know. Joan kept wishing that Ed hadn't been there. She never did find out why Brandt had really come, and she had the feeling that she never would.

Although she hadn't seen him yet, Joan knew he was in his office. She'd heard the usual clicking of a computer keyboard and paper rustling and footsteps inside the room when she arrived. Following their routine, she picked up the appointment book folded open to today's date and the mail and a notepad. At the last minute she included the letter of resignation, folded inside an envelope this time.

"What do I have scheduled this morning?" was all Brandt said when she walked in. There was no greeting and no comment about the weekend or his visit.

In near-record time, Brandt dictated replies to the morning mail that she would fill out into finished letters. His brusque manner didn't invite small talk. In fact, his studied remoteness made it impossible for Joan to bring up her resignation. In the end, she didn't have the heart for it and she rose to leave his office when the routine meeting was over. She was nearly at the door when Brandt's voice stopped her.

"Joan," he said curtly, not glancing up when she turned around. "I'm ready to accept your resignation. Contact our usual employment agency and have them submit a list of applicants and their resumes and references."

"Will do," Joan murmured numbly. Her spirits sank as she realized she'd been secretly hoping Brandt would try to persuade her to stay. Blindly she reached for the doorknob.

"By the way—" His gaze pinned her on the spot. "Make it clear that I want someone experienced and mature. Someone I can rely on not to be carried away by ridiculous flights of imagination—but don't tell them I said that," he added.

"Right," she snapped, "I wouldn't want to insult anyone."

"Is something the matter?" He looked at her blandly.

Joan could feel tears beginning to well, but she blinked them back. It just wasn't worth it to cry or argue with him. She'd be out of here soon enough. "No. Is that all?" she asked in a controlled voice.

"As soon as you've compiled a list of candidates, you can arrange interviews. Thursday is best."

"Got it." The two little words had to be forced through the constricted muscles in her throat.

He shot her a cold look. "You are giving notice today, right?"

She riffled through the papers in her hand for the letter. When she found it, her head lifted proudly. "I haven't changed my mind, if that's what you mean. It's right here."

Brandt didn't glance at the envelope when she

walked back and put it on his desk, but kept his gaze on her. "I know I can trust you to find someone good," he said finally in dismissal.

Joan murmured a thank-you laced with irony that undoubtedly escaped him and fled the room, fighting back the emotions that threatened to engulf her. She'd once told herself that Brandt would be glad to see her go, but hadn't really believed it until today.

After getting through the rest of the day, she had the feeling she could survive anything. Even the moment when she would finally walk out of the office for the very last time—and never come back. Knowing that gave her the strength to return the next day, determined to carry out her duties and not give in to misery.

Her mask of efficient practicality seemed to be firmly in place. Her voice hadn't trembled at all when the employment agency had called later that day asking for more specific information on the company's requirements.

She glanced at her watch. It was almost eleven thirty. Kay would be calling soon to go to lunch with her. Joan arched her back, stretching her tense muscles as she printed out the last of the morning's correspondence and read it over for errors that spell-check might have missed. The door to her office opened from the hall and she glanced up absent-mindedly. Then she sat up totally straight, not prepared for the vision of rose pink femininity that floated into the room.

"They told me I could find Brandt here." The woman's perfect lips curved into a charming, porcelain-figurine smile.

Somehow Joan snapped out of her surprise to reply. "This is Mr. Lyon's office," she said. "I'm his assistant."

"Oh. Then you must be the person I talked to on the phone a week or so ago." The petite blonde glided softly to her desk. "I'm Angela Farr. Brandt is supposed to have lunch with me today." Baby blue eyes peered at the diamond watch around her slender wrist. "I'm early. I was hoping to persuade him to play hooky with me so we would have more time."

Aww. Just like high school kids, Joan thought with annoyance. But she kept her outward composure. "There's someone with him at the moment," she said. "But I can let him know you're here."

A conspiratorial smile flashed, revealing pearl white teeth. "Maybe that will hurry him up," Angela purred.

Joan wanted to roll her eyes, but there was no Kay around to see. She could only nod and be polite. As Angela looked around, clearly not impressed by a place where actual work got done, Joan pressed the intercom button to Brandt's office.

"What is it?" There was more than a trace of impatience in the voice that responded to her summons.

"Angela Farr is here to see you." Her voice took on a frigidly cold tone in spite of her desire to sound indifferent.

There was the slightest pause before Brandt replied. "Ask her to wait. I . . . shouldn't be long." His voice was distinctly warmer. That hurt.

As the connection between the two offices was broken, Joan glanced at the blonde. "Please take a seat."

"Thank you." Angela sank gracefully into the straight chair beside Joan's desk. "You're so nice. And young. The way Brandt talks about you sometimes, I had the feeling you were much older."

Joan didn't know how to take that odd remark, but it would be easy to read something into it, considering the mood she was in. She would have preferred Angela to be a catty bitch instead of so openly friendly.

"That's what I get for working hard," she finally replied.

"Have you been Brandt's assistant long?"

Shuffling papers on her desk that didn't need to be shuffled, Joan forced a smile. She didn't want to tell the woman who was obviously Brandt's significant something-or-other that she'd just given notice.

"For about three years," she answered.

"You must know him pretty well," Angela sighed, a whispery sound that wafted the flowery fragrance delicately scenting her skin to Joan.

"Not really." Joan decided suddenly that she hated flowers and most especially pink rosebuds.

"Do you go with Brandt when he visits those construction sites?" Big blue eyes gazed at her, their roundness emphasized by naturally long curling lashes.

"Whatever gave you that idea?" Joan softened the tart question with a sweet smile.

Angela shrugged in pretty confusion. "Don't you have to take notes or something?"

"Sometimes he uses a mini tape recorder. And then I transcribe what's on it when he comes back," Joan explained.

"I see." Angela nodded. Then she looked right through Joan and smiled flirtatiously. "There you are, Branny. I knew you wouldn't keep me waiting long."

Branny? Yikes. Joan's cheeks flamed as she involuntarily turned to the connecting door where he was standing. The man with him, a sales rep, nodded politely and left. Brandt's gaze flicked over Joan, then Angela, as though he was comparing them. Joan knew perfectly well who was second-best and she tried to convince herself it didn't matter. But a tear slid down her cheek when the mighty jungle lion walked out of the door with the precious pink rosebud.

She told herself to stop it and scrubbed away the betraying tear. Brandt had a point about her ridiculous flights of imagination.

Chapter 9

The sandwich Joan had eaten was caught somewhere between her throat and her stomach, a hard lump of bitterness and misery that refused to go away. It was one thing to wish silently for Brandt's happiness and it was another to see him with the woman who was providing it. Only a saint would be immune to the pangs of jealousy, Joan thought.

Her head pounded unmercifully as she tried not to look at her watch. Resolutely she kept typing, concentrating on the rough draft Brandt had scribbled for her to shape into a business letter, feeling as if she was hearing his voice. Before she realized it, she'd left out an entire sentence.

Frustrated and impatient and all too aware that Brandt's lunch was stretching out longer than he'd ever been gone at that hour, she reread the letter and noticed a missing phrase that had conveyed the gist of it. With a defeated sigh, she leaned back in her swivel chair, staring at her monitor without really seeing the document she was typing on it. Maybe if she relaxed for a moment and looked elsewhere, she would find the strength to control her wandering thoughts.

The doorknob turned and Joan quickly bent over her keyboard, pretending to concentrate on the words on the screen again. She knew who it was—she had heard those firm strides for too many years. Her gaze darted to the time display in the lower right corner. It was a few minutes before two.

"Any messages?" Brandt asked.

Her head only half-turned—she was deliberately not looking directly at him. "They're on your desk," she replied in a carefully controlled tone of professional indifference.

His footsteps paused somewhere near her desk and waited. The nape of her neck tingled and Joan held her breath, saying a silent prayer that Brandt would go away.

"Is there anything else?" Her question was cold, but then she was unable to stop visualizing just why his lunch break had lasted so long.

"Yes, there is," Brandt responded grimly. "Eye contact would be nice. It makes it easier to communicate with people, I think."

Her pulse accelerated alarmingly as his statement caught her off guard. The desire to do anything to please him was strong, but he already took up way too much space in her thoughts, even if he didn't know it. More of a share than even a lion was entitled to. She kept her fingers over the keyboard, correcting a word letter by letter.

"Okay," she said, still not looking at him. "Eye contact it is—I'll keep that in mind."

She let out her breath with a whoosh as her chair was spun around. Hands gripped each side of the

back, effectively holding her prisoner in its seat as
Brandt towered above her.

"Good," he said calmly. "Let's start right now."

The lenses of her glasses brought his face into
sharp focus. She was stunned by the assertiveness in
his expression. Never once had she seen Brandt quite
this determined.

"Start what?" she murmured, unsure of whether to
protest what could be called an order. She had no
idea what he would do next.

With care, he lifted the tortoiseshell-framed glasses
away from her face by the earpieces and set them on
the desk before she could stop him.

"Nice," he growled.

He'd made his move with finesse, but it still irked
her.

"I need those," she said crisply. "And don't touch
me in the office, Mr. Lyon. Or anywhere else."

"I didn't touch you. I took your glasses off."

She gave him a thin smile. "That's a fine line. Don't
cross it again." Joan stood up, pushing her chair into
a spin that thunked him below the belt. Unfortunately, he seemed not to care as his hands grabbed
the back of the chair again.

"Not a problem. I won't. But I really want to kiss you."

"What?" She looked at him in disbelief.

"You heard me. I'm asking your permission before
I cross another fine line. Or hear from your lawyer."

So he wanted a kiss. Well, she wanted to give him
one that would make his knees weak, a kiss that
would be as good as telling him off. Her heart
pounded as she nodded, silently allowing him to get
up close and personal.

His hands slid around her back, one moving to the
nape of her neck and the other to her waist as he

pulled her against him. Hotly possessive, his mouth closed over hers. Joan took the kiss from there, not surrendering to her own hunger as she teased his lips with little bites, then pretended to yield to his ardent intensity.

The door to her office opened and Brandt roughly pushed her from him. Lyle Baines was standing in the doorway, gaping at them in surprise. Joan twisted away, her face coloring in shame at being caught in the act. Without saying a word, Lyle stepped back into the corridor and closed the door.

Not until they were alone again did Brandt say anything himself. His fingers closed over her chin, raising it so she had to look into his face.

"That was fun," he said in a low voice. "But I wasn't expecting it. You took me totally by surprise."

"I had to do something after you whipped off my glasses," she retorted. "How corny is that? Next you'll beg me to take down my hair again. I wonder what you do to get Angela into your arms," she said acidly.

"Joan—"

"But I'd bet anything she doesn't critique your moves."

"She's nothing like you, if you really want to know," Brandt muttered. He took one last look at her and strode away into his office.

By Monday of the following week every employee of Lyon Construction was aware that Joan was leaving and that her replacement would be learning the office routine under her supervision. And everyone had heard of the passionate scene witnessed by Lyle Baines. The office grapevine was buzzing with rumors and speculation as to Joan's true reason for leaving. There was nowhere in the building Joan could go without being stared at.

But the scorching kiss had still been worth it, in her secret opinion.

Her replacement, Mrs. Mason, was a small, gray-haired woman with a ready smile and plenty of experience. She was quick on the uptake, something that reassured Joan, who hoped to leave before the week was over.

Mrs. Mason went with Joan when she entered Brandt's office first thing on Monday morning to deal with mail and appointments. Brandt seemed eager for the new hire to learn quickly, addressing all his questions and notations to her instead of Joan. Except for an initially brusque greeting, he ignored Joan almost completely, not even glancing in her direction. It was something of a relief when everything had been covered and she and Mrs. Mason could leave.

"Would you stay a moment, Joan?" Brandt asked calmly as she started to rise from her chair.

She looked over at the older woman, preferring the buffer zone of her company, but there was really no choice. "Of course," she said, and resumed her seat as Mrs. Mason walked out of the office.

His expression was bland when he directed his attention toward her, revealing none of his thoughts. An uncomfortable silence settled in the room, unbroken until Brandt got up and walked to the window, folding his hands behind his back.

"Have you heard the rumors making the rounds?" The question was tossed almost casually over his shoulder.

Joan blinked, stunned that Brandt would be aware of them. "Yes," was all she said.

He half-turned to look at her, arching one eyebrow.

"So you're aware that everyone thinks we're having an affair."

"You could say that."

"Have you tried to deny it?"

"What's the point?" she replied nervously. "I'll be gone by the end of this week and the stories will die naturally."

Slowly Brandt turned around and went back to his desk, stopping in front of her chair and leaning against the edge of his desk.

"Do you know what they say about you resigning?" His gaze was concentrated on her.

Joan felt the heat rising up from her neck. "That we quarreled," she answered.

His mouth curved into a cynical smile. "Oh, there's more to it than that," he said with a tired sigh.

"I can imagine. I wish I know why people say such awful things sometimes." Joan averted her eyes, speaking her thoughts aloud.

"Who knows?" he answered exasperatedly. "I suppose we gave them plenty to talk about after we were stuck here during the blizzard. It didn't help when I lost my temper the other day. I'm sorry, Joan."

"I . . . I don't blame you, Brandt," she said softly. Her agitation got her on her feet again and she walked awkwardly to the window.

Brandt followed her, stopping beside her and staring out through the thick glass. "Will you reconsider your resignation?" he asked quietly.

"What?" She glanced sharply at his profile.

His level gaze darted to her. "It's the only way I can think of to put an end to the rumors. After a few months, they can see for themselves that it isn't true. If you leave, they'll assume they're right."

It was difficult to breathe. His suggestion was so

logical she almost didn't want to think about it. "I can't. I just can't." She shook her head. "I'm leaving at the end of the week and that's that."

"What would another few months matter?"

"Mrs. Mason's already been hired to take my place," Joan reasoned. "We both know there isn't any truth to the stories and I'm not going to let idle gossip change my mind."

"The trouble is," Brandt corrected, "we both know there's some truth in what's being said, which is why the rest of it is all the more believable."

"No." She didn't want to believe it.

He shrugged. "Have it your way. I thought I should bring it up, that's all. But it's obvious that you don't care."

"Of course I care," she protested.

"Not enough to do anything to stop it."

Joan couldn't face his cobalt gaze. "I can't work for you anymore. It's become impossible."

"Oh? You didn't find it difficult for three whole years."

"But that was before—" She nearly said it was before she truly fell in love with him.

"Before what?" he chided her. "Before I tried to make love to you? I honestly didn't realize you weren't willing. It never occurred to me that you felt you owed me because I was your employer."

Joan drew in a sharp breath. "That's not it. You only used me as a stand-in for Angela." There. She'd said the worst.

"If I'd wanted Angela, I wouldn't have come to you," he replied curtly.

Amazement mixed with confusion as she stared at him, wishing she could see behind his expressionless face and read the true meaning of what he'd just said.

"Why did you show up on New Year's Eve?" she murmured.

"I don't want to get into another argument with you, Joan. Let's skip the analysis." Their discussion was over, Joan could tell by the firm set of Brandt's jaw. "Mrs. Mason probably has some questions. I suggest you go help her."

"Yes," she sighed, turning toward the door, then hesitating. "I—I have an appointment for a job interview tomorrow at one. Would it be all right if I take my lunch hour then? Mrs. Mason should be able to manage the office by herself for an hour."

"I don't care." Brandt frowned and resumed his seat behind the desk. "Make whatever arrangements that need to be made with her."

The interview the next day went badly. Joan kept thinking of things she should have warned Mrs. Mason about and had forgotten. Her interviewer had to repeat the standard questions several times. Joan didn't have to be told when she left the insurance office that she wasn't going to be considered for the position.

Her steps lagged as she walked down the corridor to her office. Before she reached the door, she could hear Brandt's voice carrying into the corridor and Mrs. Mason's anxious replies.

"Found it yet? I have the guy on hold. What do I tell him, that we lost his quotation?"

Was nothing going to go right today? Joan pushed open the door, preparing herself. The frustrated expression on Mrs. Mason's face turned to one of immediate relief at the sight of Joan.

Brandt sighed heavily. "It's about time you came

back." He looked accusingly in her direction. " Would
you please show Mrs. Mason where the folder is for
the A.B. King Company? I hate keeping a client waiting and I need my handwritten notes."

Fumbling through her purse, Joan removed her
glasses case and slipped the tortoiseshell glasses on
her nose. Her coat got slung over a chair—she didn't
have the time to hang it up. She walked quickly to the
filing cabinet where Mrs. Mason was hovering nervously.

"I think I have the right drawer," Mrs. Mason said.
"I checked the others, but I couldn't find it."

Joan smiled a quick reassurance. "This is the
drawer the folder should be in. Sorry it's so crammed
with stuff—there's a lot of files in here from before
we got computers and new files too." She flipped
quickly through the file folders in the "K" section
with no success. Darting Brandt a puzzled look, she
asked, "When did you last have it?"

"Friday. And it's not on my desk," he retorted.

The corners of her mouth twitched in amusement
as she directed her attention to the front of the
drawer under the "A." There was the missing folder.

"Aha. You know what?" she asked Brandt with a
rueful look. "If you would stay out of the filing cabinet, maybe the recent folders wouldn't get misfiled."

His only answer was an impressive scowl. But it
didn't intimidate her in the least.

"Mrs. Mason, you should know that Mr. Lyon tends
to put folders wherever it seems logical to him.
Whenever possible, keep him away from the files if
you want to avoid this kind of thing."

Brandt cleared his throat. "Thank you, Joan." He
barely glanced at the folder she handed him.

When his office door closed, Roberta Mason cast

Joan a grateful look. "Thank goodness you came back
when you did. I knew you were so meticulous it never
occurred to me that the folder might be misfiled. For
a moment I thought Mr. Lyon was going to tell me to
find another job."

"I wouldn't worry about that." Joan walked over to
retrieve her coat and hang it up. "The filing system is
one of his pet peeves, but I don't think this is ever
going to be a paperless office."

Mrs. Mason nodded. "There's no such thing
anyway," the older woman laughed.

"Did anything else come up while I was gone?"
Joan lightly touched the bracelet on her wrist. A wist-
ful feeling came over her as she realized that Brandt
would no longer be turning to her to solve the end-
less puzzle of the files.

"No. Everything else went very smoothly." Mrs.
Mason glanced hesitantly at Joan. "May I ask you a
personal question?"

Unconsciously Joan stiffened, wondering if the various rumors had gotten this far already. "Sure, go
ahead."

"I know you're looking for another job and I wondered why you're giving up this one."

A guarded look was about all Joan had to offer for
a moment. At last she spoke. "I guess you've heard
some of the stories that have been circulating," she
said coldly.

"Oh yes." Mrs. Mason smiled, her eyes twinkling.
"The gossips hope I'll give them an inside look at
what's going on. Nothing doing."

Joan tilted her head to one side in amazed disbelief. Her hair, worn down the way Brandt liked it,
shimmered over one shoulder.

"Don't you believe what they're saying?" she asked cautiously.

"You're a very lovely girl. If Mr. Lyon hasn't noticed that, he needs an eye examination. Those rumors are confined to only a few employees. No one believes them, including myself."

"Thank you." Joan smiled gratefully. "Sometimes I feel as if everyone's talking about me. It's an awful sensation."

"I can imagine. But I don't think you have to worry about it."

Mrs. Mason didn't say anything more and Joan realized that she hadn't answered her first question yet. "Okay—you wanted to know why I was leaving. It's pretty simple." She gave a little shrug. "I've enjoyed working here, but I'd like to try something new. You know, a change of scene." Which was partially true.

"Oh, it can do wonders. And a new job is challenging," the older woman agreed, apparently satisfied with Joan's answer. "When you've worked at one place for too long, you can definitely get in a rut."

By Friday, Joan knew that there was nothing left to show Mrs. Mason. Every minor problem that might crop up couldn't be predicted in advance, and it wasn't as if Joan wanted to micromanage the office from her new job, whatever it might be. Mrs. Mason's experience would help her solve things without Joan's supervision. Her presence was unnecessary by this point.

Too much of her time had been spent gathering impressions of the office, storing up memories of the way it was. This last day was winging by too fast. Although she had been on two more job interviews, she still hadn't found a new position or even been called back.

Last night Kay had suggested calling temp agencies, which seemed like the best solution for a lot of reasons. Her life was already in limbo, and a variety of jobs and work locations might help her through the transition period. No matter how she reminded herself that she was doing the right thing, Joan was reluctant to work for anyone other than Brandt permanently.

During her lunch hour on Friday, there had been a small going-away party given by the rest of the employees. Mrs. Mason's assurances that most of them were on Joan's side turned out to be true. Practically everyone was sorry to see her leave. Brandt had arrived in the conference room just as Kay handed over the beribboned present with everyone's signature on the accompanying card.

The most difficult thing had been listening to Brandt's carefully phrased regret at seeing her leave and accepting his thanks for the fine work she'd done. Joan knew his appearance had been motivated by a sense of duty. The routine speech had been expected of him. She didn't doubt the sincerity of his compliments, but she didn't believe he was sorry to see her go.

As she walked with Kay out of the building that evening for the last time, Joan pressed her lips tightly together and blinked at the tears burning her eyes. She couldn't help feeling sorry for herself.

"So help me, Joan," Kay muttered beneath her breath. "If you start crying, I'll hit you with a brick."

Joan's short burst of laughter was caught back by a sob. "It's stupid, isn't it? I couldn't bear to stay and I can't stand to leave."

"I'd quit my job too, if it wasn't for the health insurance and paid vacation time. John and I plan to take two weeks for our honeymoon. But I don't think I'll be working here much longer after we're married. Life is different when someone's got your back," her roommate declared.

"That reminds me." Joan swallowed the tight lump in her throat. "Brandt gave me my vacation pay, so I have two weeks, theoretically speaking, to get another job. No pressure, right?"

"Well, you were entitled to that." Kay bridled automatically at any mention of Brandt.

Joan had never been able to make Kay understand that the fault for what had happened didn't rest with Brandt alone. She had contributed to their problems. She'd worked with Brandt too long not to know he never would've attempted to make love to her if she hadn't indicated that she wanted him. But then, friends were friends because they stood beside you no matter what.

"We're going to celebrate this weekend," Kay announced, refusing to let Joan's moodiness affect her. "The first thing we're going to do tonight is stop at the grocery store and buy some big fat steaks. Tomorrow we'll hit the thrift stores and buy some outlandishly ridiculous clothes. Doesn't that sound like a great idea?"

"I thought buying flowered hats was the way to forget your problems," Joan teased to hide her lack of enthusiasm. Kay had a dozen in her closet.

"Who wears flowered hats except at Easter?" Kay shrugged as their bus pulled up to the curb. "Besides, I stopped at this crazy little secondhand store last week and they have a lot of fun stuff."

As long as Kay was around, Joan knew she would never be allowed time to be miserable. It was kind of scary to think what it would be like when Kay was married and gone six months from now. Suddenly she wondered if she would ever get married. She somehow doubted it. Before she'd ever met Brandt, she'd spent most of her weekends alone or hanging out with girlfriends. After knowing Brandt Lyon and loving him, she didn't think she could settle for anyone else.

"Yoo-hoo!" Kay waved her hand in front of Joan's face. "I asked you twice what you wanted to eat with your steak."

"I'm sorry. I was thinking," Joan said hastily, trying to clear her mind of Brandt's image.

"And I know what about. Really, Joan, you have to forget him. Men like that aren't worth crying over," her roommate answered impatiently. "Anyway, let's get back to the really important questions in life. Do we want baked potatoes mashed with butter or stuffed with cheese? Or . . ."

But Joan had already let her thoughts drift back to the weekend when she and Brandt had shared what they could scrounge up with a cold north wind rattling the windows and fresh snow drifting over the disappearing world outside.

Chapter 10

"Yes, you are going to put it on now!" Kay declared, tearing open the bag and shaking out the floor-length robe of Oriental silk. "What did you buy a lounging robe for if it wasn't to wear around the apartment?"

"I already have one that Mom and Dad gave me for Christmas." Joan laughed. "I don't know how I let you talk me into buying another."

"You bought it just so I would shut up and you know it!" Kay gave her a mischievous smile. "And you looked absolutely gorgeous in it. Besides, it was a steal at the price you paid."

"It is beautiful," Joan agreed as the sleek material slipped luxuriously through her fingers.

The brilliant colors had seemed to give her hair a richer shade when she'd tried it on at the second-hand store with Kay. Wearing it, Joan had felt like some exotic flower. She secretly wished that Brandt had seen her in it. But now, back in their plain old apartment, the robe didn't seem right for her.

"Go and try it on again," Kay ordered impatiently. She pushed the robe into Joan's hand and turned her toward the bedroom. "I'll make some tea while you're changing."

Kay was trying too hard to cheer her up for Joan not to agree. The robe seemed to lose some of its magic as she slipped it over her head and stood in front of the dresser mirror. Or maybe it was just that some of the delight had gone out of her eyes when she wished Brandt could see her. She tried smiling at her reflection, but it wasn't much of a smile at all. Quickly she ran a brush over her golden hair, determined not to reveal her inner unhappiness to Kay.

"Well, we don't have fortune cookies," her roommate said when Joan walked into the room, "so we can't predict whether you will be going on a long trip or winning the lottery. But it's a fact that you look fantastic."

That got a genuine smile from Joan. "We can make do with vanilla wafers," she suggested.

The kettle began whistling merrily. "That'll work," Kay said, getting up to turn it off.

"And now it's your turn to put on your gypsy outfit," Joan said. "You can read tea leaves to make up for forgetting to buy fortune cookies on your spending spree."

"Wait until John sees me in it!" Kay laughed, pausing by the couch to pick up her own bag from the secondhand store. She paused in the bedroom doorway. "Can I borrow your gold chain necklace?"

"Sure. It's in my jewelry box. Help yourself." Joan reached into the cabinet for the cups and saucers while the tea steeped.

She was just pouring the brewed tea into the cups when Kay whirled into the room, her bare feet skipping over the carpet. She stopped, posing in the center of the room, the calf-length skirt swirling around her legs.

"What I really need is a long brunette wig," Kay declared.

"You'd scare John half to death." Joan chuckled, carrying the cups to the coffee table in front of the couch. "Where can you ever wear that outfit?"

"Who cares?" Kay settled in front of the table on the floor in true gypsy fashion. There was an impish gleam in her brown eyes as she glanced at Joan. "He's supposed to come over this afternoon for an hour. Do you really think he'd be shocked to see me dressed like this?"

"Well, maybe not shocked," Joan qualified. "He's probably beginning to realize he should expect anything from you, but he will be surprised."

There was a knock at the door and Kay bounded to her feet. "Holy cow! He's here already!" She quickly smoothed her skirt and pulled the gathered elastic neckline of her peasant blouse daringly low.

With a wink at Joan, she dashed to the door, swinging it open with a flourish. But instead of almost throwing herself in John's arms, she stopped inside the door.

"What do you want?" she demanded as Joan sat up straighter on the couch, startled by the harshness in her friend's voice.

"Is Joan here?"

Her heart turned over at the rich, low sound of Brandt's voice. She rose, not knowing whether to run from the room or out the door, and instead waited like a statue beside the couch.

"If she was," Kay was saying, "she wouldn't want to see you."

"Well, I would like to see her. Please tell her I'm

here," Brandt responded. Joan sensed the patience in his tone—and the underlying irritation too.

"If it has to do with business," Kay was still blocking the door, "Mrs. Mason is who you want. I believe she now works at Lyon Construction."

"It's Joan I want to see, not Mrs. Mason."

Joan knew that tone, the one that said Brandt wouldn't put up with interference. Her fingers twisted together in agitation.

"That's not going to happen. You've caused enough trouble," her roommate retorted. "Why don't you leave her alone?"

"I understand that you have reasons for protecting Joan. She's your friend," Brandt said crisply. "However, I'm not leaving until I speak to her."

"You're in for a long wait!" And Kay started to slam the door.

It moved only a few inches and it was stopped by a stronger force pushing it open. Nothing was going to deter Brandt. Drawing a deep breath to steady her shaking nerves, Joan stepped around the coffee table, accepting the inevitable.

"It's all right, Kay," she said softly. "Let me talk to him."

An angry glance flashed at her as Kay stayed stubbornly in front of the doorway. "You don't have to, Joan. We can call the police. He doesn't own you and you don't have to do what he tells you."

"Kay, please!"

"You're a glutton for punishment." Kay stalked away from the door to stand beside Joan, her arms crossed in front of her as if she was ready to do battle at a moment's notice.

Brandt came into the small apartment, his hands shoved deep into the pockets of his coat. He stopped just inside, his diamond-sharp gaze riveted on Joan's pale face. Then he took in all of her, gloriously dressed in bright Oriental silk. She felt her legs quaking beneath her at the impassive expression on his compelling face.

It was barely twenty-four hours since she had seen him. Yet that last time hadn't had a physical impact anything like what she was feeling now—probably because she'd convinced herself she would never see him again. Her heart throbbed with pain.

"What do you want, Brandt?" She had to force herself to speak.

"Just to talk to you. I thought I had made that clear." He frowned slightly.

"There really isn't anything we have to talk about." She couldn't meet his gaze any longer and lowered her own.

"I believe there is."

"If it has to do with work—like Kay said—contact Mrs. Mason." As if he would follow an order from either of them, Joan thought.

He gave her an exasperated glare. "I know you don't work for me any more, Joan. If you would please ask your watchdog to leave the room, I'll explain why I'm here."

Joan glanced hesitantly at Kay, who was still glowering at Brandt. She knew she should insist that whatever he had to tell her could be said in front of her friend. Kay's presence made her feel stronger, a lot stronger. Without her, Joan might ignore her own common sense. But she weakened inwardly.

"Kay," her voice shook as her treacherous emotions took over, "would you mind waiting in the bedroom?"

A bare foot stamped the carpet almost noiselessly. For an instant Joan was positive Kay was going to refuse. Then blazing dark eyes looked daggers at Brandt, a silent warning that she would be out of the bedroom like an avenging mother bird if Joan needed her. The full gypsy skirt whirled around her legs as Kay flounced out of the room.

Joan's gaze was drawn back to Brandt, but she felt incapable of looking at him without revealing the fluttering in her heart. Her fingers were still clenched in front of her and they clenched harder when Brandt took a step forward. The hard line of his mouth tightened as his blue eyes raked her from head to toe.

"That robe is beautiful." The words were said with what seemed like indifference, but something in his gaze told Joan that wasn't so. But Brandt had to spoil it. "Too bad it makes you look even more untouchable and aloof."

Nervously she smoothed her hands over the silk, then stopped. "You didn't come here to talk about my clothes," she reminded him with a flash of pride.

He heaved a sigh that had a definite edge to it. "Can you tell me why we can no longer have a simple conversation?"

"Actually, we never were very good at that," Joan reminded him.

"I disagree." Unbuttoning his coat, he gave her a weary look. "Mind if I take my coat off? Or are you going to swoon if I do?"

The dry sarcasm in his voice made her look down to conceal the anguish in her eyes. She gave a wave that was meant to signal permission, because her voice failed her.

He took a few steps toward the rocker, where he deposited his coat, and noticed the teacups. "Well, well. Looks like tea is served. I'll have some."

Joan flinched at the prospect of him making himself at home. Nothing doing. "Why?" Her velvet brown eyes, wary and hurt, slid to him. He was accustomed to taking over, but she didn't have to allow it here.

"Because it's cold outside and in this apartment. I need something to raise the temperature and tea will do it. I don't think you're going to volunteer to warm me up." The quirk of his mouth lacked humor.

"Not for what you have in mind, no. But you can have a cup of tea." Let him drink it and let him go, Joan thought. She hastened to the kitchen where the teapot still sat on the stove. The cup clattered in the saucer as she tried to hold it steady and pour tea into it at the same time.

Brandt was seated on the couch. Joan ignored the vacant space beside him as she set his cup down on the low table and chose the safer distance of the rocking chair, pushing his coat aside and sitting primly. Her actions got her a glittering look of masculine amusement.

His hand was iron-steady as he picked up the cup. "Have you found a job?"

"Not yet." Her chin tilted a fraction of an inch to show it didn't matter.

"What are you looking for? I have a lot of connections. I can help." He was settled lazily against the back of the couch, controlled and seeming untouched by the tension that had Joan's nerves jumping.

"No, thanks," she said sharply. "I don't want to be under any obligation to you."

A muscle in his jaw twitched. His narrowed gaze moved from her face to the hands in her lap. "I see you're still wearing the bracelet."

Too late, her hand raced to cover the filing-cabinet

charm. "It's pretty," was all she said. She wished she hadn't worn it constantly—it was too easy to forget that it was on her wrist.

"Yes, it is." His brows knitted together as he stared at the amber-colored tea in his cup.

Silence pounded in the room. The strain of sitting immobile, hardly daring to breathe, maintaining the unconvincing pose that they were now strangers to each other, made her want to scream with frustration.

"Brandt, why are you here?" she burst out suddenly.

There was a gleam of satisfaction in his gaze when he picked up on the note of desperation in her voice. He glanced in the general direction of the bedroom, probably thinking that Kay had her ear pressed to the door. Then he set down the untouched cup of tea.

"I want you to have dinner with me tonight." Brandt held his head high, looking rather leonine—almost ready to pounce.

Her fingers closed over the curving arms of the rocker and she pushed herself to her feet, leaving it rocking wildly behind her. "No." Her refusal was vehement, making her hair dance over her shoulders.

She went swiftly to the window overlooking the street below. Concentrating her attention on the traffic, she still knew the instant Brandt got up. His steps were muffled by the carpet, but that didn't matter. She refused to turn her head even when her peripheral vision registered his profile beside her.

He radiated strength and purpose from the set of his mouth to his broad shoulders. Brandt stared down into the street too and then his gaze lifted to the pale winter sky.

"What I wouldn't give for a January blizzard." His glance at her was unexpected and he caught her covert study of him.

The thought of Brandt being marooned in her apartment flashed through her mind. The consequences of such an event were just too painful to contemplate.

"What for?" Her voice was cold, but she'd been praying for the same thing.

"Well," Brandt began in a mocking tone, "I suspect we're thinking along similar lines. Unless you have no emotions at all."

That biting comment was beyond tolerating. Emotionless? Every cell in her body tingled with him so near. She still craved his caresses, knowing how wonderful he could make her feel—and knowing that he would leave her to return to Angela.

It was payback time.

She spun sharply around, her brown eyes flashing with vengeful anger. The open palm of her hand swung at his face, headed for the infuriating curl of his mouth. A few inches from his face, the slap was checked by an iron hand around her wrist. Her awakened temper mixed with her pride and she blew up at him.

"Who do you think you are?" Joan cried out. "You can't force me to do what you want—or act like what I feel doesn't matter—oh, let go!"

He did but not completely, using his hold to draw her nearer to the rock-hardness of his body while he circled her waist to mold her more closely against him. It only took his touch to spark the fires of her love to new life. A shudder of surrender raced through her and her velvet eyes asked silently for what she craved.

Their mutual arousal made him bolder. His gaze moved to her parted lips, but not a sound came from her throat as his sensual mouth moved hypnotically closer. Joan didn't want to resist as his lips claimed hers.

Her wrist was released, yet her arms were pinned against his chest, the thudding of his heart hammering against them. Overwhelmed by the intensity of his embrace, Joan was lost to everything but his passionate demand for more.

Suddenly his fingers dug into her silken sleeves, moving her an arm's length away. Her lips throbbed pleasurably from his kiss and she looked away to hide the desire aching with her. A scarlet blush heated her face.

"Joan, what do you want?" Brandt asked huskily. "Tell me to go or tell me to stay."

"I can't let you stay," she whispered.

"Why?" His troubled gaze caught hers. "Don't you feel the way I do?"

"Brandt—"

"I'm a man and you're a woman. There are no other bonds between us, no business, no rules that apply, no obligations. If you don't want me, then tell me to leave."

"No!" The despairing cry beseeched him to say nothing more. "I don't want just an affair with you!" She drew in a ragged breath. "Leave. Go to Angela."

"Angela? Who's talking about Angela?" he asked harshly. "She has nothing to do with this. I'm talking about you and me."

"But ultimately she is involved." Joan took a step back, trying to put distance between them before she melted into his arms.

"Answer me one question," Brandt demanded. "Do you believe I love Angela?"

"Of course!" she cried out, hating the way he said her name. "She's perfect. She's ideal."

"She's a little too perfect and madly in love with herself. She doesn't run around in bare feet. She isn't a stubborn blonde who can't see two inches in front of her nose without her glasses!" His voice grew louder and more forceful.

Joan's mouth opened in disbelief. The look in the brilliant eyes that studied her held a message that she was sure she didn't understand. She shook her head just a little.

"If you could see what's in front of your nose," Brandt continued more calmly, "you could see that I love you."

"But what about—" she breathed.

"Angela is a pretty china doll, just as you said. I've known her a long time, but she was never a woman I wanted. I swear I haven't been alone with her, except for that lunch, since that weekend we were stranded." His gaze narrowed. "I love you, but do you, ah, care about me?" He hurried on before she had a chance to respond. "I'll settle for that right now. Anything for the time being. All I want is a chance to make you care as much as I do."

"Care!" Joan laughed, happiness bubbling in her heart. She ran a hand across her forehead as if erasing the idea of him loving anyone else. "I've loved you nearly every day that I've worked for you."

In the next instant she was caught up in his arms. This time there was nothing but trust as he tenderly and gently kissed her again and again, touching her as if she were a fragile blossom. She cradled his rugged face in her hands.

"Brandt, is this real? Am I dreaming?" she murmured achingly.

"If it's a dream, I never intend to wake up unless it's with you in my arms," Brandt vowed. "If it hadn't been for that blizzard—hell, I keep asking myself how long it would have been before I saw you for the woman you are. When I hired you, I was afraid it wouldn't work. But you were always so reserved."

"So were you." Joan slipped her arms around his neck. "How come it took five feet of snow dropping on Chicago to break you out?

"Good thing the power failed." He smiled, brushing his mouth warmly over her cheek. "And it was so natural and right to sleep with you in my arms. But that warm woman was impossible to find when the lights came back on."

"She was hiding, afraid you would guess that she loved you." Joan curled into his arms, those strong arms that felt so protective. His embrace would always thrill her.

"Not afraid of losing the job?" Brandt asked lightly.

"I gave it up, remember?" she whispered.

"I remember." A soft kiss touched her lips before he lifted his head. "Kay!" He kept Joan in his arms, smiling at the stars in her eyes. "You can come out now."

The bedroom door opened and Kay hesitantly stepped out. Her dark eyes took in the unexpected sight of Joan in Brandt's arms.

"I think Joan would like you to be maid of honor at our wedding," Brandt announced.

At Joan's startled look, his smile broadened, the love light in his blue eyes bringing out a soft glow of happiness in hers. She bit her lip to keep from crying out.

"Did I forget to ask you?" he teased, unmindful of Kay's astonished stare. "Well, I'm asking. Would you do me the very great honor of becoming my wife?"

"Yes." Softly at first, then with a little cry of joy, Joan repeated her acceptance. "Yes, yes—oh, yes."

"Then tonight we'll have dinner with my parents and tomorrow we'll drive to your hometown. Am I going too fast?" He searched her face for a sign of uncertainty.

"Oh, Brandt . . ." Joan laughed through her sparkling tears. "If anything, you aren't going fast enough!"

His arms tightened around her an instant before his mouth captured hers. Neither of them heard Kay, a tear of shared happiness slipping from her dark lashes, go back into the bedroom and close the door behind her.